THE SILVER LODE

Jerome Mysteries
Book 2

Suzanne J. Bratcher

Scrivenings
PRESS
Quench your thirst for story.
www.ScriveningsPress.com

Published by Scrivenings Press LLC
15 Lucky Lane
Morrilton, Arkansas 72110
https://ScriveningsPress.com

Printed in the United States of America

Paperback ISBN 978-1-64917-080-4

eBook ISBN 978-1-64917-081-1

Library of Congress Control Number: 2020940046

Cover by Diane Turpin, www.dianeturpindesigns.com

(Note: This book was previously published by Mantle Rock Publishing LLC and was re-published when MRP was acquired by Scrivenings Press LLC in 2020.)

Published in association with Jim Hart of Hartline Literary Agency, Pittsburgh, PA

ACKNOWLEDGMENTS

Writing a book for publication is an adventure. Each book follows a unique route with curves, switchbacks, and stops. All along the journey to *The Silver Lode*, friends encouraged me.

Before I began this trek, my publisher, Kathy Cretsinger, saw the possibility of other Jerome mysteries with the same characters. As I began to imagine the second story, *Copper Box* readers gave me the courage I needed by asking for the next book. The six Hot Springs Village (HSV) book clubs that invited me to their meetings to discuss this first mystery helped me conquer my hesitation to claim the title "author" as my own. By inviting me to speak to larger groups, the Friends of the Coronado Center Library, the HSV Kiwanis Club, and the HSV chapter of PEO helped me find my public speaking voice.

When it was time to hit the road and start *The Silver Lode* journey, my daughter, Jorie, made a trip back to Jerome with me to gather new ideas. When I started writing, my friend Marlene immediately wanted the first three chapters. Once I got those to her, she wanted the next three, and then the next until I had a complete draft. Whenever I ran off the road, she helped me brainstorm how to get back on.

On the last leg of the journey, as I worked to turn the draft into a manuscript ready for editing, my publisher Kathy Cretsinger offered me the grace of three extra weeks when I couldn't meet my deadline. During that last month of intense effort my bonus sister Becky, who also lives with MS, cheered me on, my friend Rhonda pitched in to keep me (and my cats) fed, and Jorie and Marlene took time out from busy schedules to help proofread.

In chapter 36 of *The Silver Lode*, Paul says, "When I'm facing something I know is bigger than my strength, I repeat Philippians 4:13 three times, adapted a bit. 'I can do all things through Christ who strengthens me,' even _____." All along this journey, I repeated, "I can do all things through Christ who strengthens me, even finish this scene…this chapter…this book." My friend Jesus kept that promise.

Thank you, one and all, for the love and support that brought *The Silver Lode* to life.

1

Wednesday, March 13

Paul Russell leaned back in his office chair and studied the serious young man standing in front of his desk. "A seventy-year-old cold case dependent solely on your grandfather's memory. You think that's a focus for a serious oral history project? If so, you've learned less in this course than I thought."

Alex Reyes's black eyes didn't drop, an adult holding his ground in the face of power. "It's the focus you assigned us, Dr. Russell."

Alex was a straight *A* student. Paul didn't believe the young man had misunderstood. "You saw the Do Not Disturb sign on my door. Five minutes. Convince me."

"The assignment was to interview a family member who lived through an important historical event and document his or her experiences. The murder of my great-uncle in 1950 was such an event. It's changed the course of the lives of my family for four generations. If I unravel the mystery, I can save my niece's life." Alex exuded enthusiasm, a teenager convinced he could conquer the world.

Amused by the young man's unconscious shift, Paul had a hard time staying out of parent mode. How much older than Scott was Alex anyway? Probably no more than four years. But he was Alex's teacher, not his dad. "The spirit of the assignment was to document a family member's experience of an important news event. You didn't provide any evidence this so-called murder happened, much less that it was an important news event."

Alex reached for the red pocket folder marked with his name. "The letter! I bet you didn't read it." He pulled out the single sheet of yellowing paper and handed it to Paul.

"I read it, but it isn't supported by anything. No newspaper story on Manuel Reyes's death, no obituary, not so much as a death certificate."

"In 1950 the copper mines were closing down. Jerome was shrinking every day. The closest newspaper was in Phoenix. No one cared about a Mexican American miner in a town that was about to become defunct."

Paul made a dismissive gesture. "I'm sure the coroner was still issuing death certificates."

"My great-uncle disappeared, Dr. Russell. Did you listen to the interviews with my grandfather on the audio file?"

"I did. No disrespect intended, but your grandfather is eighty-six and living in an institution."

"My grandfather's mind is as clear as yours or mine. And it's not an institution. He has his own room in a private home that provides residents with the help they need to stay out of an institution!"

Paul checked his watch. "Your five minutes is about up. Even if I decide to accept the evidence you turned in, you haven't convinced me your great-uncle's death was historically important."

Pulling a cell phone out of his pocket, Alex bent his dark head, frowning in concentration. Finding what he wanted, the boy thrust the phone at Paul. A thin-faced little girl, black curls framing a serious heart-shaped face, pale despite the warm brown tones of her smooth skin, smiled at him.

"Look at that photo, Dr. Russell, and tell me Manuel's death wasn't historically important. Aurora is four years old, and she's going to die if she doesn't get a heart transplant. Do you know how much that surgery costs? A million and a half dollars! My family doesn't have that kind of money. If Manuel wasn't murdered and he mined the silver lode he discovered, our family could pay for everything Aurora needs with some left over."

In spite of his determination to stay in teacher mode, Paul felt a pang of sympathy, such a small child. He didn't have a daughter. If Linda had lived... But she hadn't. How did Marty feel about children? Paul forced his attention back to Alex and the problem of the oral history project.

As if he sensed Paul's weakening, the young man said, "At least talk to my grandpa. He'll convince you it's real. I know he will. I didn't believe him at first. I kept trying to get him to talk about his experiences in Korea, but he wouldn't. He said Manuel's murder was more important than anything he saw in Korea. Lots of men saw fighting in Korea. He's the only one alive who knows about his brother's murder, at least the only one except the children of the killer."

"What makes your grandfather think a murderer would tell his children what he did to make his money?"

"Nothing. My grandpa says the killer would probably tell his children he found the silver lode himself. So, if we find the fortune from the silver lode and look back a generation, we find the killer."

"How does your grandfather plan to convince a son or grandson his father was a murderer?"

"With the letter!"

"I don't know, Alex. A good-hearted person might be willing to help with Aurora's medical expenses, but no one's going to accept the idea his father was a cold-blooded killer."

"We have to try!"

Paul checked his watch again, 4:45. If he was going to get any writing done this afternoon, he had to extricate himself from this conversation. "All right, Alex. I'll promise you this. Before I write that zero in the grade book, I'll talk to your grandfather. Email me his name and contact information."

"So you'll go see him?"

"I didn't say that. I said I'd talk to him on the phone. After I have a conversation with your grandfather, I'll decide whether to go see him."

Alex frowned.

The kid was skating on thin ice. Paul shook his head. "Next week is spring break. You're supposed to be on vacation. I'm supposed to be finishing a book. That's the best you're going to get today. Take it or leave it."

Alex reached for his backpack. "I'll take it," he said between clenched teeth. "But think about this, Dr. Russell. Without a new heart, Aurora won't be around next spring break. I don't have time for a vacation. And which is more important, your book or a little girl's life?"

The shot went home, and Paul's chest tightened. He wasn't in charge of who lived or died. To emphasize that the interview was over, he swiveled to face the computer and moved the mouse to wake up the screen.

"I'm sorry, Dr. Russell."

Alex sounded truly contrite. Paul let out his breath and turned to look at the young man.

"I feel so helpless," Alex said. "We all love Aurora. This is the only chance we've got to get the money we need. If you'll help me…"

Paul raised his eyebrows.

"I have to pass your course," the boy hurried on. "I can't do it with a zero on the mid-term project. More important than my grade, I need help to find my great-uncle's killer. I did all the research I know how to do. You're an expert in oral history. I hope you'll tell me what to do next."

"I'm a teacher, Alex, not an investigator."

"I know, but if you'll just talk to my grandfather, you and he might think of what to do next. If you give me an incomplete instead of a zero, I'll get whatever evidence you want me to. I'll prove this is a worthy project."

"I've already promised to talk to him. After that, we'll see."

"Thank you, sir." Alex extended his hand.

Just managing not to roll his eyes at the sudden formality, Paul shook his student's hand. What Alex thought they were shaking on, he wasn't sure. He decided not to ask.

As soon as the door closed behind Alex, Paul took a deep breath. That was one thing about teaching, he never knew what hook pass a student might toss his way. But Alex and his family drama had to wait. Five pages. That was how much he needed to get written before he went home.

Closing his eyes, Paul counted backwards from twenty. He had to clear his mind, escape the present, and return to Thomas Jefferson's office at his Monticello home. By the time Paul got to five, he could see the past president in his mind. Jefferson, his white hair sparse, lined up the same New Testament passage in Greek and Latin on one side of the blank paper and matched it with English and French on the other.

The "Beatitudes" from the fifth chapter of Matthew were there, but none of the references to healing in the eighth and ninth chapters. Jefferson included the moral teachings of Jesus in his version of the Bible but none of the miracles.

Paul started to type. "Thomas Jefferson held the teachings of Jesus in the highest regard, but he deliberately excluded any account of miracles in all four gospels." Aurora Reyes looked at

Paul from his computer screen, younger than the synagogue leader's daughter in the ninth chapter of Matthew. But if it had been Sr. Reyes in that story, Paul knew Jesus would have gone with him to heal the little girl.

Paul stood up and stretched. He couldn't afford to think about sick children. He had to keep his mind on his work. His continued employment at the university depended on finishing the manuscript by the first of June. He'd worked too hard, accumulated too many degrees, to let this job go. All his work experience was in education, and he needed this position.

He sat back down, closed his eyes, and started counting backwards from twenty again. At zero he opened his eyes. The little girl with the large black eyes still looked at him, but he ignored her and typed doggedly on "...that Jefferson considered the corruption of the gospel writers' rendition..."

What if Alex had stumbled onto a seventy-year-old murder and a wealthy family thrived because a grandfather or a great-grandfather murdered a lucky Mexican American miner for a fortune he found in the side of Cleopatra Hill?

Paul gritted his teeth and hit the keys. "...of the life of Jesus Christ." He paused, took a deep breath. What came next? He toggled to the page labeled Outline and ran his eye down the subtopics for the chapter he was supposed to finish before going home. It was no use. Instead of the next subtopic, he saw a picture from his childhood Bible, a picture of Jesus with little children on his lap. One of the girls had a heart-shaped face, Aurora Reyes.

Paul got up and went to the single window in his office. Turning the old-fashioned crank, he let in the cool March air. The sun, three-quarters of the way down the western sky, deepened the blue of the San Francisco Peaks to almost black. He knew he wasn't going to get any writing done. He might as well go home.

Turning back to his desk, he opened the red folder marked

Alex Reyes and pulled out Exhibit One, a letter on faded letter-head. It was in Spanish, but Alex had attached an English translation with a red paper clip.

Paul ran his eyes down the translation for the third time. The first time he read the letter, he was astonished, and disappointed, that a serious student like Alex Reyes would turn in something so unbelievable. But here it was, the letter that began "My dear brother Enrique" and ended "Love to you and our family, Manuel." In between lay a preposterous story of the discovery of a large deposit of silver ore in a rarely used tunnel.

A fascinating tale, but surely that's all it was. How could he find out if the story was worth the paper it was written on?

He paused, struck by an idea. The paper could be a clue. Maybe he could discover if it was genuine. He looked at the letterhead, faded and incomplete. The only letter in the name he could be sure of was an *r*. The address was hopelessly smudged, a number that included a *2* and a street that began with a *D*.

Who would know about old stationery? An answer he liked came in a breath. Marty Greenlaw. She'd been in Clarkdale for six weeks.

Their relationship, instead of progressing toward an engagement as he'd expected, was cooling, and he had no idea why. She'd turned down his last three invitations, claiming she was too busy or too tired to go to dinner. He picked up his cell phone from his desk and scrolled through the pictures until he came to the last selfie he'd taken with her.

They were standing in front of the 1920s house she'd bought to use as showroom, workshop, and apartment. Marty, arm around his waist, leaned her head against his shoulder. Her auburn curls shone like burnished copper against the blue of his shirt, her green eyes danced, and her generous mouth laughed with delight. His own face mirrored her elation. They looked like what he'd thought they were—a couple in love.

So what happened?

Maybe he could find an answer to that question if he could convince her to work with him on a quasi-professional basis to look into Alex's research. But he wasn't going to call to ask. He would show up at her house. If she refused this invitation, it would be to his face.

2

E xcitement bubbled up as Marty Greenlaw looked around the living room she was transforming into the showroom of Old and Treasured, her new antique furniture workshop. "Thank you, Granny Lois," she whispered. "I couldn't have bought this house without the money you left me in your will. I wish you were here to celebrate with me."

Flinging out her arms, she whirled across the expanse of floor between the Weber square grand piano and the Shaker table with its yellow painted top and straight poplar legs. Closing her eyes, she imagined Paul's arms around her as they waltzed to "The Blue Danube" after their wedding, the two of them dancing into the future.

A knock at the door brought her back to the present. Paul Russell, as if he'd materialized from her thoughts, stood in the doorway. Momentarily confused by his sudden appearance, she almost beckoned to him to join her.

"Marty." His deep voice shattered her fantasy.

Of course, he couldn't hear the music in her head. Doing her best to ignore the flush she knew was staining her cheeks, she dropped her arms. "Hello, Paul. I was just celebrating."

His brown eyes twinkled. "I can see why. You've made significant progress."

But she knew he'd seen through her attempt to hide her real reaction to his unanticipated presence. Guilt pushed away her embarrassment. She'd been trying so hard to convince him, and herself, she wasn't in love with him. Now she'd be forced to start the process over.

The back door slammed. "Found it!" Scott's triumphant voice drifted in through the kitchen.

Grateful for a reason to turn away from Paul's amused expression, Marty hurried to take the piano stool from her young helper.

"Dad," Scott said, "what are you doing here?"

"Unscheduled supervisory visit to make sure you're giving fair work for your generous wage."

Scott rolled his eyes. "English translation, you came to check up on me."

Marty laughed. "I understood perfectly well what he said, Scott."

Paul reached out and ruffled Scott's hair. "I keep telling you it's the downside of spending too many years in school. When a guy reads too many academic books, he starts talking like one. Train for a trade like plumber or electrician if you're determined to speak the vernacular."

Scott groaned. "What kind of word is *vernacular?*"

Paul snorted. "A perfectly good word that subsumes both informal language and slang."

"Subsumes? Come on, Dad. Use the vernacular now and then, can't you?"

They both laughed.

Marty laughed with them, enjoying the joke but appreciating the word play between father and son even more. Putting on an exaggerated frown of disapproval, she said, "Boys! Back to the subject at hand." She smiled up at Paul, wishing for the umpteenth time she wasn't a full foot shorter than he. "Scott's doing great."

Paul winked at his son. "He's a great kid. I wouldn't expect anything less."

The caution light in Marty's head blinked yellow. The reasons she couldn't follow her emotions into anything more than friendship with this man lined up like cars at a stoplight. First, Scott was Paul's son, so mature for his age sometimes she forgot he was only fourteen, mature enough she couldn't fill the role of his mother. Second, she was ten years younger than Paul, not at all sure she was mature enough to be Paul's wife. Third, she was a foot shorter than Paul, making them look ridiculous as a couple. Last came the semi that threatened to block the intersection. Her track record with men was appalling, and that was being kind to herself.

She took a deep breath, exhaled slowly. "Maybe we should start over. Hi, Paul. As always, Scott's been a big help this afternoon, but if you need him to leave a little early today, we're at a good stopping place."

"You're the one I've come to see. I have a favor to ask."

Marty tried to keep her expression neutral. She didn't want Paul to make an invitation she'd be forced to turn down in front of his son. On second thought, maybe turning Paul down with Scott right here was what needed to happen. She knew Scott didn't want his dad to be in love with her.

Paul gave a tiny shake of his head. "A professional opinion."

Marty almost smiled. She'd always suspected he could read her mind. One of the things that continued to draw her to him, despite the caution light.

"I've run across a letter from approximately 1950, and I have no idea whether it's genuine."

"I know old furniture, not old documents."

Raising his hand, Scott stepped between them.

"Yes," they said in unison.

Paul winked at her, obviously aware they were reading each other's minds. Marty swallowed a giggle. She couldn't admit to an inside joke with him. That was dangerous territory, territory she needed to back away from.

Oblivious to the unspoken conversation, Scott said, "What now, Miss Marty?"

She drew a blank. She wondered if Paul's mind was blank too.

Grasping for a chore to keep Scott in the room with them, she blurted, "Polish the piano. Linseed oil and rags are in the right-hand cupboard in the workroom." She needed to clean the intricate carving with a soft toothbrush, but she could do that through a thin film of oil.

As Scott headed for the workroom, the original dining room of the 1920s house, Marty knew Paul was thinking she was afraid to be alone with him. Paul didn't wink again, but he might as well have. Marty felt herself start to blush. What was going on in her head? She knew a romantic relationship with Paul wouldn't work, so why couldn't she relax into a simple friendship?

"It's looking good in here," Paul said. "When is the grand opening?"

Glad to grab the lifeline of small talk Paul tossed her, Marty said, "April 24, a little before the tourist season begins. I plan to invite serious collectors from Sedona and local business owners." She surveyed the relatively empty room. "That's a little over a month, but I've got lots left to do."

"Let me know if I can help."

She wanted to say, "Help me by staying away. You confuse me, Paul Russell." Instead she said, "Maybe when I'm down to the wire." Now it was time to shift the attention from her. "What makes dating this letter important?"

"Maybe nothing." Paul nodded at the Shaker table and sent her a questioning look.

She nodded.

With two strides of his long legs, he was across the room. Setting his messenger bag on the table, he unzipped a pocket and pulled out a red folder. Extracting two sheets of paper attached with a red paper clip, he handed them to her.

The top page didn't look like much, a yellowed piece of inexpensive paper stamped with a faded letterhead from a boarding house whose name she couldn't decipher. At the bottom of the sheet, all that was left of the address was Jerome, Arizona. She began to read, "*Mi querido hermano.*" She looked up. "It's in Spanish. I wish I could help, Paul, but I don't know more than a half dozen words of Spanish, *buenos días, gracias, el baño.*" She gave him a half smile. "You get the picture. I'm sure you can find someone in the Modern Languages Department to help you."

"I have an English translation. It's the second sheet. What I need to know is if the letter's genuine."

She handed it back to him. "I know next to nothing about dating old documents. Surely someone at the university—"

"I need something quick, an informed guess. You can see it's from Jerome. Even information about boarding houses of the era would help."

Marty shook her head. "The only Jerome history I know is sketchy Baker family stories."

"I was thinking about The Jerome Historical Society. Have you met any of the members? I think it's a small group of volunteers."

She started to shake her head again then paused. "I met someone who mentioned it. Patricia something. Late fifties, early sixties, on the tall side, expensively put together. She came in to ask if I wanted to join. Preserving original documents from the days before Jerome became a ghost town would be fascinating work. But this isn't the right time for me."

She turned to look at Scott. Oiled rag in hand, he was clearly keeping up with their conversation. "You were here. Do you remember her last name?"

"Osborn. Osborn Savings and Loan is on Main Street."

Marty nodded. "Scott's right. Patricia Osborn offered to give me a good rate on a small-business loan, which I don't need, thanks to Granny Lois's will."

"If I remember the little research I've done on Clarkdale, Osborn is the name of one of the original settlers," Paul said. "She might know something about the Reyes case, especially if Manuel's disappearance excited any publicity. Do you mind approaching her?"

"How soon?"

"Yesterday would be best. I gave a good student a zero on an important assignment based on the assumption he'd made the whole thing up. If I'm wrong, I need to go back and adjust his grade. No matter what her guess is, I'd feel better than just going on my initial reaction. Alex claims the solution to a serious problem depends on the letter being genuine."

"Because..."

Paul separated the papers and handed her a typed English translation. "Read this and tell me what you think."

Scott moved to stand beside her. "Can I read over Miss Marty's shoulder?"

"May I," Paul said. "You can. You're tall enough."

Scott rolled his eyes. "May I read over your shoulder, Miss Marty?"

"You can, and you may." It didn't take long to absorb the gist of the letter. Manuel Reyes claimed to have found a silver lode that would make the whole family wealthy.

Scott whistled. "A silver lode! I never heard of one around here. I wonder where it was."

"Silver wasn't as plentiful as copper," Paul said, "but it wasn't rare."

"No, Dad. A silver lode isn't just silver. It's a deposit of silver and gold mixed together. There's no telling how much it would be worth."

Marty looked at Paul. "Did Alex know what a silver lode was?"

"He didn't appear to. At least he didn't explain it to me."

"This has got to be real, Dad! If the guy doesn't know what a silver lode is, he's way underestimating the worth of what Manuel found."

Marty studied Scott. "How do you know what it is?"

"Rocks are Scott's hobby," Paul said. "He's made a serious study of this entire area."

"I'm going to be a geologist, Dad! You want to know about a silver lode? In 1859 prospectors discovered the Comstock Lode. Virginia City, Nevada boomed for twenty years. Seven mines took out $400,000,000 in silver and gold before the lode gave out. A small silver lode would be worth several million."

"Wow!" Marty said. "Where does Alex claim to have found this letter?"

"He got it from his grandfather, the brother of the writer, Manuel Reyes."

"Is the grandfather still alive?"

Paul nodded. "He lives in some sort of assisted living in Cottonwood. I was thinking of visiting him to see what else he might be able to tell us."

Marty ignored the *us*. "This investigation sounds like it's above and beyond the call of duty for a university professor, even for an excellent student."

"Yep. It's probably because I never had a daughter."

"I don't understand."

"Alex showed me a picture of his four-year-old niece, a little girl named Aurora. She needs a heart transplant, and the family doesn't have the money. Alex wants to track down whoever inherited Manuel's find and ask them to pay for Aurora's surgery."

"Wait. I'm confused. What do you mean 'inherited Manuel's find'?"

"Sorry. I skipped a few important details. This letter is the last time Alex's grandfather heard from his brother. The grandfather believes someone murdered Manuel for his discovery."

"A silver lode would definitely be worth killing for," Scott said.

"Okay," Marty said. "But how could anyone pull a fortune out of the ground and keep it secret? A mine, even a small one, takes people and machinery."

"Not necessarily," Scott said. "In the early days, a miner would stake a claim and mine the ore by hand. It's a long, hard job, but they did it. You'd need some dynamite and years to do it, but it could happen."

"But the wealth would accumulate," Marty said. "Someone would ask where it came from."

Scott shook his head. "Dad said this all happened around 1950. Jerome was becoming a ghost town. It would be possible to operate a small mine under the radar. Dig out enough ore to make a trip worthwhile, take it to a processing plant in Phoenix, and put your cash in a bank anywhere but in Jerome. Who would know?"

"It would take years," Paul said.

"If I had a real gold mine to work on, I wouldn't care how much time it took."

Marty looked from father to son. Amazing similarity, not in looks, but in the intensity of their expressions—eyebrows drawn together, chins jutted out, lips pursed. Still, it was a crazy quest. "A seventy-year-old murder?" she said.

Paul nodded. "I know. But come with me to hear the grandfather's story. This opportunity is why I assign oral history projects. We hear history from someone who lived it."

Seeing the intense curiosity of this man, Marty knew full well if she accepted the invitation to be part of that *us,* she would step on a bridge over a river filled with her personal crocodiles. It was on the tip of her tongue to plead too much work.

To be fair, though, she shouldn't refuse Paul this request. He'd helped her solve her personal mystery last summer, and they'd made a good team. If they could help a four-year-old girl, a child Ruthie's age...

"Okay," she said, "make an appointment. Right now, I can close up shop just about any time for a couple of hours."

"I want to go too," Scott said. "Make it after school."

"We'll see," Paul said, taking out his cell phone. "There may be regular visiting hours or other restrictions."

"But, Dad—"

"Let it go, son. I'll see what I can work out." Paul stepped away from them.

"Back to the piano," Marty said. "It may not be a silver lode, but it needs to be polished. It's one of the focal points for the showroom."

Scott picked up the bottle of oil and the rag he'd set on the floor while he read over her shoulder. As he made his way back to the piano, Marty moved to stand beside Paul.

He looked down at her and gave her a half smile. Something funny happened in her stomach. Don't be ridiculous, she told herself. You haven't agreed to a date.

"Yes," he said into the phone. "I'd like to make an appointment to visit Mr. Reyes. I understand he lives in your home." He paused to listen then said, "Paul Russell. I don't know if he'll recognize my name or not. I'm a history professor at the university. Alex Reyes, Mr. Reyes's grandson, is one of my students. I'd like to discuss a project Alex did for my class." He paused again. "Tomorrow at eleven?" He looked a question at Marty. She nodded.

When he turned his attention back to the phone, she closed her eyes. She'd taken leave of her senses. After she'd gotten to know Scott better and come down out of the castle in the air she'd built from long distance phone calls between Virginia and Arizona, she'd promised herself she'd back away from Paul. They could be casual friends. So far she'd avoided three dates. But now, the first time he showed up in person after she made her decision, she was giving in.

Relax, she told herself. This is not a date!

3

Thursday, March 14

P aul parked in the wide driveway of the single-level brick home and got out. The large front yard was landscaped with multi-colored gravel and a variety of desert plants. Prickly pear cacti blooming pink, gray-green saw-toothed agave, a delicate palo verde tree covered with tiny yellow blossoms.

He watched Marty's pickup turn into the cul-de-sac and head toward the house. He'd asked her to lunch before their appointment, but she'd insisted on meeting him here, blaming errands. He'd succeeded in drawing her into this puzzle, but he'd never discover the reason behind her determination to put the brakes on their relationship as long as she refused to be alone with him.

As the pickup pulled in behind his Jeep, he got out and went to meet her. She appeared to be lost in thought, but when he opened her door for her, she looked up at him and smiled. His heart skipped a beat. Maybe he was borrowing trouble. Maybe this project would give them the outside focus they needed to get past this bump in the road. He returned her smile. "Ready to solve the mystery of the lost silver lode?"

She tossed her keys into the enormous leather shoulder bag she always carried and got out. "You've decided the letter is real. What changed your mind?"

"I haven't changed my mind. I want to meet Sr. Reyes. What I've decided is that Alex believes the letter is real. Now I want to discover how reliable his grandfather's memory is."

"Fair enough. It's easy to embellish memories as the years go along."

They followed the path of white stepping-stones across the colorful gravel to the front door and stepped up onto the concrete porch. Paul pushed the doorbell.

Marty turned and looked out at the yard. "I didn't think I'd ever say this, but I'm beginning to like the desert. I'm surprised at the variety of spring flowers."

The door opened, and a short, heavy-set man with thinning blond hair and twinkling blue eyes stuck out a pudgy hand. "Dr. Russell, I presume?"

Suppressing a groan at the joke he'd heard too many times, Paul arranged his face into what he hoped was a friendly grin. "Definitely not Livingston. I wouldn't be any good in the wilds of Africa. You must be Mr. Sweet."

The proprietor of Sweet Home chuckled. "I'm Sweet, all right, though the wife might not agree. But call me Joe." He stepped back. "Come in! Enrique is waiting for you on the patio."

Paul circled Marty with his arm, an automatic gesture. "This is Marty Greenlaw." Catching himself just in time, he managed to keep from hugging her.

Joe turned his attention to Marty. "Welcome, Miss Marty. Enrique will be happy to have a pretty face to look at while he lets the doc quiz him."

Marty gave Paul a disbelieving look, but when she spoke, it was without a trace of sarcasm. "I have a few questions I'd like to ask Sr. Reyes myself."

"I'm sure he'll be happy to answer them. Just follow me, folks."

Paul stepped back to let Marty go first. He didn't know what he'd expected the host of this guest home for the elderly to be like, but Joe Sweet was a definite surprise. Maybe hearty exuberance was what it took to deal with what was sure to be a depressing environment at times. He wondered what kind of person Mrs. Sweet was. Practical, probably.

The view from the patio made Paul forget he was in a home for the elderly. Three or four miles away at the bottom of a long gentle slope, the Verde River snaked south toward I-17 and Camp Verde on its way to join the Salt River in Phoenix. On the other side of the Verde, the ancient ruins of Tuzigoot pueblo stood three stories high, a reminder of those who had gone before. Beyond, the undulating line of the Black Hills watched over the modern-day sprawl of Yavapai County.

In the shade of a cedar pergola, an old man sat in an Adirondack chair painted a bright red. A Mexican blanket woven with blue, red, and yellow stripes lay across his knees. Paul knew they had found Sr. Reyes. Alex had inherited his grandfather's Roman nose and square jaw. Despite the old man's receding hairline, his white hair was as thick as Alex's dark hair.

Joe stopped beside the chair and, with a theatrical flourish, said, "Let me introduce Enrique Reyes to you. Enrique, this is Dr. Russell. He's brought a friend along, Miss Marty. Do you want me to make up a batch of my special mango milkshakes?"

"Thank you, not for me," Paul said.

"Nor me," Marty said.

"Enrique, how about it? I know you love them as much as I do."

The old man shook his head. "This isn't a social meeting, Joseph. We have serious business."

"Okeydokey. If you change your mind, just holler."

Extending her small hand with its trimmed bare nails, Marty said, "Buenos días, Sr. Reyes."

The old man raised friendly dark eyes to hers. Giving her a warm smile, he responded with a flow of Spanish.

Paul had assumed Alex's grandfather spoke English. Now he realized he had no idea who had provided the translation of the questionable letter, Alex or Enrique Reyes.

Tilting her head to one side, Marty gave the weathered patriarch a rueful smile and said, "I'm sorry. I don't know any more Spanish than 'Good morning.' I did a silly thing in high school and studied French. Not a useful language, I'm afraid."

"But a beautiful language," Sr. Reyes said in lightly accented English. "A sister language to Spanish." Releasing Marty's hand, he turned his attention to Paul. "I would get up to greet you, Dr. Russell, but these old legs…"

"Not at all, sir. We appreciate your sharing your time with us."

"You've been a good teacher to my Alejandro." He paused and frowned. "At least until now."

Another similarity between grandfather and grandson, come straight to the point. "I hope I'm still being a good teacher to Alex, following up on what at first glance sounds like an unbelievable story. Alex is a diligent student, but I need to hear your brother's story from you."

Sr. Reyes nodded gravely and indicated two patio chairs. "Both of you sit. I understand why you might not believe a murder has gone unsolved for seven decades, but surely my Alejandro brought you the recording of my account of Manuel's death. You've heard my story."

Paul was glad he wasn't easily intimidated. "True enough, but I need outside corroboration. Alex didn't turn in Manuel's death certificate. I'd like to see it."

Sr. Reyes shook his head. "Never got one."

Marty touched the old man's knee. "How do you know he

died? Perhaps he went away and started a new life."

"Away from his family? Not Manuel. He never came home. That means only one thing. *Está muerto.*" He paused as if daring Paul to challenge his assertion.

Paul didn't comment. He had no desire to argue with this gentleman.

After a moment, Enrique said, "Maybe my Alejandro didn't explain about us. Manuel and I, we came from Mexico with our parents. Arizona was our new life. We came to work at the rich farms." He frowned. "Those farms are gone now, turned into roads and parking lots as Phoenix conquered the valley."

He shifted his gaze to Marty. "Even back then, the selling of the farms was starting. When Manuel heard about the mining in Jerome, he got excited. He told me he would dig for silver, enough to bring our grandparents from Mexico. I told him it was copper up there, but copper was okay, so I agreed. If my brother found silver, great! But copper was better than what we got paid picking oranges and grapefruit." His eyes went to the river below, sparkling in the bright morning. "Then I got the letter Alejandro turned in with his project."

Paul unzipped his messenger bag and drew out the letter. Leaving it in its plastic sleeve, he handed it to the old man. "Can you help us with the name on the letterhead?"

Sr. Reyes picked up a pair of reading glasses from a TV tray that sat within easy reach of his chair and put them on. After a moment of intense scrutiny, he shook his head. "Too faded. Too many letters missing."

"I think it's a boarding house," Paul said. "Do you remember where Manuel lived?"

"He moved a lot. Trading problems, he told me. Whenever he got tired of one set of problems, he moved. I don't think he lived at that place long." The old man handed the letter back.

"Alex told me it was the last letter you ever received."

Sr. Reyes nodded.

Marty said softly, "Someone killed him for the silver lode he found. Did Manuel have a partner or a good friend he might have told about his discovery?"

Paul studied her. She was clearly enchanted by the old man. He didn't blame her. The intensity of Sr. Reyes's conviction, the cadence of his voice, the sincerity in his black eyes were all compelling. Paul didn't doubt Alex's grandfather believed the story he'd woven from the letter, but if he was going to take the project seriously as an oral history, he needed some kind of objective corroboration, and Marty's question was an excellent one. If a death certificate didn't exist, finding someone else who knew or at least believed Manuel had died would give him grounds for accepting Alex's work.

The old man, who was studying the excavated ruins across the river, didn't reply. After a few moments, Paul touched his arm gently. "Sr. Reyes?"

"I was remembering Manuel. My older brother. So strong. So young." He began to cough, a rasping deep in his chest that hurt to hear. Marty picked up a glass of water from the TV tray and offered it to the old man, but his hand shook so violently he couldn't hold it. Getting to her feet, Marty held the glass for him while he took a sip. When the coughing subsided, he nodded his thanks to Marty and turned to Paul. "Mesothelioma," he said. "When I was a plumber, we worked around a lot of asbestos."

"A high price to pay for feeding your family," Paul said.

Sr. Reyes shrugged. "No one knew. I've had a long life in spite of it. The doctor says I'm running out of time, but I won't go until I see my little Aurora running and laughing like a child should. You must find the thief who killed my brother!"

Marty touched the old man's arm. "Don't get upset, señor. You don't want the coughing to start again."

"I try to stay calm, but I still miss Manuel. Seventy years and I still miss him!"

Linda's face flashed across Paul's memory. "Time doesn't

matter when we've lost someone important." Letting the vision go, he looked across at Marty. He'd always remember Linda, but he would gladly go into a new future if this young woman would have him.

He turned back to Sr. Reyes. "We want to find out what happened to Manuel. Was there someone your brother might have told about the silver lode, someone we might talk to?"

"Franco Sanchez was Manuel's partner. I don't know what happened to him, but I know he loved Manuel like his own brother. Franco wouldn't kill Manuel. Perhaps he was killed too."

"Maybe we can find his family," Marty said.

Sr. Reyes shrugged.

Paul decided to approach from another angle. "What about other letters from Manuel?" If any existed, they might mention his partner and give them clues to start their search. If not, other samples of Manuel's handwriting would at least prove the letter Alex had turned in was genuine.

"*Sí.* Every week I had a letter." Sr. Reyes held up both hands, spread all his fingers and one thumb. "Nine months he was in Jerome. Thirty-six letters."

"Do you still have them?" It was too much to hope, but what a find for a working historian if they still existed!

Dropping his hands in his lap, the old man began to twirl the white fringe on the colorful blanket that covered his knees. "Some of them got away. You know how it is, a letter from a family member circulates. Sometimes it comes back, sometimes not. What can you do?"

"How many survived?" When the old man's face fell, Paul realized the question sounded harsher than he had intended.

"The number doesn't matter," Marty said. "With your permission, Sr. Reyes, we'd like to see any you still have."

The statement covered the unintended accusation so smoothly Paul wondered if she'd read his mind.

"Fifteen, maybe twenty letters."

Paul's disappointment slipped away. Fewer than thirty-six, but still a substantial number.

"Enough?" the old man said, his eyes amused.

Aware his face must have shown his earlier dismay, Paul smiled. "Yes, sir. More than I could have hoped for."

"I'll translate them for you." Leaning forward, Sr. Reyes tapped Paul's chest with one crooked finger. "Do you understand what's at stake? Lots more than Alejandro's grade. More than finding out what happened to Manuel. Did Alejandro tell you about my great-granddaughter?"

"He showed me a picture of her and explained about her heart condition."

"Sí. That's why Alejandro must find the person who robbed Manuel." The old man pulled a small photo from the pocket of his chambray shirt and handed it to Marty. "This precious little one is running out of time. Her heart is no good, no good since she was born. Her papa, my grandson Hernando, doesn't have money to get my Aurora a new heart. He was a teacher, but he went to work as a plumber to get more money for medicines and other surgeries. Still it's not enough."

"What about insurance?" Marty said.

"A bad joke. Aurora's mama, Belinda, is an accountant. She stays home to take care of the little one, but she figures out the money. After the insurance pays, we will still owe almost a million dollars. We're a hard-working *familia*, but all together we can't get that kind of money." The old man sat up straight and looked at Paul, anger blazing in his eyes. "It's only fair! Whoever killed Manuel Reyes should pay to save Aurora Reyes."

"Yes sir, but you must know the murderer is most likely dead." Paul wasn't convinced there was a murderer, but the old man had to face the facts of the years that had passed.

"Sure. If Manuel had lived, he'd be ninety this year. He was just a boy when he died, nineteen. My grandson Alejandro's age. The murderer not only robbed him of his great find, he robbed him of seventy-one years of life." The old man's voice shook, and his face turned a worrisome red.

"Sr. Reyes," Marty said, "we're not here to upset you."

"No, of course not. Forgive me." Enrique took a deep breath and looked out at the river. When he finally spoke, his voice was calm. "What you say is true, Dr. Russell. Whoever killed Manuel is, no doubt, dead. But if we cannot get justice for the murder, the money this killer made from Manuel's discovery will be here. A son or a grandson must have what's left."

He brought his gaze from the river back to Paul. "Belinda figured that out too. Whoever dug out that silver turned it into cash and invested it. Silver isn't so high now, but those investments, they're probably worth a lot more. The Reyes familia doesn't want it all. Just enough money to save our little Aurora, the dawn of my old age." The anger drained away as quickly as it had flashed, and two tears rolled down the old man's cheeks.

Marty dug in her bag, produced a tissue, and put it in his hand. He nodded his thanks and dabbed his eyes.

Paul still wasn't sure he believed the story, but he heard himself say, "We'll help your family, Sr. Reyes." He didn't know how, but he knew they couldn't leave this family to struggle alone. "Do you have Manuel's letters here?"

"Sí." Stuffing the tissue in his shirt pocket, the old man placed his hands on the arms of his chair and started to rise. As Paul got to his feet and reached for Sr. Reyes's arm to help him get up, he noticed without surprise that Marty was doing the same on the patriarch's other side.

"No, no!" Joe Sweet called from the doorway. "I'll bring his wheelchair."

A look of disdain crossed the old man's face. "José thinks I can't walk, but every night I come outside to sit under the stars. Out here I'm not afraid to die."

Paul studied Alex's grandfather with new interest. Was he afraid to die at other times? Paul wouldn't have thought so.

"Here we go," Joe said. Guiding the wheelchair between Marty and Sr. Reyes like an experienced sheepdog cutting a bothersome ewe out of the flock, he positioned it so the old man sat down whether he wanted to or not. "Time for your morning nap, Enrique. Then we have chili and cornbread for lunch. One of your favorites."

Marty gave Paul a look that was just short of rolling her eyes. Paul nodded his understanding. "Sr. Reyes, when may we return?"

"Not tomorrow," Joe said. "Fridays we all go into town to shop."

"I don't need anything," Sr. Reyes snapped.

Turning the wheelchair and starting toward the doorway, Joe said, "Not true, Enrique. You're about out of two of your prescriptions."

"Someone else can pick them up for me. I have cash."

"No, no," Joe said. "We can't become dependent on others."

Paul saw Marty's jaw clench. Before she could erupt, he dropped his arm lightly on her shoulders. "No problem. Tomorrow's a teaching day for me. Would Saturday work, Joe?"

"It will work!" Sr. Reyes roared. "You come at eight o'clock."

"Let's make it ten o'clock," Joe said. "We'll get everyone finished with breakfast so we can have coffee and sweet rolls out here on the patio."

"It's not a party," Sr. Reyes said. "I'm going to give the professor some letters. Eight o'clock! Before breakfast."

Paul put a hand on the old man's shoulder. "I have a teenager at home. Ten o'clock will work out well."

"You come, too, girl," Sr. Reyes said. "I can tell you are a team."

Paul winked at Marty. "We are indeed."

4

Scott dumped his books on the kitchen table and hurried to his dad's study. Dad was at his computer, so intent on his writing, he'd forgotten all about Rahab. Evidently enjoying the challenge, the Siamese cat was jumping from one stack of books to the next. Scott knocked on the door frame.

Dad looked up and stared like he was trying to remember who Scott was. Then he managed to get back into the present. "Hi there, bud! How was your day?"

Scott felt almost shy. He wasn't used to his dad focusing his full attention on him. "Fine."

"How about a few details? Fine as in 'everything went as expected' or fine as in 'something super happened.' Fine on the bus, at lunch, in debate, or because you talked to Sara."

Scott held up his hands. "My day was good. Except for one thing."

"Okay."

"I had to sit in health class and learn the names of the muscles I might strain running track instead of going with you to find out about the silver lode."

"Fair enough. Sit down, and I'll report."

As usual, the straight chair beside the desk was stacked with books. As was the window seat, the old coffee table, and the floor in front of the bookcases. Scott picked up the books from the chair, looked a question at Dad, and got a nod. As Scott handed the books over, he glanced at his dad's computer screen. "Been Verified? That website won't have anything on Jefferson."

"I'm playing hooky this afternoon."

"Because?"

"My report will explain. Sit."

"I could have studied the muscles at home, Dad."

Paul shook his head. "Marty and I had an interesting visit with Sr. Reyes, but we didn't find out anything about the silver lode. He doesn't know anything but what's in the letter."

Scott didn't like the sound of "Marty and I" run together like they were one word. He liked Marty for a boss, but Dad didn't need a girlfriend. "So the trip was a waste of time."

"I didn't say that. Marty was amazing with the old man. She asked him about a partner. We got a name, Franco Sanchez. Any kids at school named Sanchez?"

"Katie Sanchez is one of the cheerleaders."

"Might be a start." Dad pulled a pen out of a red and yellow flowered coffee mug Scott remembered his mom using and jotted a note on the edge of a paper.

"Is that all you found out?"

"No. But tracking down confirmation of Manuel's partner is my assignment. Marty's job is to raise funds to help little Aurora."

"The old guy didn't have any idea where his brother was looking?"

Dad shook his head.

"I know Cleopatra Hill. If I talk to Sr. Reyes, I can figure out where Manuel was searching."

"I'm not sure Sr. Reyes knows what a silver lode is. He was a plumber, not a miner."

Scott's heart picked up speed. He leaned forward. "I want to find that silver lode, Dad, more than anything I've ever wanted." Except for Mom to live. Scott pushed the ache away.

"We reviewed for a test in history. Mr. Akery let me go to the library, and I started researching silver lodes. I looked up what conditions create them, what kind of rock formations surround them, and where they've been discovered. Things like that. I'm going to study the topo map of Cleopatra Hill to figure out where to look."

"You're welcome to study the maps and come up with a theory."

It was almost too easy, so before Dad could add conditions, Scott got up to leave.

Dad said, "Same rules as always, Scott. You're not to go alone. On Cleopatra Hill or anywhere else."

"I won't get lost."

"Maybe not, but you could get hurt."

"I always have my cell phone."

Paul shook his head. "Not good enough. I mean it, Son. If you go exploring, take someone with you. And text me telling me when you're leaving, who's coming with you, and when you'll be home. If you fail to follow either of those stipulations, you won't go again."

"But who would go with me, Dad? My friends all think rocks are boring!"

"Trade hours tutoring one of the kids who's flunking science or history, one hour of tutoring for one hour hiking with you. If you don't like that option, ask the librarian who else checks out geology books and make a new friend. One way or the other, find someone. I'm not budging an inch on this."

"Okay. Okay." Having Dad's full attention had its downside. Or not. Scott couldn't figure out his own feelings. Giving Dad a quick hug, he raced from the room. Like a little kid.

Scott couldn't help it. He was filled with a feeling he hadn't had in a long time, maybe since Mom died. He didn't know how to name it, so he did what he always did when his feelings confused him. He went out to the street, turned right, and started to jog.

At the end of the block, he picked up his pace. The closer he got to Verde River Greenway, the faster he ran. The emotion, whatever it was, spurred him. By the time he passed the flagpole at the park entrance, he was winded. The feeling had settled. Slowing to a walk, he searched for a name. Whatever the emotion was, it wasn't familiar.

Instinctively he knew it was an adult emotion. Different from excitement. More than happy. Where had it come from? One second, he was feeling resentful about the rules Dad was laying down for him, and the next this feeling welled up in him. Could it be joy?

The name echoed in his heart, and he knew that's what it was. He even knew where it came from. Dad was completely back in his life. There in the study, Scott realized his dad was paying attention. He didn't say what Scott expected, that it was silly to think he could find a silver lode. He took it for granted that his son knew enough to look for a rare geological formation. Then he went one more step. He thought through what Scott would be doing and made two simple rules to keep his son safe.

As he walked along the dirt path under the spring green cottonwoods, Scott realized his dad had been back in his life for a while. He just hadn't noticed the change. After Mom died, Dad had sunk into himself. Dad wasn't neglectful. He made sure Scott ate on time, kept to the bedtime Mom had set for him, and went to school every day. But he wasn't really there. Every once in a while, Dad tried to talk to him, but mostly those talks wound up being arguments. Now Dad was back. Joy filled Scott.

When he reached the Verde River, he sat on the bank and watched the water flow lazily toward Mingus Mountain and the

Black Hills. A hundred yards upriver a male mallard's head flashed green as it dove to fish. Nearby a brown female led six ducklings out into the middle of the river. Scott lay back and closed his eyes. The warmth of the sun relaxed him. Gradually joy subsided into contentment. Another adult emotion. He began to imagine finding the silver lode. It would be mined out, of course, but he would see veins in the rock too small to be profitable.

Scott opened his eyes and sat up. He had to think of someone fun to go with. Dan would be perfect, but Dan was back in Colorado in college after his spring break. Bill might be willing to go, but if he asked Bill, Carly would be sure to find out, and Carly talked too much. He wasn't kidding when he told his dad his friends thought exploring geological formations was boring. No way was he going to tutor some jock to bribe him to go along. So who?

The mallard family had made their way to the bank and were scavenging for insects. He had to have more friends. Who was he forgetting? *B.T.* The name flashed in his mind, starting a guilty tape. He shouldn't have gotten too busy for his friend. Friends should be more important than the debate team. B.T. might not want to get together now.

Scott sighed. Only one way to find out. He pulled his cell out of his pocket and punched in the number of the Harpers' land line. Even if B.T. was home, when his name showed on caller ID, B.T. might not answer.

"Hey, Scott! Great to hear from you, dude."

No hostility, no reproaches. Scott felt worse. "Sorry I didn't call sooner, buddy."

"No big deal. I could have called you. What's up?"

Scott didn't know what to say. He couldn't open the conversation by asking for a favor. He said something he'd overheard Marty say on the phone. "Just thinking about you. How's it going?"

B.T. was quiet for so long, Scott checked to make sure he still had a signal, three bars.

Finally, B.T. said, "Okay. Pop is working nights. I only see him on weekends."

Everything B.T. didn't say hit Scott with more guilt. He should have kept up with his friend. But if B.T. was interested, the search for the silver lode could take up a lot of weekends and keep him away from his dad. "Want to climb Cleopatra Hill Saturday?"

"You bet! Will your dad let me pick you up?"

"Yeah. You're high on his list. He's not going to be happy when he finds out how long it's been since I called you."

B.T. whistled. "Well, then dude, we won't tell him."

"He wouldn't hit me or anything." As soon as the words were out of his mouth, Scott wanted to call them back and swallow them. He and B.T. had agreed never to talk about B.T.'s dad unless B.T. started the conversation.

"You're lucky, Scott."

It was the first time B.T. had said anything like that. Scott murmured, "I know."

The phone was quiet. Then B.T. cleared his throat. "What time Saturday?"

"Nine o'clock. I'll bring us a lunch."

"Eight-fifteen too early? Pop gets home from work at eight-thirty."

Scott got the message. "Eight-fifteen is better. We can get going."

"Why are we hiking Cleopatra Hill?"

"It's complicated, but get ready to find silver and gold."

5

Marty pulled into the parking lot at the Osborn Savings and Loan at four-thirty. Except for a silver Lexus, the lot was empty. It was a little before closing time, but she hoped Patricia Osborn would give her a few minutes. All afternoon Marty had thought about Aurora Reyes. Four years old, the same age her sister Ruthie was when she died.

All Marty had was her determination that Aurora would get the chance at life Ruthie had lost and a sketchy plan for a fund raiser, but she had enormous hope that Patricia Osborn would want to help. She didn't know why she had the courage to approach the older woman, but something about their first meeting had suggested they might become friends.

Marty smoothed her hair and slipped into the denim jacket she'd grabbed to dress up her jeans. Before she lost her nerve, she got out of the pickup and headed for the lobby. Except for one customer at a teller's window and a receptionist at a heavy oak desk, the spacious room was empty. The receptionist, an older woman with dark skin and short, curly, white hair, looked up from her work and smiled. "May I help you?"

Marty returned the smile. "I hope so. I'd like to see Ms. Osborn."

"Do you have an appointment?"

"No, but she called on me at my shop Monday." My shop. The words came almost naturally this time. "Ms. Osborn invited me to stop by any time."

The receptionist raised her eyebrows. "It's late." She consulted her computer screen. "How about nine-thirty tomorrow morning?"

Marty knew she shouldn't be surprised, but the urgency of her hope rebelled at the idea of waiting a few more hours to begin her campaign. A nameplate engraved Carol Evans sat on the corner of the desk.

Marty smiled again. "I only need a couple of minutes, Carol."

"Honey, I'm not Carol. She took her youngest to the doctor, and I offered to cover for her. I'm Joan Lincoln, Pat's executive assistant."

"Marty Greenlaw. I'm new to the community. I'm opening an antique furniture workshop in Clarkdale."

"Welcome to the Verde Valley, Ms. Greenlaw. Tell me what's so important it can't wait until tomorrow morning."

"I want to ask Ms. Osborn to help a four-year-old child who needs a new heart."

Joan studied Marty. "Your child?"

The older woman's tone was neutral, and Marty wondered if many people came here looking for help for their children. Marty shook her head. "I'm organizing a fund raiser to help the family. They're local, and I hoped Osborn Savings and Loan might participate."

"I can't speak for Miss Pat, of course, but she loves kids. Sadly, she was never blessed that way. I'll check to see how busy she is." Joan typed a short message on her computer and turned back to Marty. "I wonder if you can help me. I have my grandmother's mahogany dining room table. With the leaves in, it seats eight, but over the years two of the chairs disappeared. I'd like to find replacements. They wouldn't have to match, just blend in."

Marty relaxed. Right here she had a potential customer. "I'll want to see the table," she said, "but I'm sure we can find something that will work for you."

A soft musical tone brought Joan's attention back to the computer screen. "You can go on up, Miss Marty. Second office on your right at the top of the stairs."

"Thanks for your help, Ms. Lincoln."

The older woman chuckled. "Call me Joanie. I'm a fixture in this office, been here since before Mr. Osborn retired." She reached under the desk for her purse and pulled out a small case. Drawing out a card, she handed it to Marty. "When you and Miss Pat have that fund raiser planned, you let me know how I can help."

Her nervousness gone now, Marty crossed the room and went up the open staircase. Three frosted glass doors marched along the back wall. The second one said CEO. Tapping twice, Marty pushed open the door.

Patricia Osborn sat at a walnut desk that faced the door. A cluster of orange bird of paradise in a green rectangular vase brightened a wide windowsill. When she stood to welcome Marty, the only word Marty could think of was elegant. Her black silk shirt and black and white geometric skirt set off her chin-length white bob and dark eyes. Marty remembered skinny black jeans and a black and white striped sweater from her visit to Old and Treasured. Did this polished woman always wear black and white?

Hand outstretched, Patricia came from behind her desk. "Marty, what a pleasant surprise!"

Marty took her hand, struck by the perfect pressure to communicate genuine welcome. Although she was several inches shorter than the CEO of Osborn Savings and Loan, Marty didn't feel at a disadvantage as she often did. She wondered how the woman had managed to put her at ease so quickly. No doubt she could learn a lot about business from Patricia Osborn.

"Joanie says you're here about a fund raiser. You haven't changed your mind about a loan, then?"

Marty smiled and shook her head. "So far I'm staying in my budget."

"Good. If you ever find you want to expand, just remember we're here to help. Neighbor to neighbor. Now sit down and tell me about a way we can help another neighbor." Patricia indicated a leather love seat grouped with two wing chairs upholstered in red paisley.

As she sat in one of the chairs, Marty said, "A four-year-old girl needs a heart transplant, and her family doesn't have sufficient insurance or personal funds to pay for it."

Patricia picked up a small notebook and pen from a walnut coffee table. "Does the family live in the area?"

Marty nodded. "If I've got my dates straight, they've been in Cottonwood seventy years."

"Good. Pillars of the community. What's the name?"

"Reyes. The child is Aurora. Her parents are Hernando and Belinda."

Patricia looked genuinely interested. "I expect we can do something to help. How did you find out about Aurora Reyes?"

Marty's cheeks warmed. Absurd. She was just friends with Paul. "Dr. Paul Russell, a member of the history faculty at Northern Arizona University, asked my opinion about the authenticity of a letter written around 1950."

Registering the question on the other woman's face, Marty paused. "Sorry. It's a long story. Do you have time?"

"I do."

"I don't know anything about antique documents, so I couldn't comment on the letter's authenticity. It's a fascinating letter, though, and I agreed to go with Dr. Russell to visit the recipient, Enrique Reyes, a gentleman in his eighties. Aurora is Sr. Reyes's great-granddaughter. As you can imagine, he's quite concerned about her condition."

"He asked for your help?"

Marty shook her head. "My sister died when she was four, and I couldn't sleep last night thinking about Aurora. I have a sketchy plan for a fund raiser, but you're the first person I've contacted. I know you're involved with the Jerome Historical Society, and I thought you might know families with connections to Jerome who might want to help."

"The Reyes family moved to Cottonwood from Jerome?"

Marty threw up her hands. "Sorry. I told you it was a long story. I've left out what the letter said and how Aurora's plight came up. Enrique Reyes's older brother Manuel, the one who wrote the letter, was a miner. He disappeared in 1950, right after he wrote the letter. I thought the old mystery might add a note of interest to Aurora's story."

"I don't know how much a mysterious a disappearance was in those days. Lots of men disappeared from the mines. Most of them left to look for a new boom town. A few found romance and went away to reinvent their lives with women of questionable reputation."

"Sr. Reyes believes his brother was murdered."

Patricia's brows drew together in a slight frown. "Bar fights happened frequently in those days, and men died. I don't know how much interest that would create."

"It wasn't like that. The letter tells of the discovery of a rich deposit of silver and gold."

"Silver was common enough. Gold was much scarcer. I've certainly never heard anything about a deposit of silver or gold."

"The letter refers to a silver lode. Paul, Dr. Russell, has a son who's a budding geologist. Scott says a silver lode would definitely be worth killing for. He's eager to find it."

Patricia shrugged, an understated, elegant gesture. "This is all interesting, but I'm afraid I don't see the connection to the little girl's heart surgery."

"There I go again," Marty said, "leaving out the important part! Sr. Reyes believes someone else knew about Manuel's discovery and murdered his brother for it. He wants the descendants of the murderer to pay for Aurora's surgery."

"Reparation three generations later? What makes him so sure his brother was murdered?"

"Because he disappeared right after he discovered the silver lode."

"Honey, sometimes men who died in mining accidents were misidentified or never identified at all. No doubt those families thought their fathers, sons, and brothers disappeared."

Marty nodded. "Even if Manuel was murdered, I don't think it's possible to solve a seventy-year-old cold case in time to help Aurora."

"But this professor, Dr. Russell, and his son are interested?"

"Only from a historical perspective. That's okay with me, but I want to raise money now. Sr. Reyes says Aurora is running out of time."

"I'm on board with helping the little girl, but I'm afraid I don't see why the connection to the dead brother is important."

"I thought families who made money mining might want to help another miner's family."

Patricia checked her watch, a wide black and white enamel cuff. "That might work. I'll have to think about it, but I imagine I know some people who would want to give back to the town that made their fortune. A child descended from a family unlucky in mining might be a popular cause." She got to her feet. "I hate to cut this short, Marty, but I have a dinner meeting in Flagstaff. I've got to get on the road if I want to be on time."

Marty stood. "You've given me more time than I asked for, Ms. Osborn. Would you allow me to use your name as co-chair of the fund raiser? It would be an honorary title. I'll do the work."

Patricia smiled and held out her hand. "Only if you call me Pat. I'd love to help little Aurora, and I imagine I can come up with a list of names to get you started." She went to a closet, retrieved a briefcase with wheels, and set it on her desk. "What about the venue and timing?"

"My grand opening is coming up in a little over a month. I thought about doing a special historical program a day or two before. Dr. Russell is willing to help me plan it." Not that she'd had time to mention it, but Marty knew she could depend on him.

"What a great idea! People interested in history are also likely to be interested in antiques. You're going to be quite a businesswoman." Patricia slid two file folders into the briefcase, snapped it shut, and set it on the floor. "I do some of my best thinking in the car. I'll give your fund raiser some thought while I drive up to Flagstaff. After I make a few contacts, I'll pass the names on to you. When you get in touch with them, they'll be expecting to hear from you."

As Pat pulled out the telescoping handle of her briefcase, Marty went to open the office door. "Pat," she said, "I can't thank you enough. We're going to make a great team."

6

Friday, March 15

P aul looked across the table at Dr. Herbert Butler, his department chair. At the moment Dr. Butler was walking a spoon through the fingers of his right hand. "You should be further along on this book by now, Russell. The final acceptance of your publisher is due on my desk no later than June 1. That gives you less than two months to compile your chapters into a complete manuscript, polish it, and forward the finished product to your editor in time for approval."

He shook his head, causing the thinning gray hair to spread out like wings at his temples. "Frankly, I don't see how you can do it." He put down the spoon, pushed back his chair, and got to his feet.

Pulling a small comb out of his pocket, he ran it expertly through the wings, settling them back into place. "It's almost eight. I'm due in a meeting in the dean's office." Dr. Butler looked down at the small, wiry man sitting next to Paul. "I know you'll do your best to get him through this, Roger."

The chair of the history department extended a hand to Paul.

As they shook, he said, "I'd hate to lose you, Russell, but you remember the contract you signed when you took this job. It specified no more than two years to publish your first book. We extended a year after your wife died, but the clock is ticking. End of the fourth quarter, and all that." He chuckled, letting Paul know the reference to his days coaching football was intentional. A joke or a veiled threat? Finish the book by the deadline or go back to teaching high school.

As Dr. Butler hurried toward the door of the coffee shop, Dr. Roger Leonard said, "What's going on, Paul? I hope you realize that was a line in the sand. Butler is always deadly serious when he makes one of his little jokes."

Paul nodded and sipped his now lukewarm latte. His mentor wasn't telling him anything he didn't know. He'd come to this meeting knowing his lack of progress on The Book was the topic of discussion, but that hadn't helped him come up with a reason for why the project was stalled.

"I wish I had an answer, Roger. I never get enough time to make serious progress on the writing."

"What's taking up your time?"

"Besides teaching?"

"Teaching is a given. You knew that from the outset."

Paul considered the week that was passing. Wednesday evening was taken up by Alex and his trip to see Marty. Yesterday they interviewed Enrique Reyes. "Lately it's been the oral history projects my students are doing for their midterm projects. The end products are more sophisticated than I expected. It's amazing the quality of work students are capable of when they're given the opportunity to choose a topic that interests them. Just yesterday a student brought in an intriguing little problem from Jerome's mining days."

"Stop right there," Roger said. "What on earth were you thinking of to tackle such a complicated project with undergraduates? If you were teaching a grad course, I'd say it was appropriate. But this is a second-year history course, right?"

Paul shrugged. "I adjusted the research topic so the students interview a family member. It's turning out to be quite effective. I worked with the students to focus their topics, and we spent class time developing good questions." Of course some of the students, like Alex, had taken off in their own directions. He remembered approving an interview with his grandfather about the Korean War, not about the death of his great-uncle.

Roger was shaking his head. "Assignments students enjoy shouldn't be a priority for you right now, my friend. Which is more important, your students or your job? Without the job, you won't have any students. 'Publish or perish' isn't just a catchy phrase. It's reality. Publish an academic book or lose your job."

All Paul's teaching instincts rebelled at the idea that writing a book no one would read except a few graduate students looking for a dissertation topic was more important than making good assignments. But before he could put his feelings into words, Roger held up a hand. "Tell me precisely where you are in the book process."

Paul shifted uncomfortably. He could predict his mentor's reaction. Roger would repeat what Dr. Butler had said in different words, words Paul understood only too well. "The research is complete," he said. "I have a solid outline."

"How many chapters?"

Paul winced. "Four."

"Out of?"

"Fifteen."

"You turned in three with the proposal, so you've only managed to get one more chapter written."

No longer interested in the coffee, Paul put down the paper cup. "I've finished all the research for the book and chosen quotations to use. I've also procured the required permissions."

"In short, you're doing all the work for the book except the actual writing. That, my friend, is writer's block."

"I know. What I don't know is how to break through it."

Roger took the plastic lid off his tea, drained his cup, and placed it on the table with an air of finality. As he stood, he said, "I have a committee meeting in twenty-three minutes. Let's walk back to campus while we talk."

Feeling a bit like a clumsy circus clown in the company of a midget, Paul followed his mentor out into the morning sunshine. Slowing his normal pace enough to keep Roger from having to jog, Paul walked along Milton Road toward the campus.

"Why did you pick the topic of Jefferson's Bible to write a book on, Paul? It's a rather eccentric topic, even for a first book. Your dissertation, I assume."

Paul shook his head. "My dissertation was an oral history of the football program at the one-hundred-year-old high school where I taught history and coached. I'm sure you can see why I couldn't turn that topic into an academic book."

"Of course. No one but the locals would care a whit about your results. Though I'm sure your oral history techniques were impeccable."

Paul chuckled. "I don't know that I've ever heard the collection of oral history described as impeccable."

Roger stopped and turned to face Paul. Pulling himself up to his full height of five feet, six inches, he said, "The source of your writer's block is as clear to me as the stones in that old fence that marks the boundary of university property. You're trying to write a book on a topic that doesn't interest you.

"At this point in your career your interest in your topic is immaterial. Many of us, including yours truly, have written books on topics we didn't care about personally. Academic books can be evaluated objectively by peers, while teaching can only be evaluated subjectively by students unqualified to pass judgment.

"In short, the only way we in the academy can justify promotion and tenure is through a faculty member's writing. Put in rather vulgar terms, you're going to be fired if you don't break through your writer's block and finish this book by the deadline."

"I understand, Roger. I just don't know what to do about the problem."

"You must put your personal feelings aside and write, the same way I assume you've written dozens of papers on topics you were not allowed to choose. To put this in perspective, you've got to realize how simple it will be to replace you, popularity with the students or not. I was on the search committee that hired you. We had one hundred and three applicants. We were able to weed out about half of them easily enough, but we found fifty with the qualifications we specified for the position. Fifty, my friend."

"Yes, I've always wondered why you chose me."

"Your passion for teaching. It's not often we get an applicant for an entry-level position with the kind of teaching experience you have."

Paul held his rising temper in check. "Yet now you're telling me it's my passion for teaching that's putting my position in jeopardy. I don't get it, Roger. I want to teach. I don't want to write a book."

As he said the words, Paul realized with a jolt not only did he not want to write a book about Thomas Jefferson, he didn't want to write an academic book on any topic. The idea terrified him. What on earth could he do with a Ph.D. in history if he didn't want to follow the rules for faculty at a university?

7

Marty stood in the half-open doorway of the storage shed and fought dismay that threatened to escalate into panic. As large as a two-car garage, the shed was piled wall-to-wall and floor-to-ceiling with what she would call junk but what her assistant Carly called "treasures we need to sort." Odd pieces of old furniture were piled with rusting trinkets that should have been thrown on the scrap heap years before.

"There you are!"

Marty turned to watch Carly hurry across the backyard. Hurry wasn't strong enough, but Carly was too young to bustle and too confident to scurry. In any case, she covered the distance in half the time it took other people. The habit of moving quickly was Carly's strength, but it was also her weakness. She accomplished more than most people, but Marty found herself re-doing more of Carly's work than should have been necessary. This morning, however, she intended to make good use of Carly's enthusiasm.

"Good morning," Marty said.

"Sorry. I guess I'm doing it again."

Marty smiled. Not again. Always. "Ready to rush into the shed and find out what we've got?"

"I've been dying to get back here ever since you got the showroom set up. Most of the antiques in this shed belonged to my grandmother." The girl clapped. "I couldn't believe it when you decided to buy Grandma Remick's house to use for your business!"

Sometimes Marty doubted the wisdom of that decision since Carly and her brother Bill had been part of the package, but this wasn't the time to look back over her shoulder. She took a deep breath and got ready to take charge. "Okay, Carly. First, let's sort by size. I've got bins in the back of my pickup. We'll put the little things in there. Once we've got all the small stuff out of the way, we'll put the bins and the boxes in the yard. We'll sort the furniture by room. Living room furniture in the northwest corner, bedroom furniture in the northeast corner. Office items in the southwest corner, miscellaneous southeast."

"Got it. First, the bins."

"I'll help you get them." As Marty started around the house, her phone rang. She checked caller ID, Patricia Osborn. "I've got to take this."

"No problem. I'll be back with the bins in a jiff."

Marty touched the phone and held it up to her ear. "Good morning."

"It is, and I've got good news to match the morning. Last night I came up with the names of three wealthy families with connections to Jerome and the mines. I emailed last night. Two have responded positively. Not necessarily for making donations, but for being willing to be interviewed. I'll follow up with the third contact this morning."

Evidently the CEO of Osborn Savings and Loan moved as quickly as Carly when she had a task, but before Marty could thank her, Pat said, "Do you have something to write with?"

"I'm out back by the shed, but I'm heading for the house now."

"When you're ready, I'll give you the contact information. Meanwhile, I'll fill you in on the details. Carol Angel is a definite yes for the interview. Her husband, Thomas Miller, owned a small mine east of town. It's possible the Reyes boy worked for him. The second yes is Jimmy Wong. His grandfather owned a successful restaurant in Jerome. I believe he went on to invest in Coca-Cola at the right time or something like that. Jimmy heads up the Wong philanthropic foundation." Pat paused.

"The one I haven't heard back from is the Sanchez family. They own a string of grocery stores. I don't remember the details, but I think they started with a food truck in Jerome."

Marty opened the back door and went into the kitchen. Grabbing a small magnetic tablet from the refrigerator, she sat down at the table. "Okay. I'm ready."

Repeating the names one at a time, Pat rattled off email addresses, phone numbers, and physical locations. "I'll let you know after I hear back from Franco Sanchez, but you can go ahead and contact Carol and Jimmy."

"Carol Angel is the contact for the Miller mine?"

Pat laughed. "Carol is a once-upon-a-time bit actress who kept her stage name when she married Thomas Miller. He was quite a bit older than she. He died when I was a girl, but I think my father knew him."

"Thanks, Pat! I can't believe how quickly you got this information."

"My work with the historical society pays off now and then. These three families were prominent enough in Jerome's past to be magnets for anyone with the slightest interest in the town's history."

Her tone edged with irony, Pat added, "When you get in touch, be sure to let them know there's a bit of free publicity in it for them. I'm sure Franco or his uncle or whoever it is that runs the Sanchez markets will jump at the chance for some positive press. Ditto for Jimmy Wong. Carol will want to see her name in lights again."

"Pat, I don't know how to thank you."

"I have an idea about that. Do you ever take on redecorating jobs?"

"Furniture restoration is my specialty, but I've dabbled in redecoration for customers who wanted to redo a room in period furniture, usually a living room or a bedroom."

"Would you consider a whole house?"

"I'm not sure," Marty said cautiously. "It would take some time to find just the right pieces, so it would depend on how soon the customer wanted the job finished."

Pat laughed. "For me, girlfriend. This is a project I've been considering for a long time, so I'm in no hurry."

Marty pinched herself to make sure she wasn't dreaming. "I'd love to, Pat! It might take a year or more, but we could have a lot of fun with the process."

"That's my goal. I don't have nearly enough fun. All I do these days is work. Joanie is always trying to get me to find a hobby. Antiques will be my new passion. Can you start today?"

Marty took a deep breath. With her grand opening and now the fund raiser, her plate was full. But this opportunity was too good to pass up. No doubt Pat did a good bit of entertaining. If she could please Pat, and Pat told her friends about Old and Treasured, her business would start on a firmer footing than she'd ever dreamed possible. "I can meet you at your house and at least get an idea of what you have in mind. What time?"

"Come for supper around six. Do you like Chinese? I can call in an order and pick it up on my way home from work."

"Six works, and Chinese is fine. All I need is your address."

"15 River Road. Head up 89A toward Sedona. River Road is a right turn just before the bridge."

"May I bring some ice cream or something for dessert?"

Pat sighed. "A question only slim young women ask. No, honey. I don't want the temptation. Just bring your pretty head and all the ideas I know you have. Gotta run now. See you this evening."

Marty disconnected and put the phone back into the pocket of her work smock. The list of names on the tablet seemed almost too good to be true. Evidently no matter what Pat made up her mind to do, she threw herself into it. Tearing off the sheet with the notes, she carried it into the large closet she'd converted into an office and put it under a millefiori paperweight that had belonged to her grandmother.

"Who was it?"

Marty jumped.

"Sorry," Carly said, looking over her shoulder at the list. "I didn't mean to sneak up on you." She laughed. "I guess that's why some people call athletic shoes sneakers. Who was that on the phone?"

Marty's first impulse was to say, "It was a business call." But her nosy, enthusiastic assistant could be a valuable asset in organizing the fund raiser and in locating particular items of furniture. "Patricia Osborn."

"I thought you didn't need a loan."

"I don't. I asked Pat for help with a fund raiser. Would you like to help me organize it?"

"Sure! What's it for?"

"A four-year-old girl who needs a heart transplant. Her name is Aurora Reyes."

Carly pulled out a chair and sat down. "Reyes. Isn't that the name of the man you and Paul went to see yesterday? The one whose brother was murdered for lost treasure?"

"That's the name of the man we went to see, but where did you get the idea his brother was murdered for lost treasure?"

"Scott was talking about it. He and B.T. are going to start looking for the silver tomorrow."

What to say? Marty didn't want to add to the gossip already starting, but neither did she want to let it spread based on inaccuracies. The best way to rein it in was to enlist Carly's help. She touched the girl's arm. "The death of Sr. Reyes's brother ties indirectly to the fund raiser. If we want to help this little girl, we need to do everything we can to keep people from gossiping."

Carly tensed ever so slightly. "I'm the last person to pass along gossip."

Right. Amazing how little self-knowledge the girl had. "Scott didn't have his facts quite straight. Sr. Reyes's brother Manuel wrote a letter home telling about finding a rich silver deposit. That letter was the last anyone in the family heard from Manuel. No one knows what happened to him. For that matter, no one knows what he found, if anything."

"But now the family needs money for heart surgery," Carly said, "and Sr. Reyes is trying to find out if there's some way to raise it from his brother's discovery."

In spite of herself, Marty was impressed. Carly was quick to grasp the ramifications of the letter. "That's right, but Aurora needs the transplant now. She can't wait for Scott or anyone else to track down whatever Manuel's discovery was."

"How do we come in?"

Just barely Marty managed to keep from smiling at the we. "Good question. When I approached Pat about donating to the cause, I suggested we tie the fund raiser into our grand opening by doing a preview for invited guests likely to donate to Aurora's medical fund."

"I get it! Manuel Reyes dates back to mining days. We bring in antiques, and we have a well-heeled, sympathetic group of future customers who just might find a piece of furniture they can't live without."

Marty winced at the way Carly phrased it, but she had to

admit the young woman had grasped the situation with lightning speed.

"What do you want me to do?"

"Right now, we need to clear out the shed. We can brainstorm a plan while we work. Remember, I only heard about Aurora Reyes Wednesday afternoon."

Carly got up and headed for the back door. "I can deal with the logistics. I know the best caterer in the area, and I know where to get extra chairs for people to sit in when it's time to make the pitch. We're going to have to work fast."

As Marty followed her outside, she wanted to ask her assistant if she ever worked any other way. Marty shuddered at the idea of putting Pat and Carly together on a task. They would work so fast she wouldn't be able to keep up with what they'd done. Still, as she went into the shed and saw Carly filling the first bin with the odds and ends that cluttered every available surface, Marty knew Carly's energy was what she needed.

Retrieving her iPad from the battered roll top desk where she'd left it, Marty pulled up the spread sheet she'd created for inventorying the furniture. "I'm going to start cataloging the larger pieces."

They worked in relative silence for an hour. While Carly bustled out with a full bin and in with an empty one, Marty inspected desks, headboards, and pianos with a small flashlight. She estimated ten percent would be worth the time and labor it would require to make it sellable. At least thirty percent of the pieces should be hauled to the landfill.

The other sixty percent could be sold as-is to the customer making the highest bid. She was standing on a sturdy step stool inspecting the soundboard of yet another upright piano with questionable ivories when Carly shouted, "Over here!"

Marty closed the piano lid and went to where her assistant squatted beside what looked like a common World War II military-issue footlocker. It was in good shape, but the relics were so common they could be bought on eBay for around forty bucks.

"It doesn't look like much," Carly said, "but wait till you see what's inside!"

Stifling the urge to remind Carly that Thomas Jefferson or his contemporaries never owned a footlocker, Marty hefted one end of the army-green trunk. It was surprisingly heavy. Maybe it was a load of silver. The ridiculous pun flashed through Marty's mind, making her want to laugh. "Let's get it outside so we can take a good look."

Getting the footlocker around a wide sofa Marty hoped was a genuine Duncan Phyfe proved to be a challenge, especially when Carly wanted to rest by setting it in the middle of the velvet upholstered seat. Finally they staggered through the shed door. "A little farther," Marty said. "If we take it into the middle of the yard, we can lay out the contents."

Once they had the footlocker positioned, Marty stretched to get rid of the kinks in her back. As she straightened, she realized the morning shadows had disappeared. They'd spent four hours in the dim, dank shed.

Flinging back the lid of the footlocker, Carly crowed, "Come take a look. Practically new tools for mining by hand." She pulled a small pickax out from under a pair of mud-stained overalls. She set it on the ground beside the footlocker. "Here's a shovel that still has the price marked on the handle. I can't quite make it out, but I'd swear that's a dollar sign." She handed it to Marty. "What do you think?"

It was a dollar sign all right, but the numbers were smeared. High numbers, though. Maybe an eight and nine or two eights. The price had to be in cents, not in dollars. Even by today's standards, this shovel wouldn't cost eighty dollars.

"There are more tools in here. A rope that's been used a lot, a headlamp that's so heavy it must have guaranteed a headache, and a bunch of little bags for ore samples. The right customer would pay a lot for this set of tools!"

Marty wasn't interested in the tools. What looked like the owner's name had caught her attention. Kneeling on the grass by the footlocker, she traced the letters with one finger, whispering the letters to be sure she was right. "M-R-E-Y-E-S. "

8

"**M**-R-E-Y-E-S," Marty repeated. Could this be what she thought it was? Hands trembling, she began lifting out the rest of the contents of the footlocker.

"Mr. Eyes?" said Carly. "Who on earth is that?"

"Not Mr. There's a period after the *M*. I think this footlocker belonged to Manuel Reyes."

"The tools of the murdered man. We could raffle them off. People would love it!"

"I told you before, Carly. This time listen to me. You must not go around talking about murder. We don't know if it's true."

"But if it is true," Carly said thoughtfully, "talking about it could stir up a hornet's nest."

"Forget the murder! Help me see if there are any letters that never got mailed in here."

But it was a disappointing jumble. A couple of threadbare shirts, a tin cup, stained underwear, a tin plate, a pair of shoes that needed new soles, a Spanish Bible wrapped in a pair of pajamas that were only fit to be used as cleaning rags. At the bottom of the footlocker, Marty spotted a cheap spiral notebook with a lime green cover.

Snatching it before Carly could claim it, Marty looked slowly through the brittle pages. Everything was in Spanish, of course, but nothing looked like the beginning of a letter. Several of the pages were covered with lines of roughly the same length in twos or threes. Poetry?

An almost personal sense of loss engulfed Marty as she pictured a young man, a teenager really, in grimy clothes working to get the words right for a poem. "The Reyes family might want this footlocker," she said.

"But if we explain the tools would be great for an auction at the fund raiser, they'd want us to keep them. Nothing else in here is worth anything to us."

"I want Paul to take a look at this footlocker before we make any decisions. Let's put everything back and return it to the shed."

"Let me keep out the tools. Listen, Marty, I'm serious about a raffle, and I won't say a word about the murder." She flung her hands wide and raised her voice as if to get the attention of an audience. "Mining tools from Aurora's great-grandfather."

"Great-granduncle."

"Okay. Aurora's great-granduncle who worked in the copper mines in Jerome." She dropped her hands and lowered her voice. "Seriously, it's the perfect come-on. If we sold raffle tickets for it at fifty dollars a pop, I bet we'd get at least a thousand dollars. If the other people who attend are in Jimmy Wong's league, no one will be hurting for spending money."

"How do you know Jimmy Wong is invited?"

Carly settled cross-legged on the ground and dusted off her hands. "I saw his name on the tablet. You do know who he is, don't you?"

"All I know is he heads up a philanthropic organization of some kind."

"Jimmy Wong is Mr. Do-Gooder Big Bucks."

A note of defensiveness in Carly's voice caught Marty's attention. "Care to explain what you mean by that?"

Carly shrugged. "He's at least a multi-millionaire, maybe a billionaire, who funds special programs for kids on drugs."

More than defensiveness, resentment. But why would this young woman resent a man who did his best to help kids who were hurting? Unless...

Marty looked at Carly, but her assistant wouldn't meet her eyes. To let it go, or to push gently? "Tell me," she said quietly.

Still refusing to meet Marty's eyes, Carly said, "I don't know what you mean."

"Have you ever met Mr. Wong?"

Carly shook her head.

"But you've had experience with one of his programs."

Carly raised her head, meeting Marty's eyes with a defiant glare. "I got busted for drugs when I was in high school, okay? My grandmother overreacted. She went to some presentation at her church on Wong Summer Camps for kids who wandered from the straight and narrow. She signed me up without asking me if I wanted to go! When my friends found out, they..."

The girl had come this far. Marty decided to prod. "What did your friends do?"

Carly sighed, all the fight going out of her. "The same thing you're probably going to do. They quit talking to me."

"I'm sorry."

"You're going to fire me, aren't you?"

"No, Carly. Of course not."

"But I just told you I got busted for drugs!"

"Are you still using?"

Carly made a disgusted sound. "I never used. I had friends who did."

"If you weren't involved with the drugs, how did you get busted?"

"Okay. So I tried something once. I just had the bad luck to get caught the first time."

"Maybe not such bad luck. Where are the kids who gave you the drugs?"

Carly drew in a quick breath. "I never thought about it, but one of them is in jail and one of them is dead. A third kid dropped out of high school. The fourth kid is a girl who went to that Wong Summer Camp with me. She's in college studying to be a counselor."

"Good for her," Marty said. "And good for you! Here you are apprenticing as an antique restorer. Now, come on. Let's go in the house and grab some lunch." She got to her feet and held out a hand to the younger woman. She was rewarded with one of Carly's rare smiles.

As they walked toward the house, Carly said slowly, "Do you think I'll meet Mr. Wong?"

"I imagine so. Why?"

"I'd like to thank him. I've spent the last four years mad about having to spend my summer that way, but as I think back on it now, I realize it wasn't so bad. We hiked all over the San Francisco Peaks. A couple of nights we slept out under the stars at Hart Prairie. Have you ever seen the stars up there?"

"No."

"Maybe one afternoon we can drive up to Flag and hike into Hart Prairie."

Marty was glad her young assistant was making a quick comeback. She'd made the right decision when she pushed Carly to tell her story. "Sounds like fun."

Carly bounced into the kitchen. As she opened the refrigerator, she gave Marty a sly smile. "Bill makes a great campfire. I know I can talk him into it if you come. He'd like to get to know you better."

Marty reached around her assistant to retrieve a bagged salad from the hydrator drawer. "Are you trying to play matchmaker, Carly Remick? If you are, forget it. I'm not interested."

"Not me! Bill's been wanting to ask you, but he told me he couldn't compete with Dr. Russell."

Marty stiffened. "Paul and I are just good friends."

"Have you told him that?" a male voice asked from the doorway.

Marty looked up to see blond Bill Remick smiling at her. She felt herself flush, whether from embarrassment at the question or frustration that Paul had so obviously refused to hear her when she told him she just wanted to be friends, she wasn't sure. Either way, she had no intention of discussing her personal life with Carly or Carly's brother.

"This isn't the time or place for this discussion," she said crisply. "It's still a workday, and the last time I looked I was both boss and landlady around here."

Bill chuckled in a rich tenor that begged for a guitar. Sitting by a campfire singing to a guitar sounded like fun. But not with a tenor on guitar, with a bass, with Paul. She shook off the momentary lapse and focused on lunch. Opening a single serving can of chicken salad, she dumped it on the lettuce. Then, armed with a fork and a bottle of water, she sat down at the table. After a quick silent prayer of thanks, she started to eat.

She was grateful when brother and sister busied themselves making their own lunches. The arrangement of buying their grandmother's house from the Remicks and renting rooms back to them had felt like a gift from heaven at the time. Now she wondered if they were about to try to take her down a path she hadn't anticipated.

She wasn't the least interested in Bill. He was nice enough, but her heart didn't do the happy jig when Bill came into a room like it did when Paul showed up. Or called. Or crossed her mind. She speared a chunk of chicken. What was wrong with her? She'd made up her mind.

She took a long swig of the cool water. Time to focus on the bins of junk that lined the perimeter of the backyard. "Carly, let's talk about the smaller items you brought out of the shed this morning."

The girl put down the slice of leftover pizza that was her lunch. "The next step is to sort the things we can sell from the things that need to be donated to the Salvation Army."

"How about the things that need to go to the dump?"

"Ladies," Bill said, "interesting as this conversation is, I'll leave you to your working lunch."

Marty studied Bill. He'd taken the dashing of his hopes in stride. It was just as well he'd overheard her comments to Carly.

"Where are you going?" his sister demanded.

Bill raised an eyebrow. "To the library at the community college, if I have your permission, Mother."

Carly ignored the jibe. "When will you be home?"

"None of your business, squirt. You'll be safe enough here with our landlady this evening. Who knows? I may decide to be daring and drive up to the university library and stay until closing." As he left the room, he said, "I hear Friday nights are great at the library."

"Funny," Carly said.

"Meanwhile, back at the antiques workshop," Marty said, "the boss lady is considering giving her assistant an order to take all the bins to the Salvation Army, unsorted."

"No way, Marty! You saw the condition of those mining tools. I didn't have time to go through everything, but I know there are bound to be some more treasures like that. We can't just turn antiques like that over to the Salvation Army!"

"Priorities. I need your help finishing the inventory of the furniture out there. And don't forget about the tasks you agreed to do for the fund raiser. You're going to be much too busy to waste time on nickel and dime stuff."

"That 'nickel and dime stuff' is a treasure trove of antiques!"

"Not antiques. Just old stuff."

Carly frowned. "What makes an old chair a more valuable antique than an old cookie jar? The amount of money you can charge for it?"

A legitimate question. One that went to the heart of the vision she had for her business. "Antique furniture is more valuable because it creates a home that reflects the personality of the owner."

"I can say the same thing about the items you call 'trinkets.' A person who chooses a pig cookie jar shows more humor than someone who chooses one painted with roses."

"Good point. Let me see if I can be more precise. You can help me write a mission statement for Old and Treasured. Hand me that tablet." She wrote for a minute, crossing out words here and there.

"How about this? 'Antique furniture, by allowing a person to inhabit a favorite period of history, creates a home that reflects not only the owner's taste but also her personality.'"

Carly tilted her head and narrowed her eyes. "Read it again."

Marty complied.

"Okay. I can see that's what you're trying to do with the showroom and the furniture. You want to help people turn vanilla houses into homes with personality."

"Correct."

"Okay. But we can do the same thing with the trinkets. I know you think I rush into everything, but I've been thinking about the shed. We could use it to draw customers in, sort of like a bargain basement. I thought of a name, The Treasure Trove."

Marty wasn't sure how buying a cookie jar would lead a customer into looking at a Weber square grand piano, but having her own corner of the business would be good for Carly. She could prove she was trustworthy with the little things, maybe get over a bit of her guilt about her stint with the Wong Foundation. "I think it's a good idea," she said. "As long as you agree it takes second priority. The jobs I give you come first."

"Agreed! Can I use Scott sometimes? When you don't have anything for him to do."

"That's fine."

Carly clapped her hands. "I'm sure that jumble is hiding some valuable items! There might be more things that belonged to Manuel Reyes."

9

P aul climbed in his Jeep and headed home, as tired from grading midterm exams as if he'd run a marathon. Traffic was heavy as students headed out of Flagstaff for a wide spectrum of destinations over the week of spring break. Most of the students were going home or to the beach.

Some, though, had more exotic travel plans. One student had asked permission to take the midterm early because her grandmother was treating her to a trip to Scotland. Two of his Navajo students were headed to Window Rock to attend a healing ceremony complete with sand painting for an elder they both admired.

His destination for the week was his study in his home in Cottonwood. He was looking forward to having time to evaluate the oral history projects his second-year students had turned in. He was also eager to explore the ramifications of Enrique Reyes's story. And then there was his book. He was supposed to be writing about Jefferson and his odd attitude toward the Bible this week. Which meant he had to break through the writer's block Roger had diagnosed so accurately.

But the first task he had was to interview Franco Sanchez, Jr., the son of Manuel Reyes's partner. Paul was eager to talk to Sanchez because he was the one person who might be able to clear up the mystery of Manuel's death by relating whatever his father had told him about his days mining in Jerome.

Paul glanced at the clock on the dashboard, two-fifteen. An unheard-of time to leave on a Friday, but today he hadn't held class, just waited for his students to turn in their midterm papers. Eager to start their vacations, many of the students had turned them in Thursday afternoon, and the last one had come in at ten o'clock this morning. He was running ahead of schedule for his appointment.

On a sudden impulse, Paul took the exit for Montezuma's Well National Monument. The name was absurd, but the tiny park was a place he enjoyed. Montezuma had never been anywhere near the well. A stray conquistador or two, but no Aztecs. The name was an excellent example of popular legend overcoming historical fact.

Paul parked and walked the short uphill path to the top of the well, a limestone sinkhole that had formed some eleven thousand years before.

Fed by a spring, the well was filled with water so clear he could see to the bottom from where he stood six or eight stories above. The people who had seen the well as a source of irrigation for farming were the Sinagua, the indigenous "people without water." Around the middle of the fifteenth century, the Sinagua built stone houses under the overhanging cliffs now referred to as "Montezuma's Castle." They farmed the rich land around the sinkhole.

Paul walked from the well down to the edge of Beaver Creek and then back into the green, quiet grotto where the spring bubbled up from an underground river. If he had any hope of breaking through his writer's block, he had to understand why he'd chosen to write on a topic that clearly didn't "light his fire," as his Grandma Dottie would have said.

He supposed he'd had several reasons. First, the manuscript was a historically significant artifact housed in the Smithsonian. Second, copies were printed and distributed to every new member of Congress beginning in 1904 and continuing until the 1950s. Third, and most compelling... His mind went blank. Why had he chosen to study the 1820 manuscript?

Squatting in the manner those early people most likely did, Paul ran his hand through the moving crystalline water. Amazingly cold. He first saw a copy of the document at Monticello, Jefferson's Virginia plantation, when he was ten. He and his dad were on the way to a football game at the University of Virginia in Charlottesville.

They stopped at Monticello because his father was fascinated by every detail of Thomas Jefferson's life. That obsession was easy enough to unravel. His father's name was Thomas Jefferson Russell. His parents and his two brothers and one sister called him Tommy when he was growing up. He'd switched to Jeff when he went to college because he thought the name sounded more adult.

Paul shook his head, remembering how annoyed his dad got at family reunions when the next generation, his cousins, called him Uncle Tommy instead of Uncle Jeff as he requested again and again. Getting to his feet, Paul followed one of the irrigation canals toward the plots of dry ground that produced corn and squash six centuries before. Paul knew it didn't take a psychologist to figure out why he'd chosen to write on Thomas Jefferson.

But why that quaint version of the Bible? Ancient people irrigating with water from a sinkhole interested him more than what Thomas Jefferson thought belonged in the Bible and what didn't. He'd grown up with his Grandpa Warren, a retired preacher, impressing on him the importance of reading every verse in Scripture in the context of its book. He'd said to never, ever take part of it and ignore what was around it.

Paul stopped on the path and almost laughed out loud, except the realization wasn't funny. The source of his writer's block wasn't a flaw in his research. It was his family tree. The passion for history was his own. No one in his family cared about the flow of the past the way he did. So at least he'd chosen his own major in college. Still, at thirty-eight was he making decisions to try to please his father and his grandfather, both of them long gone from this life?

Paul walked slowly back to the Jeep. Nice to understand the forces driving his decisions. But now he had come up with his own topic, one he could write a book about. He'd have to locate a publisher and renegotiate his deadline with Dr. Butler. A challenging process, to say the least. As he got back on the interstate, he didn't even know how to start thinking about the problem.

10

P aul blinked as his eyes adjusted from desert brilliance to the low light of the sports bar. The place was almost empty, not surprising at four in the afternoon. A white-haired man at a table in the center of the room watched golf on a big screen TV. His companion, a much younger blond woman, studied a cell phone in one manicured hand.

The only other occupant, a man focused on a basketball game, sat at a table not far from the bar. Franco Sanchez, Jr.? He was Hispanic, but he didn't look any older than Paul. The son of Manuel's partner would be in his sixties.

As Paul started toward a table with a good view of the door, the young man beckoned to him. The grandson? Paul changed direction. When he reached the table, the young man said, "Dr. Russell?"

"Yes. Is your father ill?"

"My father?"

"I have an appointment with Franco Sanchez, Jr."

"That's me. My father died when I was ten."

As Paul pulled out a chair, he did a quick calculation. That would put Franco Sanchez at sixty something when his son was born. Unexpected, but not impossible.

The other man laughed. "I know what you're thinking, but you're wrong. Papa was about my age when I was born. His name was Pedro. He idolized his father, and since there wasn't another Franco anywhere on the Sanchez family tree, I got to be a junior. At least on my birth certificate. I never liked that name. I've been Frank since I started kindergarten."

Paul mentally reviewed the questions he'd hoped to get answered. How much would this young man know about his grandfather's early years? Probably not much, not enough anyway.

"Sorry to disappoint."

Paul summoned a smile. "I don't mean to be rude. It's just that my research is on the early 1950s. Your grandfather's era."

"Your email didn't say."

"No. I guess I'll have to add another line on my genealogical research checklist. Do you know anything about your grandfather's early life?"

"More than I wanted to as a kid. How about a beer?"

Paul shook his head. "Iced tea would be good."

Frank caught the bartender's eye. "An iced tea and an order of wings. Bring us the jalapeño dipping sauce."

"Coming up."

Frank nodded at the TV. "You keeping up with March Madness?"

Paul shrugged. "I'm not enough of a basketball fan to keep up with the college teams. The NBA's enough for me."

Frank narrowed his eyes and studied Paul. "I bet you played football."

"Guilty."

"College?"

"A couple of years. After I graduated, I taught history in high school and coached football."

Their order arrived. Paul reached for his wallet.

"Put it on my tab," Frank told the bartender.

"Let me," Paul said. "It's the least I can do for taking up your afternoon."

Frank waved the comment away. "You said you coached a few years. Why'd you give it up?"

Paul shrugged. "I got bored."

"So, you went back to school?"

"You sound surprised."

Frank laughed. "I was never much of a student. When I get bored, I travel."

Paul took a long drink of the iced tea. Cold and tangy. At least in this part of the country he didn't have to specify unsweetened. Frank turned back to the TV. Paul said, "Mind if I ask you a few questions?"

Without taking his eyes from the game, Frank said, "Nope. That's what we're here for. This game is a rerun of last night's match between the Duke Blue Devils and the North Carolina Tar Heels. Duke won."

Frank obviously had a short attention span. Suppressing his annoyance, Paul opened the file folder he'd brought with him. He might as well skip the preliminary questions and go straight to the point. "How did your grandfather make his money?"

Frank picked up a wing and dipped it in the sauce. "Grocery business. You know the Sanchez Markets? He and his brother built that chain. My father and my two uncles carried on the family tradition."

"Now the responsibility is on you and your cousins?"

Frank looked away from the TV, visibly surprised. "My uncles are still in charge. One of my cousins is working his way up the ladder."

"You're not involved?"

"Why would I be? I have plenty of income from my dad's

share of the business. My grandfather was the original owner. He brought his brother in when he opened his second market."

"I see." Keeping his tone neutral, Paul said, "Where did your grandfather get the capital to open his first market?"

"He sure didn't inherit it. He worked hard for it, a real self-made man. The reason I got stuck with the name. Papa didn't want me to forget we came from nothing." As Frank dipped a second wing in the sauce, his eyes flicked back to the TV. "Not that there was ever any chance of that. After Papa died, Mama kept it up. She thinks I should double our capital by the time I'm forty."

"I take it you don't aspire to that goal?"

"It's not like we need it. The stock market is doing just fine. Even if it flattens out, I've got enough to last me into my golden years."

Paul decided his time with Frank Sanchez was running out. "Do you have enough to make a serious donation to a fund for a little girl who needs a heart transplant?"

Frank transferred his gaze from the TV to Paul's face. "I thought you were doing research. You didn't say anything about a charity organization. You'll have to take that up with my accountant. He makes sure I donate enough to keep my taxes in line. Email me. I'll give you his name."

Annoyed at the curt dismissal, Paul said, "Did your grandfather make his money mining in Jerome?"

His eyes back on the TV, Frank said, "What's this really about?"

Paul hadn't decided how much of Enrique's story to reveal. Now he said quietly, "There's a question of theft. A serious question."

Frank sat up and looked straight at Paul. "What theft? Who's asking?"

Paul handed Frank a photocopy of Manuel's last letter to Enrique.

Frank glanced at it. "Sorry," he said. "No *hablo español*. You'll have to translate."

"Turn it over. Translation's on the back."

Frank read it through slowly. Finally, he looked up, his expression bland. "So who is this Manuel? And what's his discovery of silver got to do with my grandfather?"

"Manuel Reyes and your grandfather were partners. Manuel disappeared shortly after his brother Enrique received this letter."

"So what?"

"Enrique believes someone found out about Manuel's discovery and killed him for it."

"First, get this straight. I never heard a whisper of a story about my grandfather discovering silver or anything else, for that matter, so I don't buy Enrique's story. But, just for the sake of argument, let's suppose there's something in it. Why wait seventy years to come forward with this accusation?"

"The little girl who needs the heart transplant is Enrique's great-granddaughter. The family can't possibly raise enough money for the operation. Enrique thinks the family that's lived off his brother's find for three generations should pay for Aurora's surgery."

"Blackmail! I pay you some amount of money, and you forget you ever saw this." Frank wadded up the letter and tossed it onto the table. "You can talk to our lawyer, Mister Researcher."

Paul checked his temper. "You asked a question," he said evenly. "I answered it. No one's accusing your family." So why the sudden defensiveness? Paul decided not to ask. That would be like tossing gasoline on hot charcoal.

"Sure sounds like it to me!"

"No. I told you the truth when I said I'm doing research on Jerome. I might use it in a book." Surprised at what he'd said, Paul realized it was true. This was the topic he wanted to write about. He filed that discovery away to examine later. "I knew your grandfather was dead. I hoped to talk to his son to find out what Manuel's partner said when he came back from Jerome. Maybe one of your uncles is more interested in your family's rags-to-riches story than you are."

"You're not dragging them into this. I told you. Talk to our lawyer."

Paul retrieved the letter, smoothed it, and returned it to the folder. "If that's the way you want it, you'd better give me his name."

"Her name is Linda Kent."

"Phone number?"

"She's got a website. Kent and Kent, Attorneys at Law."

Paul got to his feet. "You can let her know I'll be calling, but I hope you'll give serious thought to looking into your family history."

He didn't get a reply. Frank had already shifted his attention back to the TV.

11

Marty turned onto River Road a few minutes before six. The sun was headed toward the horizon, and she was relieved to have it behind her. The dirt road was packed and graded to a surface almost as smooth as pavement.

On her left, the wide driveway of 3 River Road curved in a graceful circle in front of a Spanish-style adobe house with arched windows. The home sat far enough back from the road to guarantee a large lot. No doubt it offered a generous stretch of riverfront as well. Marty had no idea of its exact worth, but she guessed it had to be close to a million dollars. Uneasy, she tapped her fingers on the steering wheel.

What had she expected? Particularly from a woman who owned a savings and loan and dressed as elegantly as any wealthy New Yorker. That was the problem, of course. She hadn't given much thought to what she might have signed up for. But it wasn't the upscale lifestyle that made her nervous.

She was used to customers with plenty of money. Good antique furniture didn't come cheap. But the Western flavor of the architecture made it hard to imagine the fanciful carving of the rococo Weber square grand plucked from her showroom and placed in the living room of a Santa Fe style house.

She stilled her fingers. It wasn't like her to get discouraged before she began a venture. Wealthy ranchers in the nineteenth century had filled their homes with European-influenced furniture. So what if Pat's redecorating job was unlike anything she'd ever tried before? It had tremendous potential as a business resource, and Pat would most likely be a cooperative client with lots of input to give her.

The perfect opportunity to learn about adapting traditional antique furniture to a variety of settings. More important than the business resource, the opportunity to work closely with Pat gave her a chance to get to know the older woman better. Without doubt, Pat was an excellent businesswoman with a lot to teach her.

"Not about you, Mart," she said to her empty pickup. This visit was about Patricia Osborn. It was about how she could help Pat redecorate her home so the furniture reflected her personality. It would be fun to get to know the woman beneath the classy exterior and wonderful to have a new friend. "Not about you, Mart," she repeated.

The mailbox in front of a boxy pueblo-revival home sported a large number 13. According to the mailbox, Pat's house was next, a much older ranch style home built of logs on a stone foundation. A sturdy chain link fence surrounded a surprising lawn as green as what Marty was used to seeing in Virginia. Beyond the house stood a stone horse barn. Marty pulled into the driveway and turned off the pickup.

She sat for a moment, trying to readjust her thinking once again. The house seemed almost at odds with its owner. Maybe it was as simple as the wrong address. She checked the address she'd entered in Contacts, 15 River Road. That's where she was. She picked up her portfolio of antique furniture styles and got out. Talk about a challenge. Bring it on!

The gate in the fence wasn't locked, so she opened it and let herself into the yard. She was halfway to the porch when two black Dobermans with tan faces and legs came charging around the side of the house, barking. Marty froze. She wasn't usually afraid of dogs, but these two had the air of guard dogs in attack mode.

Before she could decide whether to retreat or go on, the dogs reached her. As she threw up her arms to shield her face, they sat, one on each side, and stopped barking, the silence somehow more ominous than the barking. Afraid to make a wrong move, Marty put down her arms slowly. "Pat!" she yelled. "Pat, it's Marty!"

Pat came hurrying from the same direction the dogs had appeared. "Hansel! Gretel! Friend." Both dogs relaxed and began to wag their stubby tails.

Marty let out the breath she was holding but didn't move.

"It's okay," Pat said. "They'll be friendly now. We were in the barn feeding the horses, and I lost track of the time. Come see my beauties."

"Okay with you, Hansel?" Marty said. "How about you, Gretel? I'm a friend." She reached out a tentative hand. Only after the two dogs let her pet them did she move.

The Pat who took her hand was a different Pat than Marty had encountered, a relaxed woman wearing fringed jeans, a turquoise and gold tunic, and leather moccasins. Even her hair was different, the chin-length bob held out of her face with turquoise combs. Marty's tension evaporated. This job was going to be fun.

Built from field stone, the horse barn with its overhang porch and three walk-out stalls looked newer and more expensive than the house. "I don't know much about barns," Marty said, "but this looks like a nice one."

Pat laughed. "The horses are housed better than I am. But we're going to fix that, aren't we?"

"You bet."

"Once I get a feel for what you have in mind for antiques, I plan to hire an architect to give the house a face-lift. It's essentially the same house my father built in the mid-1960s. I had the barn built fifteen years ago." She opened a door in the end of the building and went in. "I've got a feed room, a grooming area, and open storage. Everything I need."

"Do you do all the work yourself?"

"Mostly. I only have two horses at the moment, so it's not too much work. I have some help exercising the horses, but that's about it."

"Do you show them?"

Pat shook her head. "They're just for my enjoyment. I've loved to ride since I was a kid. I get a feeling of freedom I can't find anywhere else."

The statement surprised Marty. She wouldn't have thought Pat was a woman who felt constrained, but that probably showed how much she didn't know about what it was like to run a savings and loan. Though she'd never given it much thought, she realized her goal was to keep her own business small.

"Meet Snow White," Pat said, reaching across a half-door to stroke the muzzle of a white horse with a shining coat. Pulling a carrot out of her back pocket, she offered it to the horse. Showing enormous teeth, Snow White plucked the treat delicately from Pat's hand.

"Next door is Rose Red," Pat said, moving to the next stall and offering a second carrot to a red horse with a white blaze.

"You must have loved fairy tales as a kid," Marty said. "Snow White and Rose Red isn't a well-known story."

"Yes, the one where the enchanted prince was turned into a bear by the wicked witch instead of into a frog. You obviously loved them too since you recognize my references."

"I did. Still do, in fact. When I've had a rotten day, I put in an old CD of *Faerie Tale Theater*. That's an antique TV series!"

Pat clapped her hands. "I'm jealous. You'll have to invite me over for an episode and popcorn one of these days."

"You bet." Marty sensed a real friendship in the making.

Pat stroked Rose Red's white blaze. "Hungry?"

"I am. I think you mentioned Chinese."

"Orange duck, sweet and sour pork, or cashew chicken. Your choice."

"Yum. How about some of each?"

"You've got it."

Marty stepped out into the cool, dry evening. Pale pink clouds lingered at the horizon, but already the ground was dark. The dogs came and sniffed her feet. "Hansel, Gretel," she said. "Remember, I'm a friend."

Marty couldn't tell whether the dogs remembered or not because just then Pat flipped off the lights and joined them. Linking her arm with Marty's, she said, "Follow the stepping-stones. They're almost as good as a lighted path except in the absolute middle of the night."

The dogs fell in step behind them, and Marty wondered if they would come inside. They were docile enough now, but they were big dogs and she hoped not. When they reached the back door, Pat opened it and went in. Marty followed with the dogs on her heels. Once Hansel and Gretel were both inside, Pat closed the door and said, "Bed." The dogs immediately went to gray plush beds on either side of a floor-to-ceiling fireplace.

Ignoring the dogs, Pat went to the laminated counter and began removing white boxes with wire handles from a tall white paper bag. "Ever eaten at Canton Heaven?" she said.

"No, but I hear it's good."

"The best north of Phoenix. Everything in the dishwasher is clean. If you don't mind, grab a couple of plates for us. How does jasmine tea sound?"

"Perfect."

In a few minutes they were seated at the round oak kitchen

table with mugs of hot tea. Automatically Marty offered her hand for grace. Ignoring the gesture, Pat started spooning rice on their plates. Disappointed, Marty closed her eyes and gave silent thanks. When she opened them, Pat was watching her. She waited for a question or comment.

But after a moment, Pat shrugged. "You like spring rolls?"

"Love them."

Pat lifted one out of a box with a pair of bamboo chopsticks and put it on Marty's plate.

Marty picked up one of the forks she'd brought with the plates. "I hope chopsticks aren't required. I've never conquered them. Like knitting. I can crochet with one hook, but knitting with two needles is beyond me."

"Not a problem."

As she reached for the orange duck, Marty said, "Do you knit?"

"My mother died when I was quite young, and my father never remarried. As the only child, I was groomed from a young age to take over the savings and loan. I was never allowed to do anything as useless as knitting. Why waste your time with tangled up yarn when you can buy perfectly nice sweaters?"

"I hope your father didn't consider dolls a waste of time."

"He did. My first toy was an abacus."

"No dolls and no needlework. What did you do for fun as a kid?" Marty took a bite of the duck. The sauce was perfect, the delicate flavor of fresh orange juice.

"I trained dogs. My father loved dogs."

"Is he still living?" As she asked the question, Marty wanted to kick herself. Pat must be sixty-something. Her father had probably died long ago.

"He's been gone for years, but let's not talk about him. I want to know about the antiques you're going to sell me."

"First, tell me what period you're thinking of using."

Pat gave her a blank look.

"What period of history?"

"Oh. Early American."

Marty reached for the sweet and sour pork. "Chippendale, Hepplewhite, or Rococo Revival?"

"Honey, I wouldn't know one of those if it came up and bit me. All I know is that I'm sick and tired of the furniture I have. Believe it or not, it's all from my childhood, which means my father picked out every single piece."

"Not that I want to do myself out of a job, but why not hire an interior decorator and do something modern?" Marty took a bite of the pork, slightly chewy, sweet with a trace of tang.

"Because antiques are classic. I don't see myself doing this another time, and I don't want to invest in a bunch of furniture that's going to go out of style almost as soon as it's uncrated."

"Good taste combined with practicality. I like that in my clients. Antiques are beautiful and a good investment. The older they get, the more they're worth."

Pat laughed. "Like me."

Marty blushed. "I didn't mean…"

"I know. I'm teasing you. To cover up the fact that I have no idea what you're talking about."

"Okay. Forget furniture styles. What period of American history are you most drawn to? Before the Revolution, the young republic, or the end of the nineteenth century? We could stretch a point and go into the early twentieth century before the two World Wars, but the investment value is in the earlier periods."

Pat put down her chopsticks and held her hands, palms up, across the table. Marty put down her fork and took the other woman's hands. Pat said, "Girlfriend, I want you to use your expertise for this project. I don't know a thing about antique furniture and not much about history. And to be honest, I don't care a lot. It should be obvious from a look around at this old John Wayne leather and oak that I don't spend much time here. All I know is that I want something totally different."

She gave Marty's hands a light squeeze and released them. "Choose the period you want to decorate your first home in. Money is no object. Surprise me."

Marty caught her breath. "You mean that?"

"Of course, I do. I don't have children. Pretend you're my daughter and have fun."

Marty thought a minute. "I'd like to do a quick walk-through of your house to get an idea of the size of the rooms. When I find a piece I think will fit the room, be comfortable, and offer a good investment, I'll show you a picture of it. You say yes or no before I purchase it to refinish or order it from a dealer."

Pat's eyes twinkled. "I'll always say yes."

"Okay. You can always say yes, but you have to agree to look at the picture and imagine yourself sitting at that table or in that chair or sleeping in that bed."

"Will that satisfy you?"

"Yes, ma'am. Those are my terms."

"Agreed," Pat said. She reached out a hand, and they shook on it. "Ready for that walk-through?"

"I am. Thanks for a delicious meal."

The house held few surprises. The large kitchen/family room where they'd eaten was modern and must have been added on. Otherwise, the floor plan was an excellent example of a 1960s ranch style layout. Living room in the center, two bedrooms and a hall bath on one end, master suite on the other.

The master bedroom was functional to the point of feeling like a hotel room, a high-end hotel room with a California king bed and wall-mounted directional reading lamps. The only picture in the room was a twelve by fourteen photograph hanging on the wall opposite the bed.

Curious, Marty went closer. A dark-haired woman in a deep rose suit stood with a middle-aged man in a dark business suit beneath a heart-shaped arch covered with white flowers. She was about to ask if the photo was Pat's parents when something familiar about the shape of the woman's face caught her attention.

Marty turned to see Pat watching her. "Since I don't have children, you assumed I'd never been married."

"I guess I did."

Pat's face softened. "John and I only had four years together, but they were the best years of my life." She turned briskly away from the photo. "Seen enough to start putting together a plan?"

"I have. Thanks."

As Marty drove home, a three-quarter moon was already climbing the eastern sky. She was tired, but it was a good tired. The free hand Pat had given her felt almost too good to be true, but the portfolio of pieces from the various periods of American history lay on the seat beside her without ever having been opened. She let her mind drift to Pat's question. What period would she choose for her own home?

The answer came almost as quickly as the question. Federal. Spanning the years 1790 to 1815, it was perhaps the most eclectic period of American antiques. Talented craftsmen from Scotland, England, and Ireland flocked to the new nation seeking to make a name for themselves. Some of the craftsmen, cabinet-makers, like Duncan Phyfe, had succeeded beyond their wildest expectations, managing to span both the Federal and Rococo Revival periods. Monticello was furnished in the Federal style, so it should appeal to Paul.

The thought brought Marty's thoughts to a full stop. True, she'd thought for a while Paul was the man she wanted to spend her life with, but the fantasy of decorating a home with him landed her squarely in reality. Paul wasn't just beginning his life. He was already fully launched. He'd had a wife. He was interested in her only because Linda had died.

Besides Linda, Paul had a son, a young teenager with a personality of his own. It was absurd to fantasize about furnishing a home for a teenager with valuable antiques, eclectic or not. It wasn't that she didn't want kids. She did. But she wanted her first child to start out as a baby and grow up into a teenager, not start as a teenager and grow into an adult. She hadn't lived enough of her life to be ready for a teenager, especially not a mature teenager like Scott.

Tomorrow she was going with Paul to pick up the other letters from Enrique. She'd already agreed to ride with him, and that would give her another opportunity to make him understand. She wanted them to be friends.

As she turned at the bridge, moonlight sparkling on the water gently reprimanded her. Okay, she'd dreamed about marrying Paul for months, but now she'd faced reality. From here on, she would hope for a lifelong friendship. End of story.

12

Saturday, March 16

Scott noticed the black eye as soon as B.T. pulled off his black motorcycle helmet, but all he said was "Thanks for picking me up."

"Your dad's okay with this?"

"Yeah. As long as we stay together and get back here before dark. He doesn't want me prospecting alone."

B.T. laughed. "Prospecting? Is that the word he used?"

"Don't laugh too hard. At least he didn't say 'looking for buried treasure.'"

B.T. reached around and unfastened a large backpack from the seat. "Okay to leave this here?"

"Sure. I'll put it inside the front door." The pack was heavy, and Scott wondered what was inside. The black eye plus the pack might equal B.T. running away. He wouldn't blame his friend. It wasn't the first time he'd seen B.T. with a black eye or a bruise in the middle of his back. But now wasn't the time to talk about it.

By the time Scott reached the end of the driveway again, B.T.

had back walked the bike into the street. Scott took the red helmet and fastened the chin strap. He climbed up behind B.T. and adjusted his daypack so he wouldn't squish their lunch.

The morning air felt cool on his face as they headed up the mountain toward Jerome. He wanted to pull the helmet off to let the wind blow his hair, but he'd promised his dad. Safety first. That was Scott's part of the compromise. His dad still worried about the motorcycle, but he trusted B.T. The two of them had reached some sort of truce because B.T. had started wearing a helmet. Like today.

The ride took less than fifteen minutes, so Scott didn't have time to consider when or where or why B.T. and his dad might have talked about the motorcycle. All he knew was that he hadn't been included in that conversation. At nine a.m. the parking lot of the Jerome State Historic Park was almost empty. As they dismounted, B.T. said, "Remind me why we're starting here."

"One of the exhibits is a 3-D model of the town that shows the ore deposits the mines were built on. I want to study it to figure out where to start our search."

"What are you looking for?"

"Smaller ore deposits not connected to the main shafts. That silver lode had to be somewhere Manuel could see it, but it can't have been too obvious or somebody else would have known about it too."

B.T. put their helmets and denim jackets in a small pack. As he slung it over one shoulder, he said, "According to the story you told me, somebody else knew about it and killed Manuel."

"Yeah, but only one other person. If more people knew about it, that silver lode would have been big news. Nothing like it was ever recorded."

Scott took the outside stairs two at a time up to the white Douglas Mansion that looked more like a fort than a family home. At the top B.T. slowed, stopping to look at a string of ore cars. Scott watched, wondering if B.T. had ever been to the park. He couldn't imagine Mr. Harper bringing his son. They'd moved to Clarkdale just a couple of years ago, too late for B.T. to get in on an elementary school field trip. But today Scott was focused on his task, and he didn't want to take the time for B.T. to look around.

Scott promised himself he'd talk to Dad about finding a time when the three of them could come and explore the exhibits. Maybe look at the 1918 headframe sitting above the mine and the shaft going almost two thousand feet down into the earth. He whistled the signal his dad always used to get his attention. B.T. got the message and hurried to join him. At the desk inside, Scott showed his state parks family pass.

The cashier, a white-haired lady with friendly green eyes, looked at the two of them skeptically. "I don't see many families with one blue-eyed blond sibling and another brown-eyed brunette sibling. Maybe one on the pass and a friend?"

Scott didn't want to lie, but seven bucks would take a big chunk out of his allowance, and he was sure B.T. didn't have that much on him. He hesitated.

B.T. elbowed him. "I'll wait outside."

Scott ignored B.T. and gave the lady his best smile. "My adopted brother?"

"I suppose it could happen that way." She smiled and held out the hand stamp.

"Yes, ma'am."

B.T. held out his hand. "Thank you."

"Ever been here before, young man?"

B.T. shook his head.

"You're in for a treat. Let me keep your packs here behind the counter."

As they handed them to her, a family of redheads came through the door. "Come on," Scott said. "The model's this way." He led the way out of the small gift shop past the period library and around the corner. No matter how many times he saw the topo exhibit, Scott never got tired of it. The artist's creation sat inside a large Plexiglass case dominating the small room that housed it.

The brown top layer had been molded to the topography of Cleopatra Hill. Tiny white boxes representing buildings dotted the hill. While there were a few outliers, most of the buildings were clustered at the foot of the hill beneath the enormous J that identified the town from miles away. But what fascinated Scott was beneath the town.

Copper colored chunks of varying sizes representing ore deposits were suspended at irregular intervals on a lattice of yellow wire. More wires showed where shafts had been sunk and tunnels blasted. White labels identified the now defunct mines.

Moving to the right side of the model, Scott directed B.T.'s attention to a smaller body of ore. "This is one of two I want to study. I think I can figure out which road to take to get to them."

Just then a man's voice came over a loudspeaker. "Our fifteen-minute film is about to begin in the auditorium."

"If you don't need me, maybe I could go watch the movie," B.T. said.

"Sure. I should have what I need in fifteen minutes, and we can head out."

B.T. nodded.

"We'll come back to the park, I promise. Spring break is next week. I'll talk to Dad, and we'll make a day of it."

"You've been here a lot. Your dad won't want to come again."

Scott rolled his eyes. "Wrong. He loves this place. Sometimes I think he'd rather be a park ranger than a teacher."

The loudspeaker crackled, and the voice said, "The film begins in one minute."

"You better go," Scott said. "The auditorium is farther down the hall we were in."

B.T. nodded and went. Scott watched him for a moment, surprised at his friend's interest in the museum. Then pulling a small pad and pencil from his pocket, he focused on the model. If he could figure out which roads to take, they'd have plenty of time to explore before it got dark.

Scott was still scribbling when B.T. reappeared. "Sorry I'm a couple of minutes late," his friend said. "I found a cool exhibit. Do you know some of the houses around here had tunnels connecting their basements to the mines? The guys could take a pickax and shovel and do some moonlighting without anyone catching on."

Scott nodded as he finished the note he was making to himself. "I've got two places for us to check out."

"I have a feeling we're going to find it," B.T. said. "That movie has lots of stories of important finds around here."

"Anything about a silver lode?"

"Nope. A lot of talk about finding the mother lode, but it never happened."

"That means it's still out there waiting for us. Come on!" After retrieving their packs, Scott led the way back out into the sunshine and down the stairs to the parking lot.

B.T. handed Scott his helmet. "Where to?"

"Perkinsville Road."

"Where's that?"

"You know where the fire station is?"

"Sure."

"Ever been on the dirt road that takes off beside the station?"

B.T. nodded. "The road to the Gold King Mine. But it looks more like a junk yard than a mine. You have to pay to go in."

"That's Perkinsville Road, but we're not going to the mine. We're going to park and do some hiking. I want to check out the area."

B.T. got on the bike. As Scott climbed on, B.T. said, "Why the gold mine? I thought we were looking for silver."

SUZANNE J. BRATCHER

Over the roar of the engine, Scott shouted, "A silver lode is a vein with silver and gold."

It was close to ten a.m. by the time they hit the one-way loop into Jerome, and the town was already starting to fill up with tourists. The bike slowed so much Scott was sure he could have walked the mile and a half faster. Eventually they reached the fire station. From there the ride got bumpy and dusty, making Scott glad to get off the bike.

"What are we looking for?" B.T. said.

"A cave or an opening in the side of a hill."

"You think Manuel had his own mine?"

"Maybe. The United Verde and The Little Daisy were the two big mines, but prospecting wasn't dead."

"Then your dad wasn't far off calling this a prospecting trip. We're prospecting for signs of earlier prospecting."

Scott grinned. "You've got it, partner."

Three hours later, they sat under a cottonwood tree that was just starting to leaf out. Scott unzipped his daypack and handed B.T. a ham and cheddar sandwich.

B.T. drained his water bottle and took a bite. "Good stuff," he said. "Did you make these?"

"Dad did."

"Does he always make your lunch?"

"Just when he feels guilty."

"What did he feel guilty about today?"

"Not taking me with him to see Sr. Reyes. This is the second time he and Marty have gone without me. And I'm the one who knows what a silver lode is." Scott heard the edge of resentment in his voice, but he didn't care. Dad was just making up excuses to be with Marty.

"I thought you wanted your dad to date Marty."

Scott gathered the empty water bottles and stuffed them in his pack. "That was last summer. He was stuck on Mom's death. I wanted him to get a life."

"Why not now?"

"Dad and I are doing good! After almost dying himself, he realized he was still alive. We don't need anybody else."

"I wish my dad would find somebody."

"He's drinking again, isn't he?" Scott said.

"Yeah. Big time."

"He give you that shiner?"

B.T. shrugged. "We didn't find anything this morning. You still want to keep looking out here this afternoon?"

Scott accepted the change of subject. Not much to say about B.T.'s dad. "There's another place I want to check out. It's not far from here. East on 89A another couple of miles. There's a small, abandoned mine off the highway. We'll have to do some rock scrambling to get to it."

"At least there's a mine there."

"Yeah. The Gold King area was a long shot, but I thought it was worth a couple of hours."

Twenty minutes later, they were standing in front of a low doorway framed with splintering timbers. The Keep Out sign with its faded lettering leaned to the left, any urgency it had ever possessed gone. Scott scanned the surrounding area. "I don't see a sign with a name on it. Do you?"

"Any name in particular?"

Scott dropped his backpack on the ground. "Miller would be super, but anything would be better than nothing."

B.T. pulled himself up on a boulder. Shading his eyes with his hand, he scanned the hillside. "If I had binoculars, I could do a better job. You got a pair in your pack?"

"Sorry. All I've got is a headlamp, and I need it." Scott slid the headband on and adjusted it to fit tightly enough to keep the lamp steady but not so tight as to give him a headache. Flipping on the light, he stepped over the sagging wire that defined the perimeter of the forbidden territory.

B.T. jumped down from his perch. "You're not going in there, are you?"

"It's the only way to find out if this is the place."

"I don't know, dude. It doesn't look safe."

Scott stared. This from a guy who never used to wear a motorcycle helmet? "I know the warning signs of a cave-in. If something starts to shift, I'll get out."

"What if you can't?"

"Call 911."

"No cell service out here. I checked. I'd have to get on my bike and go back to the fire station!"

Scott studied B.T. "You act like you've never been inside a cave. It's safe enough if you know what to look for. These mines are just man-made caves."

"No caves in L.A., dude. Natural or man-made."

"Take my word for it. I've been in lots of caves and lots of old mines. I'm going in, and you're staying out here in case..."

"In case the roof collapses."

"No. In case the sheriff drives by. That sign doesn't look like much, but it's as good as a fancy No Trespassing sign. I don't want a ticket."

"Going in that mine is why your dad didn't want you prospecting alone, not because of cops."

"So?"

"So be careful."

"I always am. Relax!" Ducking to keep from hitting his head on the crooked crossbeam, Scott went in. While he waited for his eyes to adjust to the dark, he thought about B.T. He was different today. Almost timid. That black eye was the worst one he'd seen on his friend. Before they headed home, he was going to ask. Scott knew B.T. wouldn't want to talk about it, but that was just too bad.

When he could see what was on either side of the beam of light, he checked for bats. He wasn't afraid, but he didn't want to disturb a sleeping colony. When he was sure he was alone, he turned his attention to the mine.

It was bigger than he'd guessed from the entrance. He could see signs of blasting and tunnels branching off from both sides. The rocks that littered the floor in this central room were flecked with the tell-tale blue of azurite that so often meant copper. And where there was copper, there could be silver. The gold needed to create a silver lode might have been deposited by the thermal waters of the underground volcano that created the ore bodies under Cleopatra Hill.

Scott moved farther back into the central room. Water seeped from the walls and the floor. Some kind of underground spring. Probably the mine was active during a long drought. He checked his watch. It was already after four. Although sunset wasn't until six-thirty in Cottonwood, it would come earlier up here in the mountains. Time to give up.

As he made his way back to the entrance, he fought back disappointment. He hadn't expected it to be as easy as one day's exploration, had he? Whatever its name, this mine was worth another look. He and B.T. would come back.

Spring break was next week. An entire week of days without school. He was sure he'd be able to work things out with Marty. Even if she was planning on using him for more hours than normal, she wouldn't need him forty hours.

Feeling hopeful, or at least less disappointed, Scott stepped out of the mine. Legs stretched out and eyes closed, B.T. sat leaning against the hillside soaking up the afternoon sunshine. But he was frowning, and his forehead was wrinkled. A bad dream?

Scott went to sit beside him.

B.T. wasn't dreaming because without opening his eyes he said, "Find anything?"

"Nope."

"No silver or gold?"

"Not so much as an old pickax."

B.T. looked at Scott. "Too bad."

Scott shrugged.

"Ready to go?"

"Nope. You have to talk to me, buddy."

"What's to talk about? Next week is spring break. We do some more prospecting."

Scott picked up a rock and tossed it toward the mine entrance. It landed several yards short. He picked up another one and threw it harder. It came closer. "We need to talk about your shiner."

Scott expected B.T. to insist it was nothing, but his friend didn't speak.

"Your dad's drinking again." Scott made it a statement, not a question.

Still B.T. remained silent.

"Tell me," Scott said.

"I can't."

The words came out sort of strangled sounding, and Scott knew B.T. was fighting tears. He'd known B.T. a year and a half, and the only emotion his friend ever showed about his father was anger. Whatever had happened, it was bad. Scott wished Dad was here. He'd know what to do. But his dad was with Marty visiting Sr. Reyes.

Scott picked up another rock, but instead of throwing it, he turned it over and over in his hand. The sharp edges cut through his reluctance. "Something different happened. What?"

B.T. took a deep breath and cleared his throat. "He had a knife. I thought…I thought he was going to kill me."

Scott didn't know what he'd expected to hear, but it wasn't this. "What did you do to set him off?"

"Nothing. I just came into the house, and he went for me. He shouted that I look just like my mom. He was drunk enough that

I was able to get the knife away from him and throw it across the room. Then he started beating me."

B.T. stopped talking. Scott waited. He knew there was more. This time when B.T. spoke, his voice was shaking. "It was just like with mom when I was little. He used to beat her. I hid under the table and listened to her scream. Then one day, she packed two suitcases. One for her and one for me.

"He came home early and caught us. He grabbed me and yelled at her to get out. She said she wouldn't go without me. That was when he got a knife. He told her he'd kill her rather than let her take me away."

Tears rolled down B.T.'s cheeks, and Scott didn't know what to do. If it was him crying, his dad would gather him up in a hug. But Scott and B.T. had never exchanged a hug, and now wasn't the time to start. So he did the other thing his dad always did. He waited.

Finally, B.T. wiped his eyes with the back of his hand. "Sorry to be such a baby," he muttered.

"You're not a baby. I'm scared to death of your father, and he's never even yelled at me."

"What about your dad?"

"My dad? What do you mean?"

"Hasn't your dad ever hit you?"

"No way! He always used time out when I was little. Now if I do something out of line, I get grounded without books. Dad doesn't yell." Except for the time when he ran out of the house defying his dad's explicit command not to get on B.T.'s motorcycle. But they'd talked it out.

"Come on," B.T. said, "you make your dad sound like a saint."

"He's cranky when he's tired. Sometimes he ignores me." That was happening more and more when Marty was around. "But most of the time, he's mellow."

"My dad threw me out."

B.T.'s voice was so low Scott wasn't sure he'd heard right. "Your dad threw you out?"

"He said if he ever sees me in his house again, he'll kill me."

"But he was drunk! Maybe he won't remember."

"He'll remember, all right. He said it just like he did when Mom left."

"You're staying with me. We'll share my room until we figure something out."

B.T. was quiet for so long Scott wondered if he'd hurt his friend's feelings. But he didn't know what to say, so he waited.

B.T. picked up a rock and started scratching on the ground with it. "Your dad doesn't like me."

"That's not true!"

"Sure it is. He doesn't want you to be my friend."

"That was last summer. Before he got to know you."

B.T. threw the rock at the mine entrance and hit dead center. "I haven't heard from you for weeks, dude. Your dad can't think I'm such a great friend for you."

Scott shifted uncomfortably. "Not Dad's fault. It's mine. I got on the debate team, and I let it take over. I'm sorry."

"Forget it." B.T. got to his feet. "It's my life, and I have to deal with it. I turned sixteen last month. I can get a job."

Scott jumped up and grabbed his friend's arm. "And live in the park like a homeless person? Talk it over with my dad. I bet he'll surprise you."

"I'll get a job. I probably can't pay much rent, but I can pay some."

The hope in B.T.'s voice made Scott want to bawl like a baby.

13

Marty looked out her bedroom window as Paul's gray Jeep pulled to a stop on the street below. Last night, riding with Paul looked like a perfect opportunity to convince them both they would be wonderful friends all their lives. Nothing more, but nothing less either.

Right now, the thought of sitting only a few inches away from him made her jittery. If thinking about being that close to Paul made her nervous, how did she think she'd have the courage to say what she needed to say?

As she went down to meet him, she did her best to convince herself this sudden attack of nerves was just her eagerness to get the relationship settled.

"Good morning, Marty! You look stunning." Paul sounded surprised. No doubt he'd expected a polo shirt with jeans.

Was the jade tunic and black leggings outfit too dressy for a Saturday appointment? Marty shook off the sudden doubt. She'd noticed the difference in the way Pat dressed for work and home. Jeans were fine for someone who specialized in antique furniture repair, but she was about to launch the next stage of her career.

She smiled. "Thank you, sir. Do I look like a successful shop owner?"

"Yes, ma'am!" Paul offered her his arm.

This was not a date. They both needed to remember that. She shook her head.

"Sorry," he said. "Businesswomen do not parade around on the arm of a gentleman."

Reading her mind again. Marty ignored the discomfort that accompanied that realization. She followed Paul out and locked the door of her house.

By the time she reached the Jeep, he was there with her door open. "This isn't a date," she said crisply. "We're going to a business meeting."

"I know it's not a date, but a business meeting?"

As Paul went around to get in the driver's side, Marty realized she hadn't filled him in on her Friday. "I had an idea for tying the fund raiser to my grand opening, and Pat liked it. We'll invite people interested in the Reyes family's mining history to a preview of my grand opening. Aurora Reyes will be the focus, but as the venue, Old and Treasured will get some publicity. Pat thinks I might make a sale or two."

"It's Pat now, is it? You work fast, Ms. Greenlaw."

"Thank you, Dr. Russell. It's Pat who works fast. I'm already learning a lot about how to make my business successful by watching her with this fund raiser. She has lots of connections through the historical society. I need to join groups that are interested in the past. Those are the folks who buy antiques."

"Makes sense. But I still don't understand how picking up the other letters has become a business meeting." Paul turned left onto the Cottonwood road and headed toward Sweet Home.

"I hope Sr. Reyes will be excited by the preliminary guest list and be able to add a few names. Pat's already sent out an informal invitation by email, and three of the families have shown interest."

"I'm impressed. I assume these families will be interested in helping Aurora."

"They're all families who got wealthy from the Jerome mines. Pat thinks they'll want to give back. Aurora is a perfect opportunity."

"You're not afraid they'll be put off by the idea that Sr. Reyes is looking for the murderer of his brother."

"That's where thinking of this visit as a business meeting is important. I need to convince Sr. Reyes to tell Manuel's story without mentioning his belief that Manuel was murdered. We don't want the guests to feel like they've been lured to a witch hunt."

"I might be able to help with that. I traced Franco Sanchez, Manuel Reyes's partner."

Marty touched Paul's arm, an involuntary gesture of congratulations, but the contact sent a jolt straight to her heart. She withdrew her hand hastily, but the damage was done. She was still attracted to this man who was all wrong for her. Silence stretched between them. She wanted to ask an intelligent question, but her mind was blank.

Paul broke the silence before it got awkward. "Finding him wasn't much of a challenge once I focused on tracing the name. You know the Sanchez Markets?"

Marty swallowed. "I've shopped in a Sanchez Market in Cottonwood. I didn't know there was more than one."

"It's a regional chain, and evidently the family has done quite well. I met with Frank Sanchez yesterday. He wasn't any help."

Before she could ask why not, Paul turned into the cul-de-sac and headed toward the brick home with the palo verde tree in bloom. An ambulance, lights flashing, sat in the driveway. An aging, blue Honda Civic was angled in at the curb.

Marty's hand moved involuntarily to her heart. "I hope Sr. Reyes is all right."

"I imagine he's fine. Except for his cough, he looked healthy enough. Remember, this is a home for people who require assistance. Someone may have fallen."

Marty prayed he was right. She was committed to helping little Aurora Reyes, and they needed her great-grandfather's help. The story of the dashed mining hopes of the family would carry much more weight coming from Manuel's brother than from one of his nephews or nieces.

Paul pulled in beside the Honda and turned off the engine.

Marty undid her seatbelt with shaking hands. "Why don't you stay here, Paul? I'll find out what's going on. Even if Sr. Reyes is fine, this may not be a good time to see him."

"It's okay, Marty. Nothing's happened to him. We can stay out of the way of the EMTs."

"I hope you're right."

"I am. Come on."

She nodded, fighting the certainty that something was terribly wrong. Their plans were going too smoothly. By the time she got out, Paul was there. Tucking her hand into the crook of his arm, he said, "I know things are going surprisingly well, but it will be okay."

He was wrong, but she didn't argue. How could she when he'd read her mind again? The feel of his arm under her hand was reassuring, so she left it there. As they moved around the ambulance, the front door opened, and Joe Sweet came out. Reaching up, he secured the screen door in an open position, and two men came out guiding a gurney that held a still form covered by a white sheet.

Marty caught her breath.

Paul said, "Seven guests live here."

A young man who looked like a much younger version of Sr. Reyes walked beside the gurney, talking excitedly with one of the EMTs.

"Not good," Paul said.

His reaction confirmed what Marty suspected. This was

Paul's student, Sr. Reyes's grandson. The EMT shook his head patiently and moved toward the back of the ambulance. The young man started to follow, but when he spotted them, he paused. "Dr. Russell! *Mi abuelo está muerto.*"

Marty's stomach clenched. She might not know the exact words, but the meaning was unmistakable. Sr. Reyes was dead.

Dropping Marty's hand, Paul moved to the young man and put an arm around his shoulders. "I'm so sorry, Alex."

Alex clenched his hands and squeezed his eyes shut, but tears escaped and rolled down his cheeks. Her own throat closing, Marty searched her bag for a tissue.

"Your grandfather was coughing when we were here Thursday," Paul said gently. "Mesothelioma is a tough way to die."

Wordlessly Marty offered Alex the tissue, but he shook his head and brushed his eyes with the back of his hand. "Mesothelioma didn't kill mi abuelo. Someone murdered him!"

14

Paul tensed when Joe Sweet rushed to them. "Young man! I warned you about slander. This home is a sanctuary for all who live here."

Alex turned to face the older man. "It isn't slander if it's true."

"I've worked five years to build the reputation of Sweet Home. Even a hint of an unexplained death makes people hesitate to bring their loved ones here. If you talk about murder, you'll ruin me!"

"Then do something to find out what happened to my grandfather!"

Before the argument escalated any further, Paul stepped between the two, using his height to suggest he was in charge. "Whoa. Let's all calm down."

"I'll calm down all right," Joe snapped. "I'll calm down enough to call my lawyer. I have an old man right now who is considering moving here. Why, he might take Enrique's room. It's bad enough to have a room where someone died, but a room where someone was murdered..."

Paul decided it was time to stop the tirade. "Alex has

suffered a terrible loss, but I know him. He wouldn't make an accusation like that if he didn't have some reason for it. Let's sit down and talk this through."

"Not interested," Joe said. "This kid is nuts."

Alex began to tremble. "I found mi abuelo. No one even knew he was dead. That's how much they care about their guests here!"

Paul put a hand on the boy's shoulder. "That's enough, Alex."

"You bet that's enough," Joe said. "Enrique was a sick old man. Sometimes sick old men die in their sleep."

"Not mi abuelo. Not now! He was determined to live until we got the money for Aurora's heart surgery. He's dead because a murderer wanted him dead."

Eyes narrowed, Joe looked up at Paul. "Get this kid off my property before I call the police."

"Let's go, Paul," Marty said. "Bring Alex. The three of us can talk in my kitchen."

Exactly what Paul wanted to do, and Marty's kitchen was the perfect place. "Come on, Alex," he said. "Mr. Sweet isn't in the mood to talk, but I am. I want to hear what you have to say."

"Listen all you want," Joe said. "Just make sure you don't talk about this. I plan to call my lawyer and find out about the slander laws in this state."

"We understand your position," Paul said, turning Alex away from the house.

Shrugging off Paul's hand, Alex stalked toward the street. "It's not slander if it's true."

"I'll file a restraining order if I have to!" Joe shouted after them.

"Don't say anything," Paul warned. "Just keep walking. We'll talk this through."

Marty looped her arm through Alex's. "My home is in Clark-dale. Why don't I ride with you? I feel like I know you, but we haven't actually met. This will give us a chance to get to know each other."

Paul watched the anger drain out of Alex as he looked down at Marty's calm face. She'd struck the right chord with him.

"My car's a mess," Alex said. "You better ride with Dr. Russell. I'll follow."

"No worries," Marty said. "My truck is usually seriously cluttered. I'm an expert at rearranging things to make room for a passenger. Besides, it'll give me a chance to talk to you for a couple of minutes. I read your great-uncle's letter to your grandfather."

If he hadn't been so concerned about the situation, Paul would have laughed at how quickly Alex gave in. He was good at reading young people, and he knew he was watching the beginning of a serious crush. For a moment he felt a flash of jealousy. Ridiculous, but there it was.

Marty was as good as her word, and it wasn't more than a couple of minutes before she was climbing in Alex's Honda. Paul started the Jeep, but he let the boy lead the way. A small thing, but he hoped it gave Alex a chance to get his emotions under control. As they turned toward Clarkdale, Paul considered what he knew of Alex.

He was a good student who could write a reasoned argument to support his conclusions. Still, he'd had a serious shock when he found his grandfather's body. Paul wanted to hear what Alex had to say, more to calm him down than because he believed anyone had killed Enrique Reyes. Joe was right when he said sick old men sometimes died in their sleep. No matter how determined people were to live, death came when it came.

Ten minutes later, Alex was turning into the driveway beside Marty's house. Paul parked along the curb and got out. In another five minutes, the three of them were sitting at the table in Marty's tiny kitchen with beverages, root beer for Alex, water for Marty, and iced tea for himself.

Paul studied his student. The young man was pale, clearly shaken. "We're listening," Paul said. "Start at the beginning."

"The beginning?"

"Why you came down from Flagstaff this morning. I wasn't expecting to see you today."

"I talked to mi abuelo last night. He told me you were coming to get the rest of the letters this morning. I wanted to be there to help translate."

Marty pushed the can of root beer closer to Alex's hand. "Have you read the other letters?"

"A few of them. I wasn't interested. Nothing but accounts of Manuel's daily life and messages for other members of the family." He ran his hand through his dark hair. "Nothing important to Manuel's murder."

Paul frowned. "We talked in class about the importance of those kinds of details to an oral history."

"I know. I got so excited about the silver lode I didn't pay much attention. Obviously, you were right, Dr. Russell. The letters must be important to make them worth killing for."

Paul raised one eyebrow. "Please explain."

"Whoever killed mi abuelo stole the letters."

"The letters are missing," Paul said. "You're sure?"

"I'm sure. I looked everywhere, starting with the drawer he kept them in."

Marty put a hand on Alex's arm. "When did you make your search?"

"As soon as I knew he was dead."

"After the EMTs were sure they couldn't help your grandfather?" Paul said.

"No! I looked for the letters before anyone but me knew he was dead."

"You didn't call Mr. Sweet for help?" Marty said.

Alex shook his head. "No one could do anything. He was dead."

"Slow down," Paul said. "This isn't making any sense. You went into his room, couldn't get him to respond, and started looking for the letters before you told anyone you thought your grandfather was dead."

Alex nodded.

"Why were you so sure he was dead?"

"His skin was cold, Dr. Russell. He was already getting stiff. I was there when my grandma died. They didn't take her away for a couple of hours, and she still wasn't stiff. He was dead. I knew those letters were important to him. I knew he'd want me to have them, so I looked for them."

"Maybe he gave them to a friend," Marty said.

"No way. He wouldn't do that. He refused to let me take them to my dorm. That's why I didn't read them all. I glanced through them, and they weren't interesting enough to warrant my taking that much time sitting in my grandfather's room."

Alex crushed the empty root beer can and got to his feet. "I should have sat there and read every single one. I should have copied them by hand. Now they're gone. Somebody wanted them enough to put a pillow over mi abuelo's head."

The first few notes of a Mariachi-style trumpet filled the room. Alex pulled his phone out of his pocket. "Sorry. I've got to answer this one." Punching the phone on, he said, "Hi, Ma..." He listened, nodded his head, said, "I'm sorry," nodded again, said, "Yes, ma'am," and clicked off. As he shoved his phone in his pocket, he said, "My mother needs me at the funeral home." He made a face, half guilty, half resentful. "Now!"

Paul pushed back his chair and got up to go with Alex. As the young man opened the door, Paul placed a hand on Alex's shoulder. "Let us know what we can do."

Alex tried to speak and then nodded.

Paul's heart went out to the young man getting into the blue Honda. He was about Alex's age when his father died. He remembered the mixture of shock, grief, and anger at God.

Anyone's first encounter with death was tough. But then wasn't every encounter with death? He'd had the same complicated emotions when Linda died. With a sigh, he closed the door and went to rejoin Marty.

She was standing at the counter, refilling her water glass. "How's he doing?"

"He's shaken up. I think it's just becoming real to him. The funeral home is going to be rough."

"At least his mother will be there."

"The person he needs most right now." The one person who couldn't help him when his father died. Retrieving his glass of tea, Paul drained it in one long swig. The cold liquid sliding down his throat brought him squarely back to the present. He held out his glass to Marty for a refill. "Just water," he said. "What do you think?"

"About Alex's murder theory? I don't know. It sounds more melodramatic than real. Would someone kill an old man for a bunch of letters filled with the details of a miner's life seventy years ago?"

Automatically Paul pulled out a chair for Marty. When she hesitated, he studied her. She looked as if she were trying to make an important decision. He said, "Did I miss something?"

She started to reply, then shook her head and sat down. "What do you think?"

Paul sat down across from her. "I'm with you, but Alex has never struck me as the kind of kid to thrive on drama. He's right about the time of death. Sr. Reyes must have died hours before Alex got there. If rigor had started, he'd been dead at least three hours, maybe more."

"That doesn't mean someone put a pillow over the old man's head and suffocated him. We heard him coughing. His lungs might have just stopped."

"Agreed. Still, it's odd the letters weren't in his room. He was eager to show them to us."

"If there's a storage room at the home, maybe Sr. Reyes was planning to get the letters first thing in the morning."

"I'll talk to Joe Sweet. Maybe he knows where they are."

Marty nodded and got to her feet. "If you find them, let me know. With more than one letter I can probably find someone interested in authenticating them."

Paul studied her. It was clear she was ready for him to leave. But he wanted to talk to her. This whole thing had started as a way to see her so they could talk about why she was avoiding him. He reached for her hand. "We need to talk."

She pulled her hand away and stepped back. "We've talked as much as we can with the information we have. When you find the letters, we'll talk again."

"You know that's not what I mean. For the last three weeks, you've been avoiding me. What's that about?"

"I agree that we need to have that conversation. But I'm not ready to have it right now. Not after what we've just been through."

Paul got to his feet. "Fair enough. It's been an emotional day."

"Try three emotional days. You do realize Aurora Reyes is the same age Ruthie was when she died, don't you?"

Paul held up his hands in mock surrender. "Leave it for now. But not for long, Marty. I don't understand what's going on. I deserve an explanation."

She sighed and pushed the red curls he wanted to run his fingers through away from her face. "Okay. Just not today. Please, Paul. Please leave."

Her tone felt like a slap, but Paul wasn't about to be pulled into an argument that would postpone the conversation they had to have. "On my way. Walk me to the door."

For a moment he thought she was going to refuse. Then she shrugged and followed him out of the kitchen through the showroom. He went outside, but before she could close the door, he put a hand on it. "Go to dinner with me tonight," he said. "Not to have a talk about our relationship or rehash anything to do with Sr. Reyes. Just to have a pleasant evening."

"I don't want to go on a date with you."

Another slap. She was doing her best to chase him off. But why? It didn't make any sense. He resisted the urge to force the conversation. If he did, he knew what she was going to say, but he wouldn't find out why.

Keeping his tone light, he said, "How about lunch after church tomorrow? Pizza at The Hideaway. I promise to have you home before dark, so the neighbors won't talk."

He got the smile he'd hoped for. While he had the advantage, he pressed on. "I'll pick you up for church. Nine-thirty for Bible study?"

The smile disappeared. "I'll meet you at The Hideaway after the service."

The door closed, not in his face, but firmly. Paul's temper frayed at the edges. He would get to the bottom of this. Not today, but within twenty-four hours. Whatever the problem was, he couldn't deal with it until she spelled it out. And he was about at the end of his patience.

15

Sunday, March 17

Paul looked across the red checkered tablecloth at Marty. Her head tilted away from him, she was watching a black-chinned hummingbird at one of the six feeders. It was clear she wasn't going to start the conversation. He'd learned with Linda and now with Scott that the best opener was the truest thing he knew about himself. He said, "I'm confused."

Marty met his eyes. "It's a confusing situation. The more I think about it, the more I think Alex was shocked and upset. His grandfather was quite elderly and—"

"Don't. Please, don't."

Marty looked away. The hummingbird was gone, so she looked farther out, at a rambling house perched across the canyon high on the red rock plateau, a house they'd discussed during the stilted small talk while they waited to place their order.

Without taking her eyes from the house, she said, "I want us to be friends, Paul."

"I'm ready to look at engagement rings. You're lucky I haven't already bought one and offered it to you."

That got her attention. He saw his confusion mirrored on her face, and he wondered how she had expected him to respond. Had she honestly expected him to say, "That's what I want too?" Sometimes he felt like he could read Marty's mind, but not now. He needed her to talk to him.

Their waiter, a nervous young man named Todd, arrived and deposited their order in the exact center of the small, square table. "Everything pizza, hold the anchovies. Would you like a refill on your Coke, sir?"

"No, thanks." More caffeine was the last thing Paul wanted right now.

"If you need anything, be sure to let me know."

"Will do." Paul held out his hands to Marty. "You want to say grace, or shall I?"

She was slow to put her hands in his, but when she did, he felt the familiar electric tingle. Did she feel it? He thought so, but he could be wrong. He still felt the way he had when she came back from Virginia, but perhaps she genuinely didn't feel it. It wasn't his place to pass judgment on her feelings. But if things had changed that much, he needed to know why.

Her voice low, Marty said, "Please pray for us."

That request could be taken two ways. He decided to take it literally. Bowing his head, he murmured, "Father, thank you for our many blessings, including this pizza. Be with us as we try to find our way through our present confusion. Amen."

She pulled her hands away as quickly as if she'd touched something hot. Maybe she did feel the electricity. But if she did, it disturbed her. He couldn't imagine why, but that was the reason they were here.

He took a bite of pizza. Hot, cheesy, juicy with fresh tomato sauce. Marty slid a piece onto her plate and attacked it with a fork. Halfway through his second piece, Paul decided it was up to him to break the silence. "Talk to me, Marty."

"You're the one who insisted we talk. You go first."

"I did. I told you I'm confused. But if you need me to spell it out, here you go. Something has changed between us in the last three weeks. What happened?"

She shook her head. "How did you jump from a few long-distance phone calls and a couple of dinners to engagement rings?"

"You'd characterize an almost daily occurrence for six months as 'a few phone calls'?" He stopped just short of adding, "I'd hate to see your phone bill if you ever talked to anyone on a regular basis." Sarcasm might relieve his tension, but it would give her a legitimate reason to shut down the conversation.

She gave him a defiant look. "How would you characterize it?"

He wanted to blurt, "I'd characterize it as a precious time, months when I was content in the present and excited for the future, months when I woke up each morning wondering what the new day would bring." But as he studied her, he knew she wasn't ready to hear those words.

As he tried to decide what to say, he looked over her head at a table near the end of the deck where a child who looked to be two years old was picking pieces of pepperoni off a pizza and dropping them on the floor. The little girl's father looked as frustrated as Paul felt. With Scott it was raisins in cereal, and their two-year-old had thrown them against the wall. He wished he could trade places with the young father.

Paul brought his gaze back to Marty, to her shiny, copper curls, green eyes, and complicated emotions. He didn't want to change places with anyone. What he wanted was to get this relationship back on track. That was evidently going to take some work.

Why was he surprised? Commitment meant work. He

considered her question again. How to explain what he'd felt was happening in those six months of conversation? He said, "Laying a foundation for a lifetime."

"What?"

"You asked me how I'd characterize our six months of phone calls. That's my answer. I'd say we were laying a foundation for a lifetime, one conversation at a time. Our histories, our dreams, our faith. Did I read it so wrong?"

"No, Paul. I…" She hesitated, checked the bird feeder, watched a ruby-throated hummingbird drink once, twice, three times, and then flit away. She looked at him and away again. "I want us to be friends for a lifetime."

Evidently friends was the word she'd chosen. She was certainly hanging on to it with dogged determination. Well, he could be just as determined as she could. "When you came out in December to make a decision on a house, we had a great time." All they'd done was visit properties for sale, eventually comparing each one to the Remick house. But they'd done it hand-in-hand. They'd laughed a lot, each trying to top the other with outrageous explanations for any quirk they spotted in a house.

Paul gave her a moment to contradict him. When she remained silent, he went on. "In January when you were packing and moving, I knew you were busy, but we kept talking. Not quite as often, but we made up for lost conversations with longer talks. We started talking about the future. I helped you unpack and settle in. You hired Scott to work for you after school."

When had the ground started to shift under his feet? They were now two weeks into March. She'd begun pulling away at least three weeks ago, maybe four. "Just when I thought it was time to start official dating, you started dodging me. At first, I thought you were still getting oriented from moving, but after three weeks, I knew something had changed. Is there someone back in Virginia you miss more than you expected to? Did Ted come back into the picture?"

"No! Nothing like that." Using both hands, she began pleating her white paper place mat, beginning at the corners and working toward the middle. "I do want you in my life," she told the place mat, "as a lifelong friend."

He reached across and captured her hands in his. "Look at me, sweetheart."

She raised her head. "Does that hurt you so much, Paul?"

"I'm long past wanting friendship with you, Marty. As precious as friendship is, I want more than that. I want you to be my life partner."

She jerked her hands out of his and sat back. "There's obviously something holding you back from moving to the next level too. Otherwise you would have bought me a ring and proposed. Are you sure?"

"Believe me, it isn't because I haven't decided whether I want to marry you. I know I want to marry you, and I'd think you'd realize my self-restraint is proof of my sincerity. Linda taught me women don't like to be surprised with jewelry. Flowers make great surprises, but not rings. If you want to give a woman something she's going to wear a lot, she wants to pick it out herself. Since I want you to wear my ring 'until death do us part,' I want to know you love it."

He couldn't interpret the look on her face. Maybe he'd made a mistake with her. After all, Marty wasn't Linda. "Of course, I realize I'm hypothesizing based on a sample of one."

Marty laughed, a delighted giggle. "Most men would say, 'I know I'm guessing from one experience.' Even when you're being romantic, you talk like a professor. I can't help but love you, Paul!"

16

M arty caught her breath. She hadn't meant to say
that. Or she didn't mean what the words she'd used
said. She didn't know which, but whatever, she'd
botched the conversation with the word love. She buried her face
in her hands and started to cry. That made everything worse, but
the more she tried to stop, the harder she cried.

Paul reached for her hands. She knew he was trying to help,
but he was confusing her more. She wished he would stop, but
she also wished he wouldn't. What a mess she was. No wonder
he was confused. So was she. As much as she thought all she
wanted was friendship with him, the truth was she was still in
love with this man. But they were all wrong for each other, and
she didn't know why he didn't see it or why she had to spell it
out for him.

He let go of her hands and put them around a glass of ice
water. "Drink something, doll."

Marty took a shuddering breath and followed his suggestion.
The cool water slid down her throat, taking the last of her tears
with it. When she put down the glass, Paul handed her a napkin

wrapped around some ice. The cold soothed her swollen eyes and burning face.

When she was calm, she gave Paul what she knew was a weak smile. "You're a great guy to have around in a storm."

He grinned. "I've had a bit of practice."

"Linda again?"

"Scott. He was a passionate toddler."

Marty winced. She supposed she deserved that. Today, at least, she was acting more like a small child than a grown woman.

"He's still passionate," Paul said, "but these days he doesn't often let anyone see his tears."

Marty thought of Scott's ardent plea to be included in the visit to Sr. Reyes. He was right too. With his interest in geology, he could have asked questions she and Paul didn't know to ask. Now it was too late.

Marty couldn't bear to just sit in this calm spot, eating and watching hummingbirds. "Let's walk."

"Sure. You go ahead. I'll get Todd to wrap up the rest of our pizza and meet you at the top of the stairs."

With a sense of escape, Marty threaded her way through the other tables to the steep steps that led up to the street. She almost ran up the stairs. By the time she reached the top, she was breathing hard from exertion but more from emotion. Dropping onto a bench outside a curio shop, she stared up at the azure sky. How could she explain her complicated feelings to Paul? She loved him, and that was why she couldn't marry him. She refused to burden him with a wife who couldn't fulfill her role.

"Walk along Oak Creek or at Red Rock State Park?"

Marty blinked. She'd been so caught up in thinking about Paul she hadn't realized when he joined her. "Red Rock." The trail was wider, and part of the way it crossed an open area. She needed to see his face when she asked about Linda. The thought jolted her, but then she knew that was the only way to convince him of what she knew in her gut.

"We can take my car," Paul said, "and pick yours up on the way home."

She shook her head. She needed to be alone while she thought through what questions she could ask that would help him see for himself that they were all wrong together. More than that, she was sure he'd want to be alone after the conversation. "I'll follow you."

He narrowed his eyes, and she wondered if he might try to force the conversation right here. But he must have thought better of it because he turned away without comment.

The drive took less than ten minutes, and Marty was still at the stage of finding her courage when she pulled her pickup into the parking place next to his gray Jeep. A picture of his green pickup the last time she saw it flashed through her mind. Pushing away an annoying impulse to start crying again, she opened her door and got out.

Paul stood beside the red adobe wall that defined the edge of the parking area, looking across the open expanse that had been Smoke Trail Ranch to the House of Apache Fire perched on a bluff above Oak Creek. He turned. "Across Kingfisher Bridge or up to Eagle's Nest?"

"The bridge." The widest trail, the most open. She needed to see the sky.

"Lead on, Macduff," he said.

Despite her somber mood, she had to smile. The reference to Shakespeare was so like Paul. The first time he used the phrase, she had to ask. He chuckled. "An old misquotation of a line from *Macbeth*. It's another way of saying, 'You first.'"

She moved automatically, down the few steps to the walkway with animal tracks in the cement, past the visitor center, out onto the field where Jack and Helen Frye had kept their horses. They walked in silence until they reached the wide bridge across Oak

Creek. She gestured toward a bench under a sycamore bursting with spring-green leaves.

They sat side-by-side, and Marty fought the urge to thread her arm through his, lean her head on his shoulder, and watch the sparkling water tumble over the modest rapid below the bridge. It was going to take more strength than she had to handle this right. Breathing a prayer, she angled her body so she could see Paul's face without twisting. "Tell me about Linda."

"You're not in competition with her."

Only because Linda was dead. It was true, but she didn't say it. "Maybe not, but I want to understand who she was."

He studied her for a long moment, and Marty wondered what he was thinking. Then he said, "What do you want to know?"

Everything. Marty wanted to know what had attracted Paul to Linda, what had kept them happily married until Linda's sudden death in a car crash, what he felt when he looked at her picture. But she couldn't start there because he would change the subject. He'd tell her what attracted him to her, why they were good together, how he saw their future.

"Start with her personality. Give me one word."

Paul leaned back and looked up at the canopy of green over their heads. "Organizer. Linda could survey a complicated situation and decide where to start. Then she could figure out the steps it would take to reach the goal."

"Your house was always tidy. You didn't have to wonder whether the socks that went with the tie you wanted to wear were clean or not."

"This can't be about housework! Do you think I care that your focus is on the latest harpsichord you're restringing rather than on laundry?"

He made her concern sound silly, but it was serious. He had expectations for what a wife would be like. "It's more than that. Give me a better example."

"Linda was a people person. She could take a problem like

how to get the kids more involved at church and figure out the place to start was to talk to the kids and discover what they wanted to do more of. If it was outdoor activities, she'd find someone in the congregation who had horses. If it was movies, she'd find the classic movie buff. Together, they'd make a plan."

Worse than a neat house. Marty remembered how quick she was to delegate the logistics of the fund raiser to Carly, the most outgoing people person she knew. But Carly wasn't right for Paul. She was just a few years older than Scott.

Taking her hand, Paul threaded their fingers. "I'll tell you something I've never admitted to anyone before. I loved Linda dearly, but sometimes I felt a bit extraneous. I don't mean she didn't love me as much as I loved her, but sometimes I felt like I was in the way. She did everything to perfection."

He rubbed his thumb along hers. "Linda cooked like a Cordon Bleu chef. She knew more about the Bible than anyone at church except the pastor and Sofia. She rarely got tired. She taught school, did most of the household chores, and still had time to be the best mom on the block."

The best mom on the block. There it was.

Paul didn't notice how everything went still around them. He kept talking. "Sweetheart, Linda was my first love, but sometimes it was tough keeping up with her."

"Stop," Marty said. "Tell me what kind of mother Linda was. Besides organized." She took her hand back and crossed her arms. She didn't want to be comforted. She wanted, no needed, the truth.

"You're worried about Scott?" Paul sounded incredulous. "But you hired him! I thought he was doing a good job."

"This isn't about Scott. He's a great kid doing a great job."

"I know he's been acting a bit jealous, but that will pass. He enjoyed being the center of my attention this fall."

"While I was back in Virginia."

"Scott likes you. He'll adjust."

Marty picked up a dry sycamore leaf as big as her hand and twirled it by its stem. The question wasn't whether Scott would adjust to her. The question was could she adjust to being Scott's mother? When she'd dreamed of being a mother, she'd imagined a tiny baby in her arms, not a teenager on his way to manhood. She was ten years younger than Paul and fourteen years older than Scott. She might love Paul, she might even love Scott, but the math didn't work. She was all wrong for the roles Paul had cast her in.

Marty crumbled the leaf and flung the fragments into the air. A sudden gust caught the largest one and tossed it above their heads. "What about B.T.?"

Paul leaned forward and propped his elbows on his knees. "That's a tough question. I take it you saw him with us in church."

It had felt odd sitting three rows behind Paul instead of beside him as she always had. But it had given her a chance to watch him with the two boys. Like a father with two sons. "I also saw his black eye. Did he and Scott have a fight?"

"I wish it were that easy." Paul stood and held out his hands. "Come on. Let's walk. You can help me."

She let him pull her to her feet. Dismayed by a sudden urge to pull his head down for a kiss, she frowned and turned away. "How?"

"Help me decide the next step with B.T."

Marty stopped herself from saying what she was thinking, that without Linda he was on his own in the how-to-proceed department.

They crossed the bridge, feet clattering on the open planks. At the other side, she turned right and headed toward the trail that followed the creek and then looped back to the parking lot. She didn't hurry, and as always, he matched his pace to hers. "Scott brought B.T. home yesterday evening."

"I don't suppose they found Manuel's silver lode."

"No, but they eliminated the area around the Gold King Mine. They also found what Scott has decided is the old Miller mine."

"Miller," Marty said. "That's one of the names on the list Pat gave me."

"Carol Angel, the actress. At least that's the cover story."

"What do you mean?"

Paul shrugged. "The gossip around Jerome is that her most important role was rejected ingenue."

"I don't understand."

"Oh, it's just a lot of talk. The kind that springs from jealousy. The story is that she was never more than a hopeful hanger-on in Hollywood until she met Miller. Then she dazzled him with an embellished version of the truth that she'd been rejected as an actress until he felt quite lucky to catch her."

"Sounds like the plot of a paperback romance."

"Or a B-movie," Paul said.

"Do you think it's true?"

"No idea. Mr. Miller died years before Linda and I ever visited Jerome. By then Carol Angel was the recluse she is now. To tell you the truth, I don't know if you should waste time with her."

Wasting time talking about half-century old gossip was what they were doing now. She hadn't wanted to have this talk with Paul, sure she could let the relationship drift into friendship. But she'd been wrong. Paul was further in his thinking than she'd imagined, and she was still drawn to him. But that had to stop before they both got so hurt they couldn't be friends.

Marty stopped walking. "Back to B.T. What are you trying to decide?"

"A little background first. His father is an alcoholic who's started drinking again. He beat B.T. up pretty thoroughly Friday night and came after him with a knife. The black eye is one of many bruises, including some invisible ones."

"So B.T. spent the night at your house and came to church with you."

Paul nodded. "Scott brought him home and asked if B.T. could share his room. I called B.T.'s father last night, and after what he said, I don't think there's much hope he'll consider any counseling. I've done a good bit of praying since that phone call. I'm not done praying, but I feel a nudge."

"A nudge to do what?"

"Get certified as a foster parent and give B.T. a home until he graduates from high school. I don't need a guest room. Hotels are designed for guests."

Marty felt a weight lift off her shoulders. This situation was what she needed to explain to Paul why they couldn't pursue a romance. She wanted to marry someone who was free to invent a life with her. Paul was committed to Scott and, by extension, to Scott's friends. Instead of the explanation she intended to offer, she heard herself say, "That's a huge decision."

"It is. I thought you could help me make it."

An even better opening. She shook her head. But instead of saying, "A foster son with an abusive father isn't in my plan for my life," all she said was, "I'm not Linda."

Paul stepped in front of her. Dropping his hands on her shoulders, he said, "I know that. In fact, I know that far better than you do. You're Marty Greenlaw, the woman I want to share the rest of my life with. I need your opinion."

Marty was confused again, so confused she was drowning. She did love this man, for his kind brown eyes and gentle hands, for his soft voice and heart big enough to want to give a troubled teen a home. But she couldn't share his life. He was too far ahead on the road. The life he was offering wasn't anything like the one she'd dreamed of for so many years.

She twisted away before she crumbled like the leaf she'd crushed in her hand. "I'm sorry, Paul. I can't be your wife. I can't be Scott's mother. And I can't cope with B.T." She put her hands flat on his chest and looked up into those captivating brown eyes, eyes dark with pain she was inflicting. "Please, Paul! I want you in my life. Please, be my friend."

Before he could answer, she turned away and started walking. She meant to keep a steady pace up the trail that led to the parking lot. But after a few steps, she found herself walking faster, then jogging, and finally running so hard the blood pounded in her ears.

17

P aul put the Jeep in the garage and headed for his office. Lunch with Marty and their walk had been a disaster. And he had no idea what he could have done to avoid her tears. Buy a ring and get down on one knee? He'd thought women wanted to choose their own jewelry.

So much for what he knew about women. He sat in the chair behind his desk and leaned back to stare at the ceiling. If he'd showed up with a ring, would that have changed the outcome?

A cobweb in one corner told him no. Marty was scared to step into his life. Maybe she was right. He had a lot more than cobwebs on his ceiling that she'd have to deal with. B.T. was the obvious complication, but he was sure there was something about Scott that scared Marty.

No doubt there were other complications inherent in a ten-year age difference. He was farther along his journey than she was on hers. But she wasn't the only one who would have to deal with the differences. He loved her enough to want to accept the challenge. He thought she loved him too, or else why the push-pull of the last few days, the tears at lunch, and the race to get away from him? Why wasn't she willing to...

That was a train of thought that would get him nowhere but more frustrated than he already was. Paul let his chair down and woke up the computer. When the menu opened, he clicked on the file titled "Jefferson Bible" and stared at the outline of the book his father and grandfather would have been proud for him to write. A ridiculous bind to have put himself into, but he'd concluded that he didn't have a choice except to write this book.

It was fine to fantasize about starting the process over, but reality was that he didn't have time to do anything but plow through the task he'd set himself, whether he wanted to or not. As Roger had said, most academics had sat in this chair at one time or another. It was his turn now.

The next chapter, titled "Influence of Deism," should be easy enough to get on paper. He could write a definition of deism without glancing at a source, "A philosophy that grants the existence of a Creator but rejects any intervention in creation through miracles."

Despite the logic that compelled him to get to work, Paul didn't start to type. He did not want to write this book. What he wanted to do was erase the entire file. That, of course, would be equivalent to erasing his job.

He glanced at the box of oral histories he'd brought home to do put final grades on. Another question Roger had asked during their walk was why he'd assigned an oral history project when he knew full well the amount of time the evaluation of their work would demand.

On one level the answer was easy. Spending time grading projects that interested him kept him from having to work on the book he was staring at on his computer. On another level the answer was just as easy but more challenging. Oral history was the branch of history he was passionate about.

With all the research data coming from the public, oral history connected scholars with their communities. Which explained why he'd gotten so caught up with the story of Manuel

Reyes. Jerome was the community he felt connected to. It was where he and Linda had dreamed of moving. It was where he'd met Marty and fallen in love all over again.

With no idea what he was doing, Paul closed the "Jefferson Bible" file and opened a new one. Without giving himself time to stop and think, he started writing what he'd already learned about Jerome in the late 1940s. He didn't bother with a title or an outline. He didn't try to decide where paragraphs belonged. Just let the words come.

He lost track of time, but finally the words slowed and then stopped. Without reading what he'd written, he saved the new file, calling it "Jerome Oral History." Not a brilliant title, but descriptive enough to allow him to find it if he ever needed it.

Pushing back from his desk, Paul got up and stretched. Well over an hour had passed like it was just a few minutes, and he estimated he'd written close to five pages. Not since his dissertation had he enjoyed writing. Could he change book topics this late in the game? If he went deeper into the information he and Marty were gathering, he knew he could write a book in record time.

Paul made his way through the stacks of books to the window that looked out at the front yard. It wasn't dusk, but the shadows were beginning to go from compact to elongated. The shadow cast by the mailbox reached halfway across the street.

The problem with turning his Jerome research into a book was the same problem that had kept him from revising his dissertation into the first book required of all university faculty. The number of potential readers was so small no press would publish it.

Still, the experience of the last hour had proved he'd never write the Jefferson book. The question now wasn't how he was going to finish the book on time. The question was what he was going to do about his job.

As exciting as the idea of walking away from teaching was,

he had a son, maybe two, to think of. At least he didn't have to consider Marty or her opinion. If, as she'd made painfully clear, she was determined to keep their relationship at the friend level, what kind of work he did wouldn't matter to her.

Though they wouldn't put it so crassly, all the boys cared about was that he bring home enough money to keep a roof over all their heads, food on the table, and the Internet and cell phone bills paid.

Paul did what he always did when he was facing a tough decision. He headed upstairs. The house was so quiet, he felt like tiptoeing to keep from waking the baby. The thought surprised him. It was years since he'd had to be careful about waking a baby. The house was empty. Scott and B.T. were at the Miller mine taking another look around, and Rahab, the cat, was outside prowling the yard in search of lizards.

He passed Scott's room, noticing with faint surprise that his son had made his bed. A glance in the guest room told him why. B.T. had made the bed and put everything where it was when Paul first showed him the room. Like the boy calling him "Dr. Russell," the precision with which he'd put the room back in order showed how ill-at-ease he felt.

Paul suspected it was going to be a challenge to win B.T.'s trust. A challenge only affection and time had the power to meet. At least Marty wouldn't have to worry about B.T. He didn't like it, but the more he thought about what she'd said, the more sense it made.

As he pushed away the complicated mix of sorrow and anger that threatened to choke him, Paul went into his own lonely room. Kneeling by the bed, he began to pray.

When the land line rang, he didn't have any answers, but he knew he wasn't alone, no matter what happened. Getting to his feet, he reached for the phone. He hoped the call meant B.T.'s father had decided to agree to counseling with the goal of getting his son back.

"Hello, this is Paul."

"Dr. Russell, this is Alex Reyes. Do you have a few minutes?"

"Sure. How are you today, Alex?"

A pause. Alex cleared his throat. "I'm sorry to bother you, sir."

"You're not bothering me. What's on your mind?"

"I wanted to ask you about the fund raiser for Aurora. Now that mi abuelo…"

"I'm so sorry about his passing, Alex. I'm grateful I had the chance to meet him. He was a special man with a deep love for his family. I know you're all going to miss him."

Alex was silent for a moment. Then he cleared his throat again. "My sister-in-law asked me to call. She and my brother want to know if you're going ahead with fund raiser."

"We're all going to work just as hard as we would have if your grandfather called us every day for an update."

"Thanks, Dr. Russell. That's what I told Belinda, but she wanted me to call to double-check. It's just that she's afraid Aurora is starting to realize how worried everyone is."

"No problem, Alex. I can understand her concern. Your grandfather was a convincing advocate for our cause. We're going to miss having his voice."

"You still have the thumb drive I turned in. In one of the interviews he talked about how important the past is to the children of today. Maybe you could use that recording somehow."

"I'm sure we can. I'll keep in touch as we get the plans finalized. Now go reassure your brother and sister-in-law. Keep me posted on Aurora's condition."

Paul hung up the phone and went back downstairs. He'd forgotten the details of that particular interview. He needed to listen to it again to make sure Enrique hadn't gone into a passionate explanation of how his brother was murdered.

If he had, they wouldn't be able to use the recording, at least not without some heavy editing. But if they had Enrique's voice talking about the importance of the past to children, what a find that would be!

Back in his office, Paul went to the box of oral history projects. When he didn't find the Reyes thumb drive the first time through, he thought he'd missed it. But after a third search that included alphabetizing each drive by student name and then by subject, he knew it was gone.

He remembered checking to see that Alex had turned it in after the young man confronted him with the zero he'd placed on the preliminary evaluation response. That was Wednesday. This was Sunday, four days since the shadow of an old murder had crossed his desk.

After moving a stack of books to the floor, Paul sat on the loveseat. Steepling all ten fingers, he opened and closed his hands thoughtfully. "An octopus doing push-ups on a mirror." The joke Scott loved when he was four flashed through Paul's mind.

The same age as Aurora Reyes. Did she giggle at the old joke? How much fun it would be to have a four-year-old in the house again, maybe a daughter this time. Paul stared at his hands. What was he thinking?

Whatever it was, he needed to focus on the missing thumb drive. He was certain it was in the box when he left his office. The box hadn't spilled, so it couldn't have fallen out. Perhaps most significantly, it was the only one missing.

He'd looked through the collection three times. One thumb drive was gone. Neither Scott nor B.T. knew or cared anything about the assignment that had started their search for a silver lode. They were interested in finding gold.

Doing his best not to leap to a conclusion, Paul went through the rest of the oral history data. But everything relating to Enrique Reyes was missing. The last letter Manuel wrote home, the transcriptions of the key interviews, the conclusions essay, the outline Alex had made of his project. All of it was gone, and nothing else was missing.

Someone had come into his home and stolen every bit of data Alex had collected. With Enrique Reyes dead, even Alex had no way to recover the information. For the first time, Paul considered seriously the possibility that Alex was right. Enrique Reyes had been murdered.

Was the thief someone willing to murder a helpless old man for a few letters? What if Scott or B.T. had been in the house?

18

Monday, March 18

Scott came out of the mine and gave B.T. a thumbs-down. "All the branch tunnels peter out to nothing. I bet this hole didn't tap into a rich vein of copper, much less Manuel's silver lode."

"Did you find anything to identify which mine this is?"

"Nope." He'd been sure it was the Miller mine, but that one made at least one fortune. He must've figured the coordinates wrong. "This looks like a spec mine that went bust."

"So where do you look for the silver lode now?"

Scott frowned. "No idea. I've got to find out more about Manuel, like which mine he worked for, where he lived, maybe who his friends were. But with Sr. Reyes dead, I don't know how to get any of that info."

"I'll help you brainstorm tonight, but right now I've got to get to town and look for a job."

Scott shouldered his backpack. He knew his dad didn't want rent from B.T. "You don't have to do this, buddy."

B.T. shrugged. "I want to. If you guys hadn't offered me your guest room, I was planning to run away. The first thing would've been to get a job and drop out of school. When I called about an apartment, I found out I need enough money for first and last month's rent plus a deposit. I would've been homeless until I could save at least a thousand bucks."

"It's March. Wait and get a summer job."

B.T. started up the incline toward the highway and his bike. "Where do you want me to drop you?"

"Might as well take me to work. Got nothing better to do till I figure out how to research Manuel Reyes." Scott fastened his chinstrap and then climbed on behind B.T. "Hey! Maybe Miss Marty will hire you to help clean out that old shed."

B.T. started the motor. As they bumped up onto the highway, he shouted, "I'm not a charity case! I'll find my own job."

Scott looked to the right where the land dropped sharply away. Through a gap in the hills he could see all the way to the town of Cottonwood, almost blue in the distance. He needed to be more careful of B.T.'s feelings. He didn't want his friend to think he felt sorry for him. B.T. was strong and independent.

They'd both lost their mothers, and Scott knew how angry he was when his dad was too sad to remember he had a son. But Dad had never taken his feelings out on him. He couldn't imagine what it was like to have your own father hit you. What should he say to B.T.?

He still hadn't figured it out when B.T. pulled up in front of the 1920s bungalow with the new sign over the doorway that read Old and Treasured. But he had to say something. He didn't want B.T. to head into town thinking Scott saw him as a charity case. As he climbed off, he said, "Miss Marty hired me because of my dad. You're going to find a great job on your own."

B.T. gave Scott a half smile. "If I know my address and phone number. You got anything to write it on?"

Scott grinned. "Do you mind a drawing of a rock on the other side?"

"I'll memorize the information and eat the paper."

Scott laughed and pulled the small pad he always had with him out of his backpack. He was kidding about the drawing of a rock, but as he flipped through the pages of sketches, he realized he needed a new pad.

When he found a blank page, he jotted the address and the number of their land line. B.T. needed a cell phone. Scott knew his dad would put B.T. on their family plan, but how to get him a phone without making it feel like a handout? As he handed the sheet to his friend, Scott said, "When's your birthday?"

"What?"

"Your birthday. You know. The day you were born."

B.T. rolled his eyes. "What do you want to know that for?"

Scott shrugged. "My family always makes a big deal out of birthdays." At least they had when Mom was alive. Maybe it was time to start doing that again. They could start with B.T.

"February 13. When's yours?"

"August 10." No way could the cell wait until February. Maybe he could convince his dad to restart a different tradition of his mom's. He remembered a long time ago. Mom carried a cherry pie into the family room singing, "A very merry un-birthday to you, to you." Then she handed him and his dad each a package.

"What's this?" Dad said.

"I know!" shouted Scott. "The Mad Hatter!" He tore the paper off the package to find his first kid's rock-hound backpack. It contained tools and a pad and pencil.

"Scott!"

Scott blinked and came back to the present.

"You okay, dude?"

"Yeah. I was just remembering something."

"You want me to pick you up later?"

Scott nodded. "Maybe you'll have a job."

"Sure hope so." B.T. started the bike and headed down the street.

Scott watched until his friend turned the corner. He hadn't let himself remember his mom much. It hurt too bad. But now, he realized it felt good to remember that Mad Hatter tradition. Maybe he and his dad could pass some of that fun along to B.T.

Turning that new thought around in his head, Scott shouldered his pack and went around the house. Carly was sitting cross-legged in the grass, sorting little colored pieces of cloth into shoe boxes. "What you doing?" he called.

She waved him over. "I bet you've never seen anything like this." She handed him a white square.

He studied it. Thin material, lace edges, and pink thread flowers in the corners. "What is it?"

"A lady's handkerchief."

"You mean instead of a tissue?"

"Yep."

"Gross."

Carly laughed. "Kleenex is a modern invention, Scottie boy."

Scott dropped his backpack and sat down beside her. "Then I'm glad I live in modern times. What are you going to do with all those?"

"Sell them. Crafters make Christmas angels or doll clothes out of fancy handkerchiefs."

"Is Miss Marty around?"

"She went to the celebration of life for Sr. Reyes. I don't expect her back for quite a while."

"You got anything for me to do?"

"I thought you were going to find gold and silver today."

"No such luck. I need to research Manuel Reyes. You got any ideas?"

Carly clapped her hands. "I found something in the shed you're going to love!"

Scott didn't get excited. No telling what Carly thought he would love.

Carly gave him an exaggerated frown. "You don't believe me. I can tell by the look on your face. Maybe I won't show you."

Scott lay back on the grass and looked up at the older girl. "Give me a hint. If it's a good one, I'll look at your find."

"Okay, Mr. Smarty. What do the letters M and R mean to you?"

"The abbreviation for Mister."

"That's what I thought. I'll give you another clue. There are six letters. I guessed they meant Mr. Eyes. I was wrong."

Scott closed his eyes and imagined the words Mr. Eyes. What else could it stand for?

"Try taking out the period and ignoring the capital letters. That's my last hint."

"Two hints." Scott tried her suggestions. In his mind, he saw mreyes. He opened his eyes. "Carly Remick, if you're fooling around, I'm going to be seriously mad."

"I'm not kidding."

"What did you find?"

"A footlocker."

Scott sat up. "You found Manuel Reyes's footlocker?"

Carly looked smug. "It took you long enough to figure it out."

"What was in it?"

"I'll show you, on one condition."

"Anything." Scott paused. This was Carly he was talking to. "Almost anything."

"Cover for me the rest of the afternoon."

"Someone you don't want to deal with is coming."

"Nothing like that. Marty didn't have any idea when she would be back. She made me promise to stay."

Somewhere there was a catch. "Why do you want to leave?"

"Don't be so suspicious. A friend invited me to a movie in Cottonwood."

Probably a new boyfriend. Whoever it was, Scott was grateful. It would give him a chance to go through the footlocker without anyone looking over his shoulder. "Deal."

"Super!" Carly typed a quick message on her cell phone.

Scott got to his feet and started for the shed. He was pulling on the door when Carly joined him. "What's in the footlocker?" he said.

"No silver or gold. Some tools in mint condition, a few old clothes, a cheap spiral notebook, and some rocks."

A notebook. Maybe Manuel had drawn a map to his find.

Carly went inside. "Lucky for you it's still here, Scottie boy. I'm surprised Marty didn't take it with her to give to the family."

"With Sr. Reyes dead, I don't think anyone would want it."

"I tried to tell Marty that. Besides, I think something belonging to Manuel would make a great addition to the fund raiser. We could raffle it off or maybe give it as a door prize."

Scott stared at the contents of the shed. Pianos, tables, chairs, boxes, and baskets of small items. "Where did all this come from?"

"A lot of it belonged to my grandmother, but some of it's older. Like Manuel's footlocker. That's from my great-grandmother's time."

"I wonder how she got it."

"No clue, but there it is." Carly pointed to an army green trunk sitting against the wall.

Scott studied the dim interior. Not a single window. "Okay if I take it outside?"

"As long as you put everything back where you found it."

"I wouldn't steal anything!"

"Take it easy, Scottie boy. I'm just repeating what Marty always says. Now help me get this thing outside. It's heavier than it looks."

She was right. Scott wondered if Manuel had stashed ore samples in the trunk. Ore would look like rocks to Carly. His heart kicked up a notch. He had the feeling he was about to discover something important.

"You want it under the tree?" Carly said.

"Yeah."

As they approached the tree, Carly's phone played a sort of dance tune. Carly dropped her end of the footlocker, pulled out her cell phone, and glanced at it. "Got to go. My friend's out front."

"Have a good time," Scott said. But Carly was already gone. A new boyfriend for sure. Carly went through them almost as often as she changed the color of the streak in her red-gold curls. Last week it was pink. Today it was blue.

Scott squatted in front of the footlocker. "Okay, Manuel," he whispered, "now's your chance to help me find the silver lode for your family." Reaching for the two locks, he flipped them open. The miner who had owned this trunk had been dead a long time, long enough to be one of the ghosts everyone talked about in Jerome. What secrets would this ghost tell him?

The top tray held the tools. As Carly had said, the tools looked almost new. Purchased for mining out the silver lode? Never used because someone was willing to kill to get sole ownership of the rare deposit? In any case, they didn't tell him anything.

He put the tray to the side and turned to the clothes. Two pair of worn overalls with empty pockets. Three threadbare flannel shirts, one with a long tear in a sleeve. More empty pockets.

The rocks were underneath the clothes. As he suspected, they were samples of ore. One of the samples caught his attention. The size of a softball, its outer layer was reddish brown. The center was a dull gray flecked with yellow. Silver with gold, the ingredients that made up a silver lode. Without a magnet or a piece of glass he couldn't be sure it wasn't pyrite, or fool's gold, but he was willing to bet.

For a moment he was tempted to put it in his backpack, but he put it back. He would bring his gold testing kit and ask Marty's permission. A large piece of quartz appeared to have gold in it, but he doubted that came from the silver lode. A dull gray rock the shape of a soccer ball with a serious leak looked like it could be lead with flecks of silver.

He found the notebook at the bottom of the footlocker. Holding his breath, he flipped through the pages looking for a map. Nothing. What he found were sketches of faces. A man with grim lines etched in his forehead and at the corners of his mouth. A woman with a wide grin that showed two teeth missing. Another man with slits for eyes and a scary frown. Scott shivered. Was he looking at the face of Manuel's killer?

He kept going back to one sketch. A half-open door with darkness behind it. A door opening into the night or into a tunnel? He thought of Alice tumbling down the long hole. What was with him today? He had Alice in Wonderland on the brain.

He closed the notebook and put it back into the footlocker. Why hadn't Manuel drawn a map? Surely he would have wanted his brother to know where to find the silver lode if something happened to him. Maybe a map had been here, and someone had torn it out of the notebook years ago.

More disappointed than he wanted to admit, Scott put everything back the way he'd found it. As he was closing the lid, he noticed a spot along the edge where the marbled paper lining was coming loose. Not just that, the lining wasn't smooth. Holding his breath, he ran his hand along the lid. Near the middle he touched an area higher than the rest. Something was there.

His pulse started to race. A map or something useless like money stashed away for an emergency? Taking care not to tear the fragile lining, Scott worked the hidden treasure to the edge of the lid. Manuel, or whoever had used this hiding place, had glued the lining back in place. He wanted to grab the loose corner and rip back the lining. But Marty would have his hide.

He sat back on his heels and considered the problem. He needed a long, flat piece of metal to slide beneath the lining. If he used his pocketknife, he risked cutting the paper. Ditto for a kitchen knife. A butter knife would work.

He was halfway to the back door when he heard a familiar voice. "Scott? You still here?"

With an odd sense of waking from a dream, Scott saw B.T. come around the side of the house.

"Good news, dude!" B.T. said.

Scott wanted to shout, "Me first!" But B.T. had been out looking for a job. Scott swallowed his own news. "You got hired?"

"At the hardware store. I start tomorrow. It's sweeping floors and stocking shelves, but the guy said I walked in at the right time. The kid that's had the job for the last year just quit. His dad got transferred or something. I think my luck is changing."

Scott knew his dad would tell B.T. it wasn't luck, but B.T. hadn't been to church before yesterday. Scott said, "It's more—"

B.T. cut him off. "I know! It started when you said I could share your room. Then your dad said we were too old to share a room, but I could have the guest room as long as I stayed in school!"

"I mean it's more than luck," Scott said. "Did you ever think God might have a hand in your life?"

B.T. stared at him. "God doesn't care about me. He might care about you, but not me."

"God loves everyone! If He loves me, He loves you."

B.T. shook his head. "If God loves me, why am I in this mess?"

"That's theology," Scott said. "You have to ask my dad or Pastor about that. Another time. I've got good news too!"

"You found the silver lode? No way. Not here in the backyard."

"I think I found a map to it. Come on, I'll show you. But first, I've got to get a butter knife."

"What?"

"Just watch." Scott dashed into the kitchen with B.T. close behind. He jerked open the drawer where Marty kept the cheap silverware she used. It rattled with a satisfying clatter, but no butter knife sat in the plastic divider tray. "If you were a butter knife, where would you be?" he muttered.

"No idea," B.T. said. "Butter knives are too fancy for the likes of me."

"Fancy! You got it." Scott remembered a small chest lined in what looked like blue velvet filled with a set of expensive forks and knives that was real silver. But where had he seen it? Marty had set it aside to display on the Duncan Phyfe table she was refinishing. "Think," he said aloud.

"Think about what?"

"A little, polished wooden chest about eighteen inches wide and ten inches tall."

"That one?" B.T. pointed to the chest Scott was looking for. It sat in plain sight in the corner on top of a scratched-up piano bench.

"Buddy, you're the best luck I've had in a long time," Scott said.

"I thought you didn't believe in luck."

Scott ignored his friend and opened the lid. Six shiny silver butter knives sat in a box made for them. He snatched one before his better judgment could take charge.

"You think you should take that outside?"

Where had this new, cautious rule abiding B.T. come from? "I'll bring it right back. It won't get scratched." Paper wouldn't scratch silver. But Scott hurried. He wanted to get done with this project before Marty got back.

For some crazy reason he was relieved when he spotted the footlocker sitting where he'd left it under the tree. The lid was still open. Scott squatted and ran his hand over the intriguing lump beneath the lining paper.

B.T. leaned over his shoulder. "You're sure that's the map under there?"

Scott didn't answer. It had to be the map. It wasn't the right size for a packet of bills. Being as careful as he could, he slid the rounded edge of the butter knife between the lid of the footlocker and the liner and pushed. As he'd hoped, the glue was old and dried. In a moment he had the liner loose.

Scott handed B.T. the butter knife. Then he resumed sliding the hidden treasure until a tiny white edge appeared from beneath the brown marbled paper. White, not money. Unless it was in an envelope. Scott resisted the urge to grab the edge and yank out whatever was there. He resumed the gentle pressure. When a half inch was visible, he saw faded blue lines.

"That's notebook paper," B.T. said. "That's not a map."

Scott kept the gentle pressure steady. When an inch was visible, he grasped it between his thumb and forefinger. The cheap paper was brittle. Which was safer? To keep going slow or pull it out with one quick motion. Before he could lose his nerve, he pulled.

A piece of notebook paper folded in half came out without so much as a torn edge. Taking a deep breath, he opened the page. Smudged pencil marks crisscrossed the evenly spaced blue lines, all converging on a large X in the top right corner.

"I don't know what that is, dude," B.T. said, "but it doesn't look much like a map."

Scott agreed, but he wasn't about to admit it. "It's just going to take some deciphering." As he spoke he held it up to the light. Some of the lines had words printed on them. Street names? He didn't recognize any of the words, and some of them were missing letters. This was going to take some time. He refolded the paper and reached for his backpack.

"You're not going to take it, are you?"

Scott squelched the guilt that was asking the same question. "I'm not going to steal it! Just borrow it for a little while." He pulled out his geography book and placed the map between the top cover and the first page. Closing the book, he slid it back into his pack. "Come on," he said. "Help me put the footlocker back in the shed."

B.T. gave him a look he couldn't interpret.

"What? You don't trust me now?"

B.T. shrugged. "Of course, I trust you."

"Good. Then help me put the footlocker back. After I make a copy of the map, I'll put it back. Scout's honor."

19

P aul stood just outside the door and surveyed the patio of
Sweet Home. Guests clustered together in small knots of
conversation. A wizened, old woman bent almost double
sat at a round wicker table with a middle-aged couple, no doubt a
daughter and son-in-law. Despite the bright sunshine, people
spoke in low voices.

Marty stood at the edge of the patio overlooking the river,
deep in conversation with a plump, gray-haired woman Paul
didn't recognize. Was it only yesterday Marty ran away from
him? If his guess was correct, she was afraid she couldn't replace
Linda as Scott's mother. She was right, but what she didn't
recognize were the different gifts she had to give Scott.

A stir by the door drew Paul's attention away from Marty. A
tall, elegant woman wearing a black dress with a long white scarf
stepped out onto the patio, carrying a black leather portfolio, and
holding hands with a thin-faced little girl. Patricia Osborn? The
shining white hair that framed her face made it almost certain.

The little girl, followed by a tired-looking man and a worried
woman, had to be Aurora Reyes. Behind the foursome came

Alex and his parents. The funeral at the Catholic church must be over. It was time to begin the celebration of the life of Enrique.

The elegant woman moved to the wicker table and lifted Aurora onto it. "If I could have your attention," she said. "For those of you who don't know me, my name is Patricia Osborn." Bingo. Paul studied her. She had a gift for drama. Her well-modulated voice carried across the patio, and the murmur of voices stilled.

"We're here to remember Sr. Reyes," Patricia said. "What better way to celebrate his life than with his great-granddaughter, Aurora? She was the light of his life since she first came into the world four years ago. Now this beautiful little girl needs a new heart, and thanks to a guardian angel named Marty Greenlaw, you can all help Aurora get that heart." She beckoned to Marty.

Paul saw a sudden flush stain Marty's neck. She hadn't expected this public introduction, but she smiled and moved to the wicker table. Patricia said, "Ms. Greenlaw is the owner of Old and Treasured, a combination showroom and workshop for quality antiques." Putting an arm around the younger woman, Pat added, "She's also becoming my good friend."

As the flush spread to Marty's face, Pat gave her a little hug and let her go. "Marty's organizing a fund raiser for Aurora, so if she calls you, say yes. Better, come over here right now, introduce yourself, and offer to help." Stepping back, Pat said, "Now I'm going to turn this over to her."

Marty smiled at the group. "First, I want to introduce Hernando and Belinda Reyes, Aurora's parents. They've made untold sacrifices to do their best to raise the money for their daughter's heart transplant."

The couple Paul had noticed following Patricia and Aurora stepped forward. "We want to thank you in advance for any help you feel led to give," Hernando said. "We don't like asking strangers for money, but when your daughter's life is at stake, you find yourself doing all sorts of things you never thought you'd do."

"You may not know us," shouted a man near the pergola, "but anyone who knew Enrique knows Aurora!"

A tiny ripple of laughter worked its way through the crowd. When it died down, Marty said, "There's another member of the Reyes family I want you to meet, Aurora's Uncle Alex. This effort started with Alex, a history student at Northern Arizona University. He brought the problem to the attention of his teacher, Professor Paul Russell, who then made me aware of the need. When I approached Patricia Osborn, it became an official fund raiser. Because Alex spoke up, Aurora's need became known." She turned to Alex. "Would you like to add anything?"

"I sure would!" As Alex swung the little girl onto his shoulders, Paul remembered doing the same thing with Scott. How long ago? Ten years since Scott was four, but Scott was a sturdy little boy. The last time Paul remembered carrying Scott on his shoulders, his son was two. Tiny for her age, Aurora looked like a strong wind could pick her up and carry her away.

The little girl settled her chin on top of Alex's head, her dark curls mingling with his. Reaching up for Aurora's hands, Alex said, "Ms. Osborn is right. Mi abuelo loved our little girl more than anyone in the world. The best way to celebrate his life is to help her get a new heart so she can live a long life like her great-grandpapa."

Joe Sweet appeared with a yellow legal pad and a pen. Handing them to Marty, he said, "Who wants to be the first one to make a pledge?"

The old woman sitting at the table raised her hand.

"Thank you, Mrs. Arbeck. I've always said you were a generous lady."

Stepping back, Joe waved a hand toward the house. "Please go inside and help yourself to finger sandwiches and cake. Be sure to have a mango milkshake in honor of Enrique." He chuckled. "He used to pester me for the recipe, but I told him I plan to take it to the grave."

Paul heard a sudden intake of breath. Oblivious to the tension that froze the group, Joe went on. "When your plate is full, come back out and visit in this beautiful afternoon. And if you know anyone as special as Enrique who's looking for a sweet home, be sure to recommend us."

Paul had encountered many young people with as little tact as Joe Sweet, but Joe was running an establishment to help older people. Adult children must be desperate to find accommodations for their aging parents if they trusted them to this insensitive man.

As people began to drift toward the house, Patricia Osborn called out, "Be sure to stop and put your name on Marty's pledge list! Don't worry, we don't charge interest on late payments." She got a few chuckles, breaking the tension.

A young couple about Hernando and Belinda's age stopped to talk to Marty. Behind them a line began to form. It looked like she'd be occupied for some time, so Paul decided to tackle Joe about the letters Alex was so sure had disappeared from Enrique's room.

The round little man stood under the cedar pergola talking to a bored-looking middle-aged woman sitting in the red Adirondack chair Sr. Reyes had occupied the day they visited. As Paul watched, the proprietor of Sweet Home gestured toward the river and back toward the house. Making a sales pitch for the now vacant room?

As Paul started toward the pergola, he heard Patricia Osborn's distinctive voice. "Professor Russell!"

Curious, he turned to wait for the power behind the fund raiser. She stopped just a little too close, the same height as Linda but twenty or twenty-five years older. He caught a whiff of exotic, spicy perfume and stepped back. She appeared not to notice, but she put a hand on his arm as if to keep him from moving farther.

"You're the historian interested in helping Aurora."

He raised an eyebrow. "I am."

She chuckled. "Alex Reyes told me all about you. He wants to follow in your footsteps."

"Alex has the makings of a fine historian."

"Not what I want to talk to you about, though. You may know I'm president of the Jerome Historical Society."

Paul hoped she didn't want an appraisal of what was stored in the crowded upstairs room the society called a library. He was interested in Jerome history, but if their collection was like other local collections he'd seen, it would be in serious disarray. Personal letters inside hat boxes. Newspapers stacked in no particular order. Crumbling architects' drawings mixed in with hand-drawn maps.

"Yesterday as I was doing my usual Sunday afternoon filing in the archives, I ran across some information about the Wong family that might provide an interesting background for the Reyes's fund raiser gala."

So it was a gala now. Paul wondered if Marty knew. Somehow he didn't think so. Her showroom couldn't handle a gathering of that size.

"I'm thinking of a panel discussion," Patricia said, "or individual presentations by each of the special guests. Marty can decide. With a formal program, we can invite everyone on the Jerome Historical Society's mailing list, and we might be able to access the Arizona State Historical Society's list."

Paul wanted to say, "Whoa, lady. Slow down." But it was an interesting idea. He said, "How can I help?"

Patricia gave him a warm smile. "I can pull together the information on each family, but that's where my expertise stops. I'd like to give you what I find and get you to evaluate which items would be of the most interest to historians, professional and amateur. Could you do that little thing for me?"

It depended on the amount of data and her timeline, but before Paul could get the words out, she rushed on. "I know the university is on spring break this week." She unzipped the leather portfolio, pulled out a manila folder, and handed it to him. "This is what I found on the Wongs. It's interesting reading, a real rags-to-riches story. I've started collecting information on the Miller Mine—that's Carol Angel—which I can get to you by tomorrow morning."

For an instant Paul understood Marty's fear of not being able to live up to Linda's legacy. If Marty thought Linda was like Patricia Osborn, the task would be daunting indeed. Linda had been this organized with information, but she'd never tried to organize people. She'd invited people to help plan, not decide for them what role they should play to get her to her goal.

Patricia was looking at him expectantly. It was his turn to talk. He smiled. "I'll be glad to examine what you've got, Ms. Osborn, as long as you understand that I'm not an expert on Arizona history."

"Please, call me Pat. As a teacher you know what interests an audience."

Audience wasn't the word he would have chosen to characterize his students, but he understood what she meant.

"The only family I haven't found any mention of is the Sanchez family," Patricia said. "But I know they were miners. Didn't I hear Manuel Reyes's partner was a Sanchez?"

"Franco Sanchez. I interviewed his grandson Friday."

"Excellent. What did he tell you?"

"Not much. He enjoys his inheritance without being troubled about what his grandfather did to acquire it."

"Disappointing."

Paul gave Pat a wry smile. "I think he'll do some research and get back to me. When I showed him Manuel's letter about the discovery of a silver lode and explained his brother's desire to solve what he considered to be Manuel's murder, Mr. Sanchez changed his tune in a hurry. I expect to hear from him or his lawyer in the next couple of days."

"We need to be careful about discussing an old man's obsession with the so-called murder of his long-lost brother. We don't want guests to feel like they're being invited to a witch hunt. Our mission is to raise money for a little girl who needs a heart transplant. We mustn't lose sight of that." Pat lifted the flap of her black and gold leather purse and took out a white leather wallet.

"I understand, but…"

Pat held out a business card. "My office number and email as well as my cell phone. Let's talk more soon. Do you have a card?"

Paul handed her one of the generic history department cards with his name printed on it. "My email address and phone numbers are on the back."

She glanced at her watch, a wide, black enamel cuff with an over-sized face. "I'll be in touch, Paul." Then she was gone, high-heeled boots clicking on the stone patio.

20

M arty kicked off her heels and dropped onto the bed, grateful to have escaped the celebration of life for Sr. Reyes. She'd been prepared for an awkward meeting with Paul, which she'd managed to avoid.

What she hadn't been prepared for was being thrust into the public role of Aurora's guardian angel. She was grateful to Pat for giving the fund raiser a kick-start, but she wished her mentor had at least warned her. The worst part had been knowing Paul was there to see her make a fool of herself.

Marty closed her eyes. Alex had made the best appeal. Maybe he would be willing to work with Carly. Alex and Carly...

The buzz of the doorbell jarred her awake, five minutes or an hour later. No matter the time, she wasn't in the mood to work or talk about the fund raiser. She lay still and studied the ceiling fan. A layer of dust outlined the edges of each blade.

The doorbell buzzed again. Maybe if she didn't answer, her visitor would go away. But the next sounds were insistent knocking and a resonant bass voice calling, "You home, Marty?"

Paul. She'd known he would show up sooner or later. She'd

botched the conversation yesterday. She was going to have to find a way to explain without emotion why she couldn't marry him. Maybe a list would work. But however she decided to handle it, she wasn't ready.

Ready or not, her pickup was in the driveway, and she didn't want to hide from Paul. Where were Carly and Bill when she needed them?

With a sigh, Marty sat up and pulled on her shoes. She needed the extra inches for the confrontation that was standing at her door.

He knocked again when she was halfway down the stairs. "Marty?"

"Coming!"

As she worked her way around the half-finished projects that cluttered the showroom, she straightened her navy sheath. What to say? "Sorry I ran out on you?" But she wasn't sorry. She was so far from being sorry she'd changed her mind about hiding. She could run out through the kitchen and hide in the shed. Absurd. Taking a deep breath, Marty opened the door.

Paul stood there, still wearing the dark slacks and gray blazer he'd had on at the Reyes's celebration of life. So she hadn't been asleep long. Thrusting a thick manila folder at her, he said, "We need to talk."

As she stepped back to let him enter, she wondered what data he had gathered to prove that step-parenting was something she could learn.

"Patricia Osborn gave me that information," he said. "It changes everything."

Marty stared at him. What did Pat have to do with their relationship?

"There's a fortune that could have originated with Manuel's silver lode."

The silver lode. Paul wasn't here to discuss her flight. She relaxed so suddenly she almost dropped the folder. She swallowed hard. "Would you like a cup of coffee?"

"Sure."

She followed him toward the kitchen. Maybe this was going to be easy. Paul might have thought through the situation and decided she was right that they needed to be lifelong friends. A wave of dismay shook her. That was what she wanted, wasn't it? To cover her confusion, she stopped in the doorway, took off the tight shoes, and set them on a workbench shoved against the wall.

Paul had the refrigerator open. "You have a carafe of coffee left from this morning?"

It struck her how much of her routine he knew. "Top shelf behind the milk."

He pulled it out and took two mugs from the dish drainer. He filled them both, put one in the microwave, and turned it on. Over the whir of the fan, he said, "Take a look. Tell me what you think."

She sat at the table and opened the folder. On top she found the most recent annual report of the Wong Foundation. The cover, light blue card stock, sported a photo of three smiling teenagers gathered around a campfire, two girls and a boy. Marty wondered when Carly had been part of a Wong Camp and if her photo appeared on that year's cover. The second page was headed "Message from the Chairman." A small photo labeled James Wong showed a smiling man with a round face, gray hair, and dark eyes. Marty guessed he was in his late fifties or early sixties. Curious about the donor Carly credited with changing her life, Marty started to read.

"As we evaluate our success with our grant making goals last year, we must look back at our mission statement. *The Wong Foundation seeks to benefit young people on the road to recovery from addictive illness by supporting established organi-*

zations and experimental projects based on network therapy principles.

"This year the Foundation distributed grants totaling $400,000. Recipients included ongoing Wong Summer Camps as well as three exciting new venues, the annual conference on network therapy techniques for pre-clinical medical school students, and an experimental program of after-school network sessions for all Wong Camp graduates from last year.

"This year brought several changes to our board. We said good-bye to Melissa Lawson, Richard Sill, and Roger Tory. We welcomed Peter Johansen, Jennifer Byrd, and Felicia Scott. I am extremely proud of the work of our board, including successful fundraising efforts..."

Paul handed Marty a mug of coffee. Skipping to the bottom of the single page, she continued to read.

"The Foundation continues to operate on a solid financial basis, with net assets in excess of three million dollars at the end of the year. Since the Foundation was established in 1965, we have put to work over nine million dollars. We look forward to continuing to fund many exciting projects that promise to further my grandfather's bold vision."

The message closed with Sincerely, James Wong, though the signature was a scrawled *Jimmy.*

Sipping her black coffee, Marty flipped through the rest of the report. Two pages of photos and credits of directors, members, and committees. Single-page reports from each of the funded projects in crisp print with eye-catching photos. A report of outside auditors. Financial statements and, at the very end, photo credits.

She looked up. Paul, his hands linked behind his head, was sitting with his chair tipped back on two legs, staring at the ceiling.

"It looks like a focused, well-run foundation to me," Marty said. "Is that what you want to know?"

Setting his chair down, Paul said, "Take a look at the rest of the contents of that folder. Then we'll talk." Getting up, he went to the counter to refill his coffee mug. "More coffee?"

Marty shook her head and resumed her reading. The next item in the folder was titled "A Brief Family History of Shen Wong." It consisted of three entries.

1. Shen Wong: born in Phoenix, Arizona, January 5, 1890; established the Wong Foundation January 1, 1965; died in Scottsdale, Arizona, March 3, 1970.

2. Andrew James Wong: born in Jerome, Arizona, June 20, 1930; CEO of Wong Foundation 1970-2005; died in Scottsdale, Arizona, October 3, 2010.

3. James Arthur Wong: born in Phoenix, Arizona, November 23, 1959; CEO of Wong Foundation 2005-present.

Marty looked up. Paul leaned against the kitchen counter, writing on the pad she used for a running grocery list. She went back to the folder. The last three entries were photocopies of newspaper articles. The first one, a brief announcement from an inside page of *The Jerome Sun* dated May 1, 1916, told readers that Mr. Shen Wong intended to open a Chinese restaurant June 1. It promised to be friendly, clean, and economical.

The second article, taken from the March 15, 1935 *Chamber of Commerce Bulletin*, reported the establishment of a new committee on tourism headed by Mr. Shen Wong of the Wong Chinese Restaurant. The last article, from a page of the September 17, 1952 *Verde Independent* reported the latest closings in Jerome. The Wong Restaurant was the fourth in a list of ten.

Marty closed the folder. "Interesting background on one of the three magnet families, but I don't see the connection to the silver lode."

Paul resumed his seat across from her. "It's there, if you look at the chronology and read between the lines."

"You're going to have to connect the dots."

He slid the grocery pad across the table. "Start with the foundation. A Jerome restaurant owner endows his foundation with one million dollars. That's still a lot of money, but in today's dollars that's equivalent to well over eight million. How did Shen Wong get that kind of money from a single 'friendly, clean, and economical' restaurant?"

"Investments?"

Paul shrugged. "In thirteen years? The restaurant closed in 1952. He didn't sell it, so there weren't any proceeds. The foundation started up in 1965. He needed a sizable chunk of change and incredible luck to grow to over a million in that length of time. You can be sure he didn't put every dollar he had into the foundation."

Marty looked at the notes Paul had written. "Our friend Shen was seventy-five when he launched the foundation and eighty when he died. That means something to you."

"Doesn't it to you?"

"I suppose an old man who feels guilty about the way he got his money might find out he's got cancer or some other terminal disease and decide to try to balance the scales before he dies."

Paul nodded.

"That's what you meant by a fortune that might have come from the silver lode. But how would a restaurant owner find out about a miner's discovery?"

"No idea. I'm not ready to accuse Shen Wong of murdering Manuel Reyes. Just as I'm not ready to accuse Franco Sanchez of killing his partner. But the grandson sure wasn't willing to talk about where the money to start that chain of markets came from."

"I thought you told me he didn't know."

"That's what he said. But I have a hard time believing it."

"I agree. It doesn't make much sense. Unless he's been so spoiled his whole life, it's never occurred to him to ask about his grandfather's life."

Marty got to her feet and stretched. She was ready for Paul to leave. She wanted to change clothes and go for a run, a long run. Long enough to give her time to sort out her confused feelings about what she wanted from him.

As if he read her mind, he said, "You're ready for me to go home, but I've got one more question to leave you with."

Marty's throat closed. Here it came. He was going to ask her to marry him.

"Do you think Alex might be right that Enrique was murdered?"

Her relief was so intense, spots swam across her field of vision. To steady herself, she put her hand on the back of her chair.

"The reason I'm asking is I had a chance to ask Joe Sweet about those letters. I thought maybe Sr. Reyes might have kept them somewhere else. Joe not only confirmed what Alex told us about his grandfather keeping the letters in his room, he also told me he read them."

Marty sat down. With an effort she turned her mind back to the Reyes family. "I thought they were in Spanish."

"Joe grew up in Yuma. He's fluent in Spanish. It was the only reason Sr. Reyes agreed to let him read the letters."

"Did he find more evidence that Manuel was murdered?"

Paul shrugged. "No idea. I didn't have much time to talk to him. He was too busy winding up things with the caterers."

Marty grasped at the side issue. She needed Paul to leave. If she could guide the conversation into trivialities, he would get bored and go home. "What about Mrs. Sweet? I'm sure he mentioned a wife."

"He did, but I haven't seen her or talked to her on the phone."

"She might be out of town."

"I made an appointment to talk to Joe later in the week. If she's around, she might know something. The letters are important because if they have disappeared like Alex thinks, someone took them. If we have the possibility of a murder in 1950, we also have the possibility of a second murder to cover it up."

Paul's words triggered a memory of a conversation she'd had before Pat arrived and pushed her into the spotlight. "I talked to the hospice nurse who was assigned to Sr. Reyes the last six months."

"A plump, gray-haired lady?"

"Mrs. Kendrick. She told me she was shocked by his death."

"A hospice nurse?"

Marty nodded. "I know. But she was upset. She told me that in the ten years she's worked with hospice, she's only had one other patient as determined to live as Sr. Reyes. A woman who wanted to see her granddaughter graduate from high school the following year. The doctors told her to do whatever she was planning for her granddaughter now because she wouldn't last another year."

"But she did."

"Not only that. She lived to see the granddaughter graduate from college. Mrs. Kendrick told me Sr. Reyes had that same determination to live to see Aurora get her heart transplant. She said that although his prognosis was grim, his condition was stable. She started to cry."

Paul tipped his chair back and studied the ceiling again. Marty looked up, wondering if the light fixture had trapped bugs again. But no, it was as clean as she'd left it three weeks ago.

"What are you thinking?"

He brought the chair down with a thud. "That Sr. Reyes may have poked a sleeping cougar with a sharp stick."

"But if he was right and Manuel was killed, the murderer is dead or very old."

"Agreed. But if a family's wealth is built on that murder, there's a lot at stake for someone in the here and now. Enough to warrant another murder."

"You're sure Sr. Reyes was smothered?"

"Not at all. What I'm sure of is that we need to stay alert as we interact with these families. Pat gave you three families to start with, right?"

Marty nodded. "Magnet families, she called them."

"She wants me to help her set up a program based on Jerome's history. If someone did kill Sr. Reyes, I'm willing to bet it's someone on that short list."

In spite of herself, Marty shivered. The last thing she wanted was to encounter another murderer.

"I've already spoken to Frank Sanchez. He's promised to get back to me, but if he doesn't, I'll follow up. With these suspicions about the Wongs, I want to interview James myself. That leaves you with the Millers."

"Carol Angel. She's ninety-two, Paul. I'm sure we can leave her off the list."

"Don't forget her money. She could have paid someone."

"But how would any of these people have known about Sr. Reyes?"

"You told me Pat contacted them before she gave you their names. How much did she tell them?"

"No idea," Marty said. "But I'm sure she didn't say anything about murder. She warned me not to make people feel like we were on a witch hunt."

"The name Reyes would be all it would take to rattle a guilty conscience."

21

P aul turned onto Fifth Avenue in Old Town Scottsdale and parked facing a life-size sculpture of four horses jumping away from a central fountain. After checking the address, he got out and headed for the north side of the square. The Wong Foundation was housed in a one-story adobe building.

He opened the cherry and glass door and stepped into a serene, uncluttered foyer. The tawny bamboo floor shone as though it had just been polished. A stylized mural of a sunrise over water on the back wall set a hopeful tone. In a corner created by two bare walls, a pair of waist-high peacocks carved from translucent white jade faced each other with quiet interest.

A pale young woman with short, dark hair sat behind a green circular counter. "Good afternoon," she said. "Welcome to the Wong Foundation. May I help you?"

"I have an appointment with Mr. Wong at four-thirty."

"Dr. Russell?"

Paul nodded and glanced at the nameplate, Sheri, Volunteer Coordinator.

"I'm afraid Mr. Wong is in a meeting."

"I don't mind waiting."

"He may not be finished right at four-thirty. Would you like to reschedule?"

"I live in Cottonwood. Since it's a bit of a drive, I'd rather wait."

Sheri smiled and gestured toward a white leather couch and two pale green leather armchairs with clean lines grouped around a low, round table. "Make yourself comfortable. May I get you a cup of coffee or a bottle of water?"

"No thanks." Paul settled in one of the chairs, picked up a book on the art of Chinese brush painting, and opened it. Graceful images of birds, fish, and flowers in delicate colors filled the pages. Flipping to the chapter on the history of the art, he began to read.

"Sorry to keep you waiting, Dr. Russell. I'm Jimmy Wong."

Paul looked up into a round, smiling face, dark eyes, and gray hair. The CEO of the Wong Foundation was dressed casually in a green and white striped shirt and khaki pants.

Returning the smile, Paul got to his feet and took the hand offered. "Thank you for agreeing to see me at such short notice, Mr. Wong."

"Please. Call me Jimmy."

Feeling awkward as he often did around people significantly shorter than he was, Paul followed the wealthy philanthropist across the room. As they passed the receptionist, Jimmy smiled and said, "You may go home now, Sheri. Thank you for everything you did today."

Turning to Paul, he said, "I'll give you the ten-cent tour." Four pairs of sliding bamboo doors opened off a hall filled with soft white light. "On the right is our board room. Across the hall are the offices of our financial wizard and our communications specialist."

Jimmy slid open a door at the end of the hall and gestured for Paul to go in. "As you see, my office is the last one." Jimmy gave him an impish grin. "I like to hide in the corner so when I'm not working, no one will know."

Like the foyer, the office was serene and uncluttered. Plants placed evenly around the room gave a feeling of outdoors even though there were no windows. Jimmy's L-shaped cherry desk sat at a diagonal facing the door. Its surface was bare except for a small fish carved from dark green jade. The single piece of wall art was a large photograph of the San Francisco Peaks hanging behind the desk.

"Are you a skier?" Paul said.

Jimmy looked at the photo. "No. I enjoy the mountains, though. I have a cabin outside of Flagstaff. When I saw this picture, I couldn't resist it."

"I can see why."

Jimmy indicated a cherry conference table across the room. "Shall we sit there?"

Paul led the way but waited for the older man to make his choice of chair first. He sat at the head of the table. As Paul took the chair on Jimmy's right, the CEO of the Wong Foundation said, "What can I do for you, Dr. Russell?"

"I'm here to ask for your help. It's a rather unusual request."

"I assume this request entails money. The Wong Foundation has a specific mission, one dictated by my grandfather in his will."

Paul nodded. "I know a young woman who benefited from one of the Wong Summer Camps. She credits the experience with giving her a new direction in life. The grant I want to apply for will give a very young girl a chance at life." Opening his messenger bag, he pulled out a folder labeled Aurora Reyes. Selecting a photo of Alex's niece, he handed it to Jimmy. "Let me introduce you to Aurora Reyes, a four-year-old who needs a new heart."

Jimmy took the picture. "I'm sorry, Dr. Russell. You've made your trip for nothing. As deserving as I'm sure this child is, she has no connection to the work of our foundation."

"I thought you might say that. May I try to convince you otherwise?"

Jimmy smiled. "You can try, but I'll warn you, you won't be successful."

Paul returned the smile. "The connection is Jerome, Arizona."

"I don't follow you."

"As I understand the history of your foundation, it all began with a restaurant in Jerome in the early nineteen hundreds." He drew out the photocopies of the three newspaper articles and passed them to the CEO. "I believe Shen Wong was your grandfather."

Jimmy cocked his head to one side. "True, but I'm getting more confused."

Was this successful businessman confused, or was he getting nervous about the direction they were headed? "We're organizing a fund raiser for Aurora, themed around the mining community of Jerome. Patricia Osborn gave us the names of three influential families she believes can help us capture the essence of the town. Your family represents people who succeeded by supporting the miners."

"Go on."

Paul decided to begin with an outline of the plan. The details could wait until he had Jimmy's buy-in. "Aurora's great-grand-uncle was a miner who died. His brother, Enrique Reyes, believed people who made a success from mining in Jerome would want to help his great-granddaughter. We're hoping you'll be part of our program and lead the way by making a donation."

Jimmy frowned. "I'm sorry, Dr. Russell. I'm going to have to turn you down. Participation in this endeavor, no matter how worthy, would set a bad precedent. My grandfather was exacting in his instructions. This foundation exists to help young people who've become addicted to drugs to find their way to a new lifestyle."

Time to take off the gloves. Paul leaned back in his chair. "My research tells me the Wong Restaurant was a modest business. How did your grandfather manage to build a fortune large enough to fund this foundation?"

"I don't understand what you're asking."

"The math doesn't work, sir. Your grandfather must have pulled more money out of Jerome than what he earned selling food to miners."

Jimmy stiffened. "How would he do that?"

Paul shrugged. "Maybe he did some mining on his own. Or perhaps one of his customers tipped him off about a find of high-quality ore."

"No. My grandfather had the foresight to invest in Coca-Cola before it became the giant company it is today. His stock split many times. That's where the money came from."

Paul studied the sixty-something executive sitting at the end of the table. A plausible story, but the math still didn't work. He'd tried it. But he couldn't see that he would gain anything by pushing harder. He nodded. "A rags-to-riches story with Jerome as the backdrop. I hope you'll at least give some thought to participating with us in our attempt to recreate something of the true nature of the billion-dollar copper camp."

Jimmy got to his feet. "I'd like to help this child, but my hands are tied. What I can and will do is give your name to my communications officer. She knows just about everything there is to know about Arizona foundations. I'll ask her to look for one that might suit your purposes better."

Paul stood. "I'd like to send you a description of the program we're planning, if I might. We're trying to put together something that will attract historians, local as well as those interested in the broader history of mining towns in the West. I believe you can bring a different perspective to our panel discussion."

"You want to support the stereotype of the Chinese immigrant, I suppose? The despised outsider whose choices consisted of running a laundry or opening a restaurant. Perhaps you want to bring up all the old accusations of serving dogs and rats as beef to the unsuspecting American?"

Paul held up one hand. "I want nothing of the sort. I apologize if I've somehow offended you, Mr. Wong. I assure you nothing was further from my mind."

Jimmy made a stiff little bow. "It is I who must apologize. I realize no historian of your stature would believe such lies. I'm afraid you touched a nerve."

Paul smiled and extended a hand to the other man. He'd touched a nerve all right. The question was, did that nerve lead to a silver lode?

22

Tuesday, March 19

Paul moved a stack of books from his desk to the floor. He put the oral history projects he'd been evaluating into the box he'd brought them home in. He gathered the pencils and pens and put them into the coffee mug where they belonged. When the desktop was empty, he dusted it with the rag he'd brought from the cleaning closet.

Tossing the rag into the box with the student projects, he sat in his chair and took a yellow legal pad from the bottom drawer of his desk. Flipping through the notes he'd taken at the last Arizona History Convention, he found a clean sheet, pulled it from the tablet, and set it in the center of the uncluttered desk.

He selected a sharp pencil with a good eraser, wrote *oral history* in the center of the page, and drew a circle around it. Having accepted he was never going to write the book on Jefferson's Bible, he'd concluded his highest priority for the rest of the week was to decide on a new career.

While he had an idea of the direction he wanted to go, he could start looking for jobs where his teaching experience might be viewed as a positive. Failing that, he would start from scratch and explore entry-level positions.

He drew five lines radiating from the circle like spokes on a wheel. Refusing to consider the reality of finding jobs, he started brainstorming occupations. Using one line for each occupation, he wrote *government researcher, historical book consultant, historical commission consultant.* Frowning, he added *university professor.* He leaned back in his chair and looked up at the ceiling. What else?

A light tap on the doorframe caught his attention. He let his chair down to see B.T. in the doorway rubbing the back of his neck. "Good morning," Paul said. "Come on in if you can find a path." Getting to his feet, Paul cleared the straight chair beside his desk and gestured to the boy.

B.T. made his way in and looked curiously at the paper on Paul's desk. "What are you doing, Dr. Russell?"

Paul laughed. "Nothing much. Just trying to decide on a new career."

"Scott said he thought you'd rather be a park ranger at the Jerome State Historic Park than a teacher. How about that?"

Paul looked down at his brainstorming. Out of the mouths of babes... His son knew him better than he knew himself. Sitting on the edge of his chair, he wrote *park ranger* on the empty line. Then he flipped the sheet over and turned his attention to the young man who had come so unexpectedly into his life.

"What can I do for you, B.T.?"

Without making eye contact, the boy said, "I don't want to bother you, Dr. Russell, but if you have a few minutes, I need to talk to you."

Paul studied Scott's friend. Three things to set straight in that single sentence. B.T. would never be a bother, they needed to find another way for B.T. to address him, and he would always make time. Before he tried to deal with all that anxiety, however, he needed to listen. "You may have solved my problem for me, B.T., so this is a great time. What's on your mind?"

B.T. finally met Paul's gaze, his brown eyes dark with worry. "I have more than one thing to talk to you about."

"No problem. I'm glad you came in. I have a couple of discussion topics for the two of us myself. But since you came to me, you get to go first."

B.T. cleared his throat. "Now that I have a job, I want to start paying rent."

Paul shook his head, but before he could speak, B.T. hurried on. "I don't know what's fair for a room, utilities, and food, but I want to pay as much as I can. Right now, about all I can be sure of is a hundred dollars a month, but when I get a raise, I'll make it more. After I graduate from high school and get a full-time job, I'll pay you back."

"I'm not planning on charging you rent, B.T. I don't need that guest room, and you need to save your money for college. Even if you stay around here and go to Yavapai Community College, you'll have tuition and books to pay for."

B.T. shook his head. "No, sir. Scott told me that's what you would say, but I'm not a bum."

Paul studied the boy. His wavy, dark hair needed a trim, and from the looks of an old scrape on his downy chin, he could use an electric razor.

"Dad!"

Paul shifted his gaze from B.T. to Scott. It struck him that B.T. looked more like his son than blond, blue-eyed Scott did. "We're in the middle of something, Son," Paul said. "I'll call you when it's your turn."

Scott took a half-step back, his face turning as red as if Paul had slapped him. Scott's reaction surprised Paul as much as his statement had evidently surprised Scott.

"I can come back later," B.T. said.

"No," Paul said. "I have plenty of time for both of you. You were here first. Whoever's in the chair has priority. It's the simplest way I've found to keep my office calm when more than one student shows up at the same time."

"News flash, Dad. We're not your students. But hey, no problem. I'll catch you later. When I have some free time."

Before Paul could respond, Scott was gone. Hardly more than a breath later, the front door slammed. Had he been that harsh? Paul didn't think so.

B.T. stood up. "Hey, Dr. Russell. I don't want to get between you and Scott. We can talk about this another time."

Paul refocused on B.T. "Sit back down. Scott's been an only child his whole life, and since his mother died, I've given in on just about everything. It's time he, and I, learned about boundaries. Have you finished what you wanted to say about rent?"

B.T. shook his head. "I insist on paying rent. I'll worry about college if I manage to graduate from high school. Do you know I'm a whole year behind in my credits?"

"I do. It's not a problem." Paul linked his hands behind his head and leaned back. "How about this as a plan? You and I decide on an amount for room and board. Then I make a list of chores. You choose what chores you want to do and keep track of your hours. You can pay as much of your rent as you want to with work around here."

B.T.'s eyes cleared, and he sat up a little straighter. "I'll keep track of the amount I don't work off. I can do the dishes every night."

"Not every night. Scott has chores to offset his allowance. The three of us will need to sit down and figure this out."

"How much do you think is fair?"

Paul did a quick calculation in his head. B.T.'s job was for ten hours a week at minimum wage. That came to a little less than three hundred dollars a month, minus the taxes B.T.'s employer would keep back. He'd let B.T. take them all out to dinner on his tax refund. "Your hundred a month is fair."

"I meant that for rent. I eat a hundred dollars a month in groceries."

"That's okay. My mortgage payment stays the same, whether you're using my guest room or not."

"What about utilities?"

Paul held up a hand. "We'll work out the details later. I'll watch the bills and see how much, if any, they go up. For now, let's leave it you're going to start by weeding and keeping track of your hours. Yesterday I noticed dandelions starting to come up along the edge of the driveway."

"Thank you, sir."

"You're welcome. Anything else on your list?"

"You get a turn now."

"Okay. I'm not comfortable being called Dr. Russell and sir in my own home. That's who I am at work. Here I'm Dad or Paul. You're not my son, and you're not my peer, so we need a new name for a new relationship. How would you feel about calling me Uncle Paul?"

B.T. stared at him. After a moment, he started to speak. When no words came out, he cleared his throat and brushed the back of his hand across his eyes. "You want to take me into your family?"

The beseeching tone in the boy's voice felt like a kick in the gut. Paul took in a slow breath. Now was not the time to bring up the idea of becoming a foster father. He needed to slow down. Marty wasn't the only one not ready to view him in that role.

"We're already in the same family, B.T. God is everyone's father. That makes your dad and me brothers, which means you're my nephew."

B.T. gave a little hiccup, and Paul picked up the box of tissues he kept on the floor under his desk for emergencies like sneezes or coffee spills. Handing it to B.T., he got up and went to the window. Scott was nowhere in sight. Oh well, he had to expect a few bumps in the road. This was new territory for all of them.

Behind him, B.T. blew his nose. "I want to change my name too. I'm starting a new chapter in my life. I can't afford to get the bat tattoo removed yet, but I can change my name."

Curious, Paul turned and looked at the young man sitting in his extra chair. B.T., or whatever he wanted to be called, was going to need to buy some new clothes soon. His cheap running shoes had holes in them. Ditto for his jeans. And he needed something more than a t-shirt. But one thing at a time. "Have you thought of what you'd like to be called?"

"Yes, sir... I mean Uncle Paul. I don't want to use my first name or my middle name because I'm a junior, and I don't want to grow up to be like my dad. I want to be called Reed. It's my mother's maiden name."

"Reed Harper. It sounds good." He moved to the boy's chair and held out his arms. "Reed, give your Uncle Paul a hug."

The boy was stiff as a board, obviously not accustomed to being hugged. Paul patted him on the shoulder and let him go.

As he watched Reed leave the room, Paul knew exactly how he was going to spend the rest of his day. First, he'd look online for information about the qualifications for a park ranger. Then he'd head up to Jerome and drop in at the park offices. And he might type up a synopsis of the book he could write based on the information he and Marty were already collecting in their oral history interviews. Visitors to Jerome were the perfect audience for that book.

23

Marty checked the large, convex mirror that revealed oncoming cars at the blind corner. The road ahead was clear. She made the sharp turn and started up the steep mountainside. Halfway up, the engine began to labor.

As she shifted from second gear into first, she said, "Come on, Snow White. You've got this." Pat had laughed when Marty told her she named the pickup after the sleek, white horse. Silly maybe, but the pickup had needed a name for a long time.

With something like a moan, the pickup topped the incline. A single house stood at the end of the road, a rambling, dusty green Victorian with faded rose gingerbread trim. Despite the color differences, it reminded her of Granny Lois's house.

She parked in the driveway that ran along the side of the house and got out. As she came around the front of the pickup, the view made her stop short. From this perspective, the winding street she'd just driven up looked as if it tumbled down the mountainside and disappeared into the earth.

She studied the little town that lay sprawled at her feet. To the south, the panorama was defined by a sprawling structure that still looked like what it once was, a hotel owned by the

United Verde Mine. Paul told her when he first saw it, the structure was nothing but a shell. Now a private home for a resident as reclusive as he was wealthy, rumor had it the structure had been redesigned to accommodate a swimming pool, a recording studio, and a helipad.

West of the old hotel and several hundred feet below, Marty identified the rusting scaffolding of the now-defunct United Verde Mine and the square, white Douglas Mansion that housed the Jerome State Historic Park museum. Far to the north she saw the San Francisco Peaks. A quaint view now, but in the time the Miller house was built, the scene would have been noisy and dark with soot.

Marty turned and headed toward the house. At ninety-two, its owner had experienced both extremes of the historical spectrum. The house looked its age. The three steps to the wraparound porch were long overdue for a new coat of paint, as was the entire house. Every one of the dozen or more windows needed washing.

A black mailbox beside the glass front door was filled to overflowing. Evidently, the old woman lived alone, and the house was too much for her to take care of.

Feeling a little sad, Marty twisted the brass doorbell, setting off a tinkle of bells. No answer, not so much as the sound of shuffling feet. When she made the appointment with Carol on the phone, the old lady was eager to meet with her, so perhaps she hadn't heard the first ring. Marty was about to twist the ornate knob again when the door swung open. A tall, thin woman with wrinkled skin, faded green eyes, and impossible red hair stood there. Dressed in a green gingham house dress with patch pockets and a row of white buttons down the front, she looked like she'd stepped out of a 1950s Sears and Roebuck catalog.

"You must be Miss Greenlaw." Her raspy voice hinted at long years of smoking.

"Yes, Patricia Osborn's friend."

"Come in." Motioning for Marty to follow, the old lady led the way through the living room into the dining room. A mahogany Chippendale table with cabriole legs and ball and claw feet sat in the center of the square room, surrounded by six carved chairs with seats upholstered in green and rose stripes.

A bone china teapot painted with yellow daisies sat on a tarnished silver tray. Beside it two matching teacups and a glass plate filled with chocolate sandwich cookies waited as if for a child's party. A scratch that looked like it had been doctored with brown magic marker peeked out from under the tray.

"Will you join me for tea?"

Ten o'clock in the morning was an odd time for tea, but Marty smiled. "I'd love to."

"I always sit at the end. You may sit on my left."

Marty obeyed. When she had a cup of pale tea and a grocery store cookie on a delicate plate, she said, "I appreciate your time, Mrs. Miller."

"I don't use that name. Call me Miss Angel or Miss Carol."

Marty blinked at the clipped pronouncement.

"Tom's been dead for forty years, ten more than I was his wife. Besides, my self-image was never tied up in being his wife."

"Pat mentioned you were an actress before you married."

"I was, and why I ever allowed Thomas Miller to convince me to marry him and move from California to this dirty mining town, I'll never know."

"Being married to a mine owner must have been exciting."

"Exciting?"

"The thrill of wondering what the miners might find."

"There's nothing exciting about copper, honey."

Marty sipped her weak, lukewarm tea. "So Mr. Miller never found silver or gold?"

Carol brushed the idea aside with bony fingers. "That's enough about the mine. Why are you here, young woman?"

"Didn't Pat tell you? We're organizing a fund raiser for a four-year-old girl named Aurora. She needs a new heart."

"You want a donation."

Another clipped pronouncement. Marty said, "Pat thought you would want to help."

"Why?"

Marty started to ask about great-grandchildren but thought better of it. "Do you have grandchildren?"

Carol put down her teacup with a decided click. "I never had children."

"I'm sorry. I didn't know."

"Nothing to be sorry about." She pushed back her chair and got to her feet. "Come with me, young woman. I have something to show you."

Doing as she was told, Marty followed the old lady into the living room. The floor was an intricate parquet design of a variety of hardwoods, scuffed and chipped. The heavy, gold brocade draperies, like those in the dining room, were frayed and ready to be replaced.

The furniture, on the other hand, was high-end. A graceful, blue damask-covered Federal sofa with a basket of carved fruit and flowers sat against one wall flanked by two matching armchairs with torn seats, antiques Pat might like.

Carol crossed to the sofa and picked up a black and white wedding photo in a gilt frame from a low table. The bride's full-length dress was overlaid with Chantilly lace. One hand was on the groom's arm. In the other hand she held a cascade of white roses. The groom, who was beginning to go gray at the temples, was wearing a tuxedo. "Tom was several years older than I was. He wanted to have children, but I refused."

"Do you ever regret that decision?" The question was out before Marty realized she was going to ask it.

Carol handed Marty the photo and sat on the sofa. "When I turned forty, I wondered if I'd made a mistake. But that was just the hormones talking. I realized I had the life I wanted. I was free to travel, to make appearances, to buy the things I wanted." She indicated the house with a sweeping gesture. "I was able to afford all of this."

Marty studied the old lady. Didn't she realize the house was falling down around her? The antiques were worth something, but only if a restorer took great care with them.

"Children would have changed everything," Carol said.

The petulance in the old lady's voice caught Marty off-guard. That was the issue, wasn't it? Scott was a nice kid, but he would change everything for her. Would she have children of her own, or would Paul insist he was through changing diapers? One more item to put on her list.

Marty put down the wedding photo and brought her attention back to the reason for her visit. As she sat in one of the armchairs, she said, "Though you don't have children, I hope you'll participate in our fund raiser. You have a distinct perspective on the mining days in Jerome."

"I don't have any money to give you." Carol patted her hair and smoothed her skirt. "I might be persuaded to make an appearance. I'm sure the name Carol Angel will still draw a crowd."

Marty considered the woman sitting on the sofa. She wore no jewelry, her dress was faded and limp, and her hair dye had come from a drugstore. Like the house, its mistress needed updating. Marty wondered when Pat had last been here. Carol Angel was not a wealthy woman, and she doubted her name would mean anything to anyone of this generation. But her participation wouldn't hurt, and it might serve as a source of excitement for the old lady.

"We'd love to have you join us," Marty said. On an impulse she added, "We could offer you a modest honorarium."

"How much?"

Marty meant to offer fifty dollars, but the hunger on the old lady's face changed her mind. "I think we could manage a hundred dollars." Ridiculous to give money to anyone else while raising funds for Aurora Reyes. But if she had to take the money out of her own savings, it would be worth it. Besides, Carol was right in one respect. A picture of her with Aurora would be eye-catching.

Carol clapped her hands. "I'll wear my green silk. It sets off my eyes."

Marty's stomach turned over. She needed to leave the decaying house and this delusional woman. She wanted fresh air. Standing, she offered the old lady her hand. "I'll be in touch about the details." As Carol started to rise, Marty added, "Please don't get up. I'll let myself out."

She didn't run away like she had from Paul, but she moved faster than necessary, not slowing until she was behind the wheel of her pickup and headed down the winding street. What was going on with her? She'd always prided herself on her ability to stand her ground and look for the truth, as she had last summer right here in Jerome. Now it seemed running away was becoming a habit.

As she took the first curve, she realized she wasn't running away from the pitiful old woman. She was trying to escape what Carol had said about not wanting children because they would have changed her life. Was her reason for running from Paul that Scott would take her life down a path she'd never envisioned?

Speaking firmly, she said, "Marty Greenlaw, it's time you faced the truth. You're in love with Paul Russell. Figure it out."

When she reached the stop sign at the bottom of the hill, she checked the mirror over the roadway. Three cars were headed up the highway from Cottonwood. A Tuesday morning in March and already tourists were arriving. She meant to turn right down the mountain to Clarkdale. She had work to do. Instead she turned left. She needed to talk to Sofia.

The drive took less than five minutes. It was still early

enough that she found a parking place in the gravel lot across the street from Sofia's gallery. As she climbed the steps to the door, she wondered if Sofia would be here. Maybe she was already at the little kiosk she used as a storefront. Marty pushed the doorbell.

She didn't have to wait long. The door opened, and Sofia stood there, one of the few women Marty knew who was shorter than she was. Sofia wore jeans and a white artist's smock with large patch pockets. Her black hair, liberally threaded with silver, was swept up and secured with tortoise-shell combs.

Throwing her arms wide, Sofia said, "Marta! How I've been longing to see you, *mi amiga*."

Marty hugged the woman who had been so close to her Granny Lois. "I should have come sooner."

Sofia put a gentle finger on Marty's mouth. "Hush. You've been busy. I know what it is to set up a workshop and open a business." Threading Marty's arm through hers, she said, "I'm busy, too, so come into my studio and talk while I work."

"I can come back."

"No. I'm working with my hands this morning. I need something to occupy my mind. You can tell me all about your move and your plans for this fund raiser I've been hearing about from my young friend Belinda Reyes."

"Aurora's mother?"

"Si. Belinda's mother, little Aurora's grandmother, was a good friend of mine. I was so sorry I was out of town when Sr. Enrique passed from this life. He was a fine man."

"I only met him once, but I know he was." Marty watched Sofia's quick movements as she smoothed a length of turquoise silk that shimmered in the sunlight coming in through the tall windows. Should she tell Sofia about Alex's conviction that his great-grandfather was murdered? Perhaps she already knew.

"Will you be comfortable in that basket chair? It wasn't the most practical piece of furniture I've ever bought, but I know the young man who makes them."

"It's all right to sit on this cushion?" Marty ran her hand over the fuzzy, yellow fabric.

"Of course. You'll be the first, I think. Most of my visitors are old women like me, afraid they won't be able to get back up. You're young. Just like the artist who makes these. When he's older, he'll make more practical chairs. But now, I keep this chair just for you."

Marty smiled. Glad she'd decided on leggings instead of jeans that morning, she arranged herself in a cross-legged position. "I love these chairs, Sofia. I don't dare put one among my antiques, but one of these days when I have a house, I'll buy one for the family room." Such a common thing to say, but it stopped Marty. Paul had a family room. Would he want a chair like this? Scott, yes. Paul, no idea.

Sofia picked up a pair of dressmaker shears. "Tell me what's bothering you, Marta."

"Maybe nothing. Maybe I just came to see you because I have a morning free."

Her black eyes twinkling, Sofia said, "If your Granny Lois was still with us, you'd be at her kitchen table right now. I can tell by the tiny frown lines you're trying not to let me see."

Marty smoothed her temples. "I've just been to see Carol Angel. Do you know her?"

"Ah. That one gives me a headache. She lives in a world all her own. What on earth took you up to that crumbling mausoleum she calls a mansion?"

Some of the tension eased out of Marty's neck. At least her assessment of Carol agreed with Sofia's more informed opinion. "Pat Osborn thought she might make a good addition to the Jerome history theme we're using to draw interest to our fund raiser."

Sofia snorted. "What did Carol say that has you so upset?"

"She said, 'Children would have changed everything.'" Was it a single sentence?

Sofia didn't look up from her cutting. "She's right. Children change lives. More than many parents are ready for."

"Do you have children, Sofia?"

Sofia shook her head.

"I'm sorry. I suppose I shouldn't have asked."

"Don't be silly, my dear. That was all many years ago. If I had children, they would be long gone from my little world. Sure, they might come to visit, but I have as many visitors as I can handle." She put down the scissors and gave the silk a slight turn. "You're still young. I think this is about you and Scott Russell."

Marty sighed, glad she didn't have to explain. "Yes. You knew Linda Russell. Don't I remember that Granny Lois, Linda, and you had a prayer group? Wasn't that one of the reasons Linda wanted Paul to redo that old house across the road from Granny's house?"

Sofia nodded. Picking up the scissors, she began to cut. "That's right. The three of us were close. It was hard when Linda died."

"Paul told me you helped him through that tough time."

"We helped each other."

"I need your help now, Sofia." When the older woman didn't reply, Marty blurted, "I love Paul, but I'm nothing like Linda. You know me well enough to realize I'm right. I can't take Linda's place as Scott's mother."

"Of course not."

Was it going to be this easy? Restless, Marty got up and walked to the window that overlooked the street. A silver BMW took the hill smoothly.

"I can't imagine Scott wanting anyone to take Linda's place," Sofia said.

Marty counted the cars parked in the lot across the street,

twelve. She'd come for Sofia's support, and she had it. So why did she feel so forlorn?

"Scott is like Paul," Sofia murmured. "He needs someone to love him. You said you love Paul. Do you love Scott?"

"I...I don't know."

"Think about it."

Marty turned back into the room. Sofia was watching her, shears resting on the table. "I like Scott," Marty said. "He's a good kid, a reliable worker."

"Then I don't understand your problem."

"My life wasn't supposed to work out like this!"

"How was it supposed to work out?"

"I was supposed to meet someone in college, get married, and have children." What Paul and Linda did. Why couldn't she have been the one to meet Paul first? Of course, that was ridiculous. She was twelve when Paul married Linda. "When that didn't happen, I realized God must want me to be single. I found my career..." She hesitated.

"But something happened at Carol's house that confused you."

"She claims to be happy with the choice she made not to have children, but I feel sorry for her. You don't have children, and I don't feel sorry for you. I don't know what to think."

Sofia didn't answer right away. When she spoke, she said, "Come here, mi amiga. Let me show you what I'm working on."

Mystified, but grateful for the change of subject, Marty complied.

Sofia settled a flowing piece of turquoise silk with a delicate fringe on Marty's shoulders. "What do you think?"

"A summer shawl. It's lovely."

"The color looks good on you. Would you like to wear it?"

Marty let the silk slide through her fingers. "I'd love to."

"I thought so. But look here." Sofia spread the shawl out on her worktable. In the center of the back, a block about three inches by six inches was missing the crosswise threads, leaving a hole.

"How sad! What happened?"

"When silk gets old, it can shatter. The warp threads stay strong and the weft threads break."

"Can you mend it?"

Sofia beamed at her as if she'd asked a brilliant question. "I'll show you and let you decide." From a box under the table, she pulled out another length of silk and put it beside the old shawl. "What do you think?"

"The color is amazing. It's so close!"

Sofia nodded. "I love this old shawl, so I did my best to dye some new silk to match. But shawls are a bit old-fashioned, so I decided to make a scarf. The question is, should I patch the old shawl with a swatch from the new scarf?"

Marty put the two lengths of silk side by side. "The color is close, but it's not exact. I'd hate to see you ruin the new scarf because I don't think it would solve your problem. I'm afraid the new silk is so much stronger that the old silk will shatter around the edges of the patch. And you'd ruin the scarf."

"You're right. That's why you're confused about Paul and Scott."

Marty frowned. She was missing something. "I'm sorry. I don't understand."

"How about a cup of coffee? It's about time for my second cup of the morning."

Marty was glad for this second change of subject. Much better to drink coffee than talk about silk. "That sounds good."

She followed Sofia into the tiny kitchen. When they were seated at the table with mugs of steaming coffee, Sofia reached for a well-worn Bible. Opening it, she found a passage. "Listen to a parable Jesus told. 'No one tears a piece from a new garment and puts it upon an old garment; if he does, he will tear the new, and the piece from the new will not match the old.'"

"I didn't remember Jesus talking about sewing."

Sofia handed Marty the Bible. "Luke 5:36."

Marty read it a second time. "I still don't understand what you're trying to tell me."

The older woman took her hands. "God doesn't want you to take Linda's place and patch up Paul and Scott's family. That wouldn't be good for any of you."

"What then?"

"That's for you and Paul and Scott to discover. What I know is God creates new things."

Marty wanted to believe Sofia. But all she could think was, B.T. too?

24

S cott stared with disgust at the jumble of small items he thought someone might buy, most of them worth less than a buck. An entire morning's work, and this was all he had to show for it. He picked up an old misshapen football he'd brought from the shed by mistake and kicked it back inside.

What would it hurt if he left work right now? Miss Marty wasn't that excited about Carly's idea of a nonstop garage sale. In fact, this sorting job was nothing but busy work to get him a paycheck for the week. He didn't care about his paycheck.

He wasn't like B.T. He had a dad, a home, and an allowance. At least he'd thought he had a dad. Until last night. He was still mad his dad kicked him out and closed the door so he could talk to B.T. in private. What did Dad and B.T. have to talk about he couldn't hear? He was the one who brought B.T. home.

Scott pulled the copy he'd made of Manuel's map out of his back pocket and frowned at it. Exploring would be a much better use of his time than trying to decide if a little kid would buy an old box of colored pencils.

The more he looked at the map, the more the faded pencil marks he'd traced with a yellow highlighter looked like a route that started at the United Verde mine and went south. The UV was a landmark anyone could find. The X was where Manuel found the silver lode.

It didn't make sense for the map to start at the X and point north to the mine. If the silver lode was in the big mine, someone would have found it long before Manuel ever did. Besides, he knew the hills around UV well enough to know the X was on Old Mine Road. What more logical place for an undiscovered vein of silver and gold than there?

Last night Scott was disappointed when B.T. said he was going to sleep in this morning. He had to work the late shift to help stock or something. But what would it have hurt his friend to run him over here on his motorcycle? He could have gone back to bed.

Now things were looking a little different. Scott was glad he'd ridden his mountain bike. He wasn't supposed to explore old mines alone, but that wasn't the same as riding alone. He rode on bicycle trails alone all the time. Old Mine Road was as safe as any of those trails. He looked back at the map, and his heart beat faster. He had a feeling…

"How's it going, Scott?"

Scott almost jumped at the sound of Marty's voice. She shouldn't sneak up on people like that. Smoothing out the frown he knew was on his face, he did his best to look bored. Not hard, all he had to do was remember back five minutes. He refolded the map and slid it into his back pocket while he turned to face her. "It's a bigger mess than I thought," he said. "I'm not making much progress."

Marty studied the pile of junk he'd collected. "Organizing is a big job, especially at first. But Carly's convinced me. Once we open Treasure Trove, people will bring items to try to sell us and then stay to browse. Some of them will come into Old and Treasured to see the larger pieces."

"Yeah, but how many of the people who want to sell Carly

junk for a couple of bucks will come in to look at the fancy furniture?"

Marty shrugged. "You never know. Maybe a few. The point is that Treasure Trove will bring us good will and a lot of traffic. When the people who bring Granddad's pipe collection or Aunt Hetty's handkerchiefs decide to clear out the attic, they'll think of us first. We may find a few treasures I can rehabilitate."

A serious long shot, in Scott's opinion. But as his dad had made quite clear yesterday, his input wasn't always welcome.

"I bet I can guess your next question. Can you take off the rest of the afternoon?"

Now they were getting somewhere. Scott grinned. "I like the way you think, Miss Marty."

"Remember, after you write down the time you leave, you stop getting paid."

Seriously? He knew girls at school who made seven bucks an hour babysitting while they played video games. Instead of raising his eyebrows like he wanted to, he nodded.

"Okay. Two things before you go. First, cover all the things you brought outside with a tarp. The forecast is for rain."

Scott looked at the dark clouds building up in the west. All the more reason to explore this afternoon. By tomorrow morning, Old Mine Road might be a great place to go mudding but not fit for exploring.

"Then come inside and have a couple of peanut butter cookies. Carly made a batch last night."

Cookies. Like he was a little kid. "Thanks, but I'm not hungry."

Marty shrugged. "Skip the cookies then, but come inside. I want to talk to you."

Scott didn't like the serious tone in her voice, but unless he wanted to walk away from this job and catch it from his dad, he had to hear her out. "You got it."

"See you in a few." She turned and went back to the house. What on earth did she want?

It only took a couple of minutes to put the tarp over the jumble of junk and weigh it down on the corners with four concrete blocks he'd found under a dining room table.

When Scott went into the kitchen, Marty was sitting at the table with a glass of milk and a napkin in front of her. Another glass of milk and napkin lay across from her, clearly meant for him. She'd put a plate of cookies in the middle of the table.

All at once he felt shy. He wasn't used to being the focus of her attention.

"Can I wash my hands in here, or should I go into the bathroom?"

She smiled. "In here's fine."

For an instant, Scott could see why his dad kept hanging around her. She was pretty with her red, curly hair and green eyes. He pushed the thought away. The way his life was going, she was going to tell him he wasn't working hard enough.

Hands clean, Scott sat down across from Miss Marty and eyed the plate of cookies. Even if Carly had made them, they looked good. As he reached for one, he said, "Do we need to say grace?"

"Do you want to?"

Scott figured she wanted him to say yes, but if he was honest with himself, he didn't feel grateful at the moment. He shook his head.

"Then we'll let it go." Marty waited for him to take a cookie and then took one for herself.

The cookies were as good as they looked, thick and chewy with chunks of peanuts and chocolate chips. He finished one and was starting on his second when Marty spoke.

"What's going on, Scott?"

He let his eyes meet hers. She looked serious. "What do you mean? Nothing's going on."

"You came to work this morning with a chip on your shoulder, and it's gotten bigger."

Scott put his cookie down on the napkin. "I don't have a chip on my shoulder."

"Yes, you do."

"What does that mean anyway?"

"It means you're looking for a fight. I saw you kick that football. You weren't just passing the time."

"I know what the saying means. I'm just wondering where it came from."

Marty shrugged. "No idea. Ask your dad. He's the historian. Quit trying to change the subject. What are you mad about today?"

Scott wanted his mother. He was always able to talk to her about his dad. She would listen, not interrupting. When he was all talked out, she'd say something that made him look at everything in a different way. Not a lecture. Just something to make him think. Then she'd give him a hug, and he'd feel better.

Scott waited for Marty to say something more. Tell him how she could always tell people were mad when they did something or other. But she didn't say anything. She just waited. When the silence got uncomfortable, he said, "I got mad at my dad last night."

"Did you tell him you were upset?"

"He knew, and he knew why too."

"Is your dad a mind reader? I never noticed that about him." Except where she was concerned.

Scott picked up another cookie and broke it in half. "He was talking to B.T., and he told me to leave. It's my house!"

"Your dad told you to leave the house while he talked to B.T.?"

Scott put down one half of the cookie and broke the other half in three pieces. "No. He told me to leave the room and close the door, though."

"Did you think maybe your dad had something he wanted to talk to B.T. about in private?"

"Of course that's what I thought! I'm not stupid. But I'm his son. B.T. is just a guest. He's staying with us until his dad quits drinking."

Marty held out her hand. Scott dropped the cookie crumbs in it. "How soon do you think B.T.'s dad is going to stop drinking?"

"Never." Scott picked up the other half of the cookie. "His dad is an alcoholic. When he's drunk, he beats up his own son! Friday night he threw B.T. out."

Marty sat across the table from him without saying anything while Scott crumbled the rest of the cookie until it was nothing but peanut butter dust. Finally, he looked up. She was watching him with her pretty green eyes, and she looked like she cared.

The words, when they came out of his mouth, surprised him. He heard himself say, "I'm an only child. I don't want a brother. I used to, but not now. Dad and I were doing just fine on our own."

"Were you?"

"Sure!"

"You know Sofia."

Scott nodded.

"She told me something that's made me start thinking in a different way. Maybe it will help you too."

Here came the lecture. Scott closed his eyes. Maybe she would get the message and leave him alone.

Instead he heard her scoot her chair back and get up. He opened his eyes. She was standing at the sink, looking out the window. He knew what she saw, the shed and the pile of junk with a tarp over it. "Sofia told me sometimes God makes something different out of our lives than we expected. It's kind of hard when that happens because we find ourselves in territory we don't have a map for."

Scott looked at her standing there. She was small, shorter

than his mom. He thought she was talking to herself as much as she was to him. Maybe more. He got up and went out the back door. Kind of like having talked to Mom without the hug.

But he didn't want to think about God making a new plan for his life. He'd already had to get used to living without a mom. Now he was supposed to accept a brother, an older brother?

Scott didn't want to think about that. He wanted to find the silver lode. Pushing the problem out of his mind, he hurried to the side of the house where his bike waited for him. He'd only had it a few months, and the heavy-duty tires were what he needed for Old Mine Road.

As he slid his arms into the straps of his pack, he knew he had to check in with his dad. Mad or not, that was the deal. He was free to change his plans for the day this week as long as he let Dad know where he was going and when he would be home.

Scott found his cell phone and pressed Dad in Favorites. As he waited for it to connect, he looked up at the clouds. They were closer now. He needed to hurry. The call went straight to voice mail. "You've reached Paul Russell. Leave me a message."

Where was his dad? He was supposed to be at home. That's probably where he was, with his phone turned off so he could have another private talk with B.T.

The beep sounded. Scott said, "Hi, Dad." He started to say "Sorry I missed you" like he always did, but right now that felt like a lie, so he skipped it. "Miss Marty didn't have much for me to do this afternoon, so I'm going to ride my bike up to Jerome. I'll be home before dark, but I'll have a cell signal if you need to call me." He left off the "Love you" too, not that his dad would notice.

Scott hoisted his pack on his back and jammed his helmet on his head. Chip on his shoulder or not, as he signaled to turn into the street, Scott's heart kicked up. He had a feeling he was going to find the silver lode this afternoon.

He didn't need to look at the map to know where he was

going. He pedaled to a bike path that paralleled Highway 89A for about a mile. Then he started watching for the turn-off. When he found the junction with Old Mine Road, he turned right without signaling. No one behind him anyway.

The road, wash boarded from snow melting and refreezing, was harder going than the bike path, but he didn't care. He aimed dead on at a deep rut, ready for a fun jolt. Instead, the bike came to an abrupt stop. Down he went with the bike on top of him.

He lay still, silently checking for injuries like he'd learned in wilderness survival training. When he was pretty sure nothing was broken, he untangled himself from the bike and got up. Holding his breath, he checked out his bike. A couple of new scratches, but the tires were fine, and all the bars were straight. That was a stupid move, something a kid with a chip on his shoulder would do. Time to forget his gripe with Dad and focus on the silver lode.

Paying closer attention to the uneven ground, Scott followed Old Mine Road east about a quarter of a mile. There it doubled back on itself, heading west. When the road began to climb, Scott downshifted to take the grade with less pedaling. In about a mile, he reached an unexpected fork in the road. Dismounting, he took the map out of his pocket and studied it.

Sure enough, up over his head he could see the Hogback and a couple of crooked crosses that meant the cemetery. This fork had to connect with Dundee Avenue, a joke of a name for a dusty track no one used anymore. No street sign, but he had to be in the right area.

Taking off his helmet, Scott scanned the barren hillside. He'd read that years ago, before the miners came, Mingus Mountain was covered with pine and scrub oak. But men had cut down the trees one by one to supply wood to power the narrow-gauge railroad that ran down to the smelter in Clarkdale. Smoke had killed off what vegetation was left. The mountain had never recovered.

Old Mine Road was the obvious place for a small worked-out

copper mine hiding a rich silver lode. He checked his location against the map. Assuming the faded pencil marks stood for streets that were now ruts in the dirt, he was in the right place. So where was the mine?

He knew the signs to look for. A hole bigger than a coyote would use for a den, pieces of broken fencing, a rusted nail, any signs men had dug into the ground. Scott squatted by a flat rock and spread out the map. It didn't take long to find his mistake.

The X wasn't at the spot where Dundee Avenue intersected Old Mine Road. Another pencil line snaked south and west an inch or two. Whatever road or track that line represented was gone now. Since he didn't know the scale Manuel had used, Scott didn't know how much he was off, but it couldn't be far. Unclipping the compass from the handlebar, he oriented himself to head southwest. Better to walk than take his bike.

He found a boulder big enough to lean his bike against and settled it so it wouldn't fall over. Then, more out of habit than fear someone would happen by and steal his bike, Scott wound the heavy-duty chain in its nylon sleeve through the rear wheel and secured the lock. Shouldering his pack, he started walking. He moved slowly, taking the time to watch for the slightest sign that a mine had once existed among the boulders and scrub.

He didn't expect anything as obvious as the Miller Mine, but when he'd walked about a mile without seeing any sign of humans other than the remains of a bonfire, he took out the map and studied it again. He checked his direction with the compass, southwest. While he didn't know the exact scale of Manuel's map, based on the distance between the cemetery and Dundee Avenue, he could make a good guess. He must have already overshot the X.

Pulling a bottle of water out of his pack, Scott sat with his back against a rock and studied the terrain he'd just covered. What else might indicate digging almost a hundred years ago? Maybe something as subtle as a depression that didn't quite fit the contours of the land. Or as obvious as the foundation of a building.

Maybe Manuel Reyes had found a tunnel opening in a basement like the one in the exhibit at the Jerome State Historic Park.

Tossing the water bottle into his pack, Scott jumped to his feet and headed for what he'd assumed was a bonfire but might be the remains of a burned-out building. A coincidence or a purposeful fire meant to keep anyone from stumbling across a silver lode?

It took less than ten minutes to walk back to the pile of burned wood. At first, the charred lumber looked like the old bonfire he'd taken it for. Disappointed, Scott aimed a savage kick at a wide board protruding from the mass. The board shifted with a creak, stirring up a satisfying shower of dust and ash. He was about to kick again when the sun reflected off something that was definitely not wood.

Curious, Scott freed a long thin board and poked through the jumble, finally dislodging pieces of corrugated tin that might have been part of a roof. Not something anyone would toss on a bonfire. Further exploration uncovered chipped and broken panes of glass, several turned newel posts, a wrought iron headboard, and chunks of ceramic.

He stepped back and studied the mountain of debris. He was sure he'd found a burned-out building. A house or, more likely, a hotel. He couldn't date it, but what were the odds of finding an irrelevant structure where Manuel Reyes had placed his X?

The proof would be to find a tunnel connecting to the old mine, a tunnel out of a basement. Somewhere under this mountain of wood and tin, he'd find steps going down into the earth. He was sure of it.

Scott checked for the position of the sun. It had dropped below the line of heavy, dark clouds, so a lot of the afternoon was gone. But he still had good light.

Scott could almost hear his dad, "Go home now and come back tomorrow with some help."

"As soon as I find the tunnel," he muttered.

Scott stepped back and studied the terrain. Above where he stood in the vicinity of Dundee Avenue, he saw the dust of a vehicle. A great spot for four-wheeling. Maybe for dirt bikes.

Scott turned his attention back to the collapsed structure. If he were building a house here a hundred years ago, where would he put the front porch? He had the answer almost as soon as the question formed in his head. The hill sloped toward the south. Not too far in the distance, he spotted Walnut Creek winding its way toward Clarkdale, the perfect view.

What if the entrance to the tunnel wasn't in a basement like at the Douglas Mansion? If the back of the house was higher than the front, maybe the lower floor backed up to a room dug into the hill. Taking the pole, Scott picked his way up the hill and around the ruin to where the back would have been.

The debris was less dense on the ground, easier to poke through. He almost fell when his makeshift pole abruptly encountered empty space. Dropping the pole, he moved boards and pieces of tin roofing out of the way. What he saw made him catch his breath.

The pole had gone through a hole in what had once been a floor. Testing each spot before he put his weight on it, he made his way to the hole. Getting down on his knees, he knelt and peered inside. He was right about the room dug into the side of the hill.

Scott checked the sun again. Much lower than before. No doubt about it, it was time to go home. Even the joy riders on Dundee Avenue had disappeared. He and B.T. were planning to look for the X in the morning anyway. They could start here.

Still, it wouldn't take long to let himself down and make sure the tunnel was here. If he found it, he'd have all he needed to convince his dad to come with them tomorrow.

Checking each handhold to make sure it would take his weight, Scott let himself down into the space probably used for cold storage. The room was dark and dank, but no different than dozens of caves he'd been in. Sliding out of his pack and opening it, he dug around until he found the headlamp he'd used for exploring the Miller mine. Adjusting the headband, he flipped on the light. Just a quick look around, and he would be out of here.

The back wall had been shored up with bricks. Almost in the exact center, he saw what he was looking for. Not an opening to a tunnel. A metal door red with rust, secured by a hasp and padlock. Three steps brought him to the door. The padlock was the combination type, and it hung open. With his pulse pounding in his ears, Scott lifted the padlock off the hasp, dropped it to the ground, and swung the door open.

A tunnel ran deep into the hillside. About sixty feet ahead, it forked. Not wanting to get trapped inside, Scott found a heavy rock and propped the door open. Slipping his arms into his pack as he walked, he headed for the intriguing fork. As he got closer, he saw the left side went straight into the mountain.

The right fork disappeared around a bend. As he started toward the bend, his light illuminated something that looked like a rusted rock pick. Scott knew he should go back, but he was so close. The silver lode, at least what was left of it after all these years, was just ahead. He was sure of it.

How perfect if he showed up at home with a nugget of silver or even gold ore! Scott started down the tunnel. He was reaching for the rock pick when a dull thud made him jump. The door? Grabbing the pick, he hurried back as fast as he could without doing a face plant on the uneven ground. The last thing he needed was to fall and break his leg.

He rounded the bend and stopped. Something was wrong. Where was the rectangle of gray light from the door? Had he taken a wrong turn, accidentally wandered up the left fork?

He knew better than to move until he had his bearings. He turned slowly in a circle, studying the rocks his light caught. It didn't take long to realize he was in the main room and that the door was closed.

He was sure he'd propped it open. Maybe the rock had slipped. Even as he thought of that explanation, he knew it was stupid. A breeze couldn't move the rock. An earthquake maybe.

When he reached the door, he said a quick prayer and leaned his shoulder into it, hoping it would swing open on its metal hinges. Nothing happened. He dropped the rock pick and pushed with both hands. Still nothing. Taking a deep breath, he turned around and pushed as hard as he could with his back. The door didn't give an inch.

Unable to keep panic at bay, he pounded on the door with both fists and yelled, "Let me out! Let me out!" The padlock rattled, but the door didn't budge.

Exhausted, Scott slumped against the door and stared into the empty cave-like space that had just become a prison. Someone came down after him, picked up the padlock, and deliberately snapped it in place. He was locked in.

25

M arty looked without enthusiasm at the tuna salad on her plate. Of course, calling the canned tuna mixed with mayo "tuna salad" was a stretch. To qualify for that title, it needed celery, a hard-boiled egg, and a few dried cranberries. It should also be nestled in a bed of fresh spinach instead of sitting alone on a piece of thin white bread. What were Paul and Scott having for supper? Who had cooked? Whatever they were having had to be more creative than this.

Disgusted with herself, Marty pushed away from the table and went into her workshop. She was tired of thinking about Paul and Scott. She wouldn't mind thinking about Paul, but Scott was a worry. And B.T. kept poking his dark, shaggy head into her daydreams. Was Sofia right that God was up to something with Paul and Scott and B.T.?

To avoid thinking about what God might have planned for B.T., Marty slid Mozart's piano concerto 21 into the CD player. As the violins led the orchestra, she lifted a cloth soaked in diluted fabric softener that covered the rush seat of a Shaker rocking chair. When the caning was sufficiently pliable, she would gradually stretch the seat back to its original position. Finding it still too brittle to clamp, Marty retrieved the linseed oil and rags from the cupboard and went into the showroom.

She crossed to the rosewood square grand and perched on the stool. Scott had made a good start polishing, but the elaborately carved music rack needed a light touch and a soft toothbrush. The quick staccato notes of the piano on the CD filled her head as she worked. She wondered if any of the owners of this instrument had ever played Mozart.

The familiar score played on, and her mind went to the news Pat had passed on about little Aurora Reyes. The four-year-old was still at home, but the doctor had ordered a nasogastric feeding tube. Try as she might, Marty couldn't imagine how Belinda Reyes must feel. How would a mother cope with the possibility of losing a child?

To add to the emotional burden, the bills were piling up. No matter how successful the gala turned out to be, Marty knew they couldn't hope to make nearly enough money. As the violins began to sing the theme from *Elvira Madigan*, Sr. Reyes slipped into Marty's mind, urging her to find the children and grandchildren of the man who murdered his brother for the silver lode.

Marty dropped the toothbrush. "Go away," she whispered. "I don't believe in ghosts."

Notes written in 1785 played on a piano two hundred years later by a now-dead virtuoso mocked her from the CD player. What kind of ghost don't you believe in?

Marty got up and went to turn off the CD player. In the sudden silence, she realized she was thirsty. She hurried into the kitchen. The ice had melted in her glass, raising the water level almost to the rim. Not trusting her shaking hand, she leaned down and sipped before picking up the glass and gulping.

The tuna sandwich still sat on her plate. Maybe she was hungry. She took an experimental bite. In just the few minutes she'd worked, the bread had dried out to almost the consistency of toast. People claimed to like the low humidity, but Marty wasn't sure she would ever adjust.

She tossed the sandwich into the garbage can under the sink and went to the refrigerator. Yogurt would do, raspberry. When the carton and a spoon were on the table, she took the notepad from the refrigerator door and sat down. With the first bite, she wrote the name *Frank Sanchez*. With the next, she wrote *Carol Angel/Miller* and with the third *Jimmy Wong*.

She crossed out Carol Angel. The old woman could have hired someone to hold a pillow over Sr. Reyes's head, but the state of her house and clothes argued that Carol Angel had nothing to lose. Manuel Reyes hadn't found the silver lode in the Miller Mine.

She put a question mark after both other names. Paul would have to give her his opinion on those two. But who else? Were they missing someone? The name came as clearly as if she had heard someone speak it aloud. "Joe Sweet."

Marty reached for her cell phone. She was punching in Paul's number when she heard a knock on the back door.

"Marty?"

The deep voice startled her. Paul. But not on the phone. Here. She took a deep breath.

"Marty? Are you in there?"

She opened the door, still holding her cell. "I was about to call you."

He looked surprised, then pleased.

"To run an idea about Sr. Reyes's murder by you."

The tiny frown appeared and disappeared so fast she almost missed it. "Okay."

She stepped back so he could come into the kitchen. "I was thinking about Joe."

"Joe Sweet?" Paul looked tired.

Marty wondered if he was also hungry. "Have you had supper?"

"No. And not much lunch."

"Do you want something?"

He gave her a wry grin. "To quote my son, 'It depends on what you're having.'"

Marty laughed. She did enjoy this man's sense of humor. "Let's look in the freezer, shall we?"

"Either you've eaten and are feeling pity, or you haven't been thinking about supper."

"The second." Marty opened the freezer compartment. "I can offer you crunchy fish fillets, chicken potpies, or pizza."

"Or we could go out."

And make a date of it. Marty didn't say the words, just shook her head. "You look fine, but I don't feel like getting cleaned up. How about I make an executive decision and we cook the pizza? Ham and pineapple. It's not bad."

"Sold to the woman with the oven."

"What about Scott?" The question came out of its own accord. She wasn't Scott's mother. She shouldn't care whether Paul had made plans for his son's supper. To cover her confusion, she slid the pizza onto a cookie sheet.

"He's not answering his cell, probably because he let the battery run down again. Scott and I made a deal. I won't micromanage his life if he keeps me informed of his plans. At the end of spring break, we'll take stock and determine if he's mature enough to run his afternoons after school."

"Did he inform you of his plans?"

This time Paul gave her a curious look, and Marty wanted to kick herself. She wasn't doing a good job convincing either one of them she wasn't concerned about Scott.

"He left me a voice mail saying he was riding his bike up to Jerome. He said you let him leave work early."

Marty grasped at the straw. "I did. Carly went up to Flagstaff, and all I had for Scott to do was sort so-called antiques I think should be tossed."

Paul sat at the table. "Tell me what you're thinking about Joe."

The preheat bell dinged, and Marty put the pizza in the oven. "I think we ought to put him on our suspect list."

"You found a connection to the past?"

She sat down across from Paul. "No. I was thinking of who had the best opportunity to put a pillow over Sr. Reyes's head."

"I'll give you that. But why would he do it?"

"He told you he read the missing letters."

"Yes."

"What if he spotted a clue to the location of the silver lode?"

"And killed Sr. Reyes so he could follow up?"

Marty nodded.

"Sr. Reyes was an old man. He couldn't drive, couldn't follow Joe. So why kill him? Why not just follow the clue without saying anything about it?"

Marty frowned. She hadn't thought of that.

"Besides that, you're assuming the silver lode is something he could retrieve easily. If Scott is right, it was a rich ore deposit that was secretly mined out years ago. Sr. Reyes wanted the fortune someone made from that ore."

Marty wasn't giving up that fast. "There are a couple of steps we still have to figure out. But think about it, Paul. How could any of the other three have gotten into the Sweet establishment? I saw Carol Angel today, and not only do I not see how she could have done it, I don't think she has two nickels to rub together."

The timer buzzed. "I'll get the pizza," Paul said.

"I'll get plates, napkins, and drinks. Do you want water, one of Carly's diet sodas, or one of Bill's bottled iced tea?"

"Water."

"Ice?"

"Sure. I feel like living it up."

He sounded just the opposite, but Marty didn't comment. "Have you seen Jimmy Wong?"

Paul put a hot pad on the table and set the cookie sheet on top of it. "Yesterday after I left here. His fortune is questionable, and he's fit enough to smother an old man." He took the knife Marty offered and cut the pizza into fourths. "But you're right. I don't see how he could have managed the actual murder. Ditto for Frank Sanchez." He put a piece of pizza on her plate and another on his own.

When they were seated, she offered him her hand and said, "Will you say grace?"

He nodded and bowed his head. After a long moment of silence, he said, "Father, thank you for this food. Tonight, I ask for your wisdom. Help us find our way through this confusion. Amen." Instead of releasing her hand, he threaded his fingers through hers.

Marty knew she should pull away, but her hand felt so right in his. Keeping her eyes closed, she let herself relax into the warmth of their joined hands.

A moment, or perhaps an hour later, he murmured, "We have to talk."

His words broke the spell. She didn't want to talk about her feelings, or his. Not now, maybe not ever. Freeing her hand, she picked up a pizza slice and said, "What if Joe was working for Jimmy or Frank?"

"I don't want to talk about murder."

"We have to talk about it, Paul! That little girl is going to die if we don't figure out what happened to Sr. Reyes. Which is more important? Aurora Reyes or feelings I can't sort out, much less explain to you."

He sighed. "All right. Have it your way for now." He picked up his piece of pizza and took a bite.

"Joe has to be involved. I don't see how anyone could break in and commit a murder without Joe knowing about it."

"If a murder was committed."

"What do you mean?"

Paul shrugged. "We're going on an old man's fixation and a young boy's interpretation. We don't have one shred of evidence that Sr. Reyes was murdered. Remember, he had mesothelioma. According to the nurse, he was living on sheer willpower."

"But what about the letters?"

"What about them?"

"Someone stole them."

"Alex thinks someone stole them. Maybe they're simply lost."

"But you told me someone broke into your house and stole all Alex's research."

"Maybe I left his file in my office at the university."

"Why would you do that, Paul? Someone doesn't want us to find out more about Manuel Reyes. I know Joe is involved. I can't tell you how I know, but I do." Marty pushed back her chair and stood up. "Let's go talk to him." She couldn't explain her sudden sense of urgency, so she didn't try. She just reached for the windbreaker hanging on a hook beside the back door.

Paul got to his feet. "Now? It's eight p.m."

"Now!"

26

Paul pulled into the driveway at Sweet Home and turned off the engine. Picking up his cell from the passenger's seat, he tried Scott again. With the same result. The call went straight to voice mail. "Son," he said, "don't forget. Curfew is at nine."

Marty's pickup drew even with his Jeep and stopped. She got out and tapped on the window. He held up a hand in greeting, glad it was dark so he didn't have to force a smile. The woman was going to drive him crazy with her double messages. To be fair, he was sure she also was driving herself crazy. Mildly cheered, he got out.

She met him in front of the Jeep. "I don't know what's wrong with me."

He wanted to tell her it was only the fear of the unknown. She probably hadn't ever imagined herself marrying a man with two teenagers. Two? When had he started to think of Reed as a permanent part of his life?

"Now that we're here, I want to turn around and go home."

He suppressed a groan. She wasn't thinking about him at all. Tucking her hand into the crook of his arm, he started toward the house. She came with him, but the closer they got, the more her steps lagged, almost as if she dreaded the interview.

"We won't be here long," he promised. "We ask Joe if he remembers anything from the letters about Manuel's partner. No matter what he says, we ask him if he knows Frank Sanchez or Jimmy Wong."

"What if he knows them both?"

"We'll have to dig deeper."

He felt a tremor run through her. She was afraid. But of what? For a moment Paul felt uneasy. He pushed the tension away. There was nothing to be afraid of here. They followed the path of white stepping-stones, hard to make out in the overcast night. Odd that the outside lights weren't on. They stepped up onto the dark porch, and he pressed the doorbell.

Inside the house, a series of chimes ran down the scale. As they waited, Paul turned to look out at the yard that had looked so cheerful the first time they came to Sweet Home. Now, the palo verde tree was little more than a dark skeleton against a darker night. More clouds had rolled in during the last hour, and Paul wondered if the predictions of heavy rain were going to be accurate.

Beside him, Marty pushed the doorbell again. "Someone's got to be home," she whispered. "Joe wouldn't leave everyone alone at night."

"Agreed." Even to himself, Paul's voice sounded loud. Silly. It was only a few minutes after eight. Giving up on the doorbell, he knocked.

"Coming." A woman's voice. Maybe they were about to meet Mrs. Sweet.

But when the door opened, Paul recognized the white-haired woman who was the first to pledge to give to Aurora's medical fund. She leaned on a sturdy cane and was so bent over, she had to turn her shoulder as well as her head to look up at them. He searched his memory for a name. Nothing came.

"Hello, Mrs. Arbeck," Marty said. "It's good to see you again. We need to talk to Mr. Sweet. Is he here?"

"He's in the house, all right. No idea why he didn't answer the door. I was watching TV when you first rang. I kept expecting Joseph to get it, but after that third ring, I decided I'd better do it myself."

"May we come in?" Paul said.

Leaning on her cane, she shuffled out of the way. "I'd be glad if you did, young man. I'm worried about Joseph. This isn't like him."

As they entered, Marty said, "Maybe Mr. Sweet has gone to bed."

Mrs. Arbeck shook her head. "That man prowls around half the night. When I first moved here, it made me kind of nervous, but then I decided he was as good as a watchdog. Makes me feel secure, like I can let my guard down and sleep, knowing he's watching."

Paul looked around the dimly lit living room. "Is Mrs. Sweet here?"

Mrs. Arbeck chuckled. "Not likely. Mrs. Sweet packed up and marched out the second year I was here. We've all been the happier for it. Right old battleax she was."

"Where should we look for Mr. Sweet?" Paul said.

"Not in the TV room, hon. You might try his office. Second door on the right down that hall. Come along. I'll show you." She moved with agonizing slowness toward a shadowed hallway on their left.

"First door goes into the kitchen. TV room is the other way. Bedrooms are all in the back of the house. We each have our own little patio. More like a square of concrete just big enough for a lawn chair, but it's all I need."

Had someone come in through Enrique's patio door Friday night? Paul thought it was a possibility.

"Are you happy here?" Marty said.

"Oh, yes, hon. Much better than the nursing home my daughter had picked out."

Mrs. Arbeck stopped in front of a closed door. "Can't imagine," she muttered. Using the handle of her cane, she knocked. "He always keeps this door open. Nothing to hide, he says. If someone's in here when you come, you just mind your manners."

The three of them listened for an invitation to come in. The house was so quiet, Paul heard the TV from down the hall.

Mrs. Arbeck knocked again.

"Mr. Sweet?" Paul called. "It's Paul Russell and Marty Greenlaw. We need to talk to you."

Silence. Paul opened the door and went in. He didn't know what he expected to find, but when he saw Joe Sweet stretched out in a recliner he let out a breath he hadn't realized he was holding.

Mrs. Arbeck tapped her cane against Paul's leg. "That man never takes a nap. I hope he hasn't up and had a heart attack. That's what took my George. We were watching *Wheel of Fortune*, and I thought he'd drifted off to sleep in his recliner. But no, that man had up and died on me. Twenty years ago next month." She tapped Paul's leg again. "You go check on him, young man."

Aware Joe should have heard them, Paul obeyed. Joe couldn't be dead. Not so soon after Enrique. Raising his voice, he said, "Joe, we need to talk to you!" When the man didn't so much as open his eyes, Paul reached for his hand. It was limp and cold.

27

Holding her shoulder bag over her head, Marty ran through the rain to her pickup. The police report was filed, the funeral home had picked up the body, and social services had sent a woman to stay with the residents of Sweet Home until permanent arrangements could be made.

Marty shivered as she unlocked her door and climbed into the driver's seat. She was soaked, but it wasn't physical cold making her tremble. She put the key in the ignition and turned on the motor. It would take a few minutes to warm up enough to run the heater.

While she waited, she needed to talk to Paul. She wanted to know if he'd found Scott, and she had to tell him what Mrs. Arbeck had said. When the coroner, who was also the medical examiner, had pronounced Joe Sweet dead from a heart attack, the police had told them they were free to leave.

She was glad when Paul, still not getting an answer to his repeated calls to Scott, had gone home. But she hadn't wanted to leave Mrs. Arbeck alone until someone came from social services, so she'd stayed. Because of what had happened next, she needed to talk to the medical examiner.

Who to call first, Paul or the medical examiner? She decided on the medical examiner. Surely Paul had found Scott by now. The simplest explanation, that Scott's phone needed recharging, was usually the right one. But what to say to Dr. Schmidt?

As he'd filled out the death certificate, Mrs. Arbeck had insisted Joe couldn't have died from a heart attack. "He bragged all the time about how strong his ticker was."

"Don't you believe it," Dr. Schmidt said as he closed his bag. "Overweight and a smoker to boot. I told him more than once he was courting disaster. But did he listen? He did not, and this is the result."

When the funeral home people came with their gurney, Mrs. Arbeck pulled Marty aside. Twisting so she could look up and see Marty's face, she said, "Did you see what was on Joe's desk? I couldn't get around all those men to check."

"All I saw was the newspaper folded to the crossword and a pen."

"How about two old-fashioned ice cream soda glasses?"

Marty shook her head. "No drinking glasses or cups."

"They should have been there."

"What makes you say that?"

"At supper Joe told us someone was coming this evening to sign a contract for Enrique's room. That man was so proud of those mango milkshakes, he practically made someone signing a contract drink one."

"He gave me one at Enrique's celebration of life. Why is it important tonight?"

"I'll tell you, honey. If I was a chemist, I'd find Joe's glass and analyze any traces of a milkshake left in it."

The old lady was calm, almost matter of fact. Marty said, "I don't understand."

"My brother, may he rest in peace, was a doctor. One night he said, 'Lorraine, if you ever need to kill somebody, make them a milkshake and spike it with antifreeze.' I thought he was kidding, but then I realized he was real upset. Did my best to get him to talk to me about it, but he never would."

Another murder in this house wouldn't be a coincidence. Was Joe prowling the halls Friday night?

Marty touched the old lady's hand. "You said someone was coming about the room. Did the person come?"

"Sure did. I always mute the TV during commercials, and around six-thirty, I heard the doorbell. I didn't get up because I knew Joe was expecting that prospective tenant."

Marty couldn't breathe. "Did Joe mention the name?"

"No, hon. He says it's confidential until he's got a John Hancock on the dotted line."

"Did you see who it was?"

"No, but if you go in the kitchen, I expect you'll find a couple of old-fashioned soda glasses washed and in the drainer."

"Why didn't you tell Dr. Schmidt all this?"

Mrs. Arbeck snorted, "Tried my best. He told me to call him when I had some evidence." She thrust a card into Marty's hand. "You take this. You're younger. Maybe he'll listen to you."

As the old lady started her slow progress back to the TV room, Marty went to the kitchen. It was tidy except for two old-fashioned soda glasses in the drainer. They'd been washed, but she put them in her bag anyway.

Now Marty listened to the rain on the roof of the pickup. Steady and strong. What did she have to say to Dr. Schmidt that Mrs. Arbeck hadn't already said? He'd wanted evidence. She had the glasses. Pulling the damp card from her pocket, she called Dr. Schmidt's number.

His voice, tired and strained, came on the second ring. "Schmidt. This better be important."

"Dr. Schmidt, this is Marty Greenlaw. I met you at Joe Sweet's tonight."

"Okay, Marty Greenlaw. I don't mean to be rude, but I'm tired and busy. What's eating you?"

Marty blinked. No point in easing into it. "Mrs. Arbeck told me she thinks Mr. Sweet was poisoned."

He sighed. "Yeah. Antifreeze in a milkshake. I don't care what her brother saw twenty years ago. Joe Sweet died of a heart attack."

"I have the glasses. Couldn't you run a test or something?"

"Antifreeze would be gone by now. Sorry, Ms. Greenlaw. I wrote down heart attack, and that's what stays on the death certificate. I've still got work to do before I can call it a night, so I'm going to let you go now." The call disconnected.

"Fine," she said to the dead phone. "But you haven't heard the last of this, Mr. Medical Examiner. No murder or two murders? If you ask me, there were two murders in this house."

But one murderer. The thought made Marty's scalp prickle. After turning on the windshield wipers and the heater, she put her phone on speaker and called Paul. As she waited for him to answer, she put the pickup in gear and headed for the main road.

He answered on the first ring. "Marty. Still no word."

"You checked with his friends?"

"Everyone I could think of. No one's heard from him. This isn't like Scott."

"The hospital?"

"Yes. And the police department and the fire station in Jerome. No report of a bicycle accident, but I'm sure something's happened. I'm going to look for him."

"Wait for me, Paul. I want to come with you."

"Go home, Marty. This rain isn't supposed to let up until morning. It's a terrible night to be out on the road."

What must it be like for a teenager, lost or hurt or both? She didn't have to say it. Paul was living that nightmare. "That's why I'm coming with you. I can watch the side of the road for any sign of Scott while you drive. I'll be there in ten minutes." At the stop sign, she disconnected, but not before realizing he wasn't arguing.

As she drove, Marty considered whether to tell Paul about Mrs. Arbeck's suspicions. If the old lady was right, whoever was protecting the discovery of the silver lode was willing to do anything. They needed to rethink the theory they'd formed and look at the other suspects again. As important as that was, Scott came first. They had to concentrate on finding him. When they had him home safe and sound, they could reexamine what they knew about Manuel Reyes.

Every light was on in the Russell house. Marty imagined Paul going from room to room switching on lights, hoping to find his son asleep in an unlikely place. The realization that he'd been disappointed every time made her stomach turn over. Where was Scott? Wherever he was, she hoped he was warm and dry.

In her mind's eye she saw Scott's face, eager and intense as he talked about the silver lode. She saw the faint frown line between his blue eyes in the same place as the deep line between his father's brown eyes and the blond hair as thick as his father's brown hair. She and Scott were the same height now, but Marty knew it wouldn't be long before he was taller than she was. Would he grow to be as tall as his father? Would she be in their lives long enough to find out?

To keep from blocking the Jeep in, Marty parked in the street instead of in the driveway. As she got out, the front door opened, and Paul came down the sidewalk with a large umbrella. Shutting her door, she ran with him to the house. When they were inside, he set the dripping umbrella in the corner of the tiled entryway. Then he opened his arms.

She went to him and hugged him hard. "We'll find him," she promised, praying it was true.

Paul didn't answer, just buried his face in her hair and held on. After a moment, he cleared his throat and let her go.

She stepped back and looked up at him. His eyes were bloodshot as if he'd been crying. To keep from bursting into tears herself, she said, "Have you got a towel I can use? I got a little wet running to my pickup."

He lifted a handful of her dripping hair. "More than a little wet. You got good and soaked, sweetheart. I think I can do better than a towel. How about some dry clothes?"

"You're kidding, right? I'd trip wearing one of your sweatshirts."

"Let's try Scott's joggers. I think they might be just about right. Come with me to the laundry room. I did a load of the boys' things this morning."

She followed him down the hall and through the kitchen. The house was silent except for the squeak of their soles on the tile. "Where's B.T.?"

"It's Reed now."

"Reed?"

"Sorry. Things have been moving fast. B.T. chose a new name. He's Reed Harper now, in honor of his mother's maiden name."

Marty blinked. An interesting way for a teenage boy to choose a new name. Maybe she needed to get to know this boy better. "So where is Reed?"

"At work helping stock shelves. He's required to turn off his cell when he clocks in, so I left him a message to call me."

"You don't think he knows where Scott is?"

"No. Since he was going to have to work late, he left the house after Scott did today. It looks like you were the last person to talk to Scott."

Marty remembered Scott's eagerness to leave early. Would he be safe here at home if she'd kept him until the end of the workday? But there was no point in playing *what-if.*

The laundry room turned out to be a washer and dryer behind a double folding door. The top of the dryer was stacked with neatly folded clothes. Paul tossed her a pair of gray sweatpants. "What do you think?"

She held them up to her waist. A little long but she could roll up the legs. "They'll do. Is there a sweatshirt?"

"Red, blue, or green?"

"Green."

He handed it to her with a fluffy yellow towel and nodded to a half-bath off the kitchen. "You can change in there. I was just gathering up some things to take with us."

"I'll be quick." Marty closed the door with a sense of relief, glad to have a moment free from the concrete reality of Scott's disappearance in his home. Her hands trembled as she squeezed water out of her hair with the towel, pulled off her wet clothes, and put on the teenager's joggers.

She had to calm down. She needed to be strong for Paul. Wrapping her dripping clothes in the towel, she went out into the kitchen.

Paul gave her a half smile. "Ready?"

She nodded. "I'll thank Scott for the clothes when we find him."

"Okay. Let's go."

Marty followed Paul into the garage and got into the Jeep beside him. She could hear the rain as the garage door opened, but it pounded the roof so hard as he backed into the driveway she didn't think they would be able to talk without shouting. Which might be just as well. What was there to say?

Paul turned on the headlights. Leaning close, he said, "I'm going to follow 89A toward Jerome. Once we pass the spot where the road from Clarkdale connects, I'll drive as slowly as I can without causing a traffic problem. You watch the side of the road for any sign of him. If we reach Jerome without finding him, I'll backtrack to Clarkdale."

Marty nodded. Paul didn't need to spell out what she was looking for. A wrecked bike, Scott on the side of the road, skid marks. Any sign of a problem with a bicycle. As she scanned the glistening pavement and the rough shoulder, she intensified her prayers.

They were about to start up the switchbacks to Jerome when Marty grabbed Paul's arm. "Stop! We have to go back."

"I can't stop in the middle of the highway! Did you see him?"

"No, but I saw something that looks like a bike path."

"Help me find a place to turn around."

Marty scanned the highway ahead, catching glimpses of roadway between swipes of the wiper blades. The rain was heavier now, and the thought of Scott out in it made her shiver. "Ahead about twenty yards on the right. Isn't that a street sign?"

"It looks like it." Paul checked the rearview mirror as the Jeep slowed. "I don't see anyone behind us. Check your side mirror for me."

"It looks clear."

"Hang on. It's a sharp turn and a steep grade."

Marty reached for the grab bar as the Jeep slowed more. As they turned, the back wheels spun. Paul downshifted, and after a breathless moment, the front wheels caught, and the Jeep started to climb.

Paul let out a long breath. "We're off the highway. Find me a place to turn around."

"Just ahead on the left. I don't see a house, but that looks like a driveway."

"Someone started to build and then thought better of it." As Paul pulled into the driveway, they hit a pothole. Even with a tight grip on the grab bar, Marty bounced high enough to hit her head on the roof. "You okay?" Paul said.

Marty rubbed her head. "I'll live. But this is making me wonder if we can take the Jeep on the bike path."

"One bridge at a time."

It took a four-point turn, but in a few minutes the Jeep was back on the connecting street. When they reached the highway,

Paul stopped, lowered his window, and stuck his head out into the pouring rain. "It looks clear."

"I don't see any headlights."

"Keep watching. Headlights won't reach as far as usual in this downpour, but they'll give us a bit of warning."

The Jeep edged onto the highway. "How far back?" Paul said.

"A mile at most. Maybe not quite that far."

Moving at a crawl, they made their way back down the road. Just when Marty was beginning to wonder if she'd imagined the bike path, she spotted the opening in the roadside brush. "Just ahead on the left. Do you see it?"

When Paul turned on the signal, Marty saw the light begin to blink on the dashboard, but she couldn't hear the familiar tick-tick over the sound of the rain beating on the metal roof.

"This turn is going to be a bit bumpier," Paul said. "No pavement at all."

Just in time, Marty reached for the grab bar. Ducking her head, she avoided a second collision with the roof. The Jeep crawled a few feet and then stopped.

"I'm going to walk from here," Paul said. "The last thing we need is to get stuck in this mud." Reaching behind the seats, he retrieved a nylon bag that looked heavy. "You stay here. I'll only be gone a few minutes."

"Absolutely not! Two sets of eyes are better than one. Besides, I want to find Scott as much as you do."

"I've got rain ponchos, but your ankles are going to get wet, and you may have to throw those shoes away."

"You think I care about these sneakers?" She wouldn't care if they were top dollar leather.

Paul handed her a neatly folded, bright yellow poncho. "This one's Scott's. It should fit."

Marty shook out the heavy vinyl and pulled it on. When she finished tying the hood under her chin, Paul handed her a flashlight. "Let's go. Either we pick up his trail in a few minutes, or we come back to the Jeep and drive on to Jerome."

"Understood." Marty thought she was prepared for the storm, but before she was out of the Jeep, cold rain stung her face, and the wind grabbed the door out of her hand, slamming it against the side of the Jeep. Struggling against the folds of vinyl wrapped around her legs, she took hold of the door and wrestled with it.

A glistening red shape loomed over Marty. She jumped. She knew it was Paul, but for a moment, she experienced the same urgency that told her something was wrong at Sweet Home just a few hours ago. *Please, Lord, keep Scott safe in this storm.*

Paul reached around her to help her push the Jeep door closed. The moment passed, but her prayer continued.

Paul offered her his hand. As she took it, he leaned down and shouted, "Watch the right side of the trail. If you see something, tug on my hand. I'll do the same."

As they struggled up the incline, the bike trail became a channel for water rushing toward the road. Within minutes Marty's shoes were soaked, making her feet heavy and clumsy. They walked slowly, only able to see a few feet in any direction.

As thunder rolled around them, a flash of lightning lit up the trail. Nothing indicated a boy on a bicycle had been this way, whether because the water had washed away all the signs or because Scott had never been on this trail was impossible to know.

"We can't find anything in this storm," Paul shouted. "Let's go back."

Returning was almost as hard as climbing the hill had been. Step and slide. Step and slide. The first time Marty started to fall, Paul caught her. The second time, she grabbed for him, and they almost went down together. In a different set of circumstances, Marty knew they would have laughed. Tonight they slogged grimly on.

Back in the relative quiet of the Jeep, Paul said, "I should have known better than to try to search on foot."

"We had to try."

"Maybe."

The discouragement in his voice made Marty want to put her arms around him and comfort him. She wanted to tell him how sorry she was for running away, how she loved them both, and how she knew he would help her learn to be more than a friend to Scott and Reed. But all of that had to wait. First they had to find Scott.

28

Wednesday, March 20

Scott woke with a start. At least he'd thought he was awake, but this must be one of those nightmares when you dream about waking up. He reached for the bedside lamp, but it wasn't there. A sure sign he was still dreaming.

A rock dug into his shoulder blade, and he sat up. He wasn't dreaming. It all came back at once. The burned-out building, the door, the tunnel, the feeling he was close to finding the silver lode. Then the thud of the metal door and his useless attempts at escape.

What time was it? Dad was sure to be mad. Scott turned on his headlamp and dug his cell phone out of his backpack. He already knew he couldn't get a signal in here, but at least he could find out what time it was.

After switching off the headlamp to save the battery, he touched the cell phone screen. It was almost one. By now Dad was worried. B.T. too. Scott swallowed. He knew he'd acted like a jerk when Dad and B.T. were talking.

He'd done it again when B.T. tried to tell him what they'd

said behind that closed door. He wouldn't even listen to B.T. Scott thought he'd always wanted a brother or a sister, and now he had one. He should have at least let his new brother explain. The three of them were a family.

And Marty. The thought came out of nowhere. She wasn't family. Marty was his boss. She'd be upset when he didn't show up for work, but she wouldn't be worried about him. Would she? Of course, she liked Dad a lot. She might worry because Dad was worried. But as he tried to convince himself it was all about his dad, he knew the truth was Marty liked him for himself.

If B.T. can be family, why not Marty? A quiet voice whispered inside his head or maybe his heart, reminding him of what Marty told him about God remaking their lives. He was too hungry to think about that. Lunch was a ham sandwich and an apple a long time ago. Supper was the last thing he thought about when he realized the door hadn't just blown shut.

He yelled and pounded for a while as if he thought maybe whoever was out there didn't know someone was inside. When he was exhausted with that, he tried to figure out how to get the door off its hinges with his rock pick, but that didn't work.

He remembered drinking some water. He'd needed the water because his throat was sore from yelling. He ought to have a couple of granola bars in his emergency kit. The thought cheered him slightly.

He dug through the pack in the dark, working by feel and setting things out in a row so he could repack. First aid kit, another water bottle, sweatshirt, his mess kit from Boy Scouts, and his Swiss army knife. But no granola bars. As he pulled on the sweatshirt, he tried to think. It came to him in a flash, the outside pocket. He remembered grabbing two protein bars and stuffing them in.

He found one, tore it open, and took an experimental bite, chocolate peanut butter. He'd rather have a cheeseburger and fries, but the bar was better than nothing. The first bar, with its twenty-seven grams of protein, made him hungrier.

He reached for the other one but decided to save it and some water. He rationed himself half of the twelve-ounce bottle. As he returned what was left of his meager provisions to the backpack pocket, Scott wondered again who locked him in here. Not just that, but why, and for how long? He hoped his captor didn't plan to starve him to death.

Dad would find him. Dad, B.T., and Marty.

Scott realized he was holding his breath and listening for any sound that might mean the return of his captor. He couldn't let fear take over. He had to stay calm to be able to think. He remembered his scout master talking about wilderness survival.

"In any dangerous situation, in the mountains or in a city, stay calm. Panic robs you of the ability to think. When you stop thinking, you make mistakes. The ability to reason can make the difference between life and death."

"Life and death," Scott said aloud. "I want to live, so I have to stay calm." He took in a deep breath the way Mr. Kennedy taught them and let it out slowly. "Breathe in calm. Breathe out fear." As his breathing slowed, so did his heart rate. "Jesus," he whispered, "I know I'm not alone. I know you're here. Help me stay calm."

Okay. He was calm. First question, what was the best use of his time right now? He decided to finish what he came down here to do, find the silver lode. Switching on his headlamp, he got to his feet. Even in the total darkness, the yellow light was dimmer than it should be.

Did he have a back-up battery? With a sinking sensation, he decided he didn't. After his second exploration of the Miller Mine, he'd meant to put another battery in his pack, but he hadn't done it.

Think. He could walk in the dark if he had some guide to keep himself from going in circles. He'd made it to the fork without seeing any other tunnels to get lost in, but that didn't mean they weren't there, just that he hadn't spotted them earlier.

Standing as tall as he could, Scott aimed the light at the fork. As he remembered, it was about sixty feet ahead. He moved to the wall and put out his hand. The rock was cold and clammy, not fun to touch, but it would keep him walking in a straight line. He switched off his headlamp and started counting his strides the way his dad had taught him.

At fifty-eight feet, he touched what felt like a corner. He had reached the fork. Guessing he was about where he'd found the rock pick, Scott stopped walking. Something about the feel of the corner made him wonder if the fork was blasted out.

He flicked on the light. It didn't take a close examination to realize this tunnel was man-made. Scott thought back to the 3-D map of Jerome that showed the ore deposits. From what he remembered, the left tunnel connected to one of the United Verde ore bodies.

Now the idea this section was blasted out got exciting. He took a few experimental steps into what he'd assumed was another tunnel. What he saw made his heart pound.

He was standing in a gaping hole, like he'd expect to find where ore was mined. Just ahead his light caught a bright white rock on the floor. Quartz, but not just any quartz. This rock had a gray band that sparkled. Most likely, he'd found a chunk of silver-bearing quartz.

Praying his light wouldn't give out, Scott moved deeper into the blasted-out area. He might be about to prove his theory that Manuel Reyes had discovered an overlooked ore deposit in an existing tunnel. Scott imagined the young miner heading down the tunnel toward a back entrance to where he worked. Scott could almost see what must have happened.

Maybe Manuel was tired or maybe he had a feeling. Either way, he started walking slowly. Then his light picked up something in the wall of the tunnel. As he examined it, his heart started to pound.

He was looking at what everyone came to Jerome for, an undiscovered bonanza! Not just silver, but gold too. He knew all about the Comstock Lode. It was mined out seventy years before, but one old-timer remembered the stories his father told. Manuel thought about his family. This was going to solve all their money problems. They would be rich beyond anything they had ever dreamed of. He couldn't wait to write to Enrique.

Scott's headlamp wavered. He had to quit daydreaming. He needed proof there was something more here than a chunk of quartz. What he needed to find was calaverite, a mineral that often contained both silver and gold. He went deeper into the blasted-out cavern. On the back wall, he saw something that looked like yellow moss.

He tiptoed, almost like he was afraid to scare it off. But there it was, a metallic smudge of calaverite. Scattered all around it were tiny flecks that glittered silver and gold. Not much left, but enough of the mineral to prove Manuel Reyes had discovered a silver lode.

The weak light flickered, but just before it went out, Scott caught a glimpse of a long box, so old the wood was rotted in places. As he stood in total darkness, Scott shivered. He had a bad feeling about that box. It made him want to turn and run away. But he didn't have anywhere to go. Besides, he had to know what was in it.

He took off his headlamp and shook it. Nothing happened. But he didn't need the light to know where the box was. One careful step at a time, he went to where he'd seen it. The toe of his athletic shoe touched wood.

Kneeling, he slid his hands along the top until he found the edge. He could feel the nails, but he could also feel how the lid had splintered. As he pulled, it practically crumbled in his hands.

Sucking in a deep breath, he reached into the box and touched the contents.

With a little whimper, he jerked his hands away and sat back on his heels. Not only had he found the silver lode, Scott had found Manuel Reyes.

29

P aul drove in silence. Marty sat beside him, probably thinking the same thoughts he was. He was grateful she didn't put those thoughts into words.

Where was Scott? With each mile, he got more worried. Useless to try to reassure himself that his son knew how to survive in conditions far harsher than a spring thunderstorm. The what ifs were too strong.

What if Scott fell and broke his leg? What if the deluge started when Scott was unconscious? What if lightning struck his bicycle? Interwoven with his questions was a wordless prayer that kept time with the windshield wipers. *Fa-ther, please.* Over and over.

When he pulled into the driveway, he pushed the automatic opener. As the heavy door slid up, a streak of white cut across the Jeep's headlight. Rahab. The dripping cat must have been huddled under the boxwoods lining the front of the house.

As Paul drove into the sudden quiet of the garage, he was struck by how much the same everything was. His tools hung on the wall where they belonged, and the large trash can was in its place in the corner. Even Reed's motorcycle was parked in the spot they'd chosen for it. Reed! Maybe he knew where Scott was.

Paul was getting out of the Jeep when the back door flew open, and Reed raced out. "Uncle Paul! Is Scott with you?"

Paul's last hope flitted out of reach. "No. I hoped you would know where he went."

Reed shook his head. "We were going to try to figure out the map tonight so we could look for the silver lode tomorrow morning before work. We were going to get up early and be on Cleopatra Hill as soon as the sun came up."

Paul wondered when Scott was planning to tell him about that plan. "What map?"

"Scott found it in Manuel's footlocker."

"Scott didn't tell me about a map." Marty's voice was sharp.

Reed shifted uneasily. "We weren't sure what it was. Just some lines scribbled on notebook paper. It was the X that made Scott think it might be a map."

"Can you remember the map well enough to draw it for us?" Paul said.

"I can do better than that. I can show you the original, at least I can if Scott put it back after making a copy."

"It's not in the footlocker," Marty said. "Carly gave me a list of the contents. There wasn't a map on it."

"It was hidden under the paper lining of the lid. That's another thing that made Scott think it was a map. Why else hide something like that?"

That last hope flitted back and hovered in the vicinity of Paul's heart. "Where is the footlocker?"

"In the shed."

"Unless Carly followed my instructions for a change," Marty said.

Paul's stomach clenched. "What do you mean?"

"I decided Alex Reyes should have the footlocker. Since

Carly was going to Flagstaff anyway, I told her to take it to him at his dorm."

"Oh no," Reed said, voicing Paul's reaction.

Marty was digging in her bag. "I'll call her. She was planning to have dinner with a friend. Maybe she's still there. If she is, she can pick it up and bring it home with her."

Paul checked his watch, almost two. Dinner should have been over long ago.

"Carly, it's Marty. Where are you?"

A strange opening for a conversation if you were Carly. It made perfect sense to the rest of them. "You're at home in bed?"

Marty frowned. "Never mind what time it is. Did you take the footlocker to Alex?"

Paul watched the frown disappear then reappear.

"What do you mean you don't know where it is?"

Marty listened then said, "I'll explain later."

"I got the footlocker's still here," Paul said, "but Carly doesn't know where. It isn't in the shed?"

Marty shrugged. "Carly looked for it in the shed, but she couldn't find it."

"It's there," Reed said. "I helped Scott put it back after he found the map."

"Then Carly should have found it," Paul said.

"Maybe not," Reed said. "We put it against the back wall under a couple of boxes of a rusty old train set."

Paul raised his eyebrows. Reed shrugged. "Scott didn't want anyone to take it until he brought back the map."

"All right then, everybody in the Jeep." He got in and started the engine, glad he'd left the door up. The rain drummed loudly on the roof as he backed out. Marty shivered. As he turned the heater on, he prayed wherever Scott was, his son was protected from the cold rain.

At that time of night, the road was deserted. The headlights of the Jeep forged a glittering yellow path through the rain, giving Paul a strong sense of being alone despite his two companions. Was that how Scott was feeling? *Father, let him feel Your presence. Remind him we're praying for him.*

No one spoke during the fifteen-minute drive. Paul was sure Marty was praying, but he wondered what thoughts were going through Reed's mind. He decided he couldn't deal with what he was sure were the boy's unspoken worries.

As Paul turned onto her street, Marty said, "Pull around to the side. There's no reason to go in the house."

"You don't keep the shed locked?"

"Are you kidding? Until twenty minutes ago, I'd have paid a thief to steal every bit of the junk in there."

As soon as Paul turned off the motor, Reed was out of the back of the Jeep and running for the shed. Marty was pulling her hood over her head when Paul opened his door and got out. He raised his face into the rain. *Please, Father, let us find the map.*

Marty met him in front of the Jeep and held out her hand. "Come on, Dad," she said. "Let's find your son."

A faint glow beckoned from across the yard. Holding hands, they ran.

As they entered the shed, Reed called out, "It's here!"

Marty pushed Paul toward Reed. "Go."

Turning on his cell phone's flashlight, Paul picked his way between a pile of garden tools and a box filled with books. He passed an iron bedstead leaning drunkenly on a couch that looked fit for a colony of mice to call home, a table with three legs, and a waist-high stack of quilts.

He found Reed in the farthest corner of the shed. "You've got the map?"

"It's here, but I'm afraid to pull it out. Scott put it back like we found it, including gluing the paper lining of the footlocker back in place."

"Be as careful as you can," Marty said, "but finding Scott is more important than whatever this footlocker might be worth."

Paul handed his pocketknife to Reed. "You saw how Scott got it out."

"It's here in the lid. Hold your light for me."

Paul moved to shine his light over Reed's shoulder. At first Paul didn't see the slight bulge under the lining, but as the boy worked, he saw what looked like the corner of a folded paper emerge. Finally, it was out. Reed handed it to Paul.

In the light from his cell phone, Paul saw the map was as Reed had described it, a few pencil lines on a piece of cheap notebook paper. The X was there, but nothing was marked except the United Verde mine, the cemetery, and one street. Paul handed the map to Marty. "Any idea where Dundee Avenue is?"

Marty shook her head.

"Do you have a map of Jerome?"

"On the wall in my office."

They trudged back through the rain and went into the house through the back door. In what had probably once been a pantry, Paul saw a map of Jerome tacked to the wall. Placing Manuel's hand-drawn map underneath the slick tourist map, Paul said, "Anybody see Dundee Avenue?"

After a moment, Marty pointed to a narrow, white line. "Doesn't that say Dundee Ave?"

Paul leaned in closer. "Yes. It's connected to a road marked Old Mine."

"A perfect place for the silver lode!" Reed said.

"That's why we didn't see any sign of Scott earlier," Marty said. "We went past Old Mine Road. I wonder why we missed it?"

"My guess is it isn't marked," Paul said.

"Let's go find it," Reed said. "If we start here, like Scott did, instead of from your house, we'll have a better chance of spotting it. When we get to the highway, we watch for an unmarked dirt road."

"You mean a mud road," Marty said. "It's still raining."

Paul checked the weather on his cell phone. "According to this, the rain won't stop until morning. As much as I hate to say it, we have to wait."

"But the Jeep can go through anything, can't it?" Reed said.

Paul shook his head. "The Old Mine road is a river right now. The Jeep can handle mud, but not a river."

"What do we do while we wait?" Reed sounded like an impatient child.

Please, Father... "We pray," Paul said.

"And rest," Marty said.

"Yes, ma'am," Paul said. "But we leave as soon as the rain stops."

"Agreed."

Paul tried to sleep, but he ended up staring at the ceiling until the window was gray instead of black. The rain, though not as heavy, was still coming down. His cell phone told him it was supposed to stop mid-morning.

Feeling like a caged bear, he went into the kitchen and made the most complicated breakfast he could find the ingredients for. A plate of bacon, three stacks of pancakes, and a bowl of scrambled eggs later, he was still frustrated.

By that time Marty and Reed were in the kitchen talking to him. Over and over about Scott, then about the weather, and finally about what to pack in the Jeep.

His watch said five after ten when the rain stopped. By ten after, the three of them were in the Jeep following the bicycle route. A few minutes later, the sun peeked out from behind the clouds. At ten-thirty, Reed said, "Up there on the right! Isn't that a road?"

"At the switchback," Marty said. "How did we miss it last night?"

Paul hit the steering wheel with the palm of his hand. "The headlights swung uphill too soon. But we should have spotted it on the way back down."

Paul checked the rearview mirror. Nothing coming up behind. Depending on the four-wheel-drive, he turned slowly off the highway. The tires squished in the mud but evidently encountered enough rock to keep turning. "Start watching. I've got to stay focused straight ahead."

"I've got the left," Reed said.

"I'm watching the right," Marty said.

Paul felt her hand on his arm. The light touch was comforting, a reminder he wasn't in this alone. *Please, Father...*

The road turned back on itself, and it took all the skill he possessed to keep from sliding off into a ditch he almost didn't see. Neither of his passengers commented. They plowed on through the mud in low gear for another several minutes. Then Reed said, "Up there, just before the Y in the road. Isn't that Scott's bike?"

Spattered so heavily with mud it was hard to distinguish from the boulder it leaned against, the red mountain bike Paul had given Scott for his fourteenth birthday sat alone. No sign of Scott.

Echoing his thoughts, Marty said, "At least we know we're in the right area."

Paul parked beside the bike and got out. On the hill above their heads he could see a cross leaning to one side in the Jerome Cemetery. He took the map from his pocket and checked the location of the X against it. "Assuming Scott went looking for the silver lode, we need to walk southwest watching for any sign of an old mine. I'll walk in a straight line from the bike. Reed, you walk on my left, Marty on my right."

The mud wasn't as deep higher on the hill, but it was still like walking through molasses. Paul's stride was enough longer than the others' that they were soon moving in a lopsided triangle. Paul first, Reed next, Marty trailing behind.

They'd gone about half a mile when Reed shouted, "There!"

Following the line of the boy's outstretched arm, Paul saw

what looked like the remains of a large bonfire. He said, "I don't see it."

"That house," Reed said. "I bet it's like in the exhibit at the Douglas Mansion, a tunnel that connects from the basement to a mine."

Paul studied the landscape. To the west and slightly to the north he spotted the metal superstructure of the headframe standing guard over the mine shaft. He didn't know the exact layout of the side tunnels, but he knew they honeycombed the hill. It wasn't hard to imagine a connector tunnel from whatever this structure had been to the United Verde Mine. Paul had seen the exhibit Reed was talking about numerous times. The boy could be right.

Once again putting words to his thoughts, Marty said, "Surely Scott wouldn't have gone in there alone."

"He might have," Reed said. "Just far enough to check it out. Maybe he found a dry place out of the rain and fell asleep."

Paul didn't wait for any more speculations. There was only one way to find out. He started walking at a normal pace, but before he'd gone far, he was running. It didn't make sense, but it was as if he heard Scott calling him.

Almost immediately, he spotted where the debris had been disturbed. "Scott?" Paul held his breath, wanting desperately, yet half-afraid, to hear his son's voice, weak from exposure.

"Over here!" Reed shouted. "I see a place where Scott might have been able to stay out of the rain for a while." He dropped to his knees under an overhang created by the rubble.

Paul hurried to where the boy knelt, not twenty-five feet away.

"Scott's shoe print," Reed said. "He has those cool flex athletic shoes with the grooved tread."

Marty came up behind Reed. "He's right, Paul. I know because Scott stepped in some varnish and tracked it across the workroom. I helped him clean up the tracks."

"One print," Paul said. "Where's the next one?"

"Maybe down there," Reed said. "I think that's a room."

Paul motioned for Reed to move. Squatting, he shone his flashlight into the hole. The narrow beam lit up what was almost certainly a beaten dirt floor. Moving the light around the area, he saw a brick wall with a space in it. "I see what looks like a doorway," he said. "I'm going down."

"Let me go first," Reed said. "I'm lighter than you are. We can test how much weight these old timbers will hold."

Paul shook his head. Marty said, "He's right, Paul. The lightest one should go first, which is me. Next is Reed. You come last. If these boards give way, we'll need you up here to get us out."

Paul considered pushing them both out of the way and going down. But he knew their reasoning was sound. With one exception. "Reed goes first," he said. "If we have a problem, he's the youngest and least likely to get hurt."

Reed said, "Yes!" Before Paul could suggest the safest entry point, the boy disappeared into the opening. A moment later they heard a heavy thud. Paul shone his light into the hole.

Reed was getting to his feet. "It's a room with a door."

"Is Scott there?" Paul stopped breathing. He didn't know which answer he dreaded most.

"No, but I know where he went. I'm going to get him."

"Wait!" Too late. Reed had already disappeared through the door, rushing into whatever danger had kept Scott from coming back out the way he'd gone in. Paul put his hands on Marty's shoulders. "I go next."

"No. Reed getting down safely doesn't mean our reasoning isn't sound. If the braces around that hole give way when I go down, you need to be up here to help me get out. I promise I won't go through that door without you."

Arguing would only waste time, so Paul held out his hands.

"I'll let you down as far as I can so you won't have so far to drop."

She landed lightly and looked back up at him. "Everything looks okay. No signs of a struggle. No blood."

Marty had read his mind. "Thanks." With a slightly lighter heart, Paul let himself through the opening. He swung for a moment, judging the distance to the floor. Less than his height. He let go, landing on his feet.

Marty was right, no signs of a struggle. Either Scott was still inside, or he'd left of his own accord. The room was empty except for a padlock on the floor behind the open door.

Marty grabbed his hand. "Let's go. Maybe everything's fine. Maybe Scott stayed here last night because of the rain and Reed found him."

Paul wanted to believe Marty was right, but the dread that gripped him when he first saw the burned-out building returned full force as he followed her through the door. It only took a moment to understand why. The beam from his flashlight picked out an empty water bottle and the wrapper from a protein bar like the ones he always bought. "Scott was here, but…"

Before he could finish the sentence, he heard Reed's voice, strained and thin. "Uncle Paul! I found something."

Something, not Scott. Where was his son? Gripping Marty's hand, Paul moved toward the boy.

"Not Scott?" Marty said.

"No." Reed stopped, almost as if he didn't want to say whatever came next.

With an effort Paul held his impatience in check. "Tell us what you found."

"Some rocks I'm pretty sure are ore." Reed stopped, cleared his throat. "And a box of bones."

arty knelt by the rosewood piano and dipped the soft toothbrush into a mixture of vinegar and soap. Working with a gentle circular motion, she began to clean the intricately carved shell on the curved cabriole leg. Headachy and groggy after her long nap, she hoped the simple work would help her wake up.

Where was Scott? She knew if they'd found him, Paul would have called. Was Paul still grimly dismantling the mountain of burned wood one plank at a time? She hoped he'd gone home to rest. Getting out of the basement was a challenge, but when Reed stood on Paul's shoulders, he was able to scramble out and get the sturdy rope Paul kept in the Jeep for emergencies.

Once they were all out, Paul reported Scott's disappearance to the police and the pastor. Word spread quickly, and an eager but chaotic search began. The church youth group, the Boy Scout troop, the school's debate team, and three volunteer firefighters from Jerome had turned out to help look for Scott.

A police officer did his best to coordinate the enthusiastic search parties, but beyond assigning specific sections of the mountain to each group, he couldn't do much. When Paul tackled the collapsed building as though he thought Scott could be trapped there, she went home.

Marty looked up.

Carly stood over her, hands on slim denim-clad hips. "At least now I know how to get your attention. I tried Marty, Ms. Greenlaw, roomie, and landlady. From now on, I'll call you boss when I need something."

Marty sat back on her heels. "Okay. You've got my attention. What do you need?"

"It's seven p.m., and I'm starving. The choices tonight are meatloaf and mashed potatoes or chicken potpie. You get first choice. Which one?"

"Neither one. Take your pick."

"I could order a pizza."

The thought of food made Marty's stomach turn over. "Thanks for thinking of me, but I'm not hungry."

Carly perched on the piano stool. "What do you want to bet Scott is home having dinner right now?"

"Paul would have called if they'd found him."

"Maybe in all the excitement, he forgot. I'll call Paul if you want me to."

Shaking her head, Marty dabbed the moisture off the piano leg with a soft rag.

"Scott's okay. He's probably lost."

"I know you're trying to help, Carly, but it's not working."

"Okay. Try eating something."

"Maybe later. After I put these tools away, I'm going to take a twenty-minute nap." Or maybe she'd go to bed.

"I'll clean this up. You go lie down. But try not to worry. Scott is smart. No matter what has happened to him, he'll come out okay."

Marty didn't bother to answer, just handed Carly the rag and got to her feet. In the light from the overhead fixture, the stairs looked as steep as the side of Cleopatra Hill. As she started up, her feet felt like she had forty-pound weights attached to her ankles. Marty couldn't remember ever feeling this tired.

It wasn't just the lack of sleep or the worry. Something was bothering her, a worrisome idea that hovered at the edge of consciousness just out of reach. She didn't need to sleep. She needed to think.

Drawn to the bed with its log cabin quilt and mound of pillows, Marty fought the temptation to sleep first and think later. Switching on the Tiffany lamp on her bedside table, she crossed to the mission-style rocking chair in the corner. Leaning against the large, quilted pillow that made the wide chair comfortable, she propped her feet on the footstool and studied the ceiling fan.

The searchers on the mountain had four theories for Scott's disappearance. Assigning each to a fan blade, she considered them one by one. First, the theory Scott was dead. No one suggested it, but they all knew it was a possibility. Unable to bear thinking about it, she rejected the idea and moved on.

Second, the theory Scott was lost. That explanation made no sense. Never mind that Scott had explored every inch of Cleopatra Hill, he had a compass. They'd found his bike, without the compass he kept clipped to the handlebar.

Hurt was the strongest possibility because of the fury of last night's storm. But Scott had his cell phone with him, and Paul tried tracking it before he reported his son missing.

Fourth, the idea Scott was searching for the silver lode some- where else. Absurd. Scott wouldn't disappear, leaving his father to worry. The fan had five blades. Did the last blade represent a theory no one had considered?

Kidnapped.

The word popped into Marty's mind, illuminating her thinking as brightly as the fan light would have lit her bedroom if she'd pulled the chain to turn it on. First, if the ore they'd found in the branch tunnel under the burned-out building was from the silver lode and second, if the bones in the box belonged to

Manuel, Sr. Reyes's belief that his brother had been murdered was right.

If Alex was right, his grandfather had been murdered, and if Mrs. Arbeck was right, Joe Sweet had been murdered. Whoever now controlled the fortune spawned by the silver lode was a ruthless killer. So many *ifs* without proof.

Marty shivered. As much as she hated the idea Scott had been kidnapped, she hated worse the thought their contemporary murderer had struck a third time. Kidnapping would work as a way to get them to stop looking for the letters. Success would depend on not letting Scott discover the identity of his kidnapper. And Scott was a determined teenager. Marty felt sick.

Should she tell Paul? Since they seemed to read each other's minds so often, he might have already reached the same conclusion. If he had, sitting alone with this possibility would be agony. No longer tired, Marty pushed away the footstool and got up. Grabbing her bag from the bedside table, she headed downstairs.

Carly was at the kitchen table eating and texting. She looked up as Marty crossed to the back door. "Going to get something to eat? I don't blame you."

Marty didn't want to explain. "I've got my phone. Call me if you hear anything."

Under any other conditions Marty would have paused to marvel at the brilliance of the stars in the high desert. Now she noticed but kept moving around the side of the house and into the pickup. She was about to start the motor when her cell rang. Paul? Shoving the key into the ignition, she dug through her bag for her phone.

"Hello?"

An eerie, distorted voice responded. "Ms. Greenlaw, I have a message for Dr. Russell."

"Why call me?"

"He didn't answer. Time is critical if you want to see Scott again."

A man, a woman, even a child might be speaking. A prank? Marty rejected the idea as it surfaced. Scott wasn't the kind of kid to think disappearing and then scaring his dad was funny.

The voice went on without waiting for her to respond. "We have his son."

She was half-expecting it, but the bald statement stung like a slap. "Is Scott…" She tried to ask the question that was the only thing that mattered, but the words wouldn't go around the lump in her throat.

"He's fine for now. How long he stays that way depends on you."

"What do you want?"

A sound resembling a laugh followed her question.

Marty wanted to shout at whoever was controlling the mechanical voice. Instead she said evenly, "Tell me what you want."

"We want you to stop looking for the silver lode."

What would the kidnapper do if he knew they'd already found it? "Done. Let Scott go."

"Not that easy, Ms. Greenlaw."

Marty waited.

"You must cancel the fund raiser."

This time Marty couldn't control her outrage. She almost shouted, "Why? How does it hurt you for us to help a dying child?"

"No more talk about the Reyes family. No more Manuel Reyes."

As furious as she was, at least that made sense. The more they mentioned the name Reyes, the more people might remember stories they'd heard as children.

She was about to demand to speak to Scott when the call dropped. The only identifying information was a string of zeros. Dropping her phone on the seat beside her, Marty headed for

Paul's house. She now had confirmation for her theory about the kidnapping.

Her stomach fluttered. When had she begun to feel the nudges she was experiencing in this nightmare? She'd felt it first right before they discovered Sr. Reyes was dead. And then when they found Joe Sweet dead. This feeling about the kidnapping had to be the same.

It couldn't mean Scott was dead. *Please, Lord.*

The drive along the dark highway took the same amount of time it always did, but she found herself pulling into Paul's driveway long before she was ready to face him. What to tell him? Everything, of course. But how to tell him?

She was getting out of her pickup when the porch light came on and Paul stepped out. "Marty! I was just about to call you."

Had he spoken to the same mechanical voice? It would be easier if he had. Either way, she didn't want to talk out here. "Let's go inside," she said. "I have news."

"I do too. Should Reed be in on the conversation?"

She shook her head. Later Paul could decide what to tell the boy.

"Okay. Let's talk in my study."

She followed him down the hall and waited while he moved books from a walnut chair that had probably come from the dining room. She'd only been in Paul's study a couple of times, but her impression was the same as before. Paul knew where every book was in what appeared to be a disorganized mess. Had she known a particular book to ask for, she was sure he could find it as quickly as any librarian on home turf.

Paul set the chair across from his own. "It's cramped in here, but if you close the door, Reed can't hear us even if he comes downstairs."

"When did they call off the search?" She knew Paul wouldn't be here if anyone was still looking for Scott.

"Just after sunset."

"Did they find any clues about what happened?"

Paul shook his head.

"I heard from the kidnappers."

Paul nodded as if he already knew.

"Did they call you too?"

"No, but I've been waiting for a call. Why on earth did they call you?"

Marty shrugged. "I guess your number went to voice mail, and the person didn't have a number to leave. It was a string of zeros."

"What do they want?"

"Two things. We're to quit looking for the silver lode and call off the fund raiser."

Paul groaned and released her hands. Getting to his feet, he moved awkwardly around her and started reorganizing stacks of books. Marty imagined if there had been space in the crowded room, he would be pacing.

"Giving up the search for the silver lode isn't an issue," he said. "I'm just glad whoever it is doesn't realize we've already found it. We can't call off the fund raiser. I refuse to trade one child's life for another."

"We can find another way to get the money for Aurora."

"There isn't time. Alex called. They took her to the hospital earlier this evening." He put down the stack of books he was holding and came back to his chair. "Besides, I don't intend to let someone who has murdered two people in cold blood go free."

So he'd decided Joe was murdered without ever hearing Mrs. Arbeck's theory. "What makes you think Joe's death wasn't natural?"

"Do you think it was?"

"No, but I have some information you don't. Why do you think he was killed?"

Paul reached for a yellow legal pad and a ballpoint pen. "Joe Sweet had to have been blackmailing someone. We know he read the other letters in their original Spanish. We also know he was an expert on the history of support businesses in Jerome."

He started clicking the pen in a regular rhythm. "That burned-out building Scott found was much too large to have been a private home. My guess is it was a hotel or a boarding house. Most important, Joe was probably awake the night Enrique Reyes was murdered. My guess is he knew what happened and why."

"Didn't he realize how dangerous that might be?"

"Evidently he thought he could protect himself from whoever this killer is. A stupid mistake that cost him his life. A mistake we're not going to repeat." He clicked the pen one last time and drew a line down the middle of the page. "We're looking at one of two people at this point, Jimmy Wong or Frank Sanchez." He labeled the columns.

Marty shook her head. "There's more than one of them."

"How do you know?"

"Whoever was talking kept saying we. We have Scott. We want you to do two things."

"That would point to Frank. The Sanchez family is in the grocery business together."

"But isn't the Wong money tied up in a foundation? Jimmy might be used to saying we when he talks to potential donors."

"Agreed," Paul said.

"You don't suppose Jimmy and Frank are working together?"

"Highly unlikely. Remember, we're going back to that silver lode. I can't believe a restaurant owner and Manuel's partner worked together and shared that fortune. I also can't see Manuel's murderer wanting to share. If he was willing to do that, he wouldn't have had to kill Manuel. How about clues from the voice?"

"None. I think I was talking to one of those voice changer programs."

"Okay. Back to the grandfathers. What do we know about how they made their money?"

"Not enough," Marty said. "Neither of the histories holds up under close scrutiny. We have to think of a way to identify the contemporary killer."

Paul frowned. Leaning back in his chair, he threw the pen like a dart at the door. It connected with a thump and fell to the floor. "How on earth do we do that?"

"I was thinking about that on the way over. What about this? We pretend to give in to the demands. I take one of them and you take the other. Tomorrow morning, we go see them, tell them we're canceling the fund raiser, and see which one is surprised."

Paul hit the floor with both feet. "That just might work. I'll take Frank Sanchez and family. You take Jimmy Wong."

31

Thursday, March 21

P aul pushed the accelerator and merged onto I-17. In utter disregard for his state of mind, the sun was shining in a morning sky bluer than any he'd ever seen growing up in Virginia. If he could order weather to match his mood, he'd insist on a hurricane.

"Where are you, Son?" he said to the empty Jeep. Who was keeping Scott prisoner? Was he tied up? Hungry?

A red Corvette shot out of his blind spot, passing him on the shoulder. His reflexes kicked in, and he narrowly missed slamming into the semi in the left lane. Shaken, he took the next exit. He'd driven less than five miles on the interstate and already almost had a major accident like the one that killed his wife. He wouldn't be any good to Scott dead.

Paul pulled onto the shoulder of the road to Montezuma Castle National Monument. He sat until he'd quit shaking, then got out of the Jeep and started to walk. He had to get control of his emotions, and he only had fifty miles to accomplish that task.

Fifty miles of interstate. He had to be clear-headed for the meeting with Frank Sanchez.

The fact that Frank had set the meeting at the corporate offices suggested an agenda. For all Paul knew, he was headed into a meeting with a battery of attorneys. He needed to focus on his own agenda, to gauge Frank's level of surprise or satisfaction to his announcement they were canceling the fund raiser. Depending on the reaction he got, he would either politely request an oral history interview with the oldest living Sanchez at some time far in the future or demand to know where his son was.

Paul checked his watch. He had just about an hour to make it for the nine o'clock meeting, and that hour included a certain amount of congested city driving. Not far by freeway standards but complicated by the traffic of a growing town hemmed in by national forest. Paul went back to the Jeep. As he merged back onto the interstate, he began to pray.

Sanchez Markets occupied a three-story building that shared a parking lot with a CPA firm and a bank in a commercial park in East Flagstaff. The office he was looking for was on the third floor. Paul took the stairs.

Frank was waiting for him by a door at the end of the hall-way. "Thanks for meeting me here, Dr. Russell. You'll understand why I chose the offices shortly."

"Not a problem. I come to Flagstaff every day when classes are in session."

Frank held out his hand. As Paul took it, Frank said, "Thank you for challenging me to look into my family history. I had a long talk with my great-uncle. What I learned made me take a long look at myself. I wasn't proud of what I saw."

"The past can transform the present if we study it."

Frank opened the door. "This is my great-uncle's office. I wanted to be sure you met him."

Paul's first impression was of light. The glass wall opposite the door looked out into acres of Ponderosa pine, and pale green carpet drew the forest inside. The only occupant of the spacious office, a white-haired Hispanic man probably ten years younger than Enrique Reyes, sat behind a desk stacked with colorful folders. Despite the apparent disorganization, Paul knew instinctively this man controlled whatever he touched. If Sr. Sanchez was behind the kidnapping, Paul suspected he'd have a hard time bluffing the truth out of him.

"Uncle Lorenzo," Frank said, "this is Dr. Russell."

"Please call me Paul."

Lorenzo Sanchez nodded, but he didn't get to his feet, nor did he offer his hand. The closed look on his face struck Paul as arrogant, and he was tempted to force the issue by going around the desk and offering his own hand. But he resisted. He was here to observe, not to establish a relationship.

"Franco, bring two chairs from the conference table," Lorenzo said.

When Frank and Paul were seated, Lorenzo said, "My nephew tells me you're doing research on families associated with the copper mines in Jerome."

Paul wondered if he should follow the older man's conversational lead or get straight to the point. It only took a split second to decide. "Frank's right, but that's not my focus today."

Frank looked surprised. "I thought—"

Lorenzo waved an impatient hand. "Go on."

Paul spoke slowly, keeping a close eye on the older man's face. "Before I hear the story of your family, I need to tell you we've canceled the fund raiser for Aurora Reyes."

Lorenzo looked surprised. "I'm sorry to hear that. I want to help the great-granddaughter of my old friend Enrique."

"You know the family?"

"When I was a young boy. Sr. Reyes, the old Sr. Reyes who was Enrique and Manuel's father, came from Mexico about the same time my father did. The two of them worked in the citrus groves together. But that's our history. Perhaps you don't want to go into that today."

Paul studied Lorenzo's lined face. The surprise was gone, replaced by the closed look, a mask to hide behind? Unsure of how to proceed to get the information he needed, Paul decided to follow his instinct into the past. The story might include a reference to mining, though certainly not to a silver lode.

Watching the other man closely, Paul said, "Do you mind giving me an abbreviated account today? I'll work up some questions for an in-depth interview later."

Lorenzo nodded.

"Okay to record our conversation? That way when we go into more depth you won't need to repeat anything you tell me today."

Lorenzo nodded again. As Paul retrieved the small digital recorder he always carried in his messenger bag, the older Sanchez moved a paperweight into a ray of sunshine so it threw colored fire across the pale carpet.

Paul turned on the recorder and identified the date, place, and speaker. "Please continue, Sr. Sanchez. It's not necessary to repeat what you've already told me."

"My father and Sr. Reyes did well working in the orchards, and after a few years they decided to pool their money to buy a small farm and a pickup truck. They were confident they could make a good living selling their produce at various markets around the valley. But their two eldest sons, Manuel and my brother Franco, wanted to make money faster. They decided to go to Jerome and work in the copper mines."

"Do you know the year?"

"1949, maybe 1950. The mines were still going, though the copper boom of World War II was over. My brother Franco, this boy's grandfather, came home after several months without Manuel."

"They think Manuel was murdered," Frank said.

"Who is 'they?'" Lorenzo demanded.

"Enrique," Frank said.

Lorenzo looked at Paul. "Did Enrique tell you that?"

"Enrique believed someone killed Manuel to get possession of a rich vein of ore Manuel discovered. He wanted help finding out who killed his brother."

"To get the money to help his great-granddaughter who needs a new heart."

Paul nodded.

"I have no idea what happened to Manuel, but I'm sure my brother didn't kill his friend. I was a young boy of ten when Franco came home penniless. He asked my father to allow him to work driving the pickup. Of course, my father had to ask permission from Sr. Reyes, his partner." Lorenzo picked up the paperweight, extinguishing the colored fire.

"What did Sr. Reyes say?"

"He wanted to know about Manuel, of course."

Sr. Sanchez hesitated. Paul prompted a second time. "What did your brother say?"

"He refused to talk about Manuel. He said it would be dangerous."

Because Manuel was afraid of a murderer or because he was guilty himself? "Do you know what he meant?"

"Like any younger brother, I tried to pester the story out of him, but he never talked about it, not even on his deathbed." He put down the paperweight and looked at Paul. "I was saddened to learn of Enrique's death."

End of story according to Lorenzo Sanchez, but Paul had a question. "If your father and old Sr. Reyes owned a farm together, why isn't the Reyes family part of your business?"

Lorenzo hesitated so long, Paul wondered if he was going to answer. Finally, the older man said, "Sr. Reyes was heart-broken when his eldest son disappeared. He went to Jerome to try to find out what happened. When he came home without answers, people said he went into a decline. Now the diagnosis would be depression. One day Sr. Reyes went out into the desert and shot himself."

As if anticipating Paul's doubt, Lorenzo added softly, "There was no question that it was anything but suicide. He talked to his wife for weeks about ending his life. She did everything, even had the priest talk to him. But no one could get through the fog of his sorrow."

Lorenzo paused as if for a moment of silence to honor the dead man. "After Sr. Reyes died, my father helped Señora Reyes as much as he could. She was already teaching English to our countrymen, and she began teaching Spanish to the American farmers. She got a teaching certificate and moved her family to Cottonwood to start a new life. My father helped her as long as she would allow it."

Paul turned off the recorder. "Thank you, Sr. Sanchez. This is far more than Enrique was able to tell me before he died. You weren't at his celebration of life, were you?"

Lorenzo shook his head. "I'm afraid I fell out of touch with Enrique many years ago. I'm ashamed to say I don't know any of his children. But I plan to change that. With or without your fund raiser, I'll help this little girl's parents with their medical expenses up to two hundred fifty thousand dollars."

Paul caught his breath. "That's a most generous offer. I know Hernando and Belinda will be thrilled. May I tell them?"

"Please do. My nephew will be my liaison." He looked at Frank.

"I'll be happy to, Uncle."

A quarter of a million dollars was a lot of money. Still, it didn't come close to what must have come out of the silver lode. Paul studied Lorenzo Sanchez. The man wasn't young, but he looked fit. His arms were muscled as if he spent time lifting weights. He could easily have stood over Enrique Reyes and held a pillow over the sick old man's face until he quit struggling.

Paul put his recorder away and got to his feet. "Thank you for your time, Sr. Sanchez."

"Thank you, Dr. Russell." Still sitting, Lorenzo backed away from his desk—in a wheelchair. He pushed a button and came around to where Paul stood. Offering his hand, he said, "I'm truly sorry for Enrique's death and the difficulty the Reyes family is experiencing, but some good things are coming out of this sorrow."

The old man looked up at Frank, who now stood beside him. "I've prayed for years for a way to reach my great-nephew. Your insistence that he learn his family history has done what I never could."

Paul saw sincerity in the older man's dark eyes. The closed look was a mask all right, a mask to hide not guilt but physical pain. He took Lorenzo's hand. "We may find a way to do the fund raiser," he said. "I'll get in touch with Frank if we do."

As Paul headed toward his Jeep, he realized they only had a single suspect left, Jimmy Wong. It was now five minutes after ten. Marty had just walked into Jimmy's office.

Marty touched the satin finish of the cherry table more suited to a dining room than an office. "A beautiful piece, Mr. Wong. I know it's Chinese, and I recognize the careful handwork of tenon and mortise joints. It looks old, though beautifully preserved. Is it an antique?"

"Almost. My grandfather built it at least eighty years ago. I don't know the exact date."

"The lines are so precise they look almost as if they were plotted on a graph. The contrast to these expertly carved roses is stunning. Is the design his?"

"Hardly. He copied the Ming style used in China between 1368 and 1644."

Marty laughed. "Now those would be real antiques. Much older than anything that would come through my workshop."

"I have a genuine Ming chair in my home as well as a few other pieces you might be interested in. Perhaps one day you would like to see them."

"I'd love to." Marty considered. She'd planned to begin with the cancellation of the fund raiser, but here was a great opening to the questions she wanted to ask about the Wong family history. "Your grandfather was an expert on Chinese antique furniture. I thought he operated a restaurant in Jerome."

"Oh, he did. But he was also a passionate woodworker."

"Did he sell his furniture?"

Jimmy leaned back in his leather desk chair and steepled his short, rather stubby fingers. "You know, I'm glad to have an antiques expert to admire my grandfather's handiwork, but I was expecting Dr. Russell."

Marty didn't comment on the abrupt change of subject. He was avoiding details of the past. She'd have to find another way to get into the subject of Shen Wong's fortune. "He called to make the appointment, but since I'm the co-chair of the fund raiser, we decided I should be the one to come."

"I told Dr. Russell…"

Marty nodded. "Yes, sir. You told him Aurora's case doesn't fit your mission. I'm here to let you know we're canceling the fund raiser. We won't be bothering you again." She watched his round face.

He raised eyebrows threaded with white. "Really?"

"You're surprised. We thought you'd be relieved."

"Quite the opposite. I'd changed my mind about helping the little girl. Drug rehab isn't involved, but I understand the idea of giving back to people who left Jerome with nothing. I know how expensive organ replacement surgery is, so I was thinking of offering the largest category of grants we can provide."

Marty felt hope for Aurora struggle to the surface. Once they got Scott home safely, they could go ahead with the fund raiser. If this foundation underwrote a substantial donation, individuals would see it as a validation of the project. "With your help," she said cautiously, "we might be able go ahead with the fund raiser. How much money are you offering?"

"We can go as high as three hundred thousand dollars."

Marty blinked. She'd never imagined they could raise that

much with one donation. But what was this man's motive? Time to dig.

"I had no idea your foundation was so well-funded," she said. "What was a Jerome restaurant owner's secret to financial success?"

Jimmy narrowed his eyes and studied her. After a moment, he straightened in his chair and put both palms flat on the shining cherry table. "I was glad when Paul called. I'd been trying to make up my mind about whether to tell him the truth about my family history."

He hesitated. Then taking a deep breath, he said, "I glossed over some unpleasant facts about how my grandfather made the money that built the Wong Foundation. I decided I'd tell him the truth today and offer to make a donation to get you folks started."

Marty's breath caught in her throat. Was he going to admit his grandfather killed Manuel? Maybe the doctor was right about Sr. Reyes and Joe Sweet. Maybe both deaths were what they appeared to be, natural causes. She forced herself to breathe. "I hope you'll tell me. While my main focus is on the fund raiser, I've been helping Paul look for the truth about what happened in Jerome seventy years ago."

"It's not a pretty story. I'm ashamed for my grandfather." Jimmy got to his feet and went to a five-tier display cabinet. He picked up a tiny figurine from a shelf of similar figurines and brought it to Marty. "Take a look at this. It's white jade."

Marty turned the three-inch dragon in her hand.

"Dragons represent good luck in Chinese lore."

She looked up at him. "You're telling me your grandfather had good luck?"

"No. He tried to convince everyone he was lucky in Jerome. Most of all himself, I suspect. He collected symbols of luck from all over the world."

Marty decided to ask. "If it wasn't luck, how did he amass his fortune?"

"He ran an opium den in the downstairs room of his restaurant."

Marty blinked. She was prepared to hear Shen Wong was a murderer, but somehow this revelation was worse.

"That's the first time I've said those words out loud." Jimmy ran his fingers through his gray hair. "Now that I've admitted the truth, I've got to decide what to do with it." Turning away, he walked to the window and looked out.

"I hope you'll help Aurora when the time comes."

He nodded distractedly but didn't turn.

After a moment Marty decided their meeting was over. She picked up her bag and got to her feet. Placing the little dragon on the beautiful table Shen Wong had built during the years he was providing opium to addicts, she left his grandson alone with the consequences.

As she walked down the quiet hall past the closed bamboo doors, she realized they only had one suspect left. Frank Sanchez had to be the murderer. And Paul was with him.

Marty began to hurry. When she was in her pickup, she pulled her cell from her bag. A tiny red three told her she'd had calls while her phone was silenced, but whoever it was would have to wait. She called Paul.

"Marty! Thank goodness. I've been trying to reach you."

"Where are you? I'll get the police."

"You need the police at Wong's office?"

Marty took a deep breath. "We're talking at cross purposes. I'm fine. How are you?"

"Listen to me, Marty, you've got to get out of there. Jimmy Wong is the only suspect left. He's the murderer."

"It isn't Frank Sanchez?"

"No."

"How sure are you?"

266

"I'm certain. Where are you, Marty? Where's Wong?"

Marty rolled down the window of her pickup. Even in March, sun coming through glass could heat up a car in the desert. "I'm in my pickup. Jimmy is in his office. He wants to make a donation to get the fund raiser back on track. He told me his grandfather's story, and it's uglier than murdering a miner to steal his claim."

"I don't follow you."

"Shen Wong ran an opium den."

Paul whistled. "It looks like we're out of suspects."

"Have we got this all wrong?"

"No. After I finished interviewing Frank and his great-uncle, I took a chunk of the ore we found to the geology lab at the university. A grad student working there told me it's quartz with silver spider veins. The mossy yellow substance is calaverite-an ore rich in silver and gold. Scott definitely found what's left of the silver lode."

"Then those bones really are Manuel Reyes."

"Have to be. Enrique was right about what happened to his brother. Combine that with the fact that Manuel's partner, Franco Sanchez, was too scared to ever talk about what happened to Manuel, and we've got as strong a case for murder as I think you'd get seventy years after the fact without a signed confession. Add in the kidnappers' demand to stop gathering information, and we've just about got proof Enrique and Joe were murdered."

Marty studied the four sculptured horses leaping in the fountain that was the center of the square. The energy rippling through their bronze muscles gave her the impression of a stampede, like the stampede of information they were caught in. She shook off the fanciful thought and put the key into the ignition. "We're out of suspects. What do we do now?"

"We have the location of the silver lode, that burned-out building."

Marty put her phone on speaker and started the pickup. "I thought you didn't find anything useful when you went through the rubble."

"I didn't. I want to find out what that building was and who owned it. It wasn't a private home, so it must have been a hotel or a rooming house. The problem is finding town records. Have you ever visited the historical society?"

Marty pulled into the traffic headed for the loop that connected to I-17. "They do the best they can, but it's overwhelming if you're looking for something specific. Call Pat. If anyone can find something in there, she can. Do you have her number?"

"We exchanged cards at Enrique's celebration of life."

"What about the letter Alex turned in with his assignment? It's on letterhead."

"Yes. Not decipherable, but even if it were, I don't have it. Whoever broke into my office took it. The other letters Enrique had are gone. We're dealing with a thorough cover-up."

Marty put on her turn signal and merged into the access lane for the freeway. She felt like the faceless murderer had them boxed in.

Paul said, "Scott told me Carly found the footlocker in the junk shed. It must have come from wherever Manuel was living when he was murdered. Does Carly have records on where any of that junk originated?"

Marty got the green light to enter the freeway. As she accelerated, she said, "I'll call her and ask. But a word of caution, Carly considers that junk to be antiques of lesser value than the furniture but still worth something. If you want her help, remember that."

"Okay. But does she have records?"

"I don't know. The house belonged to Carly's grandmother. A lot of the contents of the shed were there when I bought it, so I'm guessing the footlocker was out there too. Whether Carly's grandmother kept records and whether Carly has them, I have no idea."

"You call Carly," Paul said. "I'll call Pat."

"Meet at my house in two hours. If we each get the same information from different sources, we'll know for sure who we're dealing with." Marty paused. She was about to add, "I love you, Paul" when the connection ended.

33

S cott woke with his pulse pounding in his temples. At least he thought he was awake. The problem was he couldn't see. He tried pushing the sheet out of his eyes, but his hands were tied together. And his ankles. Gradually what he thought was a nightmare resolved into memory. The tunnel under the burned-out house. The calaverite that meant silver and gold. The bones in the box.

Scott shuddered. As much as he wished the box was a nightmare, he knew it was as real as the locked door or the granola bar. He remembered using his backpack as a pillow and thinking he'd never be able to sleep. But he had because the door screeching like a banshee woke him. He remembered being happy it was his dad and confused when it wasn't. The light in his eyes made it impossible to see who had come.

Scott decided to move. He rolled from his back to his right side, banging his knees against a wall. He maneuvered to his back again. The cold floor wasn't carpet or tile. Wood maybe, but not a polished hardwood floor. The rest of his memory of the night before was fuzzy, but Scott continued the replay, looking for a clue.

He was trying to decide how to duck away from the light when his tormentor showed him the gun. A hand inside a heavy work glove holding an old pistol, the gun that killed Manuel. He knew in his gut that was the gun, but whoever was holding it moved too fast to be as old as Manuel's murderer would be.

A man or a woman? A little taller than he was, so a short man or a tall woman. Not a word spoken. Always that gun, pointing or prodding. Walking in the dark wasn't easy. He fell a few times, only to be kicked by a heavy hiking boot.

His captor had brought a ladder, so getting out of the basement was easy. He thought about making a run for it, but the gun was poking him in the back all the way to the top. The rain was coming down hard, making it almost as dark outside as it was in the tunnel.

Then the SUV, so covered with mud he couldn't be sure of the color when the flashlight slid across the side. Shoved into the back seat. The disgusting sweet smell of the handkerchief held over his face. He must have passed out because he didn't remember anything between the handkerchief and this headache.

Scott had no idea how long or the direction they'd driven. He didn't even know how his captor got him out of the SUV to wherever he was now. He couldn't have walked, so it had to be a man, a strong, short man. Scott scanned his memory for a face to go with that body. Maybe his gym teacher. But what would Mr. Becker have to do with the silver lode?

Scott gave up. Thinking crazy was worse than not thinking at all. But no wonder he couldn't think. Besides the demon with the jackhammer in his head, he was lying on a sheet of ice. He decided to move again.

He tried turning to his left side. That was the way he always got out of bed. Maybe it was a nightmare after all. He knew it wasn't, but he liked hoping. This time he encountered space that stretched out farther than his feet. At least he wasn't in a closet.

"What you doing over there, wiggling like a fish on a hook?"

Not Mr. Becker, but definitely a man. "I'm uncomfortable. How about untying my hands?"

The laugh wasn't real, more like a grunt of satisfaction. "Next you'd be asking me to let you remove the blindfold, and that wouldn't be a good idea. You don't want to wind up like Manuel Reyes, do you?"

Scott's mouth felt like it was stuffed with cotton balls. Could he be talking to the murderer? He swallowed and did a swift calculation. His dad told him Manuel would be ninety if he'd lived. His murderer was at least as old as Manuel, probably older. That meant if this was the killer, he was over ninety.

Scott swallowed. "How old are you, sir?"

This time it was a real laugh, but the sound made the hair on the back of Scott's neck stand up.

"Ninety-six."

Scott's stomach flopped the way it always did before he vomited. He took a deep breath and did his best to let it out slow like his mom taught him. Instead it came out in a whoosh. He tried again. He couldn't throw up. The man probably wouldn't let him clean up the mess. The idea of lying in a pool of his own vomit almost made him throw up. He thought about riding his bike on the path that followed the Verde River. He imagined the little rapid that wasn't much more than bubbling water. That's what he needed, a drink of water.

Scott did his best to keep his voice from shaking. "Sir, could I have a glass of water?"

"I ain't going to feed it to you like I was your daddy."

More like his great-great-grandfather. The thought stiffened Scott's spine. He was young and strong, and he could take an old man easy. "If you untie my hands so I can drink, I promise I won't take off the blindfold."

Scott heard a chair creak and footsteps that sounded like the heels of cowboy boots. Who was this guy? A door opened, and a tiny current of air colder than the floor brushed Scott's face. If he was that close to the refrigerator, this had to be a small room.

The sounds repeated in reverse order. The refrigerator door closed, shutting off the cold air. Manuel's murderer stomped the short distance and jerked Scott up to a sitting position.

"Scoot over and lean on the wall you hit with your knees."

A kick from a sharp toe propelled him in the right direction. Scott swallowed the complaint that threatened to erupt. It was slow going with his hands and feet tied, but at least he didn't have far to wriggle.

When he was sitting with his back to the wall, Manuel's murderer leaned over and undid the knot in the rope that rubbed so painfully on his wrists. The old man smell he associated with Grandpa Joiner engulfed him. Where the faint odor always meant safety before, now it meant danger.

Thinking of a faceless man made him extra scary, so Scott imagined a person to go with what he knew. Cowboy boots meant jeans, probably as old as the man and ragged around the hems. Grandpa always complained about it being cold in the house, even when it wasn't. This room was cold, so the old man was wearing a heavy shirt, wool or flannel. Maybe a coat.

What about the face and hair? Grandpa didn't shave often enough. Since he couldn't see the white stubble, he thought no one else could see it either. Manuel's murderer was older, so Scott imagined a white beard. No doubt he was bald.

The image Scott now had in his head made the surprise kick less threatening, the bad temper of a broken-down old coot. "Here's a bottle of water."

The bottle practically hit Scott in the face, but at least he knew where it was. He took a long drink. The cold water tasted better than anything he'd ever put in his mouth.

"Drink up, but don't try any tricks. Remember, I've got my gun."

Scott didn't need to be reminded. And he didn't want the guy so focused on the gun he decided to use it. He had to get this murderer talking and keep him talking. He said, "Did you grow up in Jerome?"

No reply. Scott waited. He couldn't see why that question would bother the old man. He tried again. "I mean, were you born in Jerome?"

"Yes."

"Was your dad a miner?"

"No. He hated mining, said it was grimy. That's the word he always used, grimy."

"If he hated mining, how did you live?"

"Two can play twenty questions, kid. My turn. What was the structure over the mine tunnel?"

"A hotel."

"Close. What makes you say that?"

"I saw bits of bed frames."

"Think again. What else would have beds besides a hotel? And before you guess, I'll tell you it wasn't a brothel. My father never admitted it, but he brought my mother home from one of those." The old man cackled. "Then he married her. Imagine that! And my old man thought mining was grimy."

The idea of his mom in one of those places made Scott's face burn.

"You're thinking she wasn't a very nice mother, but you're wrong. She was a great mother. It wasn't her fault the church ladies and the city council kicked her out of town. What was Pa supposed to do? He couldn't leave his business and follow her."

The old man's voice dropped almost to a whisper. "I wanted to go with her, but Pa said no. In the end, she agreed with him. What kind of life would that be for a six-year-old kid?"

"It's hard not having a mother," Scott said. "Mine died three years ago." He could have kicked himself. He and this old murderer weren't anything alike.

"Makes you tough losing your mother. That's a good thing.

Makes you learn how to take what you want since ain't nobody going to give it to you."

Was he getting tough? Scott hoped not. Having Marty in the family was starting to grow on him. He tried a different subject. "If the building wasn't a hotel or one of those other places, what was it?"

"You guess, kid. And if you're too stupid to figure it out, I just might have to kick you in the head to help you think."

At least the old man wasn't still talking about the gun. Scott thought back to what he knew of Jerome's history. The miners didn't make much money, so they couldn't rent an apartment. The poorest of them rented a bed for eight hours and then went back out on the street or more likely to a bar. What did the ones who had a little more money do? "A boarding house," he guessed. "Your daddy rented rooms to the miners."

"Just rooms, no board. No one to cook, so they were on their own for food."

Scott thought the old guy was relaxing. He decided to try to sneak up on the question he needed an answer to. "I don't know if your partner told you or not—"

"My partner?" the old man hooted. "That's a good one. I never had no partner. If I decide to do something, I do it. If I need someone to do part of the work, I'm in charge."

"Sorry. I meant your helper."

The old man snorted. "If you want to call a greedy, power-hungry daughter a helper."

Daughter? Scott thought a man brought him from the tunnel. If it was a woman, she was tall. What tall woman...

"You're thinking too much, kid. Did I say something to make you think?"

A shiver ran down Scott's spine. He had to change the subject to something that would get the old man's attention. He could figure out who the daughter was later. "I was wondering if I should tell you I saw the silver lode."

"How do you know you saw it?"

"I'm going to be a geologist one day."

"Maybe. Maybe not."

Scott ignored the threat. They didn't plan to kill him. Why else would the old guy keep him blindfolded? "I saw enough of what was left to guess it wasn't as big as the Comstock Lode, but I bet it was pretty big."

"Big enough to make me a wealthy man and then some."

"What was that tunnel? It looked like it led up to the United Verde."

"Yep. In the old days, some of the roomers dug it so they could go in at night and put in overtime, if you know what I mean." The old man laughed. "Pa let 'em do it, long as they paid him extra. Worked out fine."

"Then Manuel Reyes saw something sparkle in that bend, didn't he?"

"Nah. That was after Pa was dead. When I was twenty, Pa went and got himself killed in a bar fight. I was planning on leaving Jerome, but there was that rooming house making decent money."

The murderer paused like Grandpa Joiner did when he was remembering. Finally he said, "It was war time and the mines were selling copper at all-time high prices. I raised the rent and collected my share. The market for copper was slowing down when Manuel saw that silver in the wall of the old tunnel."

"It was the mineral calaverite, wasn't it? Silver and gold."

The old man whistled. "You do know a thing or two, don't you, kid? You know what they say, 'A little knowledge is a dangerous thing.' Might be extra dangerous for you."

This time Scott kept quiet, but the old guy had started telling his story.

"The Reyes kid spotted the calaverite. He thought no one knew, but I heard him telling his partner, Sanchez. So when those two were gone on a shift, I went down there and looked. I grew up on stories of the Comstock Lode. Course it gave out forty years before I was born, but some of the old-timers knew about it. They kept dreaming of finding a silver lode here in Cleopatra Hill."

The chair legs scraped on the floor, and Scott heard the old man stand up. He walked a few steps, making the floor creak.

"When I saw that calaverite, I decided my pa had been too generous with his roomers. The deposit was on my property. That night I told Reyes and Sanchez to meet me in the tunnel. When I told Reyes to clear out, he gave me guff."

The old man walked a few more steps, like he was nervous or excited. "I wasn't in the mood for talking, so I shot him with this gun I'm pointing at you, kid. I let Sanchez get away because I knew he was too scared to talk. Now it's time for you to be too scared to talk."

34

Paul wanted a cup of coffee. After his meeting with Lorenzo and Frank Sanchez, he'd been certain Jimmy Wong was the murderer. And with over an hour between where he was and where Jimmy and Marty were, he hadn't known how to protect her. He was beyond grateful she was safe, but after a serious scare he needed coffee. He'd call Pat while he sipped.

Pat wasn't at the savings and loan. Her assistant didn't know where she was or if she'd be back before Monday. And Pat wasn't answering her cell phone. He left what he hoped was an urgent, though not hysterical, plea for a return call. He texted her, asking for help with historical records of property ownerships. No reply.

With or without Pat's help, Paul was determined to find out who had owned the burned-out building over the silver lode. If he had to do it without records, he knew an oral history source who might have the information in his head, Bernie Lyons. Paul had a good idea he'd find Bernie at the grill on Main Street in Jerome, a favorite hang-out until the flood of summer tourists curious about the ghost town overwhelmed the four hundred locals.

He was exiting the freeway to head for Jerome when his phone chirped, letting him know he had a text message. Pat was getting back to him just in time. He pulled off the road into an empty lot beside a gas station and checked the caller ID. No name, no phone number. Three numbers, a dash, and two numbers. The beginning of a message, "You haven't canceled the fund raiser. We're…"

He clicked on the message. "…running out of patience and Scott is running out of time."

Was there more than one of them? Or maybe it was a trick to make him think he was up against a gang. He typed his own text message. "Nothing happens until I talk to Scott."

The reply was quick. "Call 928-170-2235."

No doubt a burner phone, but Paul didn't waste an instant. He heard the number ring once, twice. Scott's voice said, "Is this my father? They said my father was going to call me."

"It's me, Scott. Are you okay?"

"You're the best father—" The call dropped.

Another text message from a different sequence of five numbers came in. "Stop your search. No more talk about the Reyes family. Cancel fund raiser on radio. Twelve hours."

Paul texted, "Give me a guarantee Scott will be safe."

The response was quick. "Call blocked."

Paul looked at his watch, eleven a.m. They, whoever they were, would be listening to the public service announcements at the end of the ten-p.m. news. Dropping the phone on the passenger's seat, he pounded the steering wheel until his hands went numb. Squeezing his eyes shut, he silently shouted, *Keep Scott safe, Father! If someone dies, let it be me.*

As he started to open his door, the blare of a car horn halted him. He pulled the door shut and leaned his head on the steering wheel. He had to get control of his emotions. It wouldn't do

Scott any good for him to die here on the highway from sheer stupidity.

Closing his eyes, he breathed, *Father, you know how scared I am. I know You've got Scott in Your hands. Help me remember You've got me in Your hands too. Give me a clear head and a direction to go.*

Using the backs of his throbbing hands, he wiped away the tears running down his face. Then, checking to make sure no vehicles were coming, he opened his door and got out. As he started walking along the shoulder, he remembered his cell phone. They had contacted him once. He couldn't afford to miss another call, so he turned around. As soon as his cell was tucked in his pocket, he started moving. Running at first, then slowing to a jog, finally walking.

When his heart stopped hammering in his ears, he turned around and walked back toward the Jeep. They had to make a public announcement on the radio that the fund raiser had been canceled and people's money would be returned. He knew Marty would agree.

Alex would be hurt, but he'd promise Alex to find another way to get the money for Aurora. Take out a personal loan from the Osborn Savings and Loan, ask Pat to not charge him interest, get Scott to show him how to set up a Go-Fund-Me account. One way or another, they would make it work.

But he wasn't giving up the search for who was behind all of this, and the key was that burned-out building. He was about to turn on the engine when his phone rang again. Snatching it from the seat beside him, he checked the caller ID. Alex Reyes.

As he answered, he inhaled a steadying breath. This wasn't a time for Alex to pick up on the stress he was under. "Hello, Alex. It's good to hear from you."

No response.

"Alex, are you there?"

"I'm here." Alex's voice was husky as if he, too, had been

crying. At the moment it seemed as if everyone he knew was worried about someone special.

"How is Aurora?" *Please, Father, let that child live.*

"She's in the hospital. On life support. The heart surgeon says her time is running out. We're praying for a compatible donor heart."

The young man paused then rushed on. "It's awful, Dr. Russell. The only way to get a heart for Aurora is for another child to die. When we pray for Aurora to get a new heart, we're praying for a child to die somewhere."

Paul's mind was blank. It was true. The complications of the situation were beyond his grasp, beyond the grasp of any person. If a young man in his late teens was terrified, what must Aurora's parents be going through? "How are your brother and sister-in-law holding up?"

"That's why I'm calling. They asked me if you would start the fund raiser early by going on the radio and asking for donations. It's not them so much as it is Aurora."

"I don't understand. Aurora wants me to go on the radio?"

"Hold on."

Paul heard Alex blow his nose.

When the young man came back, his voice was steadier. "You have to understand, Dr. Russell. Aurora is only four, but she knows a lot of things about life. She knows about God and dying and heaven. She knows more than I do, and I'm almost twenty."

Alex cleared his throat.

Paul said gently, "So you think she understands about the fund raiser?"

"No. Not that. But she knows it costs money to be in the hospital. And she knows her dad is worrying about money. She sees right through her mom's cheerful talk. She knows her mom is at the end of her rope. Aurora told me today she was ready to go to heaven because her parents could be happy again if they didn't have to worry about her so much."

Paul's heart ached for the little girl and her parents. Most kids understood more than adults thought they did, but Alex was right. His little niece understood even more than most children.

Paul said, "You think jump-starting the fund raiser will give everyone a dose of hope to keep them going."

"Yes! If you go on the radio, all their friends will hear about it and strangers who have had sick children will hear. Even if we don't get that much money, knowing that other people care will let Hernando and Belinda feel less alone."

Father, breathed Paul, *I need the wisdom of Solomon.* He had to decide not between two mothers but between two children. "I'll check into it. You'll hear from me no later than tomorrow morning." The instant he had Scott back.

Paul ended the call and placed one to Marty. She answered on the first ring. "Are you driving?" he said.

"You're on speaker. What's up?"

"Change of plans, at least for me. I got a second ransom call."

He heard her quick intake of breath. He said quickly, "I talked to Scott. Not for long, but it was his voice. He's okay for now."

"But they want something else. What now?"

"A radio announcement, no later than the end of the late news. I have eleven hours to find Scott."

"So we announce it's canceled on the five o'clock news, get Scott back, and find another way to raise the money the Reyes family needs. Maybe someday we'll solve Manuel's murder and get the silver lode money as Enrique hoped, but for now we let that source drop."

"It's more complicated than that. Alex called. Aurora is in critical condition, and her parents are under more stress than they can handle. Alex asked me to go on the radio and jump-start the fund raiser to give the family enough hope to keep going."

"Oh, Paul! How can we make that decision?"

"I refuse to decide between two children," Paul said grimly. "The only option is to find Scott. Finding out who owned that burned-out hotel is the only lead we have left. I'm going to Jerome to track down an old-timer I interviewed a couple of days ago. I'll be at your place as soon as I get the information we need." He ended the call.

Paul headed for Jerome. He had no idea where Bernie Loomis lived, but if the old man wasn't at the grill, he'd find someone who could take him to Bernie's house.

35

Marty opened the back door and went into the kitchen. Carly wasn't at the table with a notebook as she'd hoped. "Carly? I'm home!"

No answer. Marty dropped her shoulder bag on the table and went into the workshop. No Carly there or in the showroom. "Carly?"

A faint answer floated down from somewhere above her head. The girl couldn't be in her bedroom! Marty was positive she'd made it clear finding Scott depended on those records. Marty went upstairs, not sure whether she was angry or disappointed. But Carly wasn't in her own room or her brother's room. "Carly?"

"In the attic!"

Marty looked around, mystified. She hadn't known there was an attic, much less how to access it. She looked at the ceiling and called, "How do I get up there?"

"Pull down...bathroom."

Marty got the gist. A pull-down ladder filled the entire floor space in the tiny bathroom. Marty started up the narrow steps.

"I've found something," Carly said. "Not what we're looking for yet, but I'm getting close. Help me look."

As cool as it was outside, the attic was warm and stuffy. Dust motes drifted in crisscross rays of early afternoon light coming through a gable vent. Carly was kneeling beside a hope chest, inexpensive in its day and not worth much more today. The girl looked up, her blue eyes sparkling. "Got it!"

"You found where the footlocker came from?"

"Not yet. But I found my great-grandmother's account books." Carly began taking spiral notebooks out of the chest and stacking them on the floor beside her.

"Great-grandma worked in Jerome cleaning for wealthy folks. Sometimes business owners called her to clear out items left behind in hotels and rooming houses. The information has got to be in one of these notebooks!"

Marty climbed the last few steps into the attic and threaded her way around boxes of books and stacks of ancient fabric. Except for the hope chest and a child's highchair, she didn't see much furniture. But she was glad she'd found the attic. Unless she wanted a fire this summer when temperatures heated up, she needed to clear every bit of this out.

Marty picked up one of the notebooks. No way to tell what it was until she opened to the first page, January-December 1922. "These can't all have belonged to your great-grandmother, Carly! I don't know when she was born, but she couldn't have been old enough to work in 1922."

Carly shrugged. "I think her mother started the cleaning business. I found one notebook that's dated 1911."

"How many notebooks are there?"

"Close to forty."

"Are they in any order at all?"

"Not that I can see. They were just all piled in here."

Marty closed her eyes. Forty notebooks, each one having to be opened to find out what year it covered. Opening her eyes, she started picking them up. "We should be grateful to have all of this. What we need is bound to be in here somewhere. Let's get these downstairs where we can see what we've got."

Carly handed Marty a stack of notebooks. Marty carried them to the top of the ladder and set them on the floor. "I'll go down and you can hand them to me. Maybe in groups of ten."

"You've got it."

The process didn't take as long as Marty had been afraid it would. As they carried the notebooks into the kitchen, she said, "Organize them in ten groups of four. That way we don't have to worry about stacks getting top-heavy and falling over."

When the notebooks were organized, each of them took a stack and started opening to the first page to find the date. "Put them in decades," Marty said. "1910-19 in one chair, 1920-29 in another chair, and so on. 1950 or later go on the table."

They'd gone through about half of the notebooks when Carly said, "1951! Isn't that the year we're looking for?"

"1950 or 51. I've got 1950."

Clearing two chairs of notebooks, they sat down at the table. Carly said, "We're looking for Manuel's footlocker, right?"

"Yes, but I doubt it will have the name. Make a note of anything identified as trunk, box, or footlocker. But don't write in the notebook."

Marty reached for the magnetized tablet from the refrigerator and tore off two blank sheets. "Tear this into bookmarks. Write the word you find on the sheet and mark the place. You may not realize it, Carly, but the women who kept these notebooks qualify for sainthood in the antique world. Being able to authenticate the origin of a piece raises the value immensely. What was your great-grandmother's first name?"

"I think it was Mildred."

"Okay, Saint Mildred," Marty said, "help us find what we need to know."

Marty opened the notebook. Four pages into the faded

looping script she saw the words she was hoping for, miner's footlocker. Instead of announcing her find, Marty wanted to close the notebook and leave it for Paul. Absurd. Still, she had to force her finger to move across the page past the date, April 19, to the place Saint Mildred had picked up the footlocker. When she saw the name, she almost cried out. Osborn Rooming House.

Across the table, Carly closed the notebook she'd been reading. "Nothing in here. Marty? Are you okay?"

Keeping her finger on the line, Marty closed the notebook. She wasn't ready to tell Carly. "I have a headache, probably from the heat in the attic."

"How about a bottle of cold water?"

Marty nodded. She wanted Paul to come bursting through the door with a different name, any name but this one. It had to be a mistake. Saint Mildred mixed up her boarding houses. Pat couldn't be the murderer. She slid a bookmark in the page and closed the notebook.

Carly handed her the water and reached for the spiral notebook. "Do you want me to finish that? The writing is hard to read."

Marty shook her head. "I'll wait for Paul. He'll be here soon." How she hoped that was true.

"I think I hear a car. Maybe that's him now." Carly's phone played its merry jig. The girl glanced at the ID and then at Marty. "Mind if I take this? It's a friend I've been playing phone tag with all day."

Marty heard a car door slam. It had to be the Jeep. "We're done for now. Thanks for your help."

"I'll be in my room. Give a shout if you need me." Then she was gone, talking even faster than usual.

Marty heard a tap at the door. Everything was going to be fine. Paul had found another name. In a few minutes they'd be laughing at her suspicions. "Come in!"

The door opened, and Paul stood framed in the doorway. She

gave him a hopeful look. He shook his head and said, "I'm sorry. I know you and Pat were becoming friends."

"I couldn't believe it when I saw Osborn Rooming House in Carly's great-grandmother's records."

"Let's make certain we're not jumping to a wrong conclusion."

As she sat down, she said, "Tell me how you found out."

"My oral history source in Jerome, Bernie Loomis, knew all about the fire that burned down the Osborn Rooming House."

Her throat closed up. No mistake. Confirmed by two independent sources. But how could Pat be the murderer? She liked Pat.

"Think back," Paul said. "You went to see Pat about a fund raiser the same day we saw Enrique. That was Thursday. Enrique was killed Friday night."

"Pat gave me the names of our suspects."

"And she gave me the information that made us question how those three families made their fortunes."

"But we never thought to ask where her family fortune came from." Marty closed her eyes. She didn't have to connect the rest of the dots this instant. "Pat won't hurt Scott," she said. "We'll get him back."

"Not we. I'm doing this alone, Marty. I'm Scott's father. You're my friend."

For answer, she got to her feet and went to him. Hugging him around the neck, she said, "I love you and Scott, Paul. If you'll forgive me for pushing you away, we'll get him back together."

He was silent for so long she wondered if she'd lost her chance with him. Finally, he got to his feet and drew her close. At least they were still friends.

Carly reappeared in the doorway, still holding her cell phone. "Reed's on the phone. I told him you found something you didn't want me to know, so it must be bad."

As they stepped away from each other, Carly came to a full stop. "Sorry."

"It's okay," Marty said.

"Reed and I want to help."

Paul gave Marty a look she understood, No help! He said to Carly, "Let me talk to Reed."

She handed him the phone. As he went out the back door, Marty said, "I have a way you can help, Carly."

"Anything!"

"You may not like what I have in mind, but you're the only person who can do it."

"Try me."

"Stay here and give us a cover story."

Carly looked disappointed. "You're taking Reed and leaving me behind?"

"No one is coming with us. Paul will explain to Reed. I need you to stay here."

"I could be another pair of eyes. I promise I'll keep my mouth shut."

"That's not it, Carly. If I leave the house and someone comes by, they'll know immediately that something is off."

"It's someone we know, and you don't want to tell me."

Marty shrugged. "The important thing is that I need you to make sure anyone, no matter who, believes I'm off on a legitimate errand. I give you permission to be as creative as you like. Say anything short of Paul and I ran off to get married. Understood?"

Carly brightened. "I can do that."

"Good. Remember, this goes for Bill too."

Carly looked surprised. "Why Bill?"

"The fewer people who know we're going to get Scott, the better. Bill wouldn't say anything on purpose, but he might accidentally let something slip."

Carly frowned. "Okay. What else?"

"Take notes on who calls and what they want. Pump without being obvious. I'll check in with you frequently to find out what's going on. But no matter what…"

Marty put a hand on each side of Carly's face to make sure she was listening with her eyes as well as her ears. "No matter what, don't call me. Under any circumstances. If the house is burning down, call the fire department. Do not call me!"

The girl nodded, and Marty let her go.

"It's important, Carly. I can't have my phone ringing. I can't have it vibrate or take a text. I don't have any idea what's going to happen in the next few hours, but it may get ugly. You have to do your part."

"Understood." Carly raised her hand like a girl scout taking a pledge. "I promise to do everything you say."

Marty gave her a quick hug. "One more thing. Pray for us. Pray hard."

36

Paul opened the passenger door of the Jeep for Marty. She said, "What did you tell Reed?"

"That I need him to stay at the house and cover for me. I told him if anyone comes by, he's got to do his best to find out everything possible without making it appear he's grilling them."

Marty climbed into the Jeep. "That's about what I told Carly."

"It's important at both our houses." Paul closed her door and went around to the driver's side. As he got behind the wheel he said, "I tried to call Pat again. I didn't expect her to answer, but I thought I might as well try. No go. We know she's with Scott. If we can just find out where!"

"Joanie, Pat's assistant, might know something. She gave me her card. It has her work number and her cell number."

"I doubt she'll be in the office after seven p.m. but try there first. We don't want her to realize how alarmed we are."

Marty punched in the number and then put the phone on speaker. It rang once, twice.

"Osborn Savings and Loan. This is Joan. How may I help you?"

"This is Marty Greenlaw. I don't know if you remember me."

"Of course, I remember you, Marty. We're closed, though. I'm just tying up a few loose ends."

"I'm looking for Pat. Is she there?"

"She hasn't been in the office since yesterday. She called in with a migraine."

"I tried her cell. She didn't answer."

"When she has one of those headaches, she turns her phone off. She can't bear the slightest sound."

Paul touched Marty's hand. When she looked at him, he mouthed, "Not home."

"I'm sure Pat's not home," Marty said. "Do you have any idea where else I can look for her?"

Joanie didn't speak, no doubt offended that Marty would contradict her. He mouthed, "About Scott."

"It's about Dr. Russell's son, Scott," Marty said. "He's missing, and I think Pat might have been the last person to see him. We need to find her. Please, does she have any family in the area, a brother or sister, a cousin, a best friend?"

"I heard something on the radio yesterday about a search for the boy. Since there hasn't been a follow-up, I assumed he'd been found."

As we hoped, Paul thought.

"Has he been kidnapped?"

Paul shook his head, mouthed, "Friend."

Marty said, "Oh no, nothing like that. We think he's with a friend. It's important that we talk with Pat, though. I'm sure she knows who Scott is with."

"Miss Pat's alone in this world except for her father."

Paul's heart kicked into overdrive.

Marty gave Paul a horrified look. "Pat Osborn's father is still living? Surely he'd be in his nineties."

"He would at that. He moved to Florida shortly after Pat's husband died. Come to think of it, it's been a while since she's gone to see him, but I never heard her talk about a funeral."

Marty looked at Paul. "Name."

"Didn't you say you started working at the savings and loan before Mr. Osborn retired?"

"I did. Mr. Ralph hired me about the time Miss Pat became the chief financial officer."

Paul touched Marty's arm, mouthed, "Somewhere he might stay."

"So you knew him well. Did Mr. Osborn have a home here?"

"Just the house Miss Pat lives in."

Paul mouthed, "A friend, a hotel, a cabin."

"How about a friend he might have stayed with or a cabin in the woods?"

Joanie was quiet for a moment. Then she said, "Now that you mention it, I do believe Ralph had a hunting cabin where he liked to go. But I'm sure it hasn't been used in years."

"Do you know where it is?"

"Sorry, honey. I never went there, but it's around here, in the Prescott National Forest."

Paul almost groaned aloud. The forest was crisscrossed with fire break roads and deer trails large enough to drive a Jeep down. He signaled to Marty to disconnect.

She took the phone off speaker and held it up to her ear. "Thanks for talking to me, Joanie."

Paul started the engine, twisted in his seat to see, and began backing out of the driveway. "They must have Scott at that hunting cabin."

"I agree. I don't know the forest at all, but I know it's too big to drive through looking for a hunting cabin. Would the county assessor's office have a record?"

"I doubt it. I don't imagine hunting cabins were recorded. Even if they were, government offices usually close by four.

However, I know Bernie Loomis, the oral history source I told you about, might be able to help." *Please, Father. Help me find Bernie. Help him remember this detail.*

"Bernie's short-term memory gets a little fuzzy now and then, but his mind is sharp as a tack when it comes to stories of old Jerome. Hunting was important for subsistence during the ghost town days in the 1960s. I imagine the residents knew where every hunting cabin was and who came and went. Maybe to use when the owner wasn't around."

Out of the corner of his eye, he saw Marty yawn. She tried to cover it, but he could guess how exhausted she must be.

She yawned again. "Sorry."

"Lean that seat back and take a quick nap. It's been a stressful couple of days, and I have a feeling it's going to get much worse before we get Scott back."

"How are we going to do it, Paul? I don't feel strong enough or brave enough for what I'm afraid is ahead of us tonight."

Paul didn't have an answer for her. He said slowly, "When I'm facing something I know is bigger than my strength, I repeat Philippians 4:13 three times, adapted a bit. 'I can do all things through Christ who strengthens me,' even find Scott and bring him home…"

Paul checked the clock again. It was seven-thirty. "…in the next two and a half hours to meet the ten-p.m. news deadline."

As she let her seat back, Marty murmured, "How about this adaptation of that verse? We can do all things through Christ who strengthens us, even find Scott in time."

37

P aul pulled the Jeep onto a secondary road that was quickly disappearing under the large, wet snowflakes drifting lazily to the ground. The rain had stopped in the Verde Valley. They were at least a thousand feet higher here, but still, snow?

The road wasn't the only thing disappearing. Their tracks were covered almost as quickly as the wheels made them. And the snow muted all sound. Maybe it would help them. They needed all the help they could get, even from the weather.

It was nine p.m. They had a little over an hour to find Scott and get him back before Pat and Ralph Osborn discovered that instead of canceling the fund raiser, they were announcing two pledges that came to a half million dollars and asking more people to pledge—to the Reyes family.

"If I'm reading the map Bernie drew for you right," Marty said, "it's the next road."

"Good. I want to walk from here. I'm not sure how far it is, and I don't want the sound of the Jeep to alert them." Paul found an opening that was probably part of a deer trail and pulled as far off the road as he could. The Jeep would be covered with snow in minutes.

Marty was pulling Scott's yellow poncho over her head. "You're sure Ralph Osborn is alive and here at the cabin. Did Bernie know something about him?"

"No. Scott told me."

"You heard from Scott! Why didn't you wake me?"

"I didn't hear from Scott."

"Then what makes you so sure Ralph Osborn is here?"

"The word father. Scott used it three times in the two sentences they let him get out. Scott always calls me dad. He always says I'm a great dad. On the phone he told me I was a wonderful father. That wasn't a slip. He was telling me Pat's father has him captive."

"Okay, but the man has to be in his nineties. Manuel was Enrique's older brother, and Enrique was eighty-six. How dangerous can Ralph be?"

Paul slipped into his own poncho. "Do you remember what Mrs. Arbeck told us happened the night Joe died?"

Marty put her hands on her cheeks. "An old man came to talk to Joe about moving into Enrique's room. You think that was Ralph."

"I do. Remember what Joe said about the night Enrique died?"

"A woman came to inquire about accommodations for her father. You think Pat came to talk to Joe to find out which room was Enrique's and then came back later to kill him?"

"Maybe. Or more likely she kept Joe occupied while Ralph went through the patio door into Enrique's room and held a pillow over his head. And remember, this is the man who murdered Manuel Reyes. If he's got a gun, he's dangerous. No matter how old he is."

Leaving the keys in the ignition, Paul opened his door. "I

want you to stay here, Marty. We may need to get out of here fast, and I need you at the wheel."

Marty reached across and grabbed his arm. "You're not going in there alone. If Ralph has a gun, you need me to watch your back. If Pat's there, I can talk sense into her. She's no killer."

"What I don't need is to be worrying about you, Marty."

"Then don't worry. Just let me help."

Before he could reply, she got out. But she didn't argue when he insisted on going first. He stayed as close to the side of the road as he could without actually knocking the snow off the trees.

Since Bernie couldn't remember anything about the road to the cabin, Paul had no idea whether the cabin was around a bend or in plain sight of the road. He hated their ponchos were red and yellow. But the snow slid right off the synthetic rubber. Good for keeping them dry. Terrible for camouflage.

The cabin, when he spotted it, sat parallel to the road almost surrounded by the forest. Whether it had been built that way or the road had come in later, he had no idea. Whichever, he was grateful. The trees provided enough cover to get them close.

Built from logs and covered with a tin roof, it had a low front porch and two doors, one in front and one in back. Only one window looked out at the road, and unless someone was actually watching out the window, he suspected they could almost knock on either of the two doors before they were spotted.

He was about to move forward another few yards when Marty pulled on his arm. He looked down to see her pointing ahead and to the right. A muscular, red horse stood among the trees, head down against the falling snow.

Marty squatted and motioned for him to do the same. When their heads were even, she cupped her hands around his ear and whispered, "Pat has two horses, this red one and a white one. She rides the white one. Maybe that means Ralph is in there alone with Scott."

Paul took in the information. It explained why they hadn't seen another vehicle anywhere on the road. He nodded. "You stay here. I'm going closer to try to get a look in that window."

She gave him a quick kiss on the cheek and then moved to stand behind a nearby tree. Keeping low, Paul approached the window. What he saw inside made his heart stop.

Ralph Osborn, clean-shaven and with a full head of white hair, looked twenty years younger than his ninety-plus years. Dressed for an upscale rodeo complete with tooled cowboy boots, he sat in a straight-backed chair with a World War II service revolver in his lap. His eyes were closed, but Paul had the sense he was wide awake.

At first Paul didn't see Scott. When he finally spotted his son, his hands clenched into fists. Scott was sitting on the floor in the corner, blindfolded with his hands and feet tied. His son looked miserable. All Paul could think of was doing a flying tackle to topple the old man on the floor. He wanted to untie Scott and tie up Ralph. Let him feel the suffering he was inflicting.

Taking a deep breath, Paul forced his hands to relax. He couldn't let his emotions get the better of him. When this was all over, he'd whale the tar out of the punching bag they kept hanging in the garage. Right now he had to figure out how to get Scott out of there in one piece.

He was about to go back to Marty and make a plan when he heard the distinctive sound of horse's hooves, muffled by the snow but clearly audible. The red horse heard too because it lifted its head and whinnied.

As Paul moved behind the house out of sight, he heard Marty call out, "Pat!"

He wanted to groan. Marty was too sure of that friendship. She'd known Pat one week, and if a murderer had to be good at one thing, it was playing the role of friend to the innocent. He hoped Ralph was the murderer, if you could hope such a thing, but for all they knew, Pat had killed both Enrique and Joe.

Undecided about making his presence known, Paul watched Pat dismount and motion to Marty to follow her as she walked the white horse to stand beside the red one. Then, hands on hips, she turned to Marty. They were too far away for him to hear what was being said, but he could see Pat talking and gesturing while Marty listened.

Then Marty held up her hand. Surprisingly, Pat stopped. Marty talked while Pat shook her head. Finally, Pat pointed at the house and grabbed Marty's hand. As much as he could guess from the body language, Pat was trying to convince Marty everything was fine in the cabin. His gut told him to stay hidden for the moment and watch the scene play out through the window.

Under the cover of the women's entrance to the cabin, Paul moved to the corner where he'd seen Scott. Hoping the wall was thin enough to allow his son to hear, Paul tapped a dash and two dots, Morse code for the letter D.

He didn't remember how old Scott was when they devised a way of communicating their positions. He was D for Dad. Linda was M for Mom. Scott was S, for Son or Scott. They never quite decided since it didn't matter. He held his breath, waiting.

How long since they'd used the code? Not since Linda's death, at least three years. Maybe longer. Paul tried again, a little louder. And waited again. As he was about to give up, he heard what he was waiting for, three dots.

Thank you, Father. Now to get inside and wait for Marty to convince Pat to disarm Ralph. If she accomplished that, he hoped Marty would distract Ralph when she saw what he was up to. He took off the bright red poncho and dropped it in the snow. Better to be wet than a neon target. Making as little sound as possible, he made his way to the back door.

As he eased it open, he heard Pat say, "Father! Why is this boy still tied up? I told you all we needed was to make sure he kept the blindfold on. He's a smart kid. He wouldn't have wanted to see your face. Even if he did, what would it matter? He couldn't possibly know who you are."

Ralph shouted an obscenity about being in charge, and Paul slipped inside. Ralph stood with his back to the door, so Paul didn't worry about him. Marty blinked several times to let Paul know she saw him. He waited for Pat to notice him, but she was focused on her father.

"Father, Marty says two people have been murdered, Enrique and Joe. You promised all you wanted to do was talk to Enrique. I'd never have taken you there if I thought you meant to kill him!"

"Marty says," mocked Ralph. "Marty doesn't know anything. She wasn't there. I was, and I'm telling you he was dead when I walked in that room. A heart attack or a stroke. Who knows? Who cares?"

Without making eye contact with Paul, Marty demanded, "Where are the letters Manuel wrote to the Reyes family?"

Paul covered half the distance between the back door and his son. Ralph jumped to his feet, waving the revolver. For a breathless moment, Paul was sure he was going to turn around. If he'd been a six-foot-two red hulk, Ralph would have noticed him for sure. Maybe the old man's peripheral vision wasn't as good as a younger man's, but in any case, Paul's brown shirt and tan khakis served him well.

Ralph shouted, "How should I know where some old letters are? I'm no historian."

"What about Joe Sweet?" Pat's voice was higher than usual. "Marty says he was poisoned."

Paul covered the last of the distance and bent down to touch his son's head with a gentle hand. Scott started, and Paul saw the ghost of a smile begin. Then Scott forced his face back into a frown.

"You can't know that!" shouted Ralph. "Antifreeze is

untraceable after the first few minutes, and I stayed with Joe until I knew I was safe."

Using his pocketknife, Paul cut through the heavy twine that held Scott's hands together. While he worked on the bulky cord wrapped around his son's ankles, Scott took off the blindfold. He didn't look the slightest bit surprised to see Pat Osborn there with Marty. But then he wouldn't. Scott had put enough of the pieces together to warn him he was dealing with a father.

"Why?" screeched Pat. "Why?"

"Joe tried a little blackmail. I don't pay blackmailers."

Paul helped Scott slowly to his feet. Pat's eyes moved to see them and widened.

Marty shouted, "Ralph Osborn, if you didn't kill Enrique, Joe couldn't blackmail you!"

Ralph whirled toward Marty, waving his gun at her. "I've heard enough out of you!"

Paul put his hand in the middle of Scott's back and pushed gently toward the back door. Scott gave him a look that said, "I don't want to go without you." Paul put a little more pressure on Scott's back, and the boy began to move.

Pat watched but didn't comment. Turning back to her father, she said in a voice empty of all emotion, "You're the devil, Ralph Osborn. I don't care if you're my father or not. I'm going to make sure you spend the rest of your days in prison."

Ralph threw his head back and laughed. "You're thinking too much, daughter. You're getting your facts all mixed up. How are you going to send me to prison for two deaths recorded as natural causes? Or a murder seventy years ago no one ever reported? That'll be a good trick."

As Scott slipped outside, a heavy burden lifted off Paul's shoulders. Now to get Marty out of here safely. He caught her eye and nodded toward the front door. As she took a step back, he took a step sideways.

Her voice almost conversational, Pat said, "I'm not getting

my facts mixed up. I think I'm seeing them clearly for the first time. You've killed everyone I ever loved, starting with my mother."

Ralph snorted. "Your mother was clumsy. She fell down the stairs and broke her neck."

"I was five years old, old enough to understand the fight you had. She was going to leave and take me with her. You told her you'd help her, and then you pushed her."

Marty took two steps back. He took two sideways.

"A year later you ran over Muffy with the car. I loved that kitty. She was all I had of my very own."

"That cat couldn't find her way out of a paper bag. She ran under the wheels of the car."

"She wasn't on the driveway. You had to work to hit her."

Marty was almost to the door. Paul wished it stood open, but at least it wasn't locked. He would create a diversion to cover the moment she'd need to get it open and slip outside. She and Scott could get in the Jeep and get away.

"That cat scratched me one too many times," Ralph said.

"What about John? He never did anything but what you told him to." Pat's voice was higher now, and her words came faster, one almost tripping over the next.

"Mrs. John Brown! What kind of name is that for my daughter?"

"A name I was proud of. Do you know how ashamed I am to be called Osborn? John was a better man than you ever were."

Ralph cackled. "Where is he now? John Brown's body lies moldering in the grave."

Marty had stopped moving, staring in horror at father and daughter. Paul tried to get her attention, let her know this was her chance. But she didn't move.

Tears running down her cheeks, Pat yelled, "John is dead because you killed him!"

"He's dead because he was a bad driver."

"You did something to his car. I know you did!"

Paul shouted, "Now!"

Coming out of her trance, Marty covered the last few feet and flung open the door.

"Where do you think you're going?" Ralph roared.

Already moving toward Ralph, Paul said, "She's going outside because you're going to give me that gun."

Ralph raised the gun and whirled to point it at Paul. "I'll give you a bullet."

Pat threw herself on her father. "I was pregnant!" she screamed. "I lost the baby." Sobbing, she grabbed Ralph's arm as he fired.

The shot went wild, and Paul moved faster. Before he could cover the entire distance, Ralph pushed Pat away and took aim a second time. The walls rushed in until the entire room was concentrated in the barrel of the revolver. Fully expecting to be shot, Paul leapt as if to catch a game-winning pass. As his feet left the floor, he heard the explosion of the gun, a moan, and a heavy thud in such quick succession all three sounds might have been simultaneous.

His feet hit the floor. As he looked around the room, he realized he was the only one standing. Marty was gone. Pat lay unmoving on top of her father. Paul reached for the gun, still in Ralph's hand. He had his hand on it when Ralph jerked it away. With a grunt, the old man untangled himself from his daughter's body. Keeping the gun pointed at Paul's head, Ralph barked, "Get back!"

Paul raised his hands and backed up. He would have another chance as Ralph got to his feet. The old man would have to shift his attention to get his balance. Paul planned to make sure he didn't have that chance.

The front door opened, and Marty rushed in. Almost at the same time, the back door opened, and Scott appeared.

"Who's been shot?" Marty cried. Taking in the scene, she

rushed to Pat and dropped to the floor.

Ralph looked wildly around. "I won't go to prison!" he shouted. Firing a shot over his head, he ran for the front door. Paul started after him.

"Let him go!" Marty cried. "Pat's alive, but she's bleeding. Getting help for her is more important than chasing Ralph. The police will find him."

Paul checked his phone. "No signal. It must be the snow."

"Out by the highway," Scott said. "That's where they took me when you wanted to talk to me. Give me your cell, Dad. I'll go call 911. You help Miss Marty."

Paul pulled his son into a fierce hug. "Watch out for Ralph. I don't think he'll head for the highway, but listen for the horse."

Scott nodded, and Paul thrust the phone into his son's hand. "Ask for the Jerome fire station. They're the closest. Tell whoever answers that we need medical assistance and the sheriff." Jerking off his jacket, he put it around his son's shoulders.

"You need your coat, Dad!"

Marty said, "Help me, Paul. The bullet went into her chest. I think it missed her heart, but she's bleeding faster. Find something to hold over it so we can apply pressure."

"Cloth," Scott said as he dropped Paul's coat on the floor and pulled off his t-shirt. "They taught us in first aid that a t-shirt works best."

Paul took the shirt and picked up the coat. "Put this on and move, buddy. Marty and I can only care for Pat a few minutes."

As Scott raced out the door, Paul tore a hole in the shirt with his teeth. As he ripped off two strips, he said, "Get her sweater away from the wound, so I can see what I'm doing." Rolling the strips into a tight wad, he knelt beside Pat and packed the cloth into the hole.

Marty winced. "Doesn't that hurt her?"

"She's in shock. She doesn't feel anything right now."

Pat said, "I feel light, like I'm floating."

"Hold her hand. Talk to her," Paul said. "She's still losing blood. We have to keep her conscious."

Marty took Pat's hand. "Pat, honey, it's Marty and Paul. You've been shot, but we're getting help."

"I'm so hot," Pat said. "Why am I so hot?"

"You'll feel better soon," Marty said. "I promise."

Paul said, "Help me sit her up. Pray that bullet went all the way through."

"We're going to sit you up now, honey, so Paul can look at your back."

"Don't help us, Pat," Paul said. "Stay limp. Let us do the work." He looked at Marty. "On three. One…Two…Three!" They got her up and Paul looked at her back. "It's bleeding here too. That's good. It means the bullet went through. I need more strips. I'll hold her up." As Marty let go, he said, "Pat, do you know where you are?"

"It's so bright," Pat said. "It's beautiful. I see my mother. I want to go give her a hug."

"Not right now," Paul said. "Later. Tell me about your kitty."

Marty handed him a tight wad, and he packed it in.

"Muffy is right here," Pat said. "I named her that because she's so soft. She's gray with the sweetest green eyes."

Voice low, Paul said, "I need more." Marty handed him a wad, and he stuffed it in.

"I see John," Pat said. "He looks just like he did when we were married." Pat's eyes began to close.

"Keep her talking," Paul said.

"Pat," Marty said, "tell me where you and John met."

"At a state conference for savings and loan directors. Father was teaching me the business, so he sent me alone. John was there with his boss. He was from Phoenix." She giggled.

Paul said, "Let's lay her down. Take it slow."

As they lowered her to the floor, Pat said, "I told John that Father would never let me see him again. But he said he didn't care. He said we could meet in different places so Father wouldn't get suspicious."

"Give me your poncho to cover her with," Paul whispered.

As Marty slid it off, he said, "Pat, I never met John. What did he look like?"

"He's handsome," she said. "It's like he hasn't aged a bit. I wonder what he thinks of me with my white hair."

"I'm sure he thinks you're beautiful," Paul said. As he said the reassuring words, he knew they were true. In an odd way Pat was more at peace than he'd ever seen her. If she looked this way at sixty, she must have been stunning when she was young. But Ralph had kept her locked up at home.

Marty covered Pat with her poncho and took the older woman's hand again. "Tell me about your wedding, honey."

Pat giggled again. "We went to Las Vegas. It was just one of those wedding chapels, but it was the cutest thing you ever saw. We had bells and flowers and everything. I didn't tell Father a word about it until the deed was done. He thought I was in L.A. at another one of those boring conferences."

In the distance, Paul heard the wail of a siren. Leaving Marty to keep Pat talking, he went to the door and stepped outside. A whinny caught his attention. The white horse was standing alone by the hitching post. The red horse was nowhere in sight. If Ralph had taken it, he'd be hard to catch up to tonight.

Rubbing his hands on his arms to warm them, Paul moved to where he could watch the road. The snow had stopped, blanketing the forest with white silence. No more than a half mile up the road, the ambulance churned its way toward the cabin, red lights staining the flocked trees in an eerie rhythm.

Scott leaned out of the passenger window and waved. Paul waved back. *Thank you, Father.*

He headed inside to let Marty know help had arrived. His hand was on the door when somewhere deep in the forest a single shot exploded.

38

Saturday, March 23

Paul pulled into the driveway of Old and Treasured, wishing he'd bought the Honda he and Scott looked at yesterday. The Jeep was too informal for a marriage proposal. Ridiculous. A responsible adult about to walk away from a predictable career with nothing but the promise of a part-time job would never make the impulse purchase of a new car, gently used or not.

He could have rented a limousine. But then he couldn't have worn the jeans and hiking boots required for their destination. Shaking his head at the inane thoughts running through his head, Paul breathed, *"Father..."*

His mind went blank. He couldn't even think how to pray. Trusting God to read through the jumble of his feelings and nudge him to do what was best, he opened the door of the Jeep and got out.

"Hi, Paul!" Marty came out of the shed dusting off the knees of her jeans.

The green and white striped polo added depth to her eyes,

making him think of a forest in spring, so dense he could get lost in there. Paul blinked. What was he thinking? He'd never thought in poetic images. Ever since they got Scott home safely, he'd found himself thinking in ridiculous metaphors, like a lovesick teenager writing sappy poetry.

"I'm glad you called. I need to get away from sorting junk into two piles, definitely trash and trash Carly might think she can sell."

"How about riding with me up to Jerome?"

"Sure. Let me wash my hands and grab a bottle of water. You want anything?"

He shook his head. "I'm good." If he told her he was nervous, she might catch on. He wanted to ask her to marry him the way she'd always dreamed. She'd said she wanted to be surprised. At least that's what he thought. He hoped he'd read her right.

"What are you thinking about so seriously?" Marty threw her arms around his waist and hugged him.

He didn't try to answer, just kissed the top of her head.

"No, honey. Let me show you how we can do this, height difference and all." Reaching up, she pulled his head down and kissed him gently.

"Let's try that again." Paul kissed her more thoroughly than she'd kissed him.

Laughing, she pushed him away. "Later! Right now, I want to go to Jerome." She ran to the Jeep and was buckled in by the time he slid under the wheel.

"What would you think of driving up to check on our property?"

She didn't answer right away, turning her head to look out the window.

He didn't think she saw much of the rocky hillside as they started up the switchbacks. Maybe he'd misjudged how she would feel about going back. Maybe this was a mistake. Did he have time to suggest an alternate location?

"Is the demolition finished?"

"All done. I drove up the road Tuesday."

"The day you found Bernie Loomis?"

"That's the day."

Turning to look at him, she smiled. "Let's do it. Maybe dream a little bit about what to do with that lovely location."

Paul relaxed. It was going to be okay. "What did you do yesterday?"

She sobered. "I went to lunch with Sofia. Then the two of us went to see Pat."

Paul whistled. "That must have been tough. I'm sorry I wasn't available."

She touched his knee. "Don't be. You and Scott needed to spend the day together."

"So how is Pat? Where is she?"

"Yesterday she was at the Verde Valley Medical Center. The EMTs took her there to get patched up. She's under arrest as an accessory to murder, but it's going to be a long time before she'll be able to stand trial."

Marty took a shuddering breath. "She's had a complete breakdown. All she does is cry. She keeps reliving everything she talked about Thursday night. She'd blocked it all out, so it's raw pain, more than she can cope with."

"Once the authorities learn the whole story, I imagine she'll be sent to rehab instead of prison."

"What about her father? I don't suppose it was an accident?"

Paul shook his head. "Suicide."

"That's terrible, another death at Ralph's hands, even if it was his own."

"I agree, but not a surprise. As Jesus told Simon Peter, people who live by violence die by violence."

The Jeep topped the switchbacks. As they passed the Jerome State Historic Park, he allowed himself a quick glance. His new career might take a few years to come together. But maybe not. He shifted his attention back to Marty. "Did Pat know you?"

"I'm not sure. She hugged me so tight I thought I was going to pass out, but whether it was because she knew I was Marty or because Sofia and I were the first people to come see her, I'm not sure."

"Doesn't she have anyone?"

"Joanie. Other than that, I may be it."

"We'll visit her. I'm sure the Caring Friends team at church will put her on the care list."

Marty dug through her bag for a tissue and blew her nose. "What did you and Scott do?"

The Jeep followed the highway into Jerome, past the little row of shops that had been "cribs" or tiny rooms where prostitutes plied their trade. "Scott slept until noon."

"Oh, poor Scott! Is he a wreck?"

Paul laughed. "Scott? He's already developing the script for the story of his adventure to tell his friends, complete with a description of how he figured out who was holding him."

"Doesn't he realize he could have been killed?"

Paul sobered. "I'm sure he does. He had a bad nightmare after he finally got to bed. I decided to spend what was left of the night sitting with him in his room. He finally fell asleep about six a.m."

"You got a few hours of sleep?"

"Mmm." It wasn't quite time to tell Marty about his morning shopping trip to Sedona. Paul braked at the stop sign and waited for an opening in the flow of traffic down Mingus Mountain. It was still too early for the tourist season, but it was Saturday.

"What did you do when he got up?"

"We drove to Flagstaff, grabbed a couple of burgers, and hiked in Hart Prairie. On the way home, we stopped and looked at a few cars."

"You're thinking of trading in the Jeep?"

Not trading, adding a family car. Not time to discuss that either. "Just something fathers and sons do together."

As Paul made the right turn at Holy Family Catholic Church and started up the road to where they'd first met nine months ago, they both fell silent. He began to doubt the wisdom of his choice of venue. But, as they'd learned last summer, you had to let go of the past in order to move forward. He prayed they both felt nudged in the same direction.

39

Marty watched out the window and let the jumble of memories come. Walking up the road in the dark, dragging her suitcase behind her. Her first glimpse of the white Victorian house with the lavender gingerbread trim. Granny Lois in her workshop in Virginia. Running smack into Paul, so shaggy back then he made her think of a bear, a cuddly bear, but still a bear.

The memories stopped abruptly as Paul pulled into the driveway. A foundation swept so clean by the wind it looked like a rock-faced patio marked where the house had stood. A wave of sorrow rushed down the mountain toward her, pushed back by the tiny blue and delicate white flowers that covered the hillside where Granny's yard used to be.

Marty clapped her hands. "Grape hyacinths! I remember those from when I was five. And snowdrops." When the Jeep stopped, she unbuckled her seatbelt and jumped out. As she ran toward the promise of spring, she spotted the distinctive yellow of daffodils. So many more than when she was five. Dropping to her knees, she began to brush brown pine needles away from the brightly colored blooms.

"Bless you, Granny," she whispered.

A breath of wind touched her face, gone as quickly as it came, almost as if Granny had blown her a kiss.

"Front porch or living room?"

Marty looked up from brushing the dirt back from a row of bright blue flowers. Paul stood in the middle of the foundation holding up two lawn chairs ready to be opened. "What?"

"Would you rather sit on the porch or in the living room?"

Mystified, Marty got to her feet. "The living room." As she walked toward the concrete slab, Paul moved to where the living room had been and opened the two chairs.

By the time she reached the house, he'd jumped down. "I didn't have time to rebuild the steps, so let me help you up onto the porch. I believe you'll be able to get in the house. I didn't lock the door."

Marty laughed. What was he up to, this serious history professor she was in love with? When she was in reach, he put his hands on her waist, and for an instant she thought he was going to kiss her, which would have been just fine. Instead he lifted her as if she didn't weigh anywhere close to her hundred pounds and set her up on the foundation.

By the time she was standing, he'd vaulted up to stand beside her. As he looked down at her, his brown eyes were dark with emotion. This time she was sure he was going to kiss her. But he didn't.

Marty started to reach up and pull his head down and kiss him herself, but his hesitation made her nervous. *Please, Lord. Please don't let me have run out of chances with this man.*

The chairs sat side by side with a sweeping view of the valley. She sat in the far one. As she watched, a dusty blue scrub jay dropped from the scorched edge of the Prescott National Forest behind them, past the first story of Jerome, and on toward the concrete plant and Clarkdale.

"Marty?"

"Oh, sorry, Paul. What did you say?"

He cleared his throat. "I'm already nervous enough. It's a spectacular view, but if you could tear yourself away long enough to hear me out, I have a question to ask you."

Marty's heart stopped. Her breathing too.

"Marty! Are you okay?"

She forced herself to take a breath. And then another one. Her heart started beating again. "Sorry. I'm fine." Brave words, but she was afraid her voice shook. *Please, Lord!*

Paul laughed. "We'd better get this over with then before one of us has a heart attack."

He dropped to one knee in front of her and held out a small dark blue box. She took it, just managing to keep from snatching it before it disappeared. But when it was in her hand, she just held it and stared at it.

"Open it, sweetheart."

She studied him, almost at eye-level. "This is for me?" It was a stupid question, but it was out before she knew she was going to ask it.

Instead of laughing at her, he put a hand on each cheek and kissed her gently. "Just for you, Marty, my love."

Ignoring the two ridiculous tears sliding down her face, she opened the little box. A platinum band with a round, brilliant-cut diamond twinkled up at her. When she drew it out, she realized the ring had four diamonds inset at equal distances around the shining band. "Art-deco, maybe 1930. Where on earth did you find it, and when?"

"At a one-of-a-kind jeweler in Sedona. Yesterday morning. Will you marry me, Marty?"

Two more tears slid down the tracks the first two had left, followed by several more. "Ye—"

Before she could finish he put a gentle finger on her lips. "Wait, sweet girl. It isn't a yes/no question. It's a discussion question."

She gave him a mock frown. "Do I have to write a paragraph of explanation?"

"No. But I have three points for discussion."

She nodded.

"First I've got to get off this concrete. It's cutting into my knee even through the denim." Rising, he pulled his chair around so he was facing her. "Honesty is required. If your impulse is to say no, then say it. A negative isn't a deal-breaker. It widens the discussion."

Marty knew Reed was on the list, but what were the other two items?

"Question number one. You know, of course, that Scott and I come as a package, but what's your honest opinion of adding Reed to my family?"

"I've thought about Reed a lot. He's Scott's friend, and Scott's a good judge of character. If the two of you think he's sincere about wanting to join the family, I'm all for it."

Paul visibly relaxed.

She touched his knee. "I'm sorry, Paul. I was scared."

"What changed your mind?"

"Not what, who. Sofia. I had a talk with her, and she reminded me of the parable in Luke about not patching an old garment with new cloth. If the old one is torn, you make a new one. I knew what she meant. God didn't want me to take Linda's place in the family you and Scott had before. He wanted us to make a different kind of family than I'd ever dreamed of."

Paul gave her a quizzical look. "I thought I told you that."

"You did, sort of. It just took Sofia to help me understand."

"Bless Sofia."

"Always! What's the second discussion question?"

Paul held out both his hands. She put hers in them. "What would you think if I decided to give up a stable career in favor of a riskier venture?"

"How you make your living is up to you. All I care about is

that you love your work as much as I love mine. What are you thinking of doing?"

"Park ranger."

She hadn't seen that one coming. Was he planning to move just as she was getting her business set up here? "That's harder because I haven't thought about it. Where would you go?"

Paul got up and came to stand beside her chair. Squatting, he lifted her right arm and pointed her hand down the hill.

She followed the line to the Douglas Mansion. "The Jerome State Historic Park? Scott told me one time how much you loved visiting there. He said he thought you'd rather be a park ranger than a teacher." She stood up and did her best to hug him. How she wished for six more inches!

Paul laughed and bent down for a real hug. "I'll take that as a yes."

She stepped back and looked up at him. "You have one question left."

He nodded, and they both resumed their seats. After a moment, he said, "The next question is part b of my career change question. How do you feel about moving into my small house with three big guys? Switching from a tenure-track position at a state university to a position at a small state park with no guarantees means I won't have the funds to buy a larger house, at least not for a while."

"What's this I? If we get married, we'll have to examine our finances before we decide what to do about housing."

He looked surprised. She wondered why. Had he assumed because she was ten years younger, she'd expect him to be in charge of their finances? If he had, it was good to get this on the table now.

"Agreed," he said. "So I'll take you moving into my house as a temporary yes, good until we can make a long-range plan."

She nodded. "But before we move out of discussion mode, I have two questions."

He looked surprised again. She said slowly, "I assume we're planning on a two-way marriage, despite the difference in our ages. I don't expect the fact you're older and have more experience to give you more than one vote."

"I'd rather not vote at all, sweetheart. I'm hoping for a consensus marriage. When we have a decision, we pray about it first. Then we talk. If we can't find a solution we're both comfortable with, we table the question for however long it takes. Does that work for you?"

"That's a fourth question, sir, but the answer is easy. Absolutely. Any more questions?"

"Just yours."

Marty went to the center of the foundation. Flinging her arms wide, she said, "What would you think of building a house right here? It has a lovely view."

He came to stand behind her. Leaning his chin on her head, he said thoughtfully, "We can put your workshop on the lot across the road and make the Remick house all showroom. You realize we'll have to build it ourselves."

"That will make it all the more special."

He laughed. "We'll see how special it feels when you're hot and sweaty and your shoulders are aching from carrying two-by-fours." He reached for her right hand, the hand that was clutching the engagement ring. "May I put the ring on your finger now?"

"I have one discussion question left." She slipped the ring in her pocket to let him know she planned to keep it, no matter what he said. This question wasn't a deal-breaker, but it would be a huge blow if he said no outright.

He cocked his head to one side and studied her face. "If you don't like the ring, the jeweler promised me I can bring it back. We can trade for something he has or get my money back and go to another store."

"I love the ring. It's something else." Before she could lose her nerve, she blurted. "How do you feel about babies... I mean, one baby?"

Laughing, he grabbed her right hand with his left. Putting his right hand on her waist, he said, "The 'Blue Danube' is playing." Drawing her into an imaginary waltz, he said, "I've been thinking about babies and toddlers ever since I saw the photo of adorable Aurora Reyes. I'd love a baby or two. More than that, we'd have to reach consensus."

She stopped dancing and pulled the ring out of her pocket. Handing it to him, she extended her left hand.

As he slipped it on her finger, he said, "Marty Greenlaw, will you be my wife until death do us part?"

To answer, she pulled his head down and kissed him. As he kissed her back, a thought flitted through her mind. Just like the "Snow White, Rose Red" fairy tale, her shaggy bear had turned into her Prince Charming. She settled in for a nice, long kiss.

40

F riday, July 12

Scott stood where his room would be. To be precise, he stood where the living room was framed-in, eight feet below his future bedroom. His back to the still sleeping town of Jerome, he stood with his head at an awkward angle hypnotized by the neon pink and orange streaks in the pale blue sky. In a half hour the sun would burst over the top of Cleopatra Hill, and the five of them would start a new chapter in their lives.

"We're getting quite a show, aren't we?" Dad's soft voice, so close behind him, loosened the bands squeezing his chest.

Dad wrapped his arms around Scott and hugged.

Scott closed his eyes and pretended he was six again. Everything was perfect. Mom was in the kitchen singing while she stirred something on the stove. He and Dad stood in the doorway like this, watching her.

Now, down the hill from where they stood, the guitarist started to play "Recuerdos de la Alhambra." Scott opened his eyes. Marty was standing off to one side pinning a corsage of daisies on Miss Sofia. Marty looked pretty in the white dress that reached almost to her ankles. Just right here on the mountain, not a fancy wedding dress, a sundress made out of something Marty called eyelet. With the shimmery blue-green scarf Miss Sofia gave her around her shoulders, Marty didn't look anything like Mom in the wedding album.

Scott said, "Marty's different from Mom."

"Does that bother you?"

Scott took a deep breath and turned around so he could look at his dad. "I think it's good. We're not trying to bring Mom back. We're doing something totally different."

Dad held up his hand for a high-five. "I see Pastor Ray motioning for people to sit down. We'd better go. Nervous?"

"A little."

"It's going to be fine, even if someone makes a mistake."

Reed motioned to him, and Scott knew Dad was right. They walked down the railroad tie steps they'd made from the driveway to the house. He couldn't believe how many people were here at five o'clock in the morning.

A lot of his friends and their families were spreading blankets on the ground. His grandma from Virginia and Marty's adopted parents from Florida were setting up lawn chairs. Miss Sofia's friends were all going to the folding chairs he and Reed had set up in two sections.

They'd made a colorful aisle out of petals from flowers the florist said he was going to throw away. It led right up to the wedding arch.

The arch looked good. It was Carly's idea, but he and Reed fastened the two old door frames Bill found with a couple of two by fours. Once they painted it white, it started to look like an arch. Carly said it was perfect for Marty's wedding because the door frames were antiques. Just a couple of old doors, but Scott didn't bother arguing with her.

Sometime during the night Carly and Bill decorated the arch with sunflowers and daisies. Like Marty's dress, the arch was perfect for Cleopatra Hill, especially with the way it framed the view of the Jerome Historic Park Mansion where his dad worked part-time.

When they got to the driveway, Scott and Dad walked to the garage to join Miss Sofia and Reed. A few feet away, Marty tickled Aurora Reyes just enough to make her giggle. Her Uncle Alex was holding Aurora's hand and grinning. Scott looked for Aurora's parents. They were sitting on the front row, holding hands and smiling at each other.

"Friends!" Pastor Ray's booming voice carried all the way to the garage even without a microphone. "Who's hungry?"

All over the yard and the driveway, people laughed and clapped.

"All right, folks. After I get in my two cents, we'll have a wedding. Then we'll adjourn to the fellowship hall for a pancake breakfast, complete with bacon and eggs."

Someone called, "Keep it short, Pastor!"

More laughter and applause.

"Will do, Taylor. I'm as hungry as you are. Let's start by singing the refrain to 'How Great Thou Art' while we look up at the brilliant colors in our Arizona sky this morning."

The guitarist played a brief introduction, and then Pastor Ray started singing, "Then sings my soul..."

Scott joined in for the first phrase, but then his throat closed up. He stopped singing and cleared his throat. Their friends were all singing, but everyone in the wedding party was clearing their throat or wiping away tears. As the song finished, the sun topped Cleopatra Hill, filling the yard with golden light.

The group gave a collective gasp. A moment later someone clapped. Soon everyone was applauding. As their friends sat down, Dad handed Scott a water bottle. He took a long drink and passed it to Reed.

Pastor Ray said, "Listen to this parable from Jeremiah 18:1-4. 'The word that came to Jeremiah from the Lord: "Come, go down to the potter's house, and there I will let you hear my words." So I went down to the potter's house, and there he was working at his wheel. The vessel he was making of clay was spoiled in the potter's hand, and he reworked it into another vessel, as it seemed good to him.'"

Pastor Ray looked around at the people who had come out so early to celebrate with them. "Friends," he said, "this morning you're going to watch five ordinary people do something extraordinary. We know Miss Sofia the best because she's been part of Community Church since its founding. We know Paul and Scott Russell well because we first met them when Linda was still with us. Later we went through a season of confusion and grief with Paul and Scott when Linda passed from this life to the next."

He paused and gestured to where Marty stood with Miss Sofia. "Over the last year we've been getting to know Marty Greenlaw, who most of you know is our dear, departed friend Lois Baker's granddaughter." He gave Reed a thumbs up. "Reed Harper is new to our congregation, but from what I hear, he's fitting in well with the youth group."

Someone clapped and soon everyone was applauding. When the group quieted, Pastor Ray said, "Each of these folks leaves behind a part of their lives they thought would turn out differently to create a brand-new family together. As you watch them take this step, think about your life. Is God nudging you to a new path? If God is, don't be afraid. You won't be alone."

Pastor Ray moved to stand under the arch and nodded at the guitarist, who began strumming the Wedding March, quietly at first and then louder. Scott started to feel like he was watching a movie.

Marty handed Aurora a basket filled with flower petals and kissed the little girl's cheek. Alex walked with Aurora to where the aisle started. Then he whispered something in her ear. She nodded and let go of his hand. Keeping her eye on her mother up front, Aurora walked slowly and solemnly up the aisle, pausing sometimes to throw a handful of flowers at whoever was sitting closest to where she stood. Gentle laughter rippled through the group.

His dad tapped Scott and Reed on the shoulder, and while everyone was watching Aurora, the three of them walked around the edge of the group to join Pastor Ray. By the time they got to the arch, Aurora was in her mother's lap, proudly showing the empty basket to her father.

The guitarist switched to "Here Comes the Bride," and the movie Scott was watching became a dream. He and his dad and Reed moved to the left side of the arch and faced the aisle. Marty started toward them with her arm looped through Miss Sofia's. When the two ladies got to the arch, Miss Sofia kissed Marty's cheek and moved to the right.

Pastor Ray said something, and Dad took the band that matched Marty's engagement ring out of his pocket. Holding her hand, he said something about loving until death parted them.

Scott thought about Mom and how Dad had said the same thing to her sixteen years ago, two years before he was born. But here his dad was, starting a life he never imagined, just like all the rest of them. Dad slipped the ring on Marty's finger, and then it was her turn.

Miss Sofia handed Marty a wide, shiny, silver band. Dad's smile lit up his face as Marty slid the ring on his finger. The last bit of doubt about what they were doing evaporated. Scott didn't know who was happiest. Dad, Marty, or himself.

Then Dad was smiling and changing places with him. Scott found himself staring into Marty's sparkling green eyes. His mind was totally blank. No idea what he was supposed to say. Then Marty reached out her hands. He hesitated then put his in hers, noticing his hands were already larger than hers.

"Scott Russell," she said, "I promise to love you until the day one of us dies." Miss Sofia handed Marty a little bag. She opened it and took out a heavy, brass chain with a silver cross dangling from it.

As she put it in his hand, she said, "Scott, you can wear this or keep it in your treasure box, but whenever you look at it, remember God brought me into your life, not to take your mother's place but to be a special friend." Then she kissed him on the cheek.

Scott felt his face grow warm. Worse, he still couldn't remember what he was supposed to say. He threw his dad a desperate look. Dad smiled and circled one wrist with the fingers of his other hand. The bracelet! Scott pulled the gold circle out of his pocket. Handing it to Marty, he blurted, "Read what's engraved. I hope you like it."

He studied her as she tilted her head to read the two words he'd told the jeweler to put, *Mom too*. Her eyes filled up with tears, and for a terrible minute, he thought he'd made a huge mistake. Then she put on the bracelet and opened her arms to see if he wanted a hug.

He stepped closer and put his arms around her. He was stiff for a moment. Then she said, "It's perfect, Scott! I'd love to be your mom too."

He relaxed. He'd struggled over the difference between too and two. He'd made the right choice. "I promise to love you until I die," he said. "Even if you die first, I'll keep on loving you. Because that's what happens, you know. I still love Mom."

Then they were both crying, and Dad handed each of them a handkerchief. "You two can finish this later," he said quietly. "We're not done here, you know."

Scott wasn't quite sure how it happened, but he and Reed changed places. Dad and Marty faced Reed. Dad said, "Reed Harper, Marty and I want to love you until death parts us. We want to provide a home for you until you graduate from college or turn twenty-five. We have a gift for you, but I didn't think I could keep a cell phone in my pocket."

Reed cleared his throat. "Uncle Paul and Aunt Marty, I'll love you both until the day I die. I made a box for you, but it was too big to bring."

All three of them laughed, and Dad said, "To be continued."

Then Dad and Marty stepped back, and Scott was facing Reed. They stared at each other, both of them dumbstruck.

Pastor Ray said quietly, "We promise to be brothers…"

They repeated it together, adding the end without prompting. "We promise to be brothers from now until we die." Scott took the rope bracelet he made for Reed out of his pocket. Reed did the same. They traded bracelets and performed the special hand-shake they'd made up.

Dad said, "Russell family, welcome our Jerome grandma." The four of them made a circle around Miss Sofia.

Reed whispered, "I never had a grandma before."

Miss Sofia, Grandma Sofia, reached up and patted Reed's cheek. Then she reached up and patted Scott's cheek. "I never had any grandchildren before." Taking one of Dad's hands and one of Marty's hands, she said, "Come to think of it, I never had any children."

"Now you have both," Dad said.

They all remembered the last part. Linking arms, they faced their friends. Pastor Ray stood beside them and said, "Friends, say hello to the Russell family."

For a moment, Cleopatra Hill was utterly still. Past, present, and future faded into a single breath. Then the guitarist began to strum "Ode to Joy."

A NOTE ON SETTING

Jerome, Arizona is a real town. Clinging to the side of Cleopatra Hill at 5,000 feet, Jerome is about halfway between Phoenix and Flagstaff on Highway 89A. Once a booming billion-dollar-copper camp and later a ghost town with fewer than 100 residents, Jerome is now a tourist destination. During the nearly thirty years I lived in Flagstaff, I made countless trips to Jerome. Every time I went, it seemed I discovered a new facet of its history. In *The Copper Box*, I drew on the ghost town side of Jerome.

In *The Silver Lode*, I draw on the mining history. One of my major sources was The Jerome State Historic Park, which I visited almost every time I went to Jerome. The descriptions of the park and its exhibits in *The Silver Lode* are as accurate as my memory (and the website) can make them. Though silver was mined in Jerome, the silver lode in the abandoned mine in my story is entirely my imagination.

While the businesses of early Jerome mentioned here are based on newspaper accounts, all of the characters came out of my imagination and are not based on any real person, living or dead. If you ever find yourself in Arizona, take the time to visit Jerome. You may find it as fascinating as I have.

DISCUSSION QUESTIONS

1. How does this story depend on its setting?
2. Who did you first suspect was the murderer? Why?
3. Everyone assumes Ralph is dead. Find the clues he's alive. (Hint: a few clues are things *not* said.)
4. The theme is Jeremiah 18:1-4. How does it apply to Paul, Marty, Scott and B.T. individually?
5. When does Ralph first reject God's desire to shape his life? How does that first rejection lead to others that occur when Pat is growing up and eventually to his role in this book?
6. When has God wanted to reshape your life? What happened when you allowed God to make your life into something new? What happened when you rejected God's desire?
7. Which of the minor characters did you like best? Why?
8. Which of the minor characters did you like least? Why?
9. Does the author do a good job with description? Why or why not?

10. Does this book make you want to visit Jerome, Arizona? Why or why not?

11. Do you think you'll ever read this book again? Why or why not?

12. Would you recommend it to a friend? Why or why not?

13. What would you like to tell the author about this book? (suzanne@suzannebratcher.com)

14. If you've read *The Copper Box*, which book do you like better? Why?

15. If you've read *The Copper Box*, what do you think happened between the two stories to Paul, Marty, Scott and B.T. individually?

The author is available for virtual visits with book clubs! Contact Suzanne at suzanne@suzannebratcher.com

ABOUT THE AUTHOR

A passionate reader since her first encounter with Dick and Jane, Suzanne J. Bratcher wanted to grow up to be a fiction writer. After college, realizing she couldn't support herself on ten cents a word, she became an English teacher, specializing in writing instruction. Over the next thirty years she taught writing to high schoolers, college students, and public school teachers. She continued her own writing: publishing professional articles, two textbooks, short stories, and poetry. Since retiring from Northern Arizona University in Flagstaff, Bratcher has returned to her childhood dream of writing fiction. *The Copper Box* (2017) and *The Silver Lode* (2019) are the first two books in The Jerome

Mysteries. Watch for the third book, *The Gold Doubloons*, in 2021. *Kokopelli's Song* (2020) is the first book in the Fantasy Folklore series. Find out more about her at https://suzannebratcher.com or connect with her via social media.

f facebook.com/authorsuzannebratcher

y twitter.com/AuthorBratcher

◎ instagram.com/suzanne.bratcher.5

ALSO BY SUZANNE J. BRATCHER

You may also enjoy these books

by Suzanne J. Bratcher:

The Copper Box

Book One of the Jerome Mysteries Series

Jerome, Arizona: the largest ghost town in America

Antiques expert Marty Greenlaw comes to Jerome to face the horror that haunts her dreams: Did she kill her little sister twenty-two years ago?

Historian Paul Russell is in Jerome to face his own horror: Was the car crash that killed his wife his fault?

Their lives become intertwined when an old lady dies on a long staircase in a vintage Victorian house. As Marty and Paul search the house for a small copper box Marty believes will unlock the mystery, accidents begin to happen.

Someone else wants the copper box—someone willing to commit murder to get it. As Marty and Paul face the shadows in the house and in their lives, they must learn to put the past behind them and run the race God is calling them to.

The Copper Box by Suzanne Bratcher

∿∽

Watch for *The Gold Doubloons*, Book Three of the Jerome Mysteries Series, coming in Fall 2021.

∿∽

Kokopelli's Song

Book One of the Four Corners Fantasy Series

New Mexico

When seventeen-year-old Amy Adams finds her father's family and a lost twin brother on the Hopi reservation in Arizona, she stumbles into a struggle between shamans and witches that spans a thousand years. After Mahu is attacked and a Conquistador's journal stolen, Amy and her new friend Diego set out on a dangerous quest to find and perform the ceremony that can stop ancient evil from entering our world.

But Amy and Diego are not alone as they race against time measured by a waxing moon. Kokopelli's song, the haunting notes of a red cedar flute, guides them along the migration route sacred to pueblo peoples: West to Old Oraibi, South to El Morro, East to Cochiti Pueblo, North to Chimney Rock, and finally to the Center—and the final confrontation —in Chaco Canyon.

Scrivenings
PRESS
Quench your thirst for story.
www.ScriveningsPress.com

Stay up-to-date on your favorite books and authors with our free e-newsletters.

ScriveningsPress.com

Made in the USA
Monee, IL
23 July 2020